FORGED
IN
FIRE
AND
STARS

FORGED
IN
FIRE
AND
STARS

ANDREA ROBERTSON

PHILOMEL BOOKS

DISCARD

PHILOMEL BOOKS
An imprint of Penguin Random House LLC, New York

First published in the United States of America by Philomel,
an imprint of Penguin Random House LLC, 2020.

Philomel Books is a registered trademark of Penguin Random House LLC.

Visit us online at penguinrandomhouse.com

Library of Congress Cataloging-in-Publication Data is available.

Printed in the United States of America
ISBN 9780525954125
10 9 8 7 6 5 4 3 2 1

Edited by Jill Santopolo and Kelsey Murphy.
Design by Ellice M. Lee.
Text set in Amerigo BT.

FOR EJO, WHO CARRIED ME THROUGH THE CRUCIBLE

SAE

FJERI

Well of the Twins

Ice Coast

Ice Mountains

Elke's Pass

Ruins of M

Fjeri
Highlands

Senn's Fury   Rill's Pass

Wellseeker's Landing

Darkfern

Teth's Camp

Silverstag

Wuldr's Grove

Port Pilgrim

Aldersprine

Shepherd's Rest

Fjeri
Lowlands

Bridgegate Cross

Westport

Oakvale   Foxgate   Hunter's Rest

Echir

Siva

DAEFRIT

Aerindross

Zeverin
Gorge

Dothris

Marik

Ghost
Cliffs   Ofrit's Cavern

Zeverin Delta

Punishing
Desert   The Bone Forest

Butcher Crow

Fortress of the Sands   Handar

Southern   Sea

The Great Mines

Isar   Zyre

Salt Coast

Blinding Cape

Forgotten Coast
N
Kelden
Nava's Ire
Fennmyr
Liflamyr
Kaenmyr
Allomyr
Five Rivers
Port Amber
The Great Market
Nava's Bounty
Sola
Nav-Nias
Tribridge
Nav-Horsa
The Gash
Nomis
Mer
Jan
Vijeri
The Tangle
Last Landing
Erlaon
Serpent Coast
Shrouded Cape

It is said that the conquest of Saetlund was
bloodless. But there was blood.

It came after the battles.
It began to seep quietly through cracks and
crevices in villages and towns and cities.
Few understood what was happening. Those
who did disappeared.

LAHVJA THE SUMMONER,
CHRONICLES OF THE LORESMITH, VOL. 1

❊ PROLOGUE ❊

langs of steel on steel announced the arrival of the black-smith's fate. Yos Steelring passed a borrowed quarterstaff from hand to hand, trying to grow accustomed to its weight and balance. It was a sorry replacement for his usual stave, having none of the life nor familiarity of that rare weapon. Nothing to be done about it. The Loresmith stave—better known by its storied name, Ironbranch—could not be among the Vokkans' spoils, which meant Yos's companion of so many years was far from the palace and his grip.

Sounds of battle were closer now, much closer. Worse than the ring and scrape of steel were the screams followed by wet, guttural moans. Yos knew that those who remained of the palace guard had attempted to barricade themselves behind broken furniture, blocking the path to the royal apartments. That pitiful bulwark must have fallen, leaving only Yos between the soldiers and their prize.

Despite his determination to hold his post, Yos couldn't keep fear-borne doubt from wriggling into his thoughts.

Is there honor in laying down one's life for a king who brought his people to ruin?

Yos ground his teeth at the question. Too many times he'd thought of what his life might have been outside of the palace and city of Five Rivers. The Loresmith hadn't always served in court. Generations ago the Loresmith roamed the provinces of Saetlund, offering aid where it was needed and joining the Loreknights in times of trouble. Together, smith and warriors had quelled threats, thwarted invasions, and crushed enemies of the kingdom.

Yos shook his head, pinpointing the moment in history when it had all fallen apart. The moment that King Nirn made the fateful declaration centuries ago. Loreknights would no longer be chosen from among the people of each province, but would instead be appointed by the monarch and take their place at the royal court. With that decree, Nirn had riddled the foundation of Saetlund's defenses with cracks. Those cracks had widened over the years, becoming fissures and faults.

Today the walls had crumbled.

Yos was close to sinking into despair.

He reminded himself it wasn't the current fool of a king, Dentroth, behind the door over which he stood watch. The royal twin toddlers were innocent and deserved his protection. If all had gone as planned, they were no longer in the nursery at Yos's back. They should be miles from the city in care of their guardians. Their destination: Port Pilgrim, a ship, and obscurity. The little princess and prince would be exiles, but they would be safe.

Yos continued to guard the room he hoped was now empty. Every minute he defended the door was another minute bought for the twins' escape. He had prayed for their safety, but most of his pleas to the gods begged for the salvation of an unborn child and its mother.

A tear rolled down Yos's cheek as he thought of his wife, Lira. It had been five years since they'd first met, but the memory of that day was so clear he felt like he could step into it.

He had been in the market district, on his way to the tanner's. The time had come to retire his smithing apron, and he wanted an exact re-creation of the garment that had served him so well. Yos had been to the tanner's before, but he took a wrong turn and found himself on a street he didn't recognize.

"Are you lost, blacksmith?" A young woman was watching him from a few feet away. She had pale pink skin and sable hair that fell down her back in a single long plait.

"I don't think I've ever been on this street," Yos admitted.

"That's your loss," she said, walking toward him. "The finest weaver in Saetlund has a shop on this street."

He could see now that her eyes were lavender-gray, a shade he'd never seen before. "Your shop, I assume?"

She tsk'd. "My mother's shop. Elke Silverthread. She creates exceptional fabrics. You could ask any of the ladies at court and they would tell you all their dresses are made of Silverthread fabrics."

"Why do you think I'd know the ladies at court?" Yos's face clouded. He wasn't dressed for court. He'd come straight from his workshop, and his clothing showed it.

Buds of blush appeared on the woman's cheeks. "I know who you are, Yos Steelring. My father is a blacksmith and a great admirer of your craft. He has pointed you out to me many times. And speaks of your generosity in sharing your knowledge with the guild, despite the king's disapproval."

"My thanks to your father for his kind words," Yos said, feeling his own cheeks redden. He cleared his throat. "As you already have my name, may I ask yours?"

"I'm Lira," she told him. "Lira Silverthread."

"Lira." For some reason, Yos could say nothing but her name. An awkward quiet stretched between them as he tried to remember how to speak. He couldn't stop staring at her, and he was horrified by his uncouth behavior.

"Tanner!" he blurted.

Lira looked startled, and Yos hurried to say, "I was on my way to the tanner."

"Ah." She nodded. Her lips quirked as she returned his gaze.

"Come to the shop first," Lira coaxed. "We will find the most beautiful scarf for your beloved."

Yos was startled to find himself blushing again. "I don't have a beloved."

She smiled at him then, and Yos knew his heart would belong to no one else.

That first meeting led to a second, a third, and before Yos knew what was happening he found himself deeply in love. He wanted to marry her, but to do so would likely put them both at risk—Lira particularly.

For years, King Dentroth had been suggesting, loudly and often, that Yos should marry. The king had taken to ushering various highborn ladies into Yos's company. He knew Dentroth was serious. Yos's parents' marriage had been arranged by the previous king. He believed King Dentroth would not go so far as to force him to marry, but he had no doubt the king would be furious if he married into a merchant family after rejecting the royal preferences.

Despite the risk, Yos and Lira did marry in secret, in the old way, at a shrine of Nava. They kept their marriage hidden from all but Lira's parents. Even if the king had welcomed Lira to court and given their union his blessing, Yos knew Dentroth would lay claim to any child of the Loresmith. The line was hereditary. Neither Lira nor Yos was willing to hand their child's fate over to the ruler of Saetlund.

Lira was six months pregnant with their first child when word of the Vokkan landings at Daefrit and Kelden reached the palace. Panic gripped the city. Given the state of Saetlund's army and the size of the invading forces, Yos knew the enemy would reach Five Rivers within a week. Though he longed to flee the city with his wife, he couldn't bear the dishonor of foreswearing his oaths. For three days, Yos and Lira had planned, debated, fought, and held each other until they came to an agreement. Those had been the worst three days of Yos's life.

The Vokkan warriors appeared from the side corridor. They were laughing. Clapping one another on the shoulder. Smiling. Yos saw splashes of red on their lips and teeth.

Servants of the Devourer.

He imagined the royal toddlers mangled and bloody; he needed to give their guardians more time. With a ragged war cry, Yos made the second-hardest choice of his life. He charged at the blood-soaked soldiers.

Having waded through so many blades and bodies to reach this corridor, the Vokkans were taken aback by this lone man's wild attack. Surely a person outnumbered ten to one would surrender rather than fight.

Their brief hesitation gave Yos the few seconds he required to sweep his quarterstaff through the first three soldiers, cracking skulls. He took some satisfaction in watching them crumple. Then, as he expected, a shudder swept through his limbs, followed by an emptiness that felt like grief.

"I am Loresmith no more," he murmured. It would mean nothing to the invaders, so Yos had indulged the impulse to speak the words aloud.

He didn't feel the sharpness of the first blade that pierced his abdomen, only a sudden pressure and the inability to draw breath.

Yos fell to his knees. Death blows came but didn't surprise him, who had known that this would be the ending to his tale. His heart had already left this room, and his mind chased after it till both reached the same place. The memory of his wife's face and his hand upon the roundness of her belly as the sun rose, after another sleepless night, when they agreed she must leave Five Rivers and go into hiding with her parents—taking Yos's stave and their unborn child with her.

The hardest choice he had ever made. In saving their lives, he'd accepted the necessity of his own death.

Had he gone with them, they all would have been hunted. The Vokkans not only conquered lands, but had gained infamy for mining the mystic of each society they consumed. Emperor Fauld craved anything with a whiff of occult power; possessing the Loresmith of Saetlund had become his obsession. If the coveted blacksmith couldn't be chased, Lira and Yos's child would disappear. Lira would be safe in the anonymity of a tiny mountain village. Their baby would be cherished by a mother and grandparents. That knowledge brought Yos comfort.

His mind remained fixed there as his life drained onto the stone floor. He took no notice of the soldiers standing over him while his blood pooled at their feet.

The soldiers did not understand whom they had killed. They could not foresee their torment and death awaiting at the hands of their emperor. As they screamed and groaned and begged while Fauld the Ever-Living watched, they still did not grasp the reason for their suffering.

What the soldiers saw as a brief skirmish, the Vokkan emperor judged an intolerable failure. It mattered not that the soldiers had been following their orders—to find and seize the young royals at whatever cost—only that in doing so they had robbed their master of another treasure.

The twins' escape gave Fauld ample reason to punish his men, though he had little concern for the toddlers who carried the blood of a pathetic king.

The emperor's real rage at his soldiers reflected fury at himself he would never admit to, nor take responsibility for. Fauld had assumed that one man facing insurmountable odds would surrender. When his soldiers insisted that the man had attacked them and not the reverse, Fauld called them liars and ordered their execution. He couldn't believe the Loresmith would raise arms against an enemy when it meant forsaking unfathomable power.

The soldiers' slow deaths brought the emperor no succor. He had conquered the kingdom he so desired, but its most precious jewel had eluded him, and the truth of it gnawed upon his soul.

The Loresmith was no more.

1

FIFTEEN YEARS LATER

By the time Ara's fate came for her she'd stopped believing in it.

Outside the smithy a wintry wind shrieked ceaselessly. Gust-driven snow flew, swirled, and shuddered with each frigid blast. All the while beads of sweat formed on Ara's forehead. Nothing existed for her but the forge, the anvil, the hammer, the heat.

Strike. Spark. Smoke.

To Ara it was a song, the smithing of metal.

Ring. Roar. Whisper.

Heat so intense it kissed the air with shimmering ripples.

Ara's hammer met the smoldering metal. Iron alive with fire. Along with the vibrations from the hammer, Ara could feel that life, that burning force racing up fingertips, coursing into her arms, her shoulders, and finally, her heart, where it continued to dance to the rhythm of her craft.

That morning Ara had the smithy to herself. When great storms swept over the village, Old Imgar's joints complained and kept him inside seeking relief using hot compresses.

Spring storms could be the most violent. Winter lashing out in its death throes. The blizzard at Ara's back was a blinding one. The sort that necessitated following the rope, hand over hand, that stretched the short distance between her grandmother's stone cottage and the smithy. On a summer day the walk from the front door to the forge would be no more than fifteen steps. A fool might assume those steps could be easily made without the rope guide. That fool would discover how easily the currents of snowdrifts pull a person from the safety of the shore. That fool would too late regret dismissing local tales of folk found frozen in place, shrouded by snow, only a few feet from shelter.

Ara was no fool. She'd been taught to revere nature's power from the moment she could comprehend it. She knew everyone in the village would be huddled in their houses, taking comfort from a warm hearth and hot spiced tea.

She had no reason to peer into the white whirlwinds, searching for danger. She thought not of attuning her ears to sounds outside the smithy.

When shadowy figures moved within the blasts of ice and snow, Ara had not seen them. When footsteps sank into the deep powder banks forming along the walls of the smithy, Ara had not heard them. Nor had she sensed the presence of another joining her in the sweltering room.

Ara remembered the viselike arm around her waist and the damp cloth pressed over her nose and mouth, its cloying scent as she drew a startled breath. Then there had been only darkness.

2

teady murmuring roused Ara from a swampy sleep. Perhaps a creek bubbling over sticks and pebbles. As her mind began to clear, Ara could pick out variations in the noise—breaks, hesitations. A rise and fall of pitch. Not running water.

Voices.

Ara went rigid, but not with fear. Fear took time, demanded awareness. Ara hadn't gotten past disbelief.

Has it happened? she thought. *Has it actually happened?*

She remembered that first warning from her grandmother. It had come on the eve of Ara's fifth birthday.

"Ara." Her grandmother had given Ara a wooden mug of warm milk, sweetened with honey and spiced with cinnamon and pepper. "You've reached an age where there are things I must tell you. Some are very nice things. Others are unpleasant. There are too many things to say all at once, so tonight I'm going to tell you one nice thing and one not so nice thing."

Ara still remembered the warmth of the milk in her belly, the way the spices tingled on her tongue and throat.

"What's the nice thing?" she asked her grandmother.

The older woman smiled. *"Your father left you a gift."*

With glances searching the room, Ara asked, *"Where is it? Do you have it?"*

"It isn't something you can hold." Her grandmother laughed gently. *"It's already inside you, waiting for you to learn how to use it."*

Little Ara looked down at her belly, giving it a curious poke. *"Inside?"*

"Your father's gift is part of you," her grandmother answered. *"And will always be with you."*

Then the older woman's face creased with regret. *"Your father was meant to teach you about this gift, but your grandfather and I will begin teaching you in his place. You have much to learn."*

While Ara puzzled over how a gift could be something learned instead of an object, the lines in her grandmother's face grew even deeper.

"It is now time for what is unpleasant," she said with a sigh.

To Ara, it appeared her grandmother's gray eyes suddenly turned a darker shade, like clouds heavy with rain.

"There are people who are jealous of your gift," she told Ara. *"Who want it for themselves. Your father died to keep them from taking it."*

A rock-hard lump lodged in Ara's throat, and the milk in her stomach no longer felt so comforting.

"Did they kill my father because he wouldn't give it to them?" Ara knew her father died fighting in the Vokkan conquest, but nothing beyond that fact.

Her grandmother's lips pressed together. *"In a way."*

"Do they want to kill me?" Tears pricked at Ara's eyes, and she was ashamed that fear could so easily make her cry.

"No," her grandmother said firmly, and she placed her hands on Ara's shoulders. Ara was comforted until her grandmother added, "They want to take you."

The memory hung in Ara's mind, glaring and insistent, but she couldn't accept that it was real. That everything she'd been told was true.

It can't be, she argued with the past. *There's another explanation.*

If you are ever taken, her grandmother had instructed, *learn all you can before you act.*

Perhaps that advice could get Ara out of this mess and back to the world she understood. After all, her kidnappers could be bandits taking advantage of the storm—though outlaws in the highlands were rare. Almost unheard of in winter.

She'd have no answers until she discovered where she was and who her captors were.

As far as Ara could tell, she wasn't hurt aside from a dull ache at the back of her skull. Keeping still, Ara used her gaze to search the space. The air was hazy and irritated her eyes. A familiar scent told her woodsmoke was the culprit.

Above her, Ara could make out a rock ceiling. To her right, pale light barely reached her eyes, and a trickle of cool air touched her cheek. From her left side came a warm, flickering glow.

Outside to the right, fire to the left—Ara knew she was in a cave. But what cave?

In this storm, Ara doubted it could be far from Rill's Pass. There were several caves to the north and west of the village.

The voices came from the direction of the fire. Ara risked turning her head, very carefully, to the right. Two cloaked figures: one hunched and huddled close to the flames, the second kneeling close by.

"We should have waited." The kneeling person had a low female voice.

A reedy male voice replied. "I-i-i-it was ou-ou-our b-best ch-chance." His teeth chattered so violently that Ara could barely make out his words.

Both sounded young—girl and boy rather than woman and man.

A low noise of disapproval came out of the girl's throat. "You can't be exposed like that. You're too weak."

"I-I-I'm fine," he argued. "I j-just need t-t-tea."

"It's almost ready." She sounded apologetic.

After wrapping her hand in cloth, the girl lifted a small kettle from the fire; then she uncorked a jar and tapped some of its contents into the kettle.

"P-pour me a cup," the boy begged.

The girl didn't look at him. "It has to steep."

"P-please." The desperation in his voice made Ara wince.

"This wasn't worth the risk," the girl said. "I don't think she can be the one."

Ara heard the sound of tea pouring into a cup.

"It has to be her," the boy said. "There's no one else."

Maybe the cave was farther from Rill's Pass than she thought. The boy's pleas seemed evidence of the north's cruelest punishments: purple-black toes that couldn't be saved, clipped ears, and blunted noses. To thaw what could be saved, the sufferer had to endure a warm bath that felt like being boiled alive, so Ara had been told. Those were the warnings children received lest they underestimate the dangers of the dark season.

Despite her predicament, Ara found herself wishing she could help them. They spoke with an accent unfamiliar to her. Their fire had been poorly constructed and placed, so it lost heat quickly and smoked too much.

Ara's brow crinkled as she watched the girl lift a wooden cup to the boy's lips.

Why these two?

They didn't look like bandits. Nor did they resemble any of the nightmares that had plagued Ara's childhood. Her dreams had conjured hordes of Vokkan soldiers. Or worse, a Wizard of Vokk, murmuring spells over her bed.

Ara had never imagined the evil coming to take her would be a girl and a boy, shivering from the cold.

She considered running. Having the advantage of surprise, Ara could get a strong head start on the girl. The boy was in no condition to give chase.

The storm quashed Ara's hope of escape. She might evade her captors, but she'd be as good as dead without a clear path home. She had no way of knowing when the blizzard would end. Spring squalls brought storms that came and went in the space of an hour, but also those that lingered for days. Ara hoped that this bout of weather would quiet before dusk. If she didn't return home by dark, her grandmother would call a search. The whole of the village would risk their lives looking for Ara. She couldn't bear the thought that anyone might be hurt on her behalf.

Ara eased onto her left side. The girl's attention remained focused on the boy. Slowly, Ara pushed herself up to sitting and felt no twinges of pain nor the burn of frostbite. She was still wearing her leather apron, but had none of her tools. Searching around the space in her immediate reach, Ara found nothing that would serve as a weapon.

The nape of her neck tingled, the hairs there standing at sudden attention.

Ara looked back at the fire.

The girl was staring at her.

Ara moved into a crouch, muscles taut. Running might be futile, but it might also be her only choice.

The girl stood up. She was very tall. Something glinted in the firelight. Ara saw the sword hilt. The girl's hand on it.

About to bolt, Ara was stopped by the boy's abrupt lurching to his feet.

"Don't run!"

The girl abandoned her aggressive stance to steady the boy.

"Please," he called again to Ara. "We need your help."

When Ara didn't move, the boy straightened. At full height, he was still a few inches shorter than the girl. His hair was a pile of soft brown curls that would not take kindly to a comb. He had wide, dark eyes.

"Take off your sword," he said to the tall girl.

She gave him an incredulous look.

"Do it." The boy's voice could be very firm when he wanted it to be.

Grumbling, the girl unbuckled her sword then tossed the belt and scabbard aside.

Ara stood up, perplexed by the unfolding situation. "Who are you?"

Now that she faced them, Ara saw that both had umber skin and bore a strong resemblance to each other. Brother and sister?

They could not be bandits. Now that they stood in front of her, Ara could see their clothing beneath their cloaks. Instead of patched trousers and spotted shirts, this boy and girl wore belted tunics of fine wool, his dyed deep blue and hers a delicate shade of green. Their legs were clad in soft leather breeches, and the cut of their boots showed impeccable craftsmanship. No one in Ara's life boasted such a luxurious wardrobe.

"My name is Eamon," the boy said.

His voice was steady now. The tea had done its work. He looked at the girl with adoring eyes.

Her hands clasped opposite elbows and her body tightened. "Please don't say it."

"You know I have to," he replied before rolling his shoulders back and addressing Ara. "This is my sister Nimhea, eldest child of Dentroth crowned by flame, son of Emrisa, daughter of Rea, daughter of Polit, son of Trin, son of Vinnea, daughter of Hessa, daughter of Imlo, son of Gright, son of Penla, daughter of Terr, son of Olnea—first of the Flamecrowned dynasty. Princess Nimhea, daughter of fire, heir to the River Throne of Saetlund. The—"

"There is no River Throne." Ara's voice was flat. Her bones felt hollow, as if they sensed Ara was about to be flooded with knowledge she didn't want.

Nimhea's expression shifted from hostile to curious, while a flustered Eamon groped for a response.

"Of course, after the conquest the Vokkans declared the end of Dentroth's line," Eamon said. "But that was—"

Ara cut him off again. "Why should I believe anything you're saying?"

Eamon elbowed Nimhea.

"Really?" She gave him a sidelong glance that hinted of disdain.

When he gestured for her to act, she sighed then reached up and pushed back the hood of her cloak.

Ara had to stop herself from gasping.

Thick curls were caught back from Nimhea's face, held by a gold cuff at the base of her skull. Its length fell to the small of her back in a sectioned twist held by three additional golden cuffs. The style was like nothing Ara had seen, but it was the color that held her gaze.

Nimhea's hair glowed in the firelight; her locks had living flames within each strand. Red, gold, copper. Its hue was ever-changing. Mesmerizing. Made even more so by its contrast to her thundercloud eyes. Fire and storm.

Ara stared at the Nimhea's long twist of flame-red hair. Something about it nagged her, like a word on the tip of her tongue that she couldn't recall.

Eldest child of Dentroth.

Ara's mouth dropped open in surprise. "Crowned by flame."

Eamon beamed at her, but Nimhea pressed her lips together and averted her eyes.

Crowned by flame. It was a phrase that made Old Imgar snort with disgust or, if he was particularly irritable, spit.

"When folks decided only a special head o' hair and a certain name made a king, that's when Saetlund was doomed."

Inevitably, the soured blacksmith would launch into a history lecture Ara had heard dozens of times before.

"Saetlund didn't always have a hereditary monarch, you know. Did fine for centuries, with a king and queen chosen by the people," Imgar would grumble, and return to work. That hadn't meant he'd stop talking. "Then there was the provincial council. Also chosen by the people. Their job to make sure the king and queen kept the good of all the provinces at the fore."

At that point Old Imgar would stop and jab whatever tool was in his hand at Ara to get her attention. "You know why it all fell apart?"

He never let her answer.

"Because people are greedy bastards." He continued to jab the air in front of Ara. "Had to ruin a perfectly good kingdom. Nava's wrath upon them, I say. She knows they deserve it. Now where are those nails I asked for, girl?"

Ara had heard Imgar's rant so many times she could recite it word for word. Those greedy bastards he hated so much. They were Nimhea's bloodline. Eamon's too.

The thought of Imgar getting the chance to jab tools and lecture at them filled Ara with a mad desire to laugh. But the stark reality of the situation quelled her glee before it could make any sound.

Ara didn't know if the Flamecrowned Dynasty had always been corrupt. Or if the seed of deceit planted at its origin had simply sprouted through generations, roots going deeper and deeper. By the time of Ara's birth, most of Saetlund accepted that it had always been that way. Only curmudgeons like Imgar railed against the system. And curmudgeons tended to be cursed at, then ignored.

How the first king and queen of that line had ensured that their child would be the next to take the throne, Ara wasn't sure. Nor did she know the details of how, over time, all key positions in the government—including the Provincial Council—became royal appointments. She'd heard court at the Five Rivers palace consisted almost exclusively of citizens from Sola and Ofrit.

Ara did recall reading that the name *Flamecrowned* wasn't coined until five generations into their rule; a result of that striking shade of red appearing with regular frequency in the royal nursery. It was widely acknowledged—to the point of being mentioned in history books—that in subsequent generations a few Dentroth monarchs had used crushed beetle shells and ochre to coax their tresses toward the royal hue.

What stood out the most clearly in Ara's mind was the reason Imgar had such vitriol for Dentroth and his ancestors. They'd let their kingdom bloat, allowed its bones to become weak and brittle. When the enemy arrived, Saetlund could do nothing but collapse.

There was no restoration. No revolt against the Vokkan Empire.

How could there be when the heir to the throne had been lost? But here she was.

More importantly, the Loresmith was gone. Would never return— so most of Saetlund believed.

But the truth coursed through Ara's veins. The blood of her father, who had been slain by the empire. She had the potential to become the next Loresmith.

I have the chance to know my father, she thought, and trembled when sorrow and anticipation mingled within her. *The only way to know who he was and what he died for.*

There was only one reason the children of Dentroth would come to a village this small and remote.

Ara hadn't wanted to accept she'd been taken. But something more astounding had happened. She'd been found.

3

imhea and Eamon tethered the horses to a tree behind the cottage where Ara lived with her grandmother. It had taken arguing, cajoling, and finally outright demanding that the royal twins should return to Rill's Pass with Ara. Despite her assurances to Nimhea that everyone in the village could be trusted, Ara admitted it would be better if no one spotted strangers for now. They entered the cottage through the cellar. In the dark, Ara guided their way around shelves, casks, and crates. Eamon kept one hand on Ara's shoulder, and Nimhea held on to Eamon's shoulder to avoid obstacles.

Ara's pulse quickened as she climbed the stairs. A heaviness on her chest was making it hard to breathe. She had the overwhelming sense that everything in her life was about to change. It felt like impending doom.

She opened the cellar door and stepped into the larder. It was almost as dark as the basement.

Ara heard a familiar whistling, and instinct made her drop to a crouch.

Crack! The sound of splintering wood came from above and to the right.

"Grandmother! It's me!"

"Ara?" Her grandmother sounded relieved, but annoyed. "Why are you creeping up the steps like a thief?"

"I have a good reason," Ara said defensively. "I'm not alone."

She moved away from the doorframe. "It's all right; you can come up."

Eamon edged into the room, followed by Nimhea, who had half drawn her sword.

Ara's grandmother huffed, squinting in the dim light. "Who are they?"

"Let's go to the hearth," Ara said. "I can barely see."

"Why do you think I nearly clubbed you?" Her grandmother shoved something into her hands. "Take this."

The familiar weight of Ironbranch was both comforting and jarring. Her fingers closed around the stave that lay at the heart of everything she feared and hoped for.

Ara's grandmother was already hanging a kettle over the hearth when Ara led Eamon and Nimhea into the room.

"Make yourselves comfortable," Ara's grandmother told the twins. "Let no one claim Elke Silverthread is a poor hostess."

Eamon whispered the name as if it were sacred. "Silverthread."

"That's the family name," Elke replied as she measured tea leaves into mugs. She cast a sidelong glance at Ara. "They don't know your name?"

Slumping into a chair, Nimhea said to Eamon, "I told you this was a fool's errand."

"No." Eamon shook his head. "I'm not wrong about this, I'm not. I told you, Silverthread is one of the names I looked for."

"But not *the* name," Nimhea snapped. Then she snarled at Ara. "Let me guess, you withheld your name because you're loyal to the Vokkans. Will you send for Emperor Fauld's cronies now?" She laughed harshly. "That's fine. I'm too tired to do anything about it."

Nimhea's words shook Ara. The princess looked like she'd lost a battle; her face was drawn with exhaustion. All the fight had gone out of her.

Eamon knelt by his sister. "Don't say that."

Ara's grandmother was holding a steaming mug and staring at the twins. Color leached from her cheeks.

"It can't be." Elke's hand began to tremble.

Turning to look at the old woman, Eamon went from crestfallen to hopeful. As he gazed at Ara's grandmother his eyes filled with fiery resolve.

"You know," Eamon said quietly.

Elke opened her mouth then closed it again.

"Nimhea." Eamon said the name like it was an order.

Nimhea slowly straightened in her chair, looking from her brother to Elke. "Are you sure?"

"Yes."

Reaching up, Nimhea pulled her hair free of its covering.

Ara's grandmother gasped. The ceramic mug shattered when it hit the floor.

"Grandmother!" Ara rushed to the older woman's side, worried her grandmother might have been scalded by the splatter of tea.

Elke didn't react when Ara put an arm around her shoulders. She continued to stare at Nimhea.

Witnessing Nimhea's revelation a second time, Ara understood why the princess doubted Ara was the Loresmith. Nimhea was everything an heir to the throne should be: tall with a proud bearing and a ready sword hand. She was statuesque in figure and observed everything around her with falcon's focus.

Ara was none of these things. The twins likely expected a brawny mountain youth with a broad back and muscles that strained the stitching of his shirtsleeves. Instead they'd come across a girl who was petite, but her stature belied her strength. Ara's hair didn't rival the fires of a forge. Her locks were dark as coal and always worn in intricate braids that kept her safe from the odd spark and were a herald of Fjeri highland traditions. Her skin never glowed like deep bronze in candlelight. She was pale as ice except for the perpetual slap of windburn on her cheeks, proving she'd danced with mountain gales.

The cottage door burst open. "Elke!"

Old Imgar's thick beard and bushy eyebrows were crusted with ice. "Something's happened to Ara. The smithy's a disaster!"

He stopped, taking in the scene. "Gods."

Nimhea was on her feet, all signs of despondence gone. She eyed Imgar warily.

"Friend." Ara threw the word at Nimhea. Imgar's craggy face, mad hair, and hulking shape could easily be taken as a threat.

"Imgar," Ara's grandmother spoke commandingly. "Close the door and lock it."

The old man did Elke's bidding, then shrugged off his cloak.

A flash of metal caught Ara's eye. It wasn't the ax Imgar took with him when he went south to fell trees. Ara hadn't seen this ax before. She immediately wanted to hold it, examine it. From across the room she could tell it was very fine. Not an ax made for chopping wood. But how had Old Imgar come to possess such an ax? He certainly didn't craft such fine weapons at his forge.

It's not the *name.* Nimhea's words sounded in Ara's mind, and she knew the time for hiding has passed.

She stepped forward, facing Nimhea and Eamon. "My name is Ara Silverthread. My father's name was Yos Steelring."

Eamon drew a sharp breath. "I knew it was you." His whole body seemed to vibrate with silent exultation.

Nimhea's gaze revealed nothing, but she responded to Ara's words with a slow half smile. "Then we have a lot to talk about."

Dusting off any shock she felt, Ara's grandmother returned to directing her household.

"Ara, collect everyone's cloaks and hang them," Elke ordered. "Imgar, clean up this mess at my feet, then bring in the bedroom chairs. After that go to the cellar and fetch a cask of mead. I don't think tea will suffice."

Imgar grumbled, "Maybe something stronger than mead."

"Mead will do," Elke said firmly.

Out of habit, the two of them set about Elke's tasks.

As Ara hung cloaks, she almost laughed at the banality of it. Her life had been upended, but some things—like following her grandmother's orders without question—hadn't changed at all. She didn't think they ever would. Ara tucked that little truth away, knowing she could call on it if needed.

A few moments later the five of them had gathered near the warm hearth, wooden cups of mead in their hands.

Old Imgar lifted his cup. Ice had fallen from his beard in chunks, revealing the gray-streaked, dark brown hair beneath. "To Saetlund."

"To Saetlund," the rest of them echoed.

After draining his cup, Imgar said to Nimhea, "We had no word you were crossing the sea. Why is that?"

Ara sat up straight. What Imgar had just said implied that he should have known the twins would arrive in Rill's Pass. And that meant he'd been in contact with them before.

For how long? Ara wondered. *And why had neither Imgar nor her grandmother talked about Nimhea and Eamon's existence as other than something hoped for?*

Nimhea's eyes shifted to her brother.

"Our friends don't know we're here," Eamon told Imgar. "We still plan to rendezvous with them at the designated time and place."

Imgar's heavy brow rose in surprise. "A bit risky that . . . venturing north on your own."

Straightening, Nimhea met the old man's eyes with defiance. "We've proven we're capable by making it here."

"Hmmmm."

Ara recognized the look on Old Imgar's face. He hadn't made a judgement about Nimhea yet. Imgar usually took the measure of a person in the first moments after meeting. His indecisiveness about the princess confused Ara.

So Imgar hasn't been communicating with the twins, Ara decided. *But he's been in contact with the rebellion.*

She'd expected clarity from her grandmother and Imgar. Instead, things were getting murkier.

Imgar nodded, but his eyes showed doubt. "Why don't they know you're here?"

"It's my fault," Eamon rushed to answer. "I've been working on something independent of our main efforts—I've kept it to myself. I wanted to be sure before . . ."

His attention fell on Ara.

"You came looking for Ara," her grandmother finished. "How did you know where to find her?"

A slight blush colored Eamon's cheeks. "I combed through everything I could find on the fall of the River Throne. The people who raised us have contacts at Saetlund's universities. They were able to get me copies of letters, diaries, and personal notes that were salvaged from the palace."

Throwing an apologetic look at Ara, he continued, "Yos and Lira did their best to hide their relationship, but I found bits of gossip about Yos avoiding the marriage King Dentroth wanted to make for him. One rejected noble lady had a servant follow Yos to the merchant quarter. The spy didn't witness anything to confirm a secret rendezvous, but the lady did note in her diary that Yos had visited the Silverthread weavers' shop."

"That's a tiny piece on the way to completing a puzzle," Elke remarked.

"I chased after any clue I found," Eamon said with a shrug. "Most didn't lead me anywhere. But that jilted woman's brief pursuit of Ara's father was enough to have me send someone to Rill's Pass looking for a girl with the name Steelring. They reported back that there was no Steelring, but they had found a girl of the right age being raised by her grandmother—whose name was Silverthread."

"You sent a spy to our village?!"

Cold grasped Ara's throat, making it hard to swallow. A diary. A jotted sentence.

"As far as they knew," Eamon continued, "Ara could never become a true Loresmith. Her father died in the conquest; thus, she had no one to teach her. When he died, the line died."

"But that's true," Ara interjected. Her initial excitement at the possibility of taking on her father's role had been tempered by the doubts she'd been harboring of late. She couldn't become Loresmith without a teacher. No ordinary blacksmith could pass on the knowledge that had been lost with her father. That fact had been at the center of her souring on anything to do with her supposed fate.

"It *was* true." Eamon moved to the edge of his seat. He looked so eager, Ara worried he might jump on her like an excited puppy. "But I've spent years looking for an answer to the problem, and I found one."

"Years?" Imgar sized up Eamon. "You're hardly more than a child."

"He has spent years on this research," Nimhea shot back. "I was there."

Eamon offered his sister a grateful smile. "And I'm not a child; we're eighteen."

Ara puzzled at Eamon not being able to say his age without including his twin.

"You know a way for Ara to come into her power?" Elke's voice was shaky.

Placing her hand over her grandmother's, Ara asked, "Do you feel unwell?"

Elke shook her head. "Not at all. It's just . . . this is all I've ever hoped for. And everything I've always feared."

"It could make an all-out rebellion viable." Imgar scratched his beard, and more ice plunked onto the floor. "The Loresmith was the spoke around which the Loreknights turned, serving as the bridge between the gods and their chosen warriors. The Loresmith not only forged god-touched weapons, but also guided the Loreknights—the heart and spirit of all they represented. If Ara brought back the Loreknights, it would provide Saetlund a near invincible force. The only real chance of driving out the empire."

Ara's pulse quickened. The gathering of Loreknights was where many of her favorite fireside tales began. How astonishing it would be to take counsel with the gods and seek out the most worthy. She suddenly felt a longing for that life.

"How?" Elke demanded of Eamon. "How could my granddaughter become Loresmith?"

Eamon quailed slightly at the force of her question. "I'm still working out the specificities, but, in short, she needs to petition the gods."

Silence overtook the room. Even the fire appeared to die down.

Ara's throat closed. *Petition the gods? Such a thing isn't possible.*

A chiding voice in her mind pointed out that Ara had little business declaring what was and was not possible considering the current state of affairs. She was finding it hard to sit still. Her limbs were abuzz with these new revelations.

"I found the solution within the origin of the Loresmith," Eamon continued nervously. "There are clues distributed through all the myths and legends. If you know what to look for they read like instructions from the gods."

"You know the tale?" Elke asked softly. "An old story, that is."

"I studied as many legends of Saetlund as I could," Eamon replied. "I had to."

Ara's grandmother nodded. "I'd like to hear that story and I'd like you to tell it."

"But—" Ara began. She stopped when Imgar gave a brief shake of his head.

The request made no sense at all. Ara knew the story by heart because she'd heard it so many times. From Elke. She wished she could speak to Eamon alone and ask every question she had. But Ara had been raised to respect her elders, so she held her tongue and sat on her hands to keep her fidgeting in check.

Eamon cleared his throat and began to speak:

In the first era, Saetlund's people prospered and the world was good.

The abundance was so great, it drew another god to the land.

The gods of Saetlund knew him, for he was their kin. Vokk, also called the Devourer, had not yet claimed a land or people for his own. He had searched the universe, but none had pleased him.

The gods gathered to greet their brother.

"We welcome you, Vokk," Eni said.

Vokk smiled his spike-toothed smile. "I thank you for your welcome."

"Why have you come to us?" Ayre and Syre asked, their light and dark always shifting, changing places.

"Stop that," Vokk complained. "You have always made me dizzy with your inconstant being."

"It is their nature," said Wuldr. The god of the hunt put his hand on the head of Senn, his great hound, to keep the beast from bristling. "Now tell us, brother, what has brought you here?"

Vokk sighed a heavy sigh, and the mountains trembled with his sorrow. "I have traveled the universe and found no people to call my own. I long for purpose. I see your people and my heart fills with envy."

"We are humbled by your admiration," Eni replied.

"It is I who should be humbled," Vokk told Eni. "To gaze upon my kindred's works and witness their mastery."

The gods murmured their thanks, but they were not at peace.

Vokk continued to speak. "I have looked beyond your land and know that this world is broad and deep and has many other lands you have not claimed."

"We need nothing more than this land, these people," said Nava, her abundant form rippling like fields of wheat as she moved.

"I marvel at your contentment." Vokk bowed deeply to her. "My only wish is to find the same."

He paused, stretching his taloned fingers. "I beg your leave, my kin, to claim the great continent on the opposite side of your world. The land is mountainous and harsh, its people are lost and need strength and tenacity to survive. I would help them, should it not displease you."

The gods of Saetlund knew one another's minds, and Eni spoke for all of them.

"We grant your wish, Vokk," Eni pronounced. "May you find your purpose in guiding the people of the great continent of this sphere."

"You are generous and I thank you." Vokk bowed once more and was gone.

At the tale's outset, Eamon had been focused and alert. Now his eyes were half closed. His words flowed in a steady rhythm.

With their brother departed, the gods were troubled.

Ofrit, with his shrewd mind, voiced what the others feared. "A neighbor like Vokk will not forever stay away."

"He hungers for war and conquest," the Twins said as one. "If he cannot be sated, he will surely devour all the peoples of this world."

Nava spoke. "We could not deny him. He is our kin."

"It is true," Eni said. "We could not deny him. But we also cannot leave our people at risk."

The gods had shaped their followers toward a kingdom of cooperation and peace, discouraging any passion for battle and blood. Saetlund's people knew not how to make war.

"How do we help them?" asked Ayre and Syre. "To make them

warlike would be to cut the bonds that tie us. We would no longer be gods of this land."

"We do not need to make warriors of them," Ofrit told the others. "Our gift to them must be one of defense. A bastion to stay Vokk should his hunger for this land overwhelm him."

The gods agreed that Ofrit's suggestion was good; thus the Loresmith came to be.

Eni searched the world for a person who embodied the best aspects of the gods:

The wisdom of the Twins.

The steadfastness of Wuldr.

The cleverness of Ofrit.

The generosity of Nava.

And Eni's own curiosity and cunning.

They were all leaning toward Eamon, enraptured by his telling.

In the land of Vijeri, Eni found a boy. The youngest of five siblings, who longed to know the world beyond his village. The boy's heart was true, his mind sharp, his curiosity boundless.

The gods visited this boy's dreams and told him what he must do to fulfill a great purpose.

Thus, the boy began his great journey: seeking and finding each of the gods to receive their wisdom in turn. To aid and instruct him, Ofrit and Eni together crafted the boy a stave infused with their magic and named it Ironbranch. When they gifted Ironbranch to the boy, they told him thusly:

He would become the first Loresmith, forger of weapons blessed by the gods, the wellspring of Saetlund's defense against all enemies.

The Loresmith's skill would surpass that of all blacksmiths, but must never forge a weapon for themself. They would manifest the protection of the gods in the form of weapons and armor, but must not be lured by the power begotten in battle, nor be consumed by vengeance, nor driven by rage. The Loresmith must shun violence and champion restoration. Should the Loresmith strike with a weapon, except in defense, their power would be taken from them.

The wielders of the Loresmith's great weapons would be chosen by the people, two from each province of Saetlund, and they would be called Loreknights—only these ten chosen could wield weapons forged by the Loresmith. The Loreknights became the invincible defenders of the people.

But neither Loresmith nor Loreknights would be immortal. All would live and die as the universe demands, but the gods-gifted protection would carry on with each new generation.

The Loresmith's legacy would be their children, one of whom would be named heir to the gods' gift, and taught the secrets of their divine craft.

The ritual of choosing two Loreknights from each province would continue, binding all the peoples of Saetlund together and to the gods.

In this way the great heroes of Saetlund were created.

After Eamon's last words came a long quiet. Ara sat very still, her eyes on the fire. Her mind transfixed by the story. Why did it suddenly feel as if she'd heard it for the first time?

Eni found a boy . . . who longed to know the world beyond his village.

I'm the same, Ara thought. *More than anything I've wished to leave the bounds of Rill's Pass. I have longed to know the world.*

The flames in the hearth blazed. Amid the spikes of orange and gold, Ara saw a picture formed of smoke and shadow. A smith at the anvil. She heard each strike of hammer upon iron. The smith paused, as if knowing that Ara watched. When the smith turned and met her gaze, Ara saw her own face.

Father? Ara's throat closed.

A small sound caught Ara's attention. Her grandmother had been watching her. Elke's hand covered her mouth—the source of the little noise.

"You understand now," her grandmother said softly.

Ara nodded, but she didn't, not completely. She did understand that her path was now the path of the Loresmith and that her father wanted her to follow in his stead. The consequences of that understanding were unknowable.

"I will not deny the power of this tale." Imgar scratched his thicket of a beard. "But the gods have faded from Saetlund. How can Ara petition them when they've left us?"

"I believe it's possible to find them," Eamon answered.

"How? Where are they?" Elke said with a gasp.

Eamon started to speak, but Imgar cut him off.

"No." The sun having set, only the firelight reached Old Imgar's face, enhancing the deep crevices time had worn into his features.

"The less we know the better," Imgar said. He pointed a finger at Nimhea. "That goes for your allies, too. Until it's fulfilled, Ara's task must be kept quiet."

"I can accept that," Nimhea replied, but her forehead crinkled. "You know more about the rebellion than I would have expected. Who are you?"

Old Imgar grinned at her. "An old man with opinions that some people want to listen to."

Nimhea pursed her lips, unsatisfied with his answer, but Imgar offered nothing further. Giving up on that front, she said, "To make our rendezvous we'll need to leave tomorrow."

Nodding, Imgar said, "We can provision you for the journey."

"Thank you."

"Imgar." Ara's grandmother gestured to the twins. "Take them to the inn. Mol and Hiffa will see that they're fed and have a comfortable place to sleep."

The old man nodded. "Get your cloaks and follow me."

Nimhea and Eamon did as they were bidden.

Ara leaned toward Imgar and whispered, "The horses are in the stand of pines behind the house."

Imgar winked at her and trudged out the door.

Ara watched him go, letting out a long sigh.

"You're troubled." Elke had been eyeing her granddaughter. "You're at a crossroads; a young person finding the way to live life on their own terms."

"Except I can't." Ara frowned. "That's what fate is, isn't it? I'm not in control of my future."

Her grandmother shrugged. "I don't think of it that way. The gods always give us a choice. They didn't want to be forgotten. But they were. Because we had the freedom to stop believing. I often think of how great their sorrow must be. To be loved and then abandoned is a terrible thing."

Ara pondered her grandmother's words. She'd only considered the gods for their marvelous feats and incredible powers. It hadn't occurred to her that gods could be vulnerable, even heartbroken. She also saw grief that must equal the gods' etched upon her grandmother's papery skin. There had been so much loss in Elke's life. Five years after Ara's father died a great fever swept across Saetlund, taking both Elke's daughter and her husband. She'd been left to raise a child on her own.

"You can choose not to be the Loresmith," Elke continued. "Whatever tasks the gods set before you, only you can complete or turn away from."

"But that would be selfish," Ara replied. "The Loresmith serves the people! If I become the Loresmith, I'm not just Ara Silverthread. A part of me belongs to the gods."

With a quiet laugh, her grandmother said, "I take issue with the idea that there is anything mundane or lacking in being 'just Ara Silverthread.' I know no matter the choices you make, you will always do right by your family and honor the gods."

Ara's face heated. She was ashamed of doubting the stories and for losing faith in the gods.

"You know," Elke whispered, "I don't think the gods are going to hold that against you. I know I won't."

That made Ara laugh, despite being embarrassed that her feelings were so plain.

"I confess," her grandmother said, "I prayed that this day wouldn't come."

Ara stepped back, not believing what she'd heard. "No you didn't."

"I did." Elke was nodding. "Accepting the role of Loresmith is an incredible honor. It's also a burden that most people couldn't bear. I would never wish such a difficult life on my granddaughter."

"But you always taught me about the necessity of the Loresmith," Ara countered. "You told me it was a gift."

"It is a gift," her grandmother replied. "But gifts from the gods are complicated. Nothing guarantees a life of ease or happiness. It would have been simpler if you could remain in Rill's Pass, marry, and surround me with great-grandchildren. That was the bliss I wanted for you."

Ara's heart swelled even as her thoughts were muddled. She had always known her grandmother loved her, but this dream for her, imagining that should could thrive in a simpler life, made that love palpable.

Taking her grandmother's hand, Ara said, "I want to become the Loresmith."

"And that's why you will." Elke squeezed her fingers.

Old Imgar stomped back into the room, clearing his throat loudly. "Don't mean to interrupt."

"Of course you do, old man," Elke said tartly, and released Ara's fingers.

Ara felt a bit of relief at Imgar's return. The well of emotions raised in the last few minutes was deep enough to drown in. She was thankful as well for the reminder that she wouldn't be leaving her grandmother alone. Imgar had arrived in Rill's Pass the summer after Elke had buried her daughter and husband. Taking Ara's grandfather's place as the village blacksmith, Imgar became a fixture in both of their lives.

Ara knew he'd been in the war, her grandmother told her as much, and he had scars on his neck and arms that hadn't come from a smithy. It had been obvious her grandmother knew him through some past connection, but she never explained how.

When Ara asked, Elke simply replied, "Another life."

For his part, Imgar carved out a place for himself in the village as a cantankerous bachelor who was good with a hammer. After a day's work at the forge he invited himself to supper in Elke's cottage and complained about the aches in his joints. That irked Ara's grandmother, given that Imgar was ten or more years her junior, so she'd taken to calling him "old man." The first time little Ara had called him "Old

Imgar," Elke and Imgar laughed until tears leaked from their eyes. The name stuck.

Imgar had stuck too. He'd been something in between father and grandfather as Ara grew. He'd taught her as much, if not more, about lore and the gods as her grandmother had. While Elke trained Ara with Ironbranch, Imgar had taken her deep into the highlands to seek out hidden shrines. He taught her to hunt and trap, all the while showing her how to honor Wuldr. She learned winter camping and wilderness survival at Imgar's side, and he shared stories of Eni, who watched over all travelers.

When Ara had proclaimed she would soon make the pilgrimage to the Well sacred to the twins—and set high among the cliffs of the highlands' tallest peaks—Elke had given Imgar the responsibility of explaining to the enthusiastic, if naive, young girl that such a trip was ill advised. At least for the time being.

She would miss him. Even his grumpiness. But Ara didn't want to show him. She'd had enough of sentiment for one day. She didn't mind sentiment, but it was draining.

Ara crossed her arms over her chest and rounded on an unsuspecting Imgar.

"Why aren't you angry at them?"

"Angry at who?" Imgar poured himself a cup, then looked at Elke. "Another?"

"No thank you," she replied.

When he turned to Ara, Elke shook her head. "None for her either. I won't have my granddaughter miserable when she rides out of Rill's Pass. I'll make some tea."

Ara wasn't bothered by her grandmother's insistence on tea. The flurry of thoughts in Ara's mind wouldn't be helped by the fuzziness of drink.

"I can't remember a day when you didn't complain about King Dentroth," Ara told Imgar. "I could list every reason you said he was a terrible king."

Imgar dropped into a chair with his cup of mead and set the cask at his feet. "He was a terrible king."

"Then why are you helping his children?" Ara asked.

"I don't know his children." Imgar took a swallow of mead. "I won't judge the princess and prince until I know who they truly are—no matter how badly their father behaved."

With a nod, Ara said, "I suppose that's fair."

"I think so." He smiled slowly. "But that's not the whole reason I'm going easy on them."

Ara recognized the gleam of mischief in Old Imgar's eyes.

Stretching his feet toward the fire, Imgar said, "Overthrowing the Vokkans is no small feat. It won't happen if we only have a like-minded group of people, even if it's enough to form an army. People need something to follow. A symbol of what was taken from them."

"Nimhea," Ara said.

"The hardest part of forming the Resistance," Imgar said, "is finding a way to unify four provinces that have been driven apart. That's why they need the heir to the River Throne. That's why they need you."

Ara considered that before returning to a point Imgar had raised before. "*Does* the Resistance have enough like-minded people for an army?"

He gave Ara a long look. While she'd known of the rebellion, Imgar had always dodged any specific questions about his allies.

Imgar nodded as if he'd come to an agreement with himself and took a long drink from his cup.

"No," he admitted. "There are rebel militias in each province—most have committed to the Resistance, some still operate independently. It's another reason we need the twins. We hope their return, once it's revealed, will significantly increase our ranks."

"Aren't you worried Nimhea will turn out like her father as soon as she's taken the throne?" Ara accepted a mug of tea from her grandmother, who snuggled into a fur-laden chair on the other side of the hearth.

"I've plenty to worry about before we come to that question." Imgar snorted. "If we get there."

"Don't scare her," Elke chided.

Imgar scrunched his face up. "Honesty can be scary."

Elke sighed and sipped her tea.

After another slug of mead, Imgar told Ara, "What you're forgetting is that Nimhea isn't taking her place in an unbroken dynasty. She has to lead a revolution. That will forge a different kind of ruler. The better kind."

"How do you know that?" Ara countered.

"History."

Old Imgar grunted as he bent down to retrieve the cask.

"Imgar, your liver," Elke said pointedly.

"Don't you remember that I replaced my old liver with an iron one years ago?" Imgar waggled his eyebrows at her as he filled his cup.

"You're impossible," Elke said with exasperation.

He feigned sorrow. "And here I thought I was brimming with the possible."

She ignored him, and he looked at Ara. "How are you feeling about all this?"

"I'm not sure," Ara admitted.

"That's very sensible of you," Imgar said. "Tell me about the things you're less sure about."

It was a relief to have permission to voice her doubts. "Traveling. The twins appear . . . unseasoned when it comes to a long journey."

Imgar nodded. "You'll catch them up."

"I don't know—" Ara was confident in her own skills, but she'd seen how ill-suited Nimhea and Eamon were for traveling rough.

"I do," Imgar stopped her. "I taught you myself. You have all the skills you need to turn those two into rangers."

Ara laughed and spilled some of her tea. Elke clucked her tongue and went to get a rag.

"What else are you worried about?" Imgar pressed.

"Everything." Ara took the damp rag her grandmother offered and mopped up tea.

"Here's my advice about that." Imgar dragged his feet away from the hearth and sat up straight. "The world is made to drown people. It's the ocean. Don't swim out there. Take your problems one puddle at a time."

"One puddle at a time," Ara repeated. She liked the sound of that.

❖ ELSEWHERE: THE SONS OF FAULD ❖

iran watched his brother Zenar's mouth curve up as though the corners of his lips were controlled by marionette strings. The resulting smile was ghastly, something between a sneer and a grin.

Though repulsed, Liran showed no reaction. He'd long ago learned to hide his feeling from his brother. At a very young age Liran discovered that Zenar was ill-suited to pleasant emotions. The younger of Fauld's two sons didn't have a happy nature and proved it through his disdain for animals and penchant for cruelty first to the nursemaids and later tutors. When he did attempt to exude joy it looked mangled on his face.

"You wanted to see me?" Liran, who carried the titles fiftieth of his name, the Dark Star, Commander of Imperial Armies, Beloved Elder Son (this generation) of Fauld the Ever-Living, addressed his brother.

Zenar, bearing the titles twenty-second of his name, the Poisoned Cup, ArchWizard of Vokk, Exalted Younger Son (this generation) of Fauld the Ever-Living, rose from his desk. "I have good news, my brother. Let us drink together in celebration."

"I'm inspecting several squadrons this afternoon," Liran told him. "Forgive me, but I need a clear head."

"How tragic," Zenar replied with a mocking sigh. "Your martial lifestyle has far too many rules. Where do you find your pleasure?"

Liran answered with a tight-lipped smile.

While Zenar poured himself a drink, Liran said, "I would like to hear your news."

Zenar took his time before answering. He lifted his crystal goblet so it caught a ray of sunshine, then swirled the bright green liquid inside, making prisms dance on the walls.

"They landed at Port Pilgrim several days ago," Zenar said at last. "By now they should have found him. I expect another report soon."

Liran rocked back on his heels. That was important news, and the last thing Liran had expected. When Zenar had concocted this scheme, Liran had dismissed it as a fool's errand. Zenar had carried on with his plans, as Liran assumed he would. Both brothers stayed out of each other's business. It was a good arrangement, as they usually moved through different worlds.

"Congratulations," Liran said. "You proved me wrong. How did you manage that?"

"Seduction is a subtler art than bribery, though either can be means to the same end," Zenar quipped.

"I'd imagine you also see bribery as the vulgar choice," Liran replied.

"How well you know me," Zenar said with a slash of a smile. "Seduction requires art, bribery merely coin."

Liran was skeptical. "Seduction from afar? Is such a thing possible?"

"How base of you, dear brother." Zenar's laugh made Liran's skin crawl. "It wasn't that kind of seduction." He paused to sip from his goblet. "There are several kinds, you know."

"I defer to your expertise," Liran murmured. He didn't want to show how alarmed he was at Zenar's revelation. It had far-reaching consequences that Liran had hoped to avoid.

"Any word from father?" Zenar asked too casually. His voice carried a familiar edge.

Liran had always been their father's favorite. Zenar believed it was due to their father's admiration of martial prowess and resented both of them for it, but Liran suspected Fauld preferred the elder son because Zenar's ever-growing occult powers presented a greater threat to the emperor's supremacy.

"He's pleased with our reports," Liran answered. "I think he will be until he crushes the uprising in Penra. He also has to contend with the rioting in Talvor because of the famine."

Zenar raised an eyebrow. "Will you be recalled?"

"Possibly," Liran said, watching hope surge in his brother's eyes. "But I doubt he'll summon me unless the situation becomes desperate. I command the conquering armies; you know Father uses specialized battalions to deal with rebels."

The gleam in Zenar's eyes dulled. "Of course."

Liran didn't say what they both knew: the emperor didn't want Zenar to have full control of Saetlund. For reasons Liran didn't yet under-stand, their father held Saetlund apart from his other conquests. Fauld wanted to keep Liran there to check Zenar's more extreme tendencies.

Clearing his throat to ease the sudden tension, Liran asked, "What further plans do you have for Dentroth's twins?"

"Ah, the twins." Zenar brightened at the mention of his success. "I'm going to let that situation unfold. I'll intervene when the time is right. But Dentroth's brats aren't the real prize."

"Of course," Liran said blandly. "How could I forget?"

Zenar licked his lips. "You shouldn't neglect your faith, brother. Vokk is a jealous god. I will bring his greatest enemy before him in chains."

"May he be sated," Liran replied.

Zenar echoed out of habit. "May he be sated."

"I'll leave you to your . . ." Liran made a vague wave at Zenar's desk.

Wearing that same tortured smile, Zenar said, "Always a pleasure to see you."

Liran offered a polite nod and left Zenar's study. He chewed on their conversation as he made his way from Vokk's temple to the barracks. A single victory was never enough for Zenar. He'd pulled off an incredible feat in finding the heirs to the River Throne. It was madness that he insisted on chasing a legend as well.

Liran wasn't without faith. Vokk was real enough, Liran knew, but all religions had their embellishments. The wizards wasted so much time searching for power that didn't exist, spirits that couldn't be summoned, magics that were nothing but charades.

Zenar's search for the Loresmith would serve only his vanity. There was no capturing a legend that didn't exist.

4

wo nights later, Ara huddled near a campfire, her body cocooned in a heavy cloak, and stared past the flames. Her gaze settled on the two strangers who'd appeared in her life without warning. Unwanted harbingers of the dust-covered destiny she'd put aside years before.

Ara's new companions were little more than misshapen lumps, buried under wool and furs that served as fiber bulwarks against the night's chill. She couldn't say what heap of blankets was sister or brother, princess or prince.

Princess or prince. Ara ground her teeth.

Even the sound of the titles in her own mind made Ara jerk from the shock of it.

She hadn't been ready for them. For this journey. This future. She still wasn't.

A sour smile curdled at the corners of Ara's lips. How fitting that all of it began with a kidnapping. After all, hadn't her life just been taken without warning?

Watching her breath smoke and curl in the air, Ara contemplated her fate. With Nimhea and Eamon's arrival, she had to accept that she was who her grandmother had always claimed: the daughter of the Loresmith. She was an heir—like the twins—and according to her grandmother and Old Imgar, she had a destiny.

She'd believed that fate was lost. It had died with her father.

The heirs to the River Throne had come seeking the Loresmith. They'd found Ara.

Will I become what they need me to be? Ara wondered. *Or will the gods forsake me because I turned away from them?*

Ara wanted to fulfill this incredible destiny, but she worried that the gods wouldn't overlook the doubts she'd clung to in her stubbornness. If Nimhea and Eamon hadn't arrived, she would still be mired in her disbelief.

As she'd grown older, Ara had balked at the stories told by grandmother and Old Imgar. Though her earliest memories were the tales of the gods and their great gift to the people of Saetlund, she'd long since given up her belief that she had any part in them. The Loresmith and Loreknights. Though she remembered the awe of learning her father was the last Loresmith, it had complicated her grief for a man she'd never known, but for whom an empty place in her heart remained. When Ara was old enough to understand what she had lost, she'd craved a father—as much to salve her mother's ongoing sorrow as to care for his daughter—but when that father was connected to the great tales of old, he became something else. A legend. She hadn't known how to reconcile her vision of a father with a man who forged the weapons of the gods. But she tried to meld the two into something she could wish for.

When she was small, Ara would sit in a corner of the smithy and envision her father working beside her grandfather, and later Old Imgar. As she grew strong enough, Ara helped Imgar with small tasks. The moment she'd felt the heat of the forge and laid hands on blacksmith tools, Ara's grandmother could hardly tear her away from that sweltering, smoky place. That was the first time she felt like her father's daughter. His blood drawing her to flame and iron. To the rhythm of the hammer and tempering of steel.

Rather than object, Ara's grandmother encouraged her to learn the blacksmith's craft. She'd given her blessing in a joyful voice tinged by sorrow. While Ara watched and sometimes worked beside Imgar, he filled her head with more stories of heroics, fate, and the gods. She became his apprentice and dreamed of the glorious weapons she would create for her Loreknights, who would avenge her father's death.

Ara constantly thought of Saetlund's deities. She stared at the Ice Mountains and imagined the Twins at their Well and gave herself a headache trying to understand how two gods could exist within one being. When Ara scouted in the forest with Imgar, she pretended Wuldr hunted beside them. At the harvest, she gave thanks to Nava and wove ornaments of dried grass with her grandmother to honor the goddess. She learned to ask Ofrit for help with puzzles and complicated tasks, as well as praying for his guidance when making ointments, salves, and other medicines. Because her travel was limited, Ara didn't often have cause to seek Eni's blessing. But Old Imgar's tales of Eni's shape-shifting, cleverness, and unpredictable antics always made her laugh.

The little girl who had prayed to those gods and delighted in those stories couldn't sustain her enthusiasm when she found no signs of power in herself as the years passed. The nails, horseshoes, tools, and knives she crafted for the village had no magic in them. In the tales, the Loresmith forged the most marvelous of weapons and impenetrable armor. Pieces known not only for their power, but for their beauty and elegance. Legendary swords and axes with names like Stormcaller and Soulcleave. Impossibly light armor with a delicate appearance that belied its strength.

At twelve Ara crafted a sword, hoping that forging a proper weapon would reveal her gift, but the sword was plain, serviceable—nothing more.

Ara took to pressing her grandmother about how exactly she could be sure she had the power of the Loresmith inside her and, more importantly, how she could become the Loresmith without her father to teach her.

Her grandmother always answered the same way. "Your fate is with the gods."

But the gods didn't seem bothered by young Ara's impatience, nor her frustration. She couldn't understand their inaction. She grew resentful of the stories and their unfulfilled promises. The gods likewise drew her ire.

Ara had spent her childhood imagining them, but she'd never actually seen any of the gods. None of them had bothered to speak to her.

When she asked for proof of her identity from Old Imgar, he told her, "Ironbranch is all the proof you need."

For most of Ara's life, Ironbranch had been her most treasured possession. The Loresmith's stave. A legendary weapon—and Ara's only connection to her father.

Another of Ara's strongest memories: it had also been a birthday, her tenth.

Ara's grandmother had offered her a strangely twisting, long stick. "This belongs to you."

Ara took it, noticing its unusual color and texture. The material it had been wrought from was strange, like a mixture of wood and steel. It was heavy and hard to grip with her small hands.

"Thank you," Ara said. "Is it a walking stick like yours?"

"This is no ordinary walking stick." Elke laughed. "It is the stave of the Loresmith, created by Ofrit and Eni for the first of your line. It has been passed down from generation to generation. Its name is Ironbranch."

"It has a name?" Ara gazed at the stave in wonder, amazed that such a thing could belong to her.

Her grandmother's mirth gave way to a careworn expression. "Your father sent it with your mother when she fled the city."

"This belonged to my father?" Ara's fingers locked around the stave. Knowing he'd left something for her made it more precious even than its legendary origin.

She gave her grandmother a puzzled look, followed by a sheepish smile. "I know it sounds strange, but holding it I feel safer. Less afraid."

"You should," Elke replied. "That stave was created to protect you and your companions. Look here." She pointed to the one end of the stave, and Ara noticed a small symbol carved into the wood. "Eni's symbol," her grandmother said, then pointed at the other end. "You'll find Ofrit's symbol carved there, on the opposite face of the wood."

"The gods made it." Ara traced the symbol with her finger and shivered when a strange sensation crackled through her limbs. It felt like recognition.

Her grandmother's voice became stern. "Ara, listen very carefully. Ironbranch must only be used for defense. I'm going to teach you how to use this stave."

Ara nodded, utterly enamored with Ironbranch. The pale, polished wood with its silvering grain. Its solidity and weight. The image of her father walking forest paths with Ironbranch at his side. Like a friend.

Her grandmother was still speaking. "Ara, listen to me. Remember the tale: should you attack, or strike out in anger or vengeance you will never become the Loresmith. The same is true for any other tool or weapon that you come to possess. Do not forget. Are you listening?"

"Yes."

But like those old stories, Ironbranch and the memory of receiving it had lost their sheen for Ara. She didn't deny it was an unusual stave. The wood from which it was carved was a silvery iron-gray. During one of her pestering sessions, Imgar had shoved Ironbranch into the forge. Ara had screamed, but grizzled Old Imgar laughed and pulled the stave from the fire. Ironbranch hadn't been scorched nor damaged and was cool to the touch. The demonstration kept her doubts at bay for a week before Ara went back to scratching at the surface of her life story.

Just because Ironbranch was different didn't mean it was the mythical Loresmith stave. After all, her knowledge was limited to the books in Rill's Pass. She had no experience of the wider world, which was surely bursting with many strange and inexplicable things.

The more she thought about it, the more the whole thing seemed cruel and unfair. What was she other than a girl whose parents had died and who was being raised by her grandmother in a tiny village in the middle of nowhere? A girl who was forbidden from going anywhere? It made her sick with rage. She considered running away.

In the end, Ara ruled out escape, but let her feelings be known in other ways. She left the room if her grandmother or Imgar tried to recite one of the tales. They had both tolerated that behavior, but Ara's grandmother would not let her stop training with Ironbranch. Ara had grudgingly continued to practice with the stave, but she put little effort into improving her skills. Her grandmother was tight-lipped and hard-eyed at the end of each lesson, but Ara ignored the disapproval. She'd decided it was better that none of it was real. That fate and the gods were simply fantasies spun from the past.

If it wasn't real, Ara didn't have to feel cheated by the universe.

She'd been picking at that scab for two years.

Ara had spent so much time convincing herself that she wasn't special, it was difficult, even in the face of the long-lost twins' arrival, to change her feelings. Becoming a skeptic hadn't been hard. After all, what signs of the gods or magic had Ara ever witnessed?

The only evidence of legends, heroes, and monsters resided in fireside stories and old books with cracked spines. Books that had to be hidden beneath the floorboards when imperial patrols came through the village. Stories that could only be told among the trustworthy.

Her grandmother's voice piped up again. *If the tales held no truth, why would the Vokkans want to destroy them? Why forbid worship of the gods, if the gods have no power?*

Ara had formulated pert answers to those questions and more as she'd rebelled against her prescribed role. Now those replies felt hollow as new knowledge seeped through the cracks in Ara's veneer of disbelief. Her rejection of the stories, of the claims made by her grandmother and Old Imgar, hadn't been built upon rational arguments and unwavering confidence. It had been the way Ara protected herself, the way she could hide from her fate.

Cowardice hadn't compelled Ara to turn her back on all she'd been taught. Shame had.

Shame for surviving in a world that had taken her mother and father. Shame for being chosen and protected, while so many others were stolen away from hearth and home by the Vokkan Empire.

The more Ara had learned about the world, the less she wanted to be special.

It laid a terrible responsibility at her feet. But she saw now that in that responsibility she could find purpose. She had to.

Ara had spent the last two years denying the truth of who she was. It was time to embrace that truth.

How can you sleep so soundly? Ara silently asked the bundled twins.

Obviously, they didn't answer.

Nettles of jealousy pricked her as she watched their peaceful forms. She didn't know how she'd ever quiet her mind enough to rest. How could she, knowing what lay ahead? Or rather, not knowing.

And they don't know either. They couldn't. Ara's stare became accusing. *They're clinging to promises picked out of folklore.*

Looking for truth in what Ara had come to believe was myth.

Maybe it was because they'd had time to accept their lot, Ara thought. More likely, their surety stemmed from having chosen their path.

Like the Loresmith, King Dentroth's lost twin children held a mythic place among the conquered people of Saetlund. The story of their escape was told near hearths in hushed whispers. Their names, especially that of Princess Nimhea, were uttered with reverence and in the company of words like *uprising* and *redemption*. The kind of words that kept embers of hope burning in the hearts of a downtrodden people.

The official records kept by the Vokkans made it clear that imperial soldiers had reached the nursery before any man, woman, or child could escape the palace. Not a soul related to King Dentroth, no matter how young, nor how innocent, was spared. The royal line of Saetlund had ended in that nursery.

Ara got the truth of it from the twins as they shared a simple dinner of bread and hard cheese in their camp.

Eamon did the telling. Nimhea remained solemn as her own story was repeated to her, as it must have been so many times before.

The twins had been secreted from the Five Rivers palace when they were toddling three-year-olds. Nimhea was a few minutes the elder to her brother, and thus named the heir. Rather than being hidden within Saetlund, the twins were sent to the Ethrian Isles—far to the southwest of their homeland. Other exiles arrived soon after. All had fled the conquest, hoping the islands were remote enough to evade the empire's grasp, their number small enough to avoid notice.

"Do you remember leaving Saetlund?" Ara asked.

Eamon shook his head. "My earliest memory is of the sea and the scent of Ethrian lemon groves."

"Sometimes I think I have flashes of Saetlund," Nimhea admitted. "Rooms in the palace. Our nanny's fear when she told us we had to leave our home. The first sight of an ocean-going vessel."

Her mouth twisted with frustration. "But they could be dreams, imaginings. We were so young."

Nimhea and Eamon were raised with full knowledge of their heritage. Nimhea grew tall and strong, bearing the telltale flaming locks of her lineage. She was drawn to combat and swordplay and proved her aptitude for both. Eamon remained slight, awkward, and prone to illness. His guardians were none too worried about his lack of martial skills. After all, Eamon wasn't the heir. He was left to pursue his own interests, borne out as obsessive scholarship that led to an unusual erudition in arcane lore.

"What made you decide to study the myths of Saetlund?" Ara asked Eamon.

He'd just bitten off a sizeable chunk of bread, and she was sorry for asking when he chewed much too fast and winced when he swallowed.

"I studied history first," Eamon told her. "Saetlund is our true home. I wanted to know everything about it. As I learned more, I came to understand that you can't separate our kingdom's history from its lore."

Ara's brow crinkled, thinking of the various books her grandmother made her read as part of her education. "Then why do scholars separate them?"

"It's hard to blame the scholars." Eamon sighed. "At least for me, but I'm sympathetic. Research is time-consuming. It's much easier to become an expert if you narrow your field. In the sources it's clear that long ago the fields weren't separated. As the population grew and history filled with more and more significant events, scholarship divided like branches shooting out from the trunk of a tree."

He took a sip of water. "The farther the branches grew from the trunk, the easier it was to forget that original connection."

Ara began to nod, but Eamon dropped his face into his hands and groaned.

"What's wrong?" Nimhea asked, putting her food and drink aside.

Eamon lifted his head. "I may as well admit my other motivation. From the first moment I stumbled across the subject of magic in the oldest histories, I couldn't help but hope that in some occult tome or scribbled scrap of paper I'd find a cure for my illness."

Nimhea mumbled her disapproval and returned to her dinner.

Ara shot a questioning look at the princess, but Eamon gave a sour chuckle.

"She thinks dabbling in magic could only make things worse for me," Eamon told Ara. "She's probably right."

Ara hesitated, turning a piece of bread in her hands. "What type of illness do you have?"

"I wish I could tell you." Eamon stared at the fire, his gaze bitter. "No healer has been able to name the ailment, nor give me relief."

His jaw tightened and he huffed out a breath. A moment later he turned to Ara and smiled.

"No matter," Eamon said. "I haven't finished our story."

Though their lives on the isles were pleasant, the twins always anticipated the future. Every day princess and prince received instruction focused on a sole purpose: the reclamation of the River Throne. Nimhea shouldered the years between herself and destiny with impatience. Her brother watched time pass with wary eyes and an increasingly nervous disposition.

Six months ago the long-awaited plan was set into motion. They would join the secret rebellion that was growing in strength and numbers with each passing day—or so they'd been assured.

That meeting had been delayed by an unexpected demand. Rather than heading directly to a rendezvous with their supporters, Eamon insisted that he and Nimhea first trek to a tiny mountain village. There, Eamon proclaimed, lived the savior of the kingdom. A hero without whom a successful uprising was impossible. A mythic figure he'd discovered in his years of research and whom he believed to be a real person.

"Mustering the courage to speak out about the Loresmith is one of the hardest things I've ever done," Eamon said with a shiver. "For a long time, I didn't believe I was capable of taking a stand."

Ara regarded him admiringly. "What changed?"

"Time," Eamon replied. "Nimhea came of age. She was about to cross the sea to take back Saetlund. I had to help her. It would have been foolish to pretend I could become a warrior, but I'd found something else. Something even better."

Rebuffed at first, Eamon's persistence finally swayed his sister. When Nimhea sided with Eamon, the others had no choice but to give in. Thus, rather than sailing to Dothring on the south coast of Daefrit, they forsook the blistering sun for the long winter of the Fjeri Highlands. They docked at Port Pilgrim and rode away from the sea toward the great peaks that formed the Mountains of the Twins. After collecting Eamon's strange relic, they would rendezvous with their allies in Silverstag.

When Eamon finished his telling, he and Nimhea both looked comforted, reassured in their purpose. The story revealed much to Ara. Nimhea's steely resolve and her protectiveness of her brother. Eamon's eagerness to please, his apologies for never being enough when his sister was everything. Ara smarted at the fact that that she hadn't always been part of the plan. In truth, she was a last-minute, unwanted addition to the rebellion. She was Eamon's addition. She went to her bedroll still wondering what to make of that.

I am the Loresmith. This is where I belong. Ara didn't want to admit that having someone in addition to Eamon championing her role would be a great comfort.

I am the Loresemith, she told herself again. *This quest is mine.*

Sleep wouldn't come, and Ara stared up, trying to catch glimpses of the night sky through the web of branches.

It would be comforting to see the same stars, Ara thought. But she wondered if that would prove true. If she looked up and saw the Fleeing Moon, harbinger of spring, and familiar constellations Senn and the Silverstag, it might instead sting of lies and loss.

Ara turned her head to look at her companions across the campfire.

Nimhea and Eamon appeared to be sleeping soundly. Ara envied them. Both cleaved fiercely to their purpose. Restless thoughts didn't make their hearts race or keep their eyes open. Ara couldn't chase away doubts about her abruptly revealed "destiny." She wasn't at all certain she believed in destiny. Things like destiny and fate existed in the tales her grandmother spun for her beside the hearth each night. Fanciful, impossible tales that had no place in the real world. Now she was expected to believe all the tales, all the mysteries of the gods, to be true. But how could a lifetime of understanding be suddenly transformed into unquestioning belief?

Yet here she was. In a strange forest, sleeping on strange, hard ground, with two strangers in her charge. Chasing after her destiny.

Ara didn't know how she was supposed to doggedly pursue her mythical role of Loresmith when she'd built up so many doubts about its very existence. She feared that meant in the end she could do nothing but fail.

Nimhea and Eamon chased after fate, while Ara had been told for years she had to wait for it. Be patient. Believe.

The twins' appearance, the very fact of their existence, proved that some truths lived within fiction. Like the tales of the gods, stories of the lost princess and prince were among those Ara had loved as a child. The secrecy surrounding the stories only added to their irresistible quality. A fallen kingdom. A stolen legacy. The promise of redemption. Those pieces fit together to create the best sort of tale.

But Ara was a real person. She'd had a life. A simple, but good life. It may not have been exciting or luxurious, but it had been hers.

Ara lifted her hands, turning them over to examine her palms. They were rough and callused, spattered with burn scars. A blacksmith's hands. That was all she'd expected, to continue as Old Imgar's apprentice.

Now Ara felt as though she'd been shoved onto a strange path. She'd become part of someone else's story.

Once upon a time it was your story, a voice like her grandmother's whispered from the recesses of her mind. *It can be your story again.*

Ara had believed in the tales before, that was true, but she didn't know how to believe again. Not only in the myths, but in what lay at their heart. What they said about who Ara was, or who she would become.

She didn't remember becoming tired enough to fall asleep, only waking to a world different from her own. Ara recognized the forest around her. She could see their campfire winking in the distance. But there were changes. The forest stirred, but there was no wind. The pine needles of each tree shimmered with drops of moonlight.

A crashing in the forest. All around her. Coming closer. Flashes of silver among the dark pines.

Then bursting from the woods, so close Ara felt the breeze from their passing, came the stags. Great beasts of legend with coats like new snow spun to silk and antlers bright as polished silver. Their namesake. The silverstags. Wuldr's sacred herd.

Ara had never seen anything so beautiful. She couldn't breathe.

After the herd came a thundering sound, heavy footfalls, then a howl, a sublime cry that made the nape of Ara's neck prickle.

Two huge shapes loomed in the trees.

The god and his companion.

Wuldr, the Hunter, patron deity of Fjeri. Twice the height of the tallest man. Hair and beard a silver to rival the stags' antlers. A bow in his hand. Quiver of arrows on his back.

Beside him, Senn, fellow hunter, constant companion. A wolfhound larger than a draft horse, with daggerlike teeth. Ara saw them when he grinned at her in the way dogs do.

With eyes on the fleeing herd, Wuldr readied an arrow and drew the bowstring.

Then he noticed Ara.

He looked upon her, into her eyes. She felt the weight of the god's mind, the power of his presence. She wasn't afraid.

Wuldr lowered his bow. "A hunter sleeps with one eye open."

Senn opened his great maw and lifted his head, sending another howl to the stars.

Ara woke to the known world. She could still feel Wuldr's presence, a rush of wind through the trees. Distant footfalls of hunter and hound. She remembered his words and became alert, though she stayed still within her blankets.

The fire undulated with low flames of orange and blue. On the other side of the shelter, Nimhea and Eamon slept.

All around Ara, the forest breathed in peace.

Nothing was amiss, but she knew to heed a god's warning. There was something out there. Something to be watched for.

5

hether from the dream or drowsiness, Ara had no trouble keeping calm and quiet. The low flames of the campfire cast little light. She could see the shadowy figures of their horses. She watched through half-closed eyes, all the while thinking she should be much more alarmed than she was.

The horses stirred. Tekki snorted. They weren't afraid, but something had woken them. A small shape, quick as a wink, darted between their legs and was gone.

Ara continued to breathe slowly, deeply, watching. The small shadow reappeared, stopping in the space between the horses and the slumbering campers. She could make out four thin limbs, a sleek body, large ears, and a bushy tail. Two glowing red eyes with slivered pupils gazed at Ara. A fox.

Satisfied with its reconnoitering, the fox slipped away from the firelight and into the forest.

Ara looked at the horses again. They had quieted, but something was wrong with Tekki's shape. One of his shoulders was too bulky. And he had an extra pair of legs.

There was someone with the horses: a figure who moved carefully and silently between the animals then disappeared.

A moment later the figure stepped into the dim light—a repetition of the fox's visit—face hidden by a hood, and crept toward Nimhea. Strangely, Ara felt no alarm or need to cry out. She was only compelled to keep watching. Pausing over the sleeping princess, the hooded figure moved so swiftly, swooping down then standing once again, Ara didn't know what had happened. Then, hanging from the stranger's hand was a slim gold chain. The thief moved away from Nimhea to stand over Eamon. Repeating that same impossibly quick motion, this time the thief retrieved a bloated coin purse. Neither Eamon nor Nimhea showed signs of waking.

Leaving the twins, the thief took silent steps toward Ara and seemed more a creature of shadow than human. When the stranger came alongside the fire, Ara seized her stave from beside her bedroll and leapt from her blankets.

The thief froze, but made no sound.

"You'll need to give their things back," Ara said, proud of her steely tone. "Now."

Tilting their head, the stranger regarded Ara for a moment then leapt away from the shelter and sprinted into the woods.

"Stop!" Ara rushed full-bore into the dark woods.

There was moon enough to keep her from stumbling or losing an eye to an errant branch. She ran, determined to catch the thief and undeterred by the fact that they moved too quietly to lead her on.

A shape appeared a few feet ahead of her.

Not the thief.

The fox.

It shimmered in and out of the trees, zigging and zagging, but always remaining in sight. Moonlight made the fox's coat glimmer, as if its fur was shot through with silver.

Suddenly the creature stopped, the glow of its fur becoming too bright to be a simple reflection of scattered moonbeams. It looked directly at Ara with eyes that burned red. The fox stared at her. Ara stared back.

She remembered the way the fox had stepped boldly into the firelight of the camp. The way the thief had mirrored the beast's path.

As if satisfied by the length of the shared gaze, the fox broke eye contact and dashed into the forest. Ara could see its coat flickering through the darkness like a beacon.

Follow the fox.

In the recesses of Ara's mind echoed the baying of a great hound.

She was on the hunt and Wuldr was with her.

Her body broke into a thrill of shivers. Here was what she'd been longing for—evidence of the gods. Hints that magic indeed dwelled in the world. It made her want to shout and cry and dance.

But Ara did none of these things. Fate had whispered a task, and she was finally ready to listen.

Giving all her focus to sighting the fox, Ara began to run. The fox moved swiftly through the forest, but Ara matched its pace. The forest seemed to part on either side of her, giving way so as not to impede her. Her footfalls became incredibly light. Each step landing then springing from the ground in near silence. Her strides grew longer and longer until it felt as if she glided through the trees.

When she came to an abrupt halt it was like being shaken out of a dream. Ara tried to get her bearings. She'd stopped because after the last flash of fox fur there had not been another. She didn't know where she was, nor did she have any sense of how far she'd run, but she could see that a short distance ahead the forest changed.

Ara moved forward cautiously, keeping watch for that telltale flash of silver fur. The fox never appeared, but something else did. Hidden within the trees was a wide, squat stone structure. Even though it was mostly a ruin, Ara suspected that despite its oval shape this building had not been a watchtower. The surrounding trees towered above the ruins. Their growth showed no sign of being impeded by an intruding spire. But she couldn't think of what else it could be.

Two-thirds of the outer wall had been demolished. The remains of a staircase rose in a spiral to a second floor. Half of the ground level was covered by what was left of the second floor, but the roof of the structure was gone.

Feeling exposed as she entered the clearing, Ara crept toward the ruin. She picked her way through broken stone, years of labor by skilled masons brought low. She closed in on the wall that remained intact. Halfway up the wall the stone blocks were different. While the rest of the wall was plain, each stone of the band that would have ringed the building bore a symbol that had been chiseled deeply into its surface. Ara recognized the symbol—it was one of the two that decorated her stave.

Eni's symbol.

A chill seized Ara as she realized she'd come upon one of Eni's shrines. She'd heard of the shrines but had never seen one. Eni's shrines were rare, and their locations were guarded secrets, as the empire forbade worship of any gods but Vokk.

In the tales, Eni guarded these sanctuaries for travelers so closely that only those seekers truly in need of the god's protection could find them. Should a person seek the sites out for adventure, curiosity, or cartography, their search would prove futile.

But that story couldn't be true. This shrine had been discovered by Fauld's wizards as they scoured the kingdom for anything connected to the gods and their powers. Discoveries were ransacked, stripped of any contents deemed valuable. At each site they found, Vokkan patrols posted decrees forbidding trespass on pain of death. Under Vokkan rule the conquered were ordered to worship the empire's god, Vokk the Devourer. Like so many other sacred sites across Saetlund, this sanctuary had been violated and destroyed.

Sadness muted Ara's anxiety. One of the stories proved false. Doubt wormed back into her heart. If Eni's shrines had been so easily found, what other promises of the gods would be revealed as lies? The stories were meant to guide her, to give her glimpses into the ways of the gods. Even if some of the tales were true, how could she know what tales to trust?

The shock of finding the shrine had put the thief and the fox out of Ara's mind, but the storm of questions crashing into her mind were driven away by a soft, lilting sound.

Someone was singing.

The song was muffled, coming from *within* the ruin.

Jolted alert, Ara pressed against the wall and slowly made her way toward the sound. The voice had a pleasant timbre and sounded like it belonged to a young man. He wasn't singing loudly, but the melody bounced off the stones, amplified in the night air.

Ara reached the jagged edge of the wall, crouched down, and peered around the corner. In the open part of the ruin, saplings and ferns crowded the space where sunlight reached. Beyond the young flora, where the stone ceiling still covered part of the ground floor, Ara saw an orange gleam. Firelight.

Sitting back on her heels, Ara pondered her next move. On the one hand, her chase had possibly led her to the culprit. On the other hand, she found it hard to believe someone would willingly occupy the ruins. Her doubts sprang from those *other* stories. Stories she hadn't let herself remember lest she lose her courage. Stories of slaughter and vengeful spirits.

The light and the voice could be a trap. A trick of ghosts to lure the hapless into the ruins.

Then again, if ghosts did sing, surely it would be a dirge and not the bright, tuneful sounds that came from within the broken stones. She listened to the melody more closely.

No, thought Ara. *Not a ghost. Someone either brave or foolhardy enough to settle in a place known for death and sorrow.*

Ara crept through the break in the wall. She stayed low, using the small trees and thick ferns as cover. When she reached the edge of ruin that had both floor and ceiling, she paused.

Something brushed against her, passing in a blur.

It was the fox, running toward the source of the firelight.

Follow the fox.

Still moving slowly, Ara kept close to the curving inner wall.

The light grew brighter. Suddenly the singing stopped and Ara froze.

"Welcome back, friend," said a voice that matched the singer's.

Ara held her breath.

"What's this—empty-handed?" the voice continued. "I was hoping for a plump grouse for breakfast. Ah well, boiled oats it is."

Is he talking to the fox?

Her curiosity almost outpaced her fear, but not quite. She suddenly felt very foolish. She hadn't considered what she would do if she caught the thief. While she wasn't unarmed, neither could she attack the culprit and demand he return the stolen property. The Loresmith couldn't attack, only defend.

But he didn't know that.

Ara decided her only chance would be to startle him so much that he'd hand over his loot without a fight. The problem was, Ara could defend herself, but she didn't know how well. She had no training in combat beyond what her grandmother had taught her. She'd never been tested by a true adversary.

Despite her fears, Ara couldn't shake the feeling that she was supposed to be here.

The dream. The fox.

She'd been led to this place. If she turned around and fled, what good would that do?

Closing her eyes, Ara sent up a brief prayer. *Wuldr, let this hunt end well. Eni, protect this traveler.*

She took Ironbranch in both hands and continued along the wall. Her steps took her into the part of the shrine that hadn't been demolished. The firelight grew brighter, and she could hear the young man humming the same tune he'd sung a few minutes ago.

The curve of the wall abruptly opened into a large open space. Ara couldn't have been more surprised by the scene laid out before her.

The fire crackled in a large hearth, wide enough to roast a boar. Not far from the fire was a simple bed with a rough-hewn frame. Similar rudimentary furniture: a small table and chair and a rocking chair shared a threadbare rug and were positioned to take advantage of warmth radiating from the hearth. The rest of the room was empty, though it could easily have held beds for a dozen or more, or long tables and benches to offer a meal to many visitors.

Eni's sanctuary for travelers, now home to one thief. And a fox, who had settled beneath the table.

The person in question was setting a cauldron in the hearth. He no longer wore a hood, but his clothes were those the thief had been wearing—dark, sueded leather trousers and a belted tunic of the same shadowy hue. His face was younger than Ara had expected. He wasn't a very tall man, a handsbreath taller than Ara but definitely shorter than Nimhea. Thick, dark hair framed his sandalwood-toned face, rising in a soft cloud from his scalp and ending in a crown of short twists. His movements were lithe and impossibly silent. Save for his humming, Ara would have had no sign that a person occupied this place.

Steeling herself, Ara strode into the light. She held her stave before her, in what she hoped was an intimidating stance.

"You." Ara got that word out, and then her mind went blank. *You what?*

The man jumped away from the hearth, landing beside the bed in a crouch. His left hand moved to his ankle and came up holding a poniard. He stayed there, body taut, and stared at her.

Ara braced herself for his attack.

But he didn't lunge as Ara expected. He kept his eyes on her; they were the color of dark honey. His gaze shifting from alarm to inquisitive.

He rose very slowly until he stood. His brow knit as he looked at Ara, like he was expecting to discover something that wasn't there.

"How did you find me?" he asked.

Ara glanced at the fox, which was grooming itself calmly beneath the table.

The thief followed her look to the fox, and the furrow in his brow deepened.

"Bringing strangers home now, are we?"

The fox ignored him.

Finding her voice again, Ara said, "You will give back what you took, thief."

Rather than anger him, her words caused the young man's body to ease, and he smiled.

"You're the first, you know." He flipped the poniard into the air, catching its hilt casually as it came spinning down. "No one has found my little refuge. It was probably too good to last forever."

Still tossing the blade and catching it, he began to cross the room. "What were you saying? You want what I took."

"Yes," Ara said. As he drew closer, she became more tense, overcome with the dreadful feeling that he was the cat and she the mouse.

Eni protect me. Ara sent up a silent plea to the god of this shrine.

The stones shuddered a reply.

Ara's eyes widened. The god of travelers had listened and replied. Joy unlike any she'd known before sang in her blood.

I am the Loresmith, and the gods are with me.

The thief froze, glancing up at the ceiling. "That's never happened before."

His eyes swept over Ara again, seeking.

"Who are you?" he asked.

"That's none of your business," she replied smoothly. Eni's powerful rumbling of the shrine filled her with resolve. The thief thought he was in charge. But Ara knew he wasn't.

He laughed softly. "I think it is. You came to my home, after all. My name is Teth, by the way."

"You're a thief." Ara gripped her stave tighter. "I don't care what your name is."

And then a dagger appeared in his right hand. "Rude." He flipped both blades into the air and caught them easily.

"You're awfully fond of that word. *Thief*," he continued. "I like to think of myself as providing a service. I teach people to be more vigilant about their possessions. You, obviously, are already quite vigilant and therefore not in need of my instruction. Apologies for having bothered you."

"You're a thief," Ara repeated, untouched by his attempt to chasten her. "And I caught you."

"I admit, the latter troubles me." Teth stood only a few feet from her. "It's been eleven years since I was last caught."

Sizing him up, Ara frowned. "I highly doubt that. How old are you?"

"I think I'm sixteen," Teth told her.

With a disgusted expression, Ara said, "You expect me to believe you were a thief at age five."

Teth shook his head. "I was a thief at age three. I was caught when I was five. How old are you?" he asked, scrutinizing her form.

"Fifteen," Ara snapped.

"Yet somehow you escaped the Embrace," he observed.

There was a sudden tightening in Ara's throat. Unwittingly, Teth had opened a deep wound Ara had lived with from the moment she'd learned about the Embrace. No one spoke about it in Rill's Pass. Old Imgar had recounted the history to Ara when she was still very young, but old enough to understand what had happened. She had borne the guilt of her existence ever since.

The Vokkan conquest had been devastating, but it was the Embrace that stoked hatred of the empire in the hearts of Saetlund's people. Soon after the fighting ended, the Vokkans sent messengers who nailed notices at the entrace of every inn and tavern announcing the imminent Imperial Embrace. The decree described the Embrace as an integral step in the process of transforming Saetlund from a conquered kingdom to a thriving imperial outpost. It promised a future of peace and abundance, but carried an unspeakable cost. Imperial patrols would move through the provinces collecting all children under the age of twelve, including infants not yet weaned from mother's milk. The children would be sent to an undisclosed location within the empire and educated. At the appropriate ages they would be tested and assigned to positions throughout Vokkan territories, including Saetlund. Many children would return to their homeland, the decree promised.

None did.

Ara hadn't always been the only child in Rill's Pass. But she had no memory of those who would have been her playmates, growing up alongside her. When the Vokkan soldiers came to reap their terrible bounty, Ara had barely taken her first steps. To her the village's lost children might as well have been characters in another storybook. They hadn't been, though. Ara caught hints of their existence in the features of her village neighbors. She saw stolen families etched in hard lines on their faces. The memory of children haunted their eyes. Rill's Pass was a gray, somber place. Ara often wondered if the village had become a ghost of its former self. If it had suffered a type of death when the Vokkans came for its youth, its future.

Teth was watching Ara closely. Something in her face made the hard glare in his eyes soften. "Say what you have to say."

After forcing herself to swallow a couple of times, Ara managed to say a few words. "I was hidden."

He studied her a few moments longer.

"It's the truth." Her voice was stronger now, and she would say no more than that. This young thief didn't need to know how or why she'd been so carefully hidden. By raising the specter of the Embrace, Teth had brought into stark relief the meaning of Ara's fate. Saetlund needed the Loresmith to overcome the horrors wrought by its imperial conquerors. She was needed.

The truth.

She'd been so caught up in the whirlwind of her own questions, doubts, and fears that she'd missed the key piece of this puzzle of unexpected events. It was her. Ara Silverthread. Daughter of Yos Steelring. Only she could become the Loresmith.

Ara hadn't fallen into the empire's clutches, despite all odds, and now she stood at the crossroads of fate. She had a choice. She could stay hidden or she could heed the call of the gods.

Sympathy flickered in Teth's eyes, but he said, "It's hard to believe you don't have imperial ties. So few avoided capture."

Ara was infuriated at the assumption she'd avoided the Embrace by somehow serving the empire. That accusation was the gravest insult to her family and all they'd sacrificed.

"How is it that you weren't taken?" Ara shot back. She wanted to deny any connection to the Vokkans, but to do so would tell him more than she thought wise. Not answering his question would have to do.

Teth shrugged. "Good fortune."

Ara's suspicion remained, but her gut told her he was being truthful.

A truthful thief? A mocking voice smirked in her thoughts. *Very unlikely.*

A good point, but Ara's instincts insisted there was more to this boy than thievery. To get there she'd have to mine him for information.

Ara's mind found its way back to something odd he'd said. "What do you mean you *think* you're sixteen?"

"Orphan." He pointed at himself.

That took her by surprise and dulled the edge of her ferocity.

"Ah," Teth said. "You've got the look. Pity. How could a child end up in such a horrible circumstance?" His laugh grew harsh. "You needn't worry. I'm one of the lucky ones. Orphans may not know their exact birthdays and don't often get a reprieve, but I was taken in by that rare person who is powerful but not cruel. Someone who taught me how to survive and more. I enjoy this life."

Irritated with herself for feeling sorry for him, Ara said curtly, "I only came here for what you stole. Give it back and I'll leave you to this life you find so enjoyable."

"But we're having such a lovely conversation," Teth replied. Then he pointed a dagger at her. "More importantly, I can't let you leave until I'm certain you're not a bounty hunter."

Startled, Ara blurted, "I'm not a bounty hunter."

She was surprisingly flattered that he thought she might be there to capture him. His wariness meant that she'd made exactly the impression she'd hoped. Fierce and unshakable in purpose.

"Mmmm." Teth shrugged. "Not convincing enough."

"I am not a bounty hunter," she repeated. Flattering or not, Ara was beginning to worry about leaving the twins alone. It was time for Teth to hand over the pilfered goods so she could be done with him.

Teth shook his head. "You'll have to find something else to say if you want me to believe that." Tilting his head in the same way he had at their camp, he said, "How about this: tell me who you really are, and if I believe you, I'll give you what you want."

Ara frowned while impatience bubbled in her blood.

"If you'd rather, we can just stand here until one of us falls over from exhaustion," Teth offered.

With a huff, Ara said, "Fine. My name is Ara Silverthread. I'm from Rill's Pass."

"I admit I've never heard of a bounty hunter from Rill's Pass." He flipped his dagger in the air and caught it again. "That's a farming village."

"It is," Ara confirmed. "I'm not lying."

"Are you a farmer?" Teth asked, still flipping and catching the dagger.

Ara didn't respond.

With a slow nod, Teth said, "I'll take you at your word . . . for the moment."

"Good."

"But you'd better not try to tell me your friends are from Rill's Pass, too," Teth added with a flash of teeth that wasn't quite a smile. "And they were hiding with you during the Embrace?"

Ara shook her head. "Wayward travelers. Lost their way in the storm. I know nothing about their past. I'm escorting them to Silverstag lest they become lost again."

"Interesting," Teth said. "Those who escort nobility are usually burlier than you."

Unsettled by Teth's recognition that Nimhea and Eamon were of high birth, Ara didn't reply. She straightened up, as if that would somehow transform her short stature into a menacing bulk. Realizing how ridiculous that was, her cheeks began to burn.

"Tell me, Ara," he continued. "Why would two young nobles from Sola have business in Silverstag?"

That he'd marked their features as those common to Solans made Ara purse her lips.

"I don't know," Ara told him. "I just didn't want to let them die in the woods."

His eyebrows lifted momentarily, then he said, "I believe you . . . at least about the latter bit. And I think for now that's good enough."

Ara had been ready to argue further. His declaration caught her off guard.

Teth either didn't notice or didn't care. He'd already turned away from her, and his daggers had disappeared. He pulled a chest from beneath his bed, opened it, and rummaged through its contents. The chest surprised Ara; along with the bed it was a sign of permanence.

Is this broken shrine his home? she wondered.

Even if he didn't always live in the ruin, he thought it safe enough to store his treasures there. Another sign that Teth believed himself under Eni's protection.

"They probably escaped the Embrace the way other highborns did," Teth continued. "It's no secret there were collaborators among the noble and merchant houses."

A wave of disgust passed through Ara at the past treachery among Saetlund's own. That anyone could witness so much sorrow while being comforted by the knowledge their own children would be safe utterly repulsed her.

Her grandmother had told her how grieving parents from every province had flocked to Nava's Bounty—her largest shrine—begging for help from the goddess of birth and earthly bounties, despite having abandoned her ceremonies and festivals years ago.

Then came the second imperial decree, forbidding worship of any gods but Vokk the Devourer. Vokkan soldiers sought out and desecrated any shrines they found, pulling down stones, setting anything that would burn aflame, and poisoning sacred springs.

When those parents pleading for mercy at Nava's Bounty attempted to protect her shrine, Vokkan soldiers surrounded the group and methodically cut them down. The soldiers went on to tear the shrine apart. They didn't collect the dead for burial or burning, leaving bodies to rot beside the smoky ruin—a clear message to the rest of Saetlund: to defy the empire meant death.

Ara hadn't heard stories of imperial patrols returning to broken shrines in search of any who still dared worship in the ruins, but that didn't mean it didn't happen. Teth had faith that either Eni would protect him or he could protect himself.

When Teth returned he bore a leather coin purse and a folded square of cloth. He looked at Ara expectantly until she realized she had to let go of Ironbranch with one hand in order to receive the stolen goods. Her fingers ached from holding the stave so tightly for so long. When she stretched them, a little smile played along Teth's lips.

Teth handed her the coin purse, which was alarmingly heavy. How much gold had he taken off Eamon?

"For your inspection." He unfolded the cloth to reveal Nimhea's gold necklace.

Ara nodded. When he refolded the cloth, Ara took it, tucking the makeshift envelope into her boot.

"And that concludes our business," Teth said. "There's little joy in things one has been caught stealing. I'm happy to return them."

With a polite nod, he returned to the cauldron over the fire.

Befuddled by Teth's abrupt pronouncement, Ara could only nod. Something felt wrong. Like she'd missed a sign that was terribly important.

Her mind nagged her as she backed away from the sheltering cavern.

Watching her awkward retreat, Teth called, "I'm not going to stab you in the back, Ara. Truth be told, I don't care to fight if it can be avoided. I'm rather delighted with how things worked out this evening. Safe journey to your camp."

Ara stopped. *Camp.* She had no idea how to find her way back. Her focus during the pursuit had been on the fox. She knew nothing of the shifts in direction they'd made, and she could only guess at the distance she'd traveled.

"Something wrong?" Teth spooned boiled oats into a wood bowl. He'd obviously been keeping an eye on her, despite seeming focused on his breakfast.

Ara had no idea what to do. At sunrise she could get a sense of where she was, but that was no help without relation to the campsite. She looked at the fox, who was still beneath the table. It returned her gaze and yipped. She wondered if she might convince the beast to show her the way back.

"Do you have a hankering for boiled oats?"

Ara drew a startled breath. Teth had appeared at her side silently in the few moments her attention was on the fox.

"I've never known it to be a food one yearns for," he went on. "But the world is full of surprises."

He was closer than he'd been during their former exchange. Her eyes caught a glimpse of metal at his shirt opening. Hanging from a leather cord was an iron talisman, hammered into the shape of Eni's symbol. It was the last bit of proof Ara needed to be certain about the significance of the hideout's location. Despite the Vokkan decree, Teth remained a follower of Eni.

Ara felt a strange confidence settle beneath her skin. *The gods have called upon me and sent me to seek my fate. Doesn't that mean I, in turn, may call upon them?*

"I need your help," she told him. Her mind rifled through Old Imgar's tales for those of Eni. The god of travelers. The god of roads and journeys. Only a person of no belief or deep belief would make a thief's hideout in a sacred place. And a person with no faith in the god wasn't likely to wear a talisman bearing Eni's mark.

Teth balked, surprised by her words. "Help is not one of my trades, I'm afraid. Unless you need me to steal something for you." His eyes brightened. "In which case we should discuss my fee."

"I don't need to you steal for me," Ara replied. She found the disappointment on his face outrageous. "I'm lost."

Teth frowned. "I beg your pardon?"

"I don't know the way to my camp," she continued, surprised she wasn't embarrassed by the admission. "I need you to take me there."

With a sigh, Teth settled into the chair and put his bowl of oats on the table. "Ara, we've had a very civil exchange. In fact, when it comes to the retrieval of stolen property, this was the most pleasant experience I've had. That does not, however, incline me to guide you to your camp. I saw the sword that girl had under her blankets. People with swords like that enjoying using them too much. I'll keep my distance."

Ara walked to the table and stood opposite Teth. "You're going to take me back to my camp."

"No." Teth's spoon clanked on the table. "I am not."

"I'm a traveler in need of your help." Ara spoke slowly, letting the words sink in. "Do you deny me aid?"

She leaned over the table and, startled by her own brashness, rested her fingertips on the iron talisman. He didn't draw back, nor did he bat her hand away. The iron under her fingers felt alive, and she could feel each beat of Teth's heart within the metal.

Teth stared at Ara, eyes narrowing. He wore the same searching expression he'd shown when she first appeared in the ruin. His jaw clenched as he failed to find what he was seeking. As his gaze once again grew shrewd, Ara could almost see the thoughts racing through his mind, searching for any open window or unlocked door through which he might escape. She knew he would find none.

"In the name of the Traveler I will give you aid," he growled.

Taking her hand in both of his, he pushed her back. "But I'm finishing my breakfast first."

The fox yipped again and snuggled against Teth's ankles.

❖ ELSEWHERE: The Room ❖

he room reeked of blood. Layers of blood. Fresh, still dripping, then blood beginning to coagulate, its thickness imparting a richer quality to the odor. Fully dried blood colored the floor dark, a rusted red, and, finally, the oldest blood seeping into the foundation of the building till it became one with the stones.

These layers of scent had purpose. They were not evidence of sloth on the part of servants or excess by the zealots—who were excessive, but not careless. Their magic demanded excess.

Liquid and lamina evoked every ritual that had been performed in this room. Echoes of that magic created the room's power. So long as the rituals were performed regularly that power would grow, and the emperor would be sated.

6

awn kissed the sky by the time Teth and Ara arrived at the camp with the fox trotting alongside. Nothing had been packed up for the onward journey. Nimhea and Eamon were awake and arguing about what to do.

"We can't go searching for her," Nimhea said to her brother. "That will only get us lost, too."

"But we're already lost," Eamon countered. He swept his hand in an arc to emphasize the dense forest surrounding them. "I don't know the way to Silverstag, do you?"

Nimhea scowled. "I don't know why I'm even discussing this with you. I woke up to find you and Ara gone!"

She knelt and began shoving items haphazardly into her pack.

"I was only gone for a few minutes," Eamon shot back. "Are you telling me that you don't have to pee first thing in the morning? Am I supposed to ask your permission?"

The fox sat down, watching the twins' spat. For a wild animal, it showed no alarm at being in the close company of four humans.

Teth leaned over, speaking softly into Ara's ear. "You must be having a wonderful time taking these two through the forest on hunters' tracks."

Ara sighed. "Thanks for getting me here." Then, more thoughtfully, she added, "Eni watch over you."

"And you, Ara of Rill's Pass."

She left him at the edge of their campsite and went to save the twins from whatever disaster they were cooking up.

Nimhea glared at Eamon, waving toward Ara's bedroll. "She has to have a map somewhere. Start going through the packs."

"That won't be necessary." Ara walked into the camp. Strangely, the fox came with her.

"Ara!" Eamon ran toward Ara with arms outstretched. At the last moment he seemed to realize that they weren't acquainted enough for an embrace. He stopped and steadied himself awkwardly. "I'm relieved to see you in good health."

Eamon noticed the fox and hopped back. "That's a fox!"

"Yes, it is," said Ara.

"What's it doing here?" he asked. "Is it sick? You should move away."

"It's not sick," Ara told him, choosing her words with care. "It's just . . . different."

Ara didn't know what made the fox behave so oddly, but now wasn't the time to worry about Teth's unusual companion. She guessed it would return to him soon enough.

Nimhea walked over, arms crossed over her chest. "Where have you been?" She made a point of looking from Ara to the fox. "I see you brought a pet. You're a very strange girl."

"It's not my pet," Ara snapped. She didn't appreciate being called strange. "An unexpected matter arose. I had to take care of it."

With a scowl, Nimhea said, "You can't just run off on a whim. What was so important that you abandoned us?"

Within Nimhea's angry glare, Ara glimpsed white flashes of fear.

She panicked when I was gone. That's what her waspish accusations are about.

Ara felt a little guilty for causing the princess distress, but not enough to endure her temper.

"I did not—" Ara began, but Teth interrupted her.

"Friends, friends." He sauntered into the camp. "No need to quarrel."

Having expected Teth to melt back into the forest once his task was complete, Ara was caught off guard by his reappearance.

Nimhea sword hissed out of its sheath.

"Look," Teth said to Ara. "Already with the sword."

"What are you doing here?" Ara asked in a tight, low voice. She didn't think any good would come of his surprise visit. The fox began to make figure eights between Ara's and Teth's legs.

Taking a menacing step toward Teth, Nimhea said, "Who are you?"

"Steady, Nimhea." Ara kept her voice calm. "I know him."

But do I? Teth's presence needled her, a warning that there was more to him than simple thievery. He'd walked into their camp for a reason and Ara was troubled that she had no inkling as to why.

Not only did I discover his hiding place, but I know him for an outlaw. He should be on the run, not lingering like an unwanted guest.

"My lady." Teth bobbed up and down in a lazy bow. "Do not blame brave Ara for her absence. It was me who caused her to leave your camp in the night hours."

Ara's eyes narrowed, suspicion stirring at his easy tone and overly familiar bearing.

Nimhea looked from Teth to Ara. "Who is he?"

"He's . . ." Ara began. How could she explain her night's adventure with its vision and mad chase. In her head it seemed reckless, but her heart cradled all of it with reverence. While she owed the twins some sort of explanation, Ara was reluctant to reveal what had taken place.

She needed time to ponder each piece so she could fully comphrehend its significance.

I will not be careless with messages from the gods.

"Is he a bard?" A bright-eyed Eamon jumped in. "He sounds like a bard."

"Thank you, kind sir." Teth removed an imaginary hat and nearly touched the ground with it in another languid bow.

Ara resisted the temptation to knock him over. He was playing games, but to what end she didn't know. That was worrying.

"Bards are useless," Nimhea pronounced, deigning to offer Teth an assessing gaze. "You're delaying us, and we have need of haste. Ara may be entertained by you, but I am not. Begone."

Eamon whined, "I love bards." He looked to Teth with wide and hopeful eyes.

His tone was so earnest Ara found herself wishing Teth was a bard.

Before Ara could intervene Teth stepped between her and Nimhea with palms up and fingers spread wide as if pleading for mercy. Surprised by his obsequious demeanor, Nimhea drew back.

"Sadly, I am not a bard." Teth put on a mournful face.

What game is he playing here? Ara kept her expression neutral while rifling through possible motives.

"Your friend came upon me practicing my real trade," he told the princess. "And was none too happy with me."

No. He wouldn't. Ara drew a shallow, sharp breath.

Nimhea frowned. "Your trade . . ."

"Thievery," Teth pronounced.

Eamon's mouth formed an O of surprise.

Ara tried to interject, but only spluttering sounds came out. She hadn't planned to tell Nimhea and Eamon about Teth's proclivities. In her mind, once they'd reached the camp she and Teth would shake hands and part ways. Obviously he had other ideas.

"Thievery is not a trade." Nimhea's blade had drooped a bit, but now it flashed up, aiming at Teth's throat. "You should die, cur."

"The story of my life proves I haven't earned an execution." Teth smiled at her and Ara's heart jumped. It was not a friendly smile. "It's understandable, however, that a highborn person such as yourself has a narrow view of my livelihood."

Nimhea scoffed. "How do you know I'm highborn?"

Having recovered her composure, Ara groaned inwardly. She needed to have a long conversation with Nimhea and Eamon about how to conceal their identities. But first she needed to find a way to get Teth to stop talking and Nimhea to calm down.

Still smiling, Teth answered, "Because only a great lady could work herself up to a tantrum over a trifle."

There it was, the fatal thrust and not delivered by Nimhea's sword.

Nimhea's eyes widened, and her bronze cheeks took on a grayish cast. Her sword arm began to tremble.

I should have seen it coming, Ara chided herself. *Too late to speak our way to peace.*

Grabbing Teth by the shirt, Ara pivoted on her heel and threw him behind her. Then she dropped to the ground and rolled to avoid the sword strike she assumed was was coming. To her credit, Nimhea hadn't swung her blade. The princess had gone very still. Slowly, her lips drew back in a snarl.

"How dare you." Nimhea's whisper was chilling. Her gaze impaling.

Eamon spoke in a very small voice. "Nimhea . . ."

Ara saw that he wanted his sister to stand down, but fear hobbled him. She didn't know if the situation alone had put him on edge, or if he was frightened of Nimhea herself.

Something had changed in the princess. Her stance no longer stiff and imperious, her limbs became sinuous. Ara watched Nimhea's transformation with growing alarm. When she'd had first encountered Nimhea and her sword, she'd been wary but never frightened. Now Nimhea didn't have the air of a contemptuous high-born; she looked like Death's handmaiden.

Teth—who'd been surprised by Ara, not to mention landing sprawled facedown—rolled onto his back and sat up. His eyes flicked to Ara first, filled with annoyance then puzzlement as she scrambled toward him. Then he looked toward Nimhea, who stalked him. Her blade bright and sharp. Teth's eyes widened, and he scuttled back a foot.

Ara glanced around for the fox, whom she expected to attack Nimhea at any moment. But the fox sat beside a trembling Eamon, calmly watching events unfold.

"Apologize," Ara hissed into Teth's ear. She could only hope he wouldn't be a fool.

He glanced at her, and she saw the beginnings of a fatal stubbornness.

"Do. It. Now." If he didn't listen to her, at worst he would die—at best he would lose a limb.

Ara's flat command put doubt in Teth's gaze.

"If I must," he muttered.

Teth climbed to his feet, brushing dirt off his breeches.

"My lady," he began. This time his voice didn't convey mockery.

Ara's breath eased when she detected no sarcasm or hostility in his tone. *Thank you, blessed Nava. Mother of mercy.*

"Sometimes my love of word sparring gets the better of me," Teth continued. "I am very sorry if my speech cut you to the quick."

His gaze settled on Nimhea's blade. "I'd be deeply grateful if you wouldn't use your sword to do the same to me."

Ara's mind churned through actions she could take if things went badly. She had Ironbranch; if necessary she could block Nimhea's sword strike . . . if she got there in time.

After a moment that stretched out terribly long, Nimhea lowered her blade. The princess didn't manage to hide the quiet wave of relief that passed over her face.

She never wanted to fight, Ara realized, then puzzled. *So why the constant front of aggression and disdain?*

Watching Nimhea, Ara understood, with apprehension and a whiff of curiosity, that she had no idea who the real person behind the princess's mask was.

"Indebted to you, my lady," Teth said.

Sheathing her sword, Nimhea turned away from Teth and spoke to Ara.

"We should take this thief into our custody and turn him in to the local authorities."

Ara blanched. In the years after the conquest some control of crimes and punishment had been returned to citizens of Saetlund, but only those who kowtowed to the empire's authority. It would take a crime far greater than theft for Ara to be willing to condemn someone to that end. Even persons convicted for petty crimes were rarely seen again. Rumors abounded regarding Vokkan prisoners: some said criminals were transported to other lands under Vokkan rule and forced to labor for the empire; others claimed that convicts were shoved into overcrowded cells ridden with vermin and disease; the worst were whispers that despite appearances it wasn't the military that oversaw the prisons, but Vokk's wizards. No one knew what the secretive wizards would do with such captives, but all imaginings were worse than death.

Whether or not Ara not cared whose hands Teth fell into, she still wouldn't risk getting anywhere near city guards. After the conquest, all martial posts had been overtaken by the Vokkans. Old Imgar had told her many times that cities had none of the life nor the spirit of the old days. All were strangled by the empire's chokehold. Turning in an outlaw wouldn't cast their trio as good citizens in the Vokkans eyes; if anything it would throw suspicion upon them and they'd end up alongside Teth in a cell.

"No," Ara told Nimhea, and said very slowly, "We're not friends of the empire, and the Vokkans own most local authorities."

Nimhea balked, then comprehension lighted her eyes. She shook her head quickly, as if chasing away unpleasant thoughts, and even had the decency to blush.

"Of course you're right," Nimhea replied, recovering from her brief lapse of composure. But when she looked at Teth again, she added. "We should tie him up and leave him. Let the forest do with him what it will."

"The forest won't harm him; it knows him too well," Ara replied. "Besides, I doubt you could tie a knot that would hold him."

"True," quipped Teth.

Why am I arguing on behalf of Teth? Ara puzzled. It would be easy enough to let the princess tie him up, knowing he'd easily escape later.

Something about the thief made Ara want to defend him. *But what? His connection to Eni? That he hasn't tried to hurt any of us?*

She suspected the truth resided in her desire to unravel the mystery of his constant shifts in character. A shallow reason, perhaps, but her curiosity was relentless.

The fox bounded up to Teth and barked at Nimhea.

"Keep your mouth shut, thief!" Nimhea did not deign to address the fox. She rested her hand on her sword hilt. "I could knock him out.

No harm done besides a sore head. By the time he wakes up and weasels out of the knots, we'll be far ahead."

Ara considered Nimhea's words. She doubted Teth would follow them. He'd been caught once. They'd already caused more trouble for him than she cared for. Giving Nimhea a small victory could put her in a better mood for the rest of the journey. That would be worthwhile.

Turning to Teth, Ara was surprised that his eyes were fixed on Nimhea, slowly looking the princess up and down. He began to smile. His eyebrows lifted as if he'd been greatly impressed. That expression vanished only to be replaced by a carefully composed blank expression.

Looking at Nimhea, then at Teth again, horror curdled in Ara's belly.

He knows. Senn's teeth. He knows who she is. At the least he suspects.

"We can't leave him," Ara blurted, a wheel of choices and consequences spinning in her mind. "We need him."

"What?" Nimhea and Teth replied in unison, then traded looks of incredulity.

"While it pains me to admit it," Ara forced herself to say in a measured tone, "Teth has done us a service."

"Of course I have." Teth's reflexive reply came though it was clear he had no idea what Ara was talking about.

Nimhea gave a firm shake of her head. "He has done no such thing. I don't understand why we're still talking with this bandit."

"I'm not a bandit," Teth snapped at the princess. "Bandits work in groups. I'm strictly a solo artist."

"But there *are* bandits in these woods," said Ara.

Teth frowned slightly. "I don't know of any woods *without* bandits. Except the Bone Forest, of course."

His mention of the Bone Forest settled the matter.

He knows the myths and respects the gods. Ara was certain now of what she should do. She allowed herself a measure of satisfaction that she'd found a way to maneuver around Teth. No only would she take control, but she'd also win the opportunity to unearth more of his secrets.

Nimhea let out an exasperated breath, but didn't speak.

"You know how they would strike," Ara continued, confident in her unfolding strategy. "Vulnerable sections of the hunting paths, ambush sites."

Teth's lips set in a thin line. He saw where she was headed and his gaze fixed on her, irked while at the same time impressed.

Turning to Nimhea, Ara said, "He's going to take us to Silverstag."

Eamon guffawed. "Is that wise?"

He appeared unnerved, but Ara could also see he was caught up in the mystery of Teth and anxious to see how the rest of the thief's story might unfold.

"It's absurd," Nimhea replied with a brittle laugh. She shared none of her companions' interest in a criminal interloper.

Ara didn't waver, offering the twins a broad smile.

"Thank you," Teth said to the princess drily. "I couldn't have said it better myself."

Nimhea's glance this time was more sour than venomous. Ara took it as a good sign.

Raising Ironbranch, Ara showed Teth the end bearing Eni's sign. "We travel under the protection of Eni."

Eamon's eyes widened. If he had lingering reservations about Teth's company, they dissolved. Ara could see he was besotted with finding himself in the midst of a yet unwritten tale of the gods.

"Not this again." Teth shook his head. "I helped you once. Once is enough."

He sounded defiant, but Ara noted the desperation in his eyes. The thief had been cornered, and he couldn't find a way out.

"You've just informed us of dangers yet ahead," Ara replied, her gaze stony even as she smiled at Teth. "You know the woods, you can guide us safely to Silverstag. Then you'll be free of your obligation and can go where you will with our thanks."

"With our thanks?" Nimhea snorted and walked away.

Good, thought Ara. *That means she's not going to fight me on this.*

Teth hadn't answered, so Ara said, "Unless you want to take the matter up with Eni."

A storm had been building behind Teth's eyes. "Eni's curse isn't invoked when a traveler's demands are unreasonable."

"How sure are you about that?" Ara shot back quickly, hoping her own doubt was masked by her sharp tone. "Do you know the god's mind so well as to decide what Eni deems unreasonable?"

Teth opened his mouth to argue further, but his gaze suddenly shifted to the campsite where Nimhea and Eamon were packing. He turned back to Ara with a complacent smile.

"May Eni guide our steps."

Teth's sudden submission undercut Ara's feeling of triumph.

He's knows I've won this game, but he's started another and I have no idea what it is.

Teth started toward the campsite, calling out to the twins. "This is a mess. Don't you know how to travel?"

Ara ground her teeth. *He's going to try to make me pay for this.*

"I don't have a horse, by the way," Teth went on. He lowered his voice. "Do you think the princess would like a passenger?"

Ara froze, her breath choked off. *He can't be serious.*

Teth walked over to the bedrolls and began to pack up as if the site was his own.

Her reproachful gaze bore into his back, and Ara startled when Eamon grabbed her arms.

"Brilliant." He was giddy. "That was wonderful!"

"I'm sorry?" she mumbled, unable to take her eyes off Teth.

"Invoking the lore!" Eamon exclaimed. "Of course the denizens of a forest like this would be superstitious. But you played him like a lyre. It was masterful."

"Thanks," Ara said, smiling slightly. It had been a good plan. "You should pack up and saddle your horse. Teth will ride with you."

Teth might think he could take charge, but she'd show him otherwise.

"Good, good." Eamon fluttered at her. "I knew you were meant to guide us. Look what you've already done."

He hurried to the campsite, chattering away at Teth while the two of them gathered the last of their gear.

Yes, thought Ara, *look what I've done.*

The fox, who'd stayed by Ara's side, jumped up, putting its front paws on her thighs, and yipped twice before bounding into the woods.

Ara was certain it had been laughing at her.

The journey to Silverstag would require a few more nights in the woods. For the most part they followed the paths Ara had planned to take, but every so often Teth would divert the group onto trails she could barely make out. Sometimes she couldn't see any signs of a hunter's track whatsoever. These alternate routes were rarely straight or clear. They wound and climbed and dropped only to climb again. Ara began to suspect Teth was making a show of his particular "guiding" techniques, which was more about hearing Nimhea, Eamon, and Ara yelp as branches snapped back in their faces, while he managed to nimbly avoid all obstacles.

But midday through the second day of traveling with Teth, the fox—who'd been absent to the point of Ara assuming it had gone home—burst out of the brush, making Nimhea's horse shy.

"Wretched beast!" Nimhea shouted at the fox while reining her horse in.

Paying no mind, the fox looked at Teth, opened its mouth, and let out an ear-scraping screech.

"Wuldr's ax," Teth snarled. "I was sure we'd cleared them."

"Cleared who?" Ara asked, when she heard something: pounding hooves behind them on the main road they'd just rejoined.

"Some unpleasant acquaintances," Teth muttered.

Ara's pulse began to drum like the sound of the approaching horses.

Hearing the hoofbeats, Nimhea drew her sword. The blade let out a metallic hiss as it slithered from its scabbard.

Teth had jumped down from Eamon's horse, eyes on Nimhea's sword. "I know you like to point that thing at people, but I hope you know how to use it, too. Braegan doesn't leave witnesses."

"Who's Braegan?" Nimhea turned only to see Teth dash into the forest. The fox vanished with him.

A lightning bolt of alarm jolted through Ara when they disappeared. Her mouth went dry. She'd expected surprises from Teth but a show of cowardice hadn't been one of them.

"Where are you going?" Eamon called after him.

When Teth didn't answer, Eamon gasped. Wide-eyed, he asked Ara. "He's abandoning us?"

"Bastard." Nimhea spit on the ground. "No doubt he's in league with this Braegan."

Ara didn't want to believe that, but at best Teth had run away, leaving only three of them to face whatever was coming.

Nimhea wheeled her horse to await the riders, face grim. "Stay back, Eamon."

She glanced at Ara. "Can you fight?"

"Yes," Ara answered. It wasn't the complete truth. The rules about being the Loresmith took more than a few seconds to explain—and a few seconds was all they had. She would do whatever she could.

"Good." Nimhea urged her horse to the center of the road.

Coming from around a bend in the road, six riders appeared. Ara's blood roared in her ears; this would be her first test in battle.

Seeing their quarry, the riders began to shout, spurring their mounts forward.

Six against two. Ara steeled herself against the unfriendly odds.

Sliding off Tekki's back, she slapped his rump hard, sending him farther up the road and out of harm's way. Hopefully.

Ara freed Ironbranch from its harness and moved to flank Nimhea. The stave felt cool in her hands, its weight reassuring, steadying her wild heartbeat. She sent a brief prayer to the gods, asking forgiveness for having begged off so many training sessions with her grandmother.

The riders were almost on them. They wore patched leather armor and wielded weapons of rust-bitten iron.

Though her horse stamped and tossed its head, Nimhea remained utterly still.

One of the riders at the rear cried out, clawing at his back before he tumbled from the saddle. The shaft of an arrow stuck out from between his shoulder blades. Another rider fell, this one clutching at her throat while blood spurted between her fingers. The third of the riders at the back wheeled his horse around to search for the assailant. That earned him an arrow through the eye.

The leader was on Nimhea. He swung a massive spiked club at her head. She feinted, bending backward to stretch her torso across her mount's flank. Then she was up, blade lashing out. Her sword caught the man's side below his ribs. Blood sprayed from the wound. He lifted his club again, but his face went slack and the weapon fell from his hands as Nimhea ran him through. She jerked her blade free, swinging around to meet the sword of the next rider.

The last of the brigands advanced on Ara. With ferocious kicks to his horse, he came at her, determined to ride her down. Ara waited until the last second then threw herself out of the path of the plunging hooves. She rolled two times and was on her feet again. Holding her stave at a diagonal across her body, Ara watched as the man swore and swung down from his saddle. He carried a battered one-handed ax and laughed as he strode toward her.

"I'll make it quick, little girl." His smile had only a few yellowed, rotting teeth.

He brought the ax down and Ara fell to one knee, raising her stave to meet the blade. She felt the vibration of the blow in her arms, but the bandit dropped back, cursing and shaking his head as if the shock of the strike had thrown him off-balance.

Ara knew it had. Ironbranch had come alive in her hands. When the bandit's ax had met her stave, the Loresmith stave had not only blocked the attack but sent a rebuke along with it like a buffeting wind. Her grandmother had often said Ironbranch had hidden powers that would reveal themselves in times of need.

Ara's instincts screamed that she should bash the man's skull while he was off-balance, but her grandmother had taught her well. She stood her ground, rooted to the earth, unwavering in purpose.

The Loresmith may only defend. She could hear Elke's voice as clearly as if her grandmother was at her side.

The man rushed at her. Instead of blocking his swing, Ara twisted away from him then came around and struck hard at the back of his knees. He toppled forward.

Again she fought the urge to bring the full force of Ironbranch down upon the bandit's head.

Ara ground her teeth. *I am the Loresmith. The Loresmith does not seek violence.*

With another font of curses pouring from his mouth, he regained his footing and came at her again.

"Time to put you down, mangy bitch."

Bracing herself as he lifted his ax, Ara heard a sharp whistling followed by a thunk. The man's eyes went wide and he stumbled back. An arrow protruded from his stomach. Another whistle and thunk and a second arrow joined the first. He fell onto his back, groaning.

Ara glanced back as footfalls reached her ears. Carrying his bow, Teth strode past Ara and stood over the writhing man. Seeing Teth, the brigand drew a dagger from his belt, jabbing futilely while Teth kicked the dagger from his hand then stomped on his arm. Ara winced at the sound of bones cracking.

"Lucket told you what would happen if you came back, Braegan." He crouched down, grasping the shaft of one arrow.

"I don't take orders from sewer rats," Braegan wheezed.

Teth twisted the arrow in Braegan's gut. He shrieked; spittle and blood leaked from the corner of his mouth.

"Someday you'll be at the bottom of Nava's Ire," Braegan said between wet breaths. "And I'll be laughing."

Teth shook his head. "You brought this on yourself."

Braegan screamed twice as Teth jerked both arrows from his body.

"Looks like he's run out of things to say," Teth said to Ara.

Her eyes were fixed on Braegan's ruined stomach. She felt ill and unexpectedly grateful that she was forbidden from dealing out that kind of punishment.

Teth wiped his arrows clean with leaves. "Who taught you to fight with a stave?"

"My grandmother." Ara looked at Teth, taken aback by how coolly he'd ended Braegan's life.

"Your grandmother?" Teth gave a low whistle. "Remind me not to tangle with her." His eyes narrowed. "This was your first real fight."

It hadn't been a question, but Ara nodded.

Teth tilted his head; his eyes became gentle. "It's different when you have a dangerous adversary. I know it appears heartless to kill a person, but you can never forget that all they want is you dead."

Ara's mouth quirked with annoyance at Teth's overly tender tone while pointing out something so obvious.

He noticed. "I only say that because you had opportunities to take Braegan out."

"I know." Ara's reply was snappy, but she didn't care. Her stubborn streak reared its head and roared.

Teth kept his eyes on her, waiting for an explanation. Feeling she didn't owe him one—after all, she barely knew him—Ara turned on her heel and went to Nimhea.

"You were magnificent," Eamon was saying to his sister. "If only Swordmaster Ilian could have seen that."

Blood spatters crisscrossed the princess's face and body, but she didn't seem to care. Nor did she react to Eamon's praise. Ara cast her eyes about, looking for the second man Nimhea had been fighting. She found the bandit's body, but not his head.

Ara looked from Nimhea to Teth. Teth wore his usual expression—pleasant but with the hint of a smirk. Nimhea's face was stern, but otherwise unreadable. Her brother continued to putter around her, praising her successful attacks, though he took care keeping his eyes averted from the bodies.

Stomach shrinking, Ara wondered if Eamon was likewise disturbed by the carnage. *How could Teth and Nimhea be so calm?*

She was, of course, relieved that they had won, but the air had an acrid tang with a disturbingly cloying overlay. Ara didn't want to think about what materials had come together to produce such a scent.

Six men dead. That fact and the foul odor made her queasy.

After shushing Eamon, Nimhea said to Teth, "You could have mentioned you were going to flank them."

"Waste of time." Teth shrugged. "Besides, I like surprising people."

Nimhea gave him a measured look. "You're a good shot."

"Thanks for noticing." He glanced up and down the road. "The horses have scattered, but they won't have gone far. Let's gather them up. Eamon, I'll ride with you again; the more skittish horses will settle if they can follow your mount."

They rode toward the bend from which the bandits had come, while Nimhea led her horse alongside Ara to find Tekki. The big, shaggy horse was only a short distance down the road, happily munching curled tops off spring ferns. Ara took a moment to rest her head on Tekki's broad shoulder. She dug her fingers into his thick winter coat. She didn't care what Nimhea thought. The adrenaline from the fight was wearing off, and she needed to breathe.

After a minute Ara climbed onto Tekki's back. Nimhea was already mounted, watching her.

"You've done that before," Ara said, searching the other girl's face, wanting to see the source of Nimhea's steadiness in the midst of violence and death. "Killed people."

Nimhea didn't answer, but clucked to her horse and rode back toward the site of the skirmish. Frustrated, Ara turned Tekki to follow.

When Eamon and Teth joined them, Teth had his own mount and two more of the bandits' horses tied behind. The remaining horses had run off in the direction of whatever home they'd come from.

"We should move on," Teth told them. "The road flattens out ahead, and I want to cover considerable distance before we camp tonight."

Chafing at Teth's assuming command, Ara said, "What about the bodies? Shouldn't we at least drag them off the road?"

"No," Teth replied. "The bodies are a message. They stay where they are."

His answer chilled her. She'd thought of Teth as clever, and sometimes entertaining, but here he was stern . . . distant.

"What kind of message?" Eamon asked nervously.

Teth's laugh was harsh. "Even thieves have rules. Braegan"—he pointed to the dead ruffian who'd attacked Ara—"broke them."

Without another word, Teth pushed his new horse into a canter, and they were travelers once more.

The road ahead was southerly, straight, and absent of the rises and dips that marked earlier paths they'd taken. Teth didn't ease their pace until the sun was low, and when he did he was quite chatty. Back to his wit and banter. Even so, the only person wanting to talk to him was Eamon. Nimhea rode quietly, not acknowledging any taunts Teth threw in her direction. Ara was still turning over his shifts in personality in her thoughts. She knew him as a thief, but he was also an adept fighter. Where had he learned all these skills? She held Tekki back and followed a short distance behind the others. Her mind was sour, tainted with conflicting ideas of bravery and honor, then compassion and mercy.

Bits of chatter floated back to her on an evening breeze.

"But it's mostly hunters in the Fjeri woods," Eamon was saying. "Don't you worry that Wuldr will take offense? Or do you only worship Eni?"

"I don't worship any gods," Teth replied.

Ara wondered if he believed that and didn't realize he worshipped Eni through his actions, or if he wouldn't admit to his faith.

"I do try to avoid offending them." Teth laughed and leaned forward in the saddle, stretching his arms. "I choose my quarry carefully. I don't harass local hunters, but since the empire took over there are plenty of trophy seekers who come to the forest looking for giant stags and bears to stuff and put in their halls. Wuldr has no fondness for them—at least that's the wager I've made—and glory hounds tend to carry heavy coin purses."

"Sound strategy," Eamon said. "Don't you get lonely in the forest?"

Tingling sensations traveled through Ara's neck and shoulders at the question. *Is Teth always alone? Has anyone but me visited his makeshift home?*

She felt a stab of jealousy at some imagined person who'd been companion to Teth in the ruins, then chided herself for being ridiculous.

Shaking his head, Teth replied, "I'm not always in the woods. My work takes me into Silverstag, sometimes to Shepherd's Rest or the coast. When I've had enough of people I come back to the lowlands."

Ara was again pestered by nagging curiosity. What did that mean— "enough of people"? What people? Who did Teth spend time with?

He'd told Ara he was an orphan, so she assumed he had no family. She wondered how he had found friends, how close he was to them.

"Do you ever go to the highlands?" Eamon asked. "Where Ara's from?"

Scowling inwardly, Ara glared at Eamon's back. She'd been content with listening to the conversation, but she had no desire to be part of it.

"Never. Much too cold." Teth looked over his shoulder and grinned at Ara. "I think it's still winter up there. In fact, I've heard they don't actually have a summer."

Ara couldn't help herself. "We have a summer!"

Summer, while very short, was a glorious time in the highlands. Its brevity only made the people who called northern Fjeri home treasure the season all the more.

"Sorry," Teth called. "Can't hear you back there."

She returned to glaring.

Teth blathered on and revealed a surprising amount of information about his thieving exploits, which Ara thought rather careless. Then again, Teth likely didn't consider Eamon any kind of threat. He was probably right.

Sunlight dwindled when they stopped for the night. Eamon and Teth continued their conversation as they all set up camp. When the time came to eat, Nimhea demurred, saying she wasn't hungry. Instead, she went to check the soundness of the new horses.

Not particularly keen on dinner herself, Ara decided to follow Nimhea. It wasn't just that she didn't have an appetite; she also wasn't convinced Nimhea knew how to check horses for soundness. Wouldn't a princess have stable hands to do that for her?

But when Ara came upon the princess, she was lifting hooves and pressing her hands against fetlocks and tendons to feel for heat.

She has more skills than I give her credit for.

Ara was about to make her presence known when Nimhea abruptly stood up. She laid her arms across the horse she'd been ministering to and rested her cheek against its back. Though the princess wasn't making a sound, Ara could see her limbs trembling in the low light. At first she thought to leave, but as she backed away, Nimhea lifted her head.

"I know you're there."

Moving between the tethered horses, Ara came to stand beside Nimhea. She could see that the princess's face was wet.

"You assumed I've killed before," said Nimhea. She did nothing to hide the fact that she'd been crying.

"Well . . . you're very good at it." Ara shifted her weight, uncomfortable at Nimhea's sudden vulnerability.

With a brittle laugh, Nimhea said, "I should be. I've been training for this from the moment I could lift a sword."

Letting out a long breath, she continued. "I thought it would be glorious."

The words riveted Ara. *That fight was a first for both of us.* She shared initation into battle with the heir to Saetlund's throne, a fact that shook her to the point of wrapping one arm beneath the horse's neck and leaning into the animal to stay focused.

"It wasn't?" Ara asked.

"In the moment it was," Nimhea answered. "I became the sword. Taking life . . . it was powerful. But after the fight, it became real. What I'd done. I killed those men. I didn't hesitate."

She paused, taking a deep breath, before she said, "I wasn't prepared for that to rattle me. Regret has a bitter taste."

The horse dislodged itself from Ara's arm and turned its head to sniff Nimhea's shoulder. She stroked its muzzle.

"Do you wish you hadn't killed them?" Ara's question was hesitant. It was deeply personal, and the princess didn't owe her an answer.

Nimhea frowned. "A part of me wishes there had been another way. But another part of me is glad it happened. I've been waiting for a real fight as long as I can remember."

As Ara watched the emotions flicker through Nimhea's eyes, she grasped another truth about her role as Loresmith. Forbidden to attack, Ara would likely never have to kill. She might always be horrified by the death around her, but she wouldn't have to bear the weight of being responsible for it. Nimhea hadn't said much, but what she had revealed was how heavy such a burden would be. That to be a warrior—even a just warrior—demanded a sacrifice, a piece of the fighter's soul.

The Loresmith is a protector. Ara found herself, rather unreasonably, wanting to shield Nimhea from that cost as much as she could. If she could.

"Teth thinks they would have killed us," Ara said softly. "Maybe there was no other way."

Nimhea nodded, falling silent.

They stood like that for several moments, with only the sounds of the horses snuffling for green shoots around them.

"You should eat something," said Ara finally.

"So should you."

They walked to the campfire together.

7

hree people were breaking bread around the crackling flames. Eamon, Teth, and an elderly woman with bent shoulders and snowy hair peeking from beneath her kerchief.

"Who is that?" Nimhea whispered.

"I don't—" Ara stopped, staring at the stranger. The stranger with Ironbranch lying across her lap.

Ara's blood frosted; she stepped stiffly into the circle of firelight.

"The ladies have finally admitted they have stomachs." Teth tore a hunk of bread off what remained of their loaf and offered it to Nimhea.

When she took it, he bit into his own bread and pointed to an object wrapped in cloth beside Eamon. "Mhper folo heez."

Picking up the object and pulling back the cloth, Eamon said, "I think he meant 'There's also cheese.'"

He cut a piece of cheese for Nimhea.

"We also have a guest, who begged the safety of our campfire," said Eamon, wearing a giddy grin as he gestured to the old woman. "Eni's blessings upon us!"

"You don't have to do that," Teth complained.

"What?" asked Eamon.

"Announce it," Teth replied, then mimicked Eamon. "'Eni's

blessings!' No one does that. It's the act of inviting someone to your campfire that matters. Not talking about it."

"Oh, leave the boy be," the old woman interjected. Her voice had the creaks of age. "Nothing wrong with a bit of enthusiasm. These are hard days. Young people grow bitter too quickly."

She pointed a bony finger at Eamon. "That one has a soul sweeter than honey."

Eamon blushed, and Teth burst into laughter.

Ara could only stare at the Loresmith stave. Should she ask for it back? Make some excuse to take it?

Why did this woman pick it up in the first place?

"Sit down, Ara." Teth chucked the heel of the loaf at her.

When she caught it, Teth quickly looked at Eamon. "Don't throw the cheese. I don't want dirt on the cheese. If she wants cheese, go over there and give it to her."

Eamon, who already had his arm lifted, hunk of cheese in his hand, looked crestfallen.

"Sit here, dear." The old woman patted the open patch of log beside her. "I was just telling your companions that I was out gathering herbs and the dark came up so quickly, I became terribly confused. I'm usually quite good at tracking the sun, so I don't know what happened. I don't think I can safely make my way back home until morning."

She lowered her voice. "It's said there are thieves about."

"Tragically, there are always thieves about," Teth said mournfully, hiding his smile with another mouthful of bread.

As her jaw worked with nerves, Ara said, "Of course you're welcome at our fire. Is there any other way we can aid you?"

"How kind of you." The woman's face crinkled when she smiled. "Might I ask, are you the owner of this stave or is the other girl?"

"It belongs to me," Ara said, her heart thudding against her breastbone.

The old woman's hands curled around the stave, cradling it. "Such a fine, fine piece of woodworking. My husband's a woodworker, you know, though I dare say he mightn't be able to craft such a thing as this beauty."

She offered Ara a wistful smile. "A young thing like you wouldn't know what a great friend a good stave is. A third leg, strong to support the others as they weaken. A friend to lean on when one needs rest. And at my age one often needs rest."

Ara took in the woman's bent back and gnarled fingers; what a burden her pain and weariness must be. Ara's grandmother had so far been spared the more severe punishments of age, but Ara knew Elke suffered aching joints and deep weariness after each lesson with Ironbranch.

I wish I'd been more grateful, Ara thought, regretting the way she'd treated their training sessions like chores. She hadn't considered the physical toll her lessons would have taken on her grandmother, nor the emotional burden of working with Ironbranch—a weapon that must have reminded Elke of all she'd lost.

Looking at the old woman sitting beside her, Ara could see the same wisdom and kindness she'd always found in her grandmother's eyes.

"Would you like to have it?" The words spilled out. Ara didn't know where they'd come from. "To help you back to your home?"

Nava's mercy. Ara's own audacity caught her off guard. Ironbranch was her most precious possession. A sign that she was truly the Loresmith's heir.

The old woman beamed.

Twins save me, she's going to take it, Ara thought, knifed by panic. *I can't give Ironbranch away . . . can I?*

Taking a deep breath, she reminded herself of Eni's hospitality. That she was honor-bound to help other travelers. If this old woman needed a walking stick, then so be it. It wasn't as though Ara could carve a different stave for her on the spot.

Ara cast her gaze around the campfire, waiting for one of her companions to object. Eamon and Nimhea were conversing quietly, paying no mind to Ara and the old woman. Teth, however, was watching the visitor with narrowed eyes. But he didn't move, nor did he speak.

When her attention returned to the old woman, Ara found the stranger staring at her, gaze bright and mischievous.

Suddenly the woman began to laugh, startling Ara so much she nearly fell off the log.

"Oh no, oh no." The woman shook her head. "A generous offer indeed, but my husband would never forgive me for bringing home a stave carved by someone else."

Able to breathe again, Ara smiled awkwardly at the old woman, who lifted Ironbranch and placed it in Ara's hands. At the stave's touch, Ara felt warmth course through her body, like a greeting, setting her at ease.

"Use it well," the woman said, her gaze still playful.

A new sensation, tingling on and under Ara's skin, passed through her, and the sound of chimes tinkled in her ears. Then it was gone.

"As thanks for your generosity, let me use some of the herbs I gathered to make you my special tea," the old woman said. "It's restorative to body and spirit. And it will give you sound sleep and lovely dreams."

"That's very kind of you," Ara heard herself say. She was still trying to puzzle out what had just happened. It felt significant, but she couldn't comprehend what it was.

The stranger touched Ara's cheek. "You look like you've seen a spirit. Be at ease, my dear."

Ara's confusion melted away, a drowsy contentment taking its place.

"Sweet boy!" the old woman called.

Eamon immediately jumped up.

She smiled at him. "Please put some water on to boil."

"Happy to be of service." Eamon set about his task, humming all the while.

Nimhea was smiling too as she watched her brother putter around the fire.

Only Teth seemed untouched by the woman's endearing character. He stood up, his face a mask.

"I'll keep watch."

Without waiting for the others to reply, he slipped into the shadows. He'd given no earlier indication that he intended to keep watch or stalk about the forest. He simply left.

The old woman joined Eamon at the fire, and soon they were humming in harmony. Ara moved to sit beside Nimhea. When the tea was ready, the woman served the steaming liquid in beautifully carved wooden bowls that Ara didn't remember seeing before. The tea was powerfully aromatic and delicious to taste. Ara found it odd that she couldn't recognize the scents or flavors of any herb in the concoction.

She could hear the woman humming as the world faded away.

Ara woke with faint memories of the loveliest dreams. She'd never had such refreshing sleep. It was the first night since they'd left Rill's Pass that she hadn't missed her bed. After indulging in a long, languid stretch, Ara sat up to see what was happening about camp.

Nimhea and Eamon still slept. There was no sign of the old woman, but Teth had returned, as had the fox. The bushy little creature hadn't made an appearance since their skirmish with the bandits, and Ara had assumed the poor beast had been, rightfully, scared off to the safety of its den. It seemed a shame for the fox to have come all this way, as their party would soon reach Silverstag. In a town, the fox would only be seen as a hide. Surely it knew better than to follow Teth into a populated area.

Crawling from her blankets, Ara began to fold up her bedroll. She hummed a sweet melody as she packed. Odd, for she wasn't much for humming or whistling or anything of that sort. But something about this tune—it was a song, she knew that—she couldn't remember the words or even what the song was called. Only the melody could she recall, and humming it now set her in good spirits.

Nimhea and Eamon stirred and stretched as Ara carried her things to the packhorse. When she returned to the campfire, the twins were sitting with Teth and eating porridge.

"Good morning, Ara," said Nimhea with a bright, open smile that Ara had never seen before. Along with her joyful expression, Nimhea's face was luminous. The deep bronze of her skin gleamed against her molten hair, which spilled over her shoulders like a waterfall of flames.

Eamon, too, had a different look to him. His friendly, eager expression was still there, but lacked the nervous shadow that usually flickered about his face.

"Good morning." Ara sat down beside Eamon. "You both look well."

With a sigh, Nimhea said, "I had the most wondrous dreams and such a deep sleep."

"So did I," added Eamon, while spooning up a bowl of porridge for Ara.

Ara took the bowl and spoon. "I did as well."

She expected a breakfast of bland porridge to dampen her happiness, but it didn't.

Teth had yet to speak, or make any sound, so Ara looked at him. The thief had not enjoyed a peaceful night. His eyes were bleary and deeply shadowed.

When he caught Ara staring at him, he scowled. "I kept watch."

"You should have woken me," Ara told him. "There's no reason we can't share night watches."

He shifted his expression to appear aghast. "Never. I couldn't have disturbed your miraculous slumber."

Ara answered with an uncomfortable laugh. While Teth had a penchant for jokes, this morning he was on edge, joyless in a way that verged on anger. It would have been easy to blame his mood on exhaustion, but behind his stony gaze Ara glimpsed fear.

"I see your pet is back." Nimhea stared judgmentally at the fox, who begged a lick of porridge from her bowl.

The fox endured her stern gaze briefly, then moved over to Eamon, who immediately set down his unfinished porridge.

"Not a pet," Teth told her. "More of an occasional accomplice."

Eamon scratched the fox behind its ears. "Does it have a name?"

"I call it Red Pestilence, Bane of Rabbits," Teth said, a hint of his usual self slipping into his wry smile.

They all stared at him, including the fox. Ara even thought she caught the fox rolling its eyes, but that was impossible.

Teth waited a moment longer for a reaction, then his shoulders slumped. "So . . . not a great joke."

"No," Eamon said apologetically.

"Fine. I don't call it Red Pestilence, Bane of Rabbits," Teth grumped. "I call it Fox."

"Fox," said Nimhea frowning. "Don't you know if it's a boy or girl?"

"Does it matter?" Teth asked.

"Maybe you'd come up with a better name," Nimhea said.

Teth waved her off. "Look, Fox and I have boundaries. If you want to find out whether Fox will let you check, that's your business, but I'd prepare yourself to be bitten."

"It bites?" Nimhea stepped back from Fox.

"Wouldn't you?"

Nimhea didn't have an answer for that.

With a self-satisfied smile, Teth stood up. "Since you're all so well rested, we should get moving. We'll reach Silverstag by day's end."

"Fox won't follow us into the town?" Ara asked, worried for the little beast.

"No," Teth answered. "Fox knows to avoid places where people congregate. That's one of the many ways wild beasts are wiser than humans."

It was said that before the conquest, Silverstag had been the great hearth to which all hunters, merchants, and fortune seekers flocked in Fjeri. Here was the place of plotting a boar hunt and pledging to a pilgrimage. Hatching a heist and settling old scores. Bustling with commerce, gossip, and the hijinks of the risk-takers so often drawn to the river town, Silverstag drummed loud the loyal heartbeat of its founding families and adoptive residents. It clapped along to the ever-changing songs of its countless visitors. Many of Saetlund's best-loved songs and oft-told tales had been first sung and spoken in Silverstag.

That made the current state of Silverstag a terrible disappointment. When the four riders emerged from the woods and looked upon the town that spanned both banks of the Fjeri River, Ara knew that the old Silverstag was no more. No rhythm carried the people who either scurried from building to building or scowled from windows and corners at passersby. The town was hunched with tension and paranoia, awaiting the next disaster that would befall it.

Old Imgar had told her as much; that towns and villages across Saetlund were strangled by the empire. The Vokkans bled dry crops, goods, and services that had been the backbone of a thriving commerce. Saetlund's people survived on the meager sustenance left over. Fauld's armies were vast, and they needed feeding. Most of Saetlund's grains were shipped to imperial territories where the soil had been stripped so nothing could grow. Artisans with the greatest skills—masons, potters, tanners, smiths, and the rest—were forced from their homes and conscripted to imperial labor.

The practice left towns like Silverstag governed by fear and bereft of their former nature.

Not that Ara had witnessed what they had been. She'd never traveled farther than the edge of the highlands. Whenever there was business to be done at a trading post, or in the rare event that certain goods could only be procured from a larger settlement, like Port Pilgrim or Silverstag, Ara had not been allowed to join her grandmother or Old Imgar on a journey more than a day's distance from the village. Inexplicably, a huge number of chores or a particularly tedious order in the blacksmith shop arrived just before a trip out of the village and whatever obligation arose fell to Ara. She'd always resented being left behind. Now she understood that her grandmother had been keeping her away as a means of hiding her in Rill's Pass. She appreciated all her grandmother and Old Imgar had done to keep her safe, but that hadn't stopped the growing anticipation of finally arriving in a place of culture and commerce.

The ease she'd felt earlier in the day ebbed as they plodded through dingy streets, faces hidden by hoods. Not that the town's residents were out in the streets to watch their passing. Though Ara knew it couldn't be, Silverstag felt empty. She caught glimpses of figures in windows. Only a handful of people crossed paths with the riders, and those few walked swiftly with their heads down.

When they reached the Antler and Tusk, an inn where the twins' contacts were meant to be awaiting their arrival, the sun had sunk below the horizon. Ara thought it was the most appealing structure she'd seen in the town. Constructed of fine timber, the inn was stained to a charcoal shade with bright white trim on the eaves and window frames. One of the inn's employees lit oil lamp sconces on either side of the building's red double doors.

Teth swung down from his horse. "You are safely delivered."

Nimhea stared at the inn, her expression unreadable.

"If you like," Teth continued, "I'd be happy to see your horses to the stables. I know the innkeeper and can get you a good price."

Ara's eyebrows lifted.

With a chuckle, Teth said, "Don't worry yourself. I know all the proprietors in Silverstag."

"Very well," said Ara, and dismounted.

The twins came down from their saddles, handing reins to Teth.

"We'll enter through the back," Nimhea told Ara, then turned to Teth. "You did as you promised. Thank you."

A corner of Teth's mouth curved up.

"As we part ways, I want to say that while I can't encourage your . . .

livelihood," Nimhea went on, "I hope . . . er . . . I hope don't you get caught."

"Hear, hear." Eamon clapped Teth on the back. "Hope we haven't inconvenienced you too much."

"Your sentiments are appreciated." Teth gave a slight bow. "As it happens, I have business in Silverstag. So no trouble at all."

"Good luck then," said Nimhea. She motioned for Eamon to follow her around the back of the inn.

Suddenly, surprisingly needing to avoid her own farewell, Ara decided to piggyback on the twins' goodbye and started after them. Teth grabbed her wrist.

"A moment."

Ara turned to face him, an unfamiliar weight pressing on her chest. She didn't understand why it should be a struggle to say goodbye to him. Having Teth around risked his discovery of their mission.

I should be relieved to have him gone.

"We need to talk," Teth said, his tone light, which did nothing to put Ara at ease. "When those two have turned in, meet me downstairs."

"You're staying at the inn?" she asked.

"No, I have other dwellings in this town," Teth replied. "I'll return after supper."

Ara pressed her lips together, but nodded.

"Till then." Teth turned his attention to the horses.

The strange weight had lifted, and she quickly tried to explain it away.

He was a helpful guide, she thought. *And it was certainly nice to have someone besides the twins to talk to.*

Satisfied with that logic, Ara was caught off guard by a quiet inner voice.

He made you feel less alone.

Tracing the twins' steps, Ara's mind churned over what Teth wanted to say to her. She hoped he wasn't foolish enough to demand a ransom for silence. Nimhea and Eamon had money, as Teth well knew, but Ara suspected whoever these allies of theirs were wouldn't take kindly to blackmail. She didn't want to see Teth imprisoned, or worse, but she also couldn't afford to have him spread word of Nimhea's identity.

The back door was set beneath a staircase that came down from a second-floor balcony, keeping the entrance shadowed. The door stood open, and Ara could barely make out the figure with whom Nimhea was speaking.

Eamon kept slightly back. In contrast to his sister, who stood tall and confident, Eamon glanced nervously from Nimhea to the street. He appeared far less than eager to go inside.

A little relief spilled into his blue eyes when Ara approached. "Everything okay?"

"Just settling the horses," Ara replied.

"Why are you dawdling?" Nimhea's harsh whisper reached them. She was signaling that they should come inside.

Passing through the door into a dim hallway, the stranger led them into a large store room, where three other people were gathered. The room benefited from the light of sconces that revealed two men, one of whom had brought them inside, and two women. All of them were elders to the travelers. Some by a handful of years, others by decades. Their cloaks didn't completely hide the steel beneath, which flashed at times in the light of the fire. Examining the strangers' features, Ara guessed that each was a representative of Saetlund's provinces, with the exception of Fjeri. The youngest was the man closest to them. He had light brown hair and the milky complexion frequently seen in Kelden; the woman seated at a small table looked to be no more than five years older than Nimhea. She had golden skin and hair dyed in stripes of ochre and cobalt, as was the tradition in Vijieri. The middle-aged man sitting opposite her had a shaved head and ebony skin common to the people of Daefrit. The last woman stood, rather imperiously, at the front of the group. Her hair was shades of iron and mahogany, cropped short, and she shared with Nimhea and Eamon the burnished skin often seen in Sola. She was the eldest of the warriors.

It was this woman who pushed her cloak back, making plain her scaled mail shirt and longsword.

Without a sign from Nimhea, Eamon took a step toward the stranger. "Behold Nimhea, eldest child of Dentroth crowned by flame, son of Emrisa, daughter of Rea, daughter of Polit, son of Trin, son of Vinnea, daughter of Hessa, daughter of Imlo, son of Gright, son of Penla, daughter of Terr, son of Olnea—first of the Flamecrowned dynasty. Princess Nimhea, daughter of fire, heir to the River Throne of Saetlund. The one who will reclaim what has been lost."

Ara recalled Eamon listing off the same titles when they'd first met. She also remembered cutting him off before he finished the last sentence.

The one who will reclaim what has been lost.

Those words lingered in her mind, like echoes of a bell ringing.

There is much more to this than a fallen king and a conquered country, thought Ara, *because much more has been lost.*

Her grandmother had said as much. *The time has come for Saetlund to remember what it was, what it must become again.*

Nimhea pushed her hood back slowly. She didn't shake out her hair, showing off, as she'd attempted with Ara. She revealed her flaming locks hesitantly, as if the act meant crossing a threshold from which there was no coming back.

Unlike Ara, the four strangers neither guffawed nor balked at Eamon's lengthy pronouncement. Nor did they laugh when Nimhea's fiery hair gleamed in the lantern light. Each warrior sank to one knee. The sight took Ara's breath away. Soldiers submitting to a young woman of whom they knew almost nothing, pledging their loyalty to a queen without a crown. To a ruler with no subjects.

Eamon's eyes were wide. He shifted his weight from foot to foot, desperate to react but forcing himself to keep quiet. His eyes were on his sister. As was Ara's gaze. The strangers remained still, heads bent. The room was a tableau, holding its breath, everything awaiting the response of the most important person there.

Nimhea appeared composed, her bearing regal. She looked upon the kneeling strangers, taking in the moment. Her expression was calm, confident.

But Ara noticed the quiver of Nimhea's lip, the sheen of her eyes, and she understood something she'd never grasped before that moment. Nimhea had been afraid. Not of sailing to the land from which she'd been exiled. Not of seeking out a strange girl with an even stranger lore tied to her. Not of facing bandits in an unfamiliar forest. None of those things had troubled the princess.

This room was what had filled her with dread. This moment was the one that truly mattered. The rightful heir to the kingdom had returned.

And she had been accepted.

Though Ara was certain it must have been difficult, Nimhea's voice was strong and clear when she spoke:

"Arise."

Rising as one, the warriors held their fists against their breastbones and responded: "Hail, Nimhea, Queen of Saetlund."

Ara shivered, for behind the voices of these four she heard echoes. A swell of hundreds, thousands of voices, all waiting to greet their queen. Then it was gone and the room was quiet again.

The woman at the front of the group broke the solemnity in the air by smiling. "Your majesty—"

"I'm not a queen yet," Nimhea interjected. "The throne I must earn. Until then, I remain a princess."

Smile growing wider, the woman said, "Your highness, I am Suli, Second Commander of our forces. I also represent your loyal followers from Sola. With me are three others, each bringing the promise of fealty from their homeland."

She gestured to the mousy-haired warrior. "Ioth of Kelden, commander of the calvary."

Next was the woman with vivid yellow and blue tresses. "Xeris of Vijeri oversees the bowmen."

The dark-skinned man she named next: "Edram of Daefrit directs our tacticians and oversees the design and construction of war machines."

"I am indebted to each of you for all you've done to bring me home," Nimhea told them. "I, too, have companions. My brother, Eamon, and Ara Silverthread . . . of Rill's Pass."

With four pairs of curious eyes suddenly upon her, Ara grasped for the right thing to say. All she came up with was:

"Hello."

"This is the person for whom you delayed your arrival?" Suli examined Ara with narrowed eyes. "You added her to your company. That was a great risk. She is of Saetlund, yet not tied in any way to our cause. We have no reason to trust her. Do you?"

Though fair, the question made Ara bristle.

"She's younger than those we recruit," Ioth said. "Most likely, she had no awareness that the Resistance exists."

Suli pursed her lips, but nodded.

"I'll buy that," Xeris quipped. "But she's here now, so who is she?"

Nimhea looked at Ara and lifted her chin to encourage a response.

"I'm a blacksmith," said Ara. She wasn't ready to offer anything more. Old Imgar had been in contact with the rebellion, but obviously had chosen to keep Ara's existence a secret. She trusted he'd had good reason to.

Eamon, however, had other plans.

"She's more than a blacksmith." He walked to Ara's side with an air of solemnity. "Ara is the Loresmith."

The warriors exchanged glances; all were taken aback, but by different emotions.

A smile played on Ioth's lips. "The Loresmith? That's a hefty title for such a small girl."

Ara straightened, making herself taller, which did little to heighten her stature. "I assure you I'm stronger than I might look. And I *am* the Loresmith."

"A smith you may be," said Xeris. "But the Loresmith is a legend. There is no such person."

Edram watched Ara with curious eyes, while Suli frowned at Eamon.

Still uncomfortable with the strangers, Ara was happy enough to let them be content with an imaginary Loremsith. But Eamon would have none of it.

"Turning the past into legends and fantasies is what brought the downfall of Saetlund," he told them. "If you want to restore the kingdom, you must have the aid of the gods."

"Stop." Ioth's good humor had faded. "If the gods want to help us, I'm happy to hear it, but it's madness to call upon old stories as our only salvation."

Suli's voice was gentler, but still firm. "We've been told you're well read, Eamon. But the books that will help us are accounts of the empire's other conquests. Turn your attention to those volumes, and you'll be a great asset to our cause."

Ara expected Eamon to back down, but he became more insistent. His cheeks had reddened, and not from embarrassment. His hands were fists.

"I *have* read those volumes," Eamon told Suli. "And I am telling you now, with all certainty, that if you rely on military histories and battle tactics alone, you will fail. My sister will never be queen."

"Listen, boy." Ioth pointed a gauntleted finger at him. "While you've been coddled in the Ethrian Isles, we've been sacrificing everything we have to build a resistance. You have no business making demands or giving orders."

Nimhea's voice was like a thunderclap. "Never speak to my brother that way again."

Ioth opened his mouth to rebuke her, then suddenly remembered who she was. "Apologies, your highness, but I don't think your brother grasps—"

"Eamon grasps our situation perfectly," Nimhea cut him off. "He hasn't spent his years memorizing nursery rhymes. He's a scholar, and he's uncovered a truth that could be the difference between winning and losing this war."

Ioth's face blanched, and Suli drew a sharp breath. Xeris sank into a chair, muttering under her breath. Edram's eyes were a mystery.

Ara looked at each of them, wondering who they were outside this room and what had driven them here. Old Imgar said the Resistance was scattered. Even before the conquest, the provinces of Saetlund had become distrustful of one another. Fjeri and Vijeri resented that power and wealth resided in Sola and Daefrit. Sola and Daefrit viewed the mountainous and jungled provinces respectively as backwaters that didn't pull their weight in the kingdom's economy.

"The hardest part of forming the Resistance," Imgar had told Ara, *"is finding a way to unify four provinces that have been driven apart. That's why they need the heir to the River Throne. That's why they need* you.*"*

"Ara is the Loresmith," Nimhea continued. "And she is the key to our victory."

As the spoke of a wheel around which this debate turned, Ara had no idea what to do. She could come to her own defense, but she had no authority that the warriors would recognize. Neither could she muster ways to cool the hot tempers blazing around her.

"Why doesn't she smith us a magic weapon?" said Ioth in a flat voice. "That will settle things."

Eamon threw up his hands. "You fool! You understand nothing!" His face became mottled with reds and purples.

Ara had never seen Eamon be anything other than wide-eyed and effervescent, if a bit anxious. When he told tales or offered details about the gods and their works, he became giddy. Now she witnessed the opposite side of the coin that was his passion for lore and history.

Ioth's hands balled into fists, but he didn't respond in kind.

"Ioth's suggestion"—Suli spoke in a calming voice and threw a chastening glance at the man from Kelden—"while delivered rather rudely, isn't unreasonable. What you claim is beyond belief—not just to the four of us—but to most of Saetlund."

Joining Suli's attempt to mollify Eamon, Ara said, "She's right,

Eamon. As you've already pointed out, Saetlund fell because the gods faded and lore was forgotten. To them, the Loresmith is a legend, nothing more."

Eamon looked from Suli to Ara, then to Nimhea, who nodded. "Yes. I suppose that's true."

He cleared his throat, abruptly appearing embarrassed by his outburst. "I apologize for my lack of civility. Please understand that while I am young, the years I've lived have been utterly devoted to these mysteries."

After a thin smile at Eamon, Suli asked Ara, "Will you demonstrate your power?"

Ara's throat filled with gravel. Their gazes dared her to perform a miraculous feat, but she did not yet have the skills of the Loresmith. Her sole purpose in joining Eamon and Nimhea was to find the key to unlocking that power. For now, she was Loresmith by blood alone. That wouldn't be enough for the rebels.

The confidence that had been building within her since leaving Rill's Pass shrank. Here she stood facing warriors. She could see in their faces what joining the rebellion had cost them and how willing they were to continue to pay that debt until Nimhea was on the throne.

What place do I have here?

Seeing her panic, Ioth muttered, "Perhaps she needs a special forge?"

"Let it be," Xeris snapped at him, but the irritation in her gaze was directed at Eamon.

Since Ara was struggling to get words out, Eamon answered for her. "She can't."

"Why?" Suli's shoulders sank as she grieved the passing of a simple solution.

Eamon brightened. He seemed happiest when giving explanations.

"The power of the Loresmith follows a bloodline," Eamon said. "Ara's father was the last Loresmith, but he was killed when the River Throne was taken. A Loresmith guides their successor through the history, skills, and rituals of their craft. The role is actively, not passively, inherited. After all, any Loresmith could have more than one child, and the eldest among siblings has not always been chosen. Ara was not yet born when her father died. She could not learn what she needed to."

Ara wanted to embrace Eamon for speaking on her behalf. He could explain her position without being burdened by the emotions she would have contended with if forced to explain the loss of her father, the elusiveness of her fate.

"If her father is gone, how can she learn?" Xeris asked, curiosity overcoming her impatience.

"The first Loresmith was chosen by the gods for his worthiness," Eamon replied. "Ara must prove she is likewise worthy."

Xeris frowned at him. "How will she do that?"

The lively current of Eamon's answers spluttered. "I . . . well . . . it's not simple. The specific manner in which Ara will be tested is hidden. No mortal can reveal that mystery."

"So," Xeris quipped. "One of the *gods* is going to tell you?"

Eamon shook his head, trying to recapture the expertise he'd fumbled. "I don't know how it will happen, only that we must go to Daefrit."

"To one of the universities?" Xeris pursed her thin lips. "I suppose the gods left a scroll in a library, as no mortal can have your answer."

"Not in libraries or archives." Eamon's face grew wistful. "Though I do hope to visit Isar and Zyre one day."

"Focus, Eamon," Nimhea murmured.

Eamon offered his sister an apologetic smile. Before he answered Xeris, Eamon tensed as if expecting a blow.

"We will petition Ofrit for guidance, by seeking him out at his apothecary . . . in the Ghost Cliffs."

The quiet that filled the room was oily; one spark and they would be engulfed by flames.

Ara had to stifle a gasp. She knew many stories about the Ghost Cliffs and the mystery of Ofrit's Apothecary. None of them ended well. That was probably the reason Eamon hadn't spoken of their trio's final destination before that moment.

Edram, who'd been a silent watcher up to that point, spoke first.

"There is truth in the mysteries Eamon speaks of." He made his way forward to stand before Eamon and Ara. His voice was deep and cool, quenching fires yet waiting to burn. "To that I can testify."

A hint of relief eked onto Eamon's face, but his body remained rigid. Nimhea's gaze followed Edram, vacillating between respect and suspicion.

Edram turned to face his peers. "The scholars of Daefrit have countless scrolls addressing these matters. Magic, the gods, their lore— though interest in them has waned—have never been abandoned as a subject of study. It has always been said that those who dedicate their minds to the understanding of the divine are transformed."

He closed his eyes, letting something well up inside him. "My great uncle was a Scribe of Ofrit, one of the rare chosen who apprenticed in Ofrit's Apothecary. Their number, while never great, had dwindled over the centuries. Few were left at the time of the conquest, but when the Vokkans came all were killed for heresy."

When he fell into a silent meditation, Ara watched, curious about the memories that had taken such a powerful hold upon him.

Edram's eyelids snapped up. "A quest to find Ofrit is not madness."

Ioth and Xeris looked unconvinced, Suli frustrated. Sympathy tugged at Ara's heartstrings. This group of fighters had come to retrieve their future queen. It should have been a triumphant moment. Instead, they'd become entangled in a web of the arcane they wanted nothing to do with.

"If Ara's journey to find Ofrit will ultimately give us an ally beyond measure, I will pray that she succeeds," Suli said, her tone overly polite. "Eamon, I appreciate that you brought her here in order to offer us insights into an aspect of our rebellion that we would not otherwise have considered."

It was a dismissal, and in the rebel leader's mind, an end to the issue.

To Ara, Suli said, "If we can help you with provisions, we would be glad to assist."

Ara was about to thank her—her discomfort at being the rift between the twins and the rebels made her eager to be gone from this room—but Eamon was shaking his head, his eyes resolute.

"You don't understand. This journey is not Ara's alone."

The openness of Suli's expression shuttered.

Despite her iron-banded stare, Eamon pressed on. "Nimhea and I must go with her."

His fervor deeply impressed Ara. For someone prone to illness, who so often demurred, Eamon showed himself to be a formidable adversary when he believed in his cause.

Ioth couldn't stay quiet. "That's impossible. The princess must be taken to a secure location where she will remain, safe and hidden, until we have forces enough to make war on Fauld."

"Ioth is right," Suli said, stone-faced. "Nimhea is at risk enough by simply being in Saetlund. For her to travel such a distance—it's unthinkable."

"Go with your blacksmith if you think you must." Xeris folded her arms on the table, leaning across it. Her posture suggested idleness, but her eyes were dangerous. "The princess, however, stays with us."

"Out of the question." Nimhea moved closer to Eamon and Ara. "Where my brother goes I go."

Ara could feel anger burgeoning in their voices, eager to become rage. She marveled at the unwavering courage in both twins. Nimhea's ferocious hunt for a stolen throne and her unflagging protectiveness of her brother. Eamon's zeal for his scholarship and his adoration of his sister. Together, Ara believed, they likely could raise a force to challenge the Vokkans.

The expressions on the rebels' faces told Ara they recognized that potential as well, and they were horrified that Eamon's obsession with a myth could rob them of their chance to rally Saetlund's people to the Resistance.

"My friends." Edram raised his hands to pacify the room. "There have been many surprises today, but let us remember we share the same goal. The hour is late and the princess has traveled long to meet us. Now is the time for rest and reflection. Tomorrow we will speak of these things again."

That no one objected revealed the threadbare trust between them.

"Wise words," Suli told Edram with a wan smile. Her face was drawn with exhaustion Ara hadn't seen before. The meeting had burdened Suli with a weight she hadn't anticipated.

To the three who had rattled her expectations, Suli said, "I will show you to your room. Food will be brought to you."

With a brief frown, she looked at Nimhea. "You do understand you must not leave the room or go into the public parts of the inn. We've made every effort to keep you safe, but only if you respect the bounds within which we can protect you."

Suli placed extra emphasis on the word *respect*, signaling that Nimhea's siding with Eamon had opened a fissure of doubt between the rebels and their would-be queen.

"Of course."

Ara had never seen Nimhea so quick to acquiesce.

Not a one among them could to stand to be in that room another moment.

8

heir small, tidy room was in a back corner on the inn's second floor. Two narrow beds with inviting feather mattresses stood parallel to each other against one wall. Two wooden chairs and a small table were the only other furniture. They'd entered the room through a panel in the wall that slid back, opening to the dim corridors where only the widowed innkeeper and his daughter were permitted.

Without being asked, Ioth had brought one of the bedrolls up from among their gear.

When he handed the bundle to Ara, he said, not unkindly, "We didn't expect you."

Ara thanked him, musing again over what reason Ioth had to become a leader of the rebellion. *Does he have a personal vendetta against the empire? Do all of the rebel leaders?*

Ara had a bit of a tussle with Eamon over who would sleep on the bedroll.

"I insist." Eamon stood beside the bedroll and pointed to one of the feather beds.

Shaking her head, Ara smiled. "It's not necessary. You should get a good night's rest."

"And you shouldn't?" Eamon countered. "I don't mind sleeping on the floor. It's much smoother than the ground in the forest."

Ara's laugh had an edge. "You take the bed, Eamon. I'm more accustomed to sleeping on the ground."

That wasn't quite true, and Ara wasn't trying to be polite. She needed to sleep on the bedroll. It gave her much better placement for sneaking out of the room once the twins were asleep.

"But—"

A little growling sound came from Nimhea. "Just take the bed, Eamon. I'm exhausted and Ara wants the bedroll. We've all been witness to your chivalry; now drop it."

Eamon's cheeks reddened, but he obeyed.

A quarter of an hour later all three were settled in for slumber. Ara stared at the ceiling, waiting for sounds of deep sleep from her companions before she could sneak from the room, and her mind began to drift. While traveling, she'd had the constant distractions of perils in the woods and Eamon's chatter. In this room, where she felt the security of a hidden place and armed warriors keeping watch, silence gave her freedom to reflect. It took her back to the room downstairs, to the incredulity of Suli and her companions.

Their disbelief had knocked down her confidence. The leaders of the rebellion had no patience for myths. Why should they? That was what she'd told Eamon—reminding him of her own reluctance to have faith in her new destiny.

Until this evening, Ara's fears about the truths in Eamon's tales had been fading, and her comfort with the idea of being the Loresmith had grown in equal measure. But it was more than just comfort; on the way to Silverstag she'd at last been shown what she'd been told by her grandparents and Old Imgar. Her dream of Wuldr. Fox guiding her to Teth. Teth's deference to Eni's oath. All these things fed her faith.

She needed to believe. Her doubts were cracks forming on thin ice. She couldn't afford them if she was to see the quest through.

Ara wished she had more than Eamon's knowledge and enthusiasm to guide her. She felt alone and ill prepared. If only her father had lived. She could have known him, learned from him. If he saw her now, what would he think: that she was brave? Foolhardy?

Tell me how to prove I'm worthy. Tell me how to face the gods. Ara let her thoughts float up to the ceiling.

Soft snoring brought her back to the present. As quietly as she could, Ara left the bedroll and gathered her cloak and stave. She went back to the hidden passageway and crept down the stairs. When she was about to open the back door, someone said:

"We asked you to stay in your room."

Ioth stepped out of the shadows.

"And the princess and prince should remain hidden." Ara spun her words quickly. "But I am no one to be recognized because to everyone in Silverstag I *am* no one."

A smile twitched onto Ioth's lips. "Clever."

He gestured to the door. "Don't get into trouble, because we won't get you out."

Ara was of half a mind to ask if that was a warning or his wish. After all, if she didn't return it meant Nimhea and Eamon would have no distraction from the rebels' cause. But she found no animosity in Ioth's voice or his gaze and was comforted. Though they were currently at odds, Ara didn't want to be an obstacle to the Resistance. They worked toward the same end: the liberation of Saetlund from its Vokkan conquerors.

Her thoughts turned again toward the reasons these men and women had chosen to become leaders of the Resistance.

Hesitating, Ara asked, "Ioth, what brought you here?"

"A horse."

"No." Ara smiled at his jest. She was about to find out how defensive it was. "How did you become a leader of the Resistance?"

Ioth's jaw tightened, then released. "If we meet again after your search for Ofrit, I'll tell you."

She didn't know if his cryptic reply was a joke or a promise. Either way he'd given Ara cause to be even more curious about his past.

Ara bid him good night and stepped outside. Her breath curled in the cool night air. Despite what she'd said to Ioth, Ara pulled her hood up. While there was no one looking for her, it was still better not to show a face that people might remember.

The Antler and Tusk's front door opened to a warm, inviting room. It bore some similarities to the Rill's Pass inn, but was much larger. The decorations were tributes to the inn's name. Stags' and boars' heads, antlers, and skulls graced walls that were polished to a sheen. A fire crackled in the great hearth, ready to welcome patrons in from the cold. If only there were patrons. The room was empty apart from the woman behind the bar and a lone man hunched on a stool. The lack of customers made Ara wonder where the innkeeper got the coin to keep his establishment in such good repair.

Is he an imperial lackey? No. That can't be. Maybe the Resistance pays useful persons for their discretion.

Teth had picked a small round table in a shadowed corner. He had a pewter tankard in his hand, and when he saw Ara he waved her over. The sudden relief she felt at seeing the thief made her skin prickle.

"Why am I here?" Ara asked as she sat down.

"There goes my offer to buy you a drink," Teth said. "It is common practice to greet the person you're joining for a nightcap."

Ara countered his merry eyes with a steady gaze. Happy as she was to see Teth, she remained wary of what he was up to.

Teth's affable features shifted to an irked expression. "You're less likely to draw attention if you act like you want to be here."

"Draw whose attention?" Ara asked with a meaningful glance around the tavern. "Where is everyone?"

"In their homes behind locked doors," Teth replied. "Imperial patrols all over Saetlund have the habit of 'recruiting' laborers at local watering holes. Business dried up quickly when word spread of whole pubs being cleared out and marched off. The empire embraces a unique interpretation of the word *volunteer*."

Though she knew the answer, Ara asked, "What happens to people who say no?"

She hoped the way Teth answered her questions would reveal something about his life.

"They decorate the city walls," Teth said with a grim smile. "And they generously donate their entrails to feed the local pigs."

Ara shuddered. Violence and gore were trademarks of Vokkan conquest.

Teth took a long drink, and when he set the tankard down again his jovial facade was back.

With some reluctance Ara pushed her hood back and forced herself to smile. "Are you always playacting? Is that how you go through life?"

"My work requires it more frequently than not," Teth replied.

The idea that Teth often showed a false face to the world troubled Ara.

How can I know when he's truly himself with me? She didn't yet have an answer to that question, but she was determined to find one.

He slid the tankard over to Ara, and she understood she was

meant to drink as part of the act. She took a swig from the tankard and wrinkled her nose. She had no taste for ale.

"I'm going to take you to a place that most people never see." Teth took the tankard back. "It shouldn't be dangerous, but stay alert."

"Where are we going?" asked Ara.

Teth shook his head. "It's better shown than told."

His vague answer irritated her, but she wanted to be taken to this place "most people never see."

He placed a few coins on the table and started to rise when a rowdy crew of men stumbled through the front door. They were armed with swords and dressed in mail shirts covered by the steel gray and crimson surcoat of the Vokkan Empire. At the center of their chests, stark in black thread against red cloth, was the spiral of eternity. The sign of Fauld the Ever-Living.

Ara's heart went mad, banging against her breastbone so hard she could feel the beats vibrate in her ears. She had never been so close to Vokkan soldiers. They reeked of iron and sweat.

Patrols passed through Rill's Pass rarely, and when they did Ara had only been able to catch brief glimpses of them before her grandmother pulled her away from the window. They'd only been frightening then because Ara had always been told the imperial patrols brought trouble. That fear had been light as mist, but what Ara felt now was a flood of cold in her limbs.

Teth rested his hand on her arm. The warmth of his touch pulled her gaze from the soldiers. To her surprise, he still wore that loose smile and mirthful eyes. She was even more amazed when he spoke without moving his lips.

"Put your hood up."

"But you said—"

"Just do it." Teth followed the soldiers with his gaze, but said to Ara, "Don't turn to watch them. Stay exactly as you are."

Ara did as he said, trying to return his smile. She even picked up the tankard and took another pull of ale.

From the corner of her eye, Ara could see the patrol swaggering toward the bar. The single patron there abandoned his drink and hurried out the door. One of the soldiers went behind the bar and grabbed the barmaid around the waist. He dragged her to the stools where his fellows gathered. The woman didn't shout or struggle; her face was simply painted with horror. Ara began to rise, but Teth caught her arm and pulled her back to her seat.

"Don't," Teth whispered.

"I can't let them—" Rage tore through her like wildfire.

"I'll take care of it." Teth stood up. "Don't move."

Ara forced herself to remain still, but she swore to herself that if Teth couldn't help the barmaid she would. It was unforgiveable that these brutes would lay hands on a woman without her consent.

"Malvo!" the soldier holding the barmaid called to one of his fellows.

Malvo strode up, grinning. "What are you up to, Tretter?"

Tretter hauled the woman in front of him, one arm around her waist keeping her pinned to his chest. "This is what I was talking about!"

With his free hand, Tretter began groping his captive, squeezing handfuls of flesh. "The northern ones, that's what you want. Not those spindly things in the south."

Ara gripped the edge of the table, fury like hot coals blazing beneath her ribs.

Teth, you need to move faster.

"I'm not convinced," said Malvo, though he joined Tretter in pinching and prodding the serving woman.

Tretter spat on the floor. "I bet you a week's wages that if you bed this cow, you'll tell me I'm right."

Stomach acid scraped at Ara's throat. *Disgusting. They should be the ones whose entrails are fed to pigs.*

"A week's wages, eh?" Malvo stopped groping and stepped back to look the woman up and down. "I'll take that bet."

The proprietor, who'd been in the back, emerged at that moment. When he saw the soldiers and his distraught employee, his face blanched.

Ara read the innkeeper's expression with a mix of sympathy and frustration. *He's too afraid to help her.*

"Sergeant Werth!" Teth strode toward the soldiers, looking delighted to see them.

A bearded man who'd scooped up the former patron's half-drunk tankard turned to squint at Teth. "Do I know you?"

"You don't," Teth answered. "But your reputation precedes you."

Werth grunted.

Teth said to the barman, "Fenser, I'd like to buy a round for these gentlemen. The last I had was a bit stale. A new cask is in order."

"Of course," Fenser replied in a shaky voice. "But I'll need Helti to rouse the boys and bring a fresh cask up from the cellar."

His gaze fixed upon the struggling barmaid.

Sergeant Werth only then took notice that his men had grabbed Helti.

"Malvo! Tretter!" the sergeant roared. "Let that woman be. That's the second time this week. If I have to tell you again, you're in for a flogging."

If I have to tell you again? *They should have been left to rot in a cell long before.*

With sour looks, Malvo and Tretter released Helti and she fled to the back room.

Ara let out a shuddering breath. She was glad Helti was free, but the sickness of what Ara had seen felt like worms crawling through her heart.

Is it like this in every town? The war was over, but Vokkan soldiers continued to prey upon Saetlund's people. So much for enfolding the kingdom into a beneficent empire.

"I appreciate your generosity, stranger," Werth said to Teth. "But I'm here on business."

Turning to Fenser, Werth let his hand rest on his sword hilt. "We've had word a group of strangers arrived this evening. We have reason to suspect they are bandits who've been harassing travelers on the road. Tell us where they are."

Ara stiffened. If Teth was going to betray her, this was the moment.

Fenser twisted a dishrag. "Sir, I—"

"If I may." Teth leaned against the bar, breaking Werth's eye contact with Fenser.

Werth's face clouded with anger, but Teth showed no alarm.

He leaned toward Werth, his tone conspiratorial. "The strangers aren't bandits. They're guests of Lucket."

Ara drank from the tankard Teth had left at the table. Just another patron. No one worth noticing.

Who is Lucket?

The sergeant lost his rage, but peered at Teth with suspicion. "You know Lucket?"

"I find myself in his employ tonight," Teth replied.

Ara didn't see Teth's hand dip into his pocket, but suddenly he was pressing a pouch of coins into Sergeant Werth's hand. "The strangers will give you no trouble."

"Hmmm." Werth tucked the pouch into his belt. "Give Lucket my regards."

Smiling broadly at his men, the sergeant pounded a mailed fist on the bartop. "Now where's our ale?"

The soldiers cheered.

Teth was already back at the table. "Time to go."

He kept his hand on the small of Ara's back, guiding her out the door and down a shadowed side street at a fast clip. He was silent, so Ara was too. Only when they'd gone a quarter mile or more did he slow and look at her.

"You did well."

"I didn't do anything," Ara protested. "I wanted to help"

"You didn't panic," Teth replied. "That helped."

A foul taste was in Ara's mouth. "Those soldiers. I wanted to kill them."

"They're brutes," Teth agreed. "That could have gone very badly. Fenser should have had a warning. The shopkeepers send word to one another if a patrol is on the way. They usually don't show up after midnight, too lazy, which means they had a serious interest in your little group of travelers."

"They can't get away with that," Ara protested.

Teth was quiet for a moment.

"They deserve—" she began.

"I know what they deserve," Teth replied. "I promise you they won't go unpunished."

Ara wanted to believe him, but she didn't see how anyone but a Vokkan could mete out justice to those soldiers for their crimes.

"Who's Lucket?" Ara asked, trying to take her mind away from the bar.

Teth smiled slyly. "He's the one who'll take care of those louts."

Ara looked at Teth sharply. "What sort of man intervenes in imperial matters without fear of retribution?"

"Lucket's sort."

They'd stopped in front of a stone warehouse. Teth pulled a key from his pocket, but before he put it in the lock two hulking shadows came at them from the side of the building.

On instinct, Ara grabbed Teth's arm, certain the soldiers had followed them and were no longer grateful for the free ale.

"That's quite the grip you have." Teth's voice was strained.

But when moonlight revealed what the shadows had masked, she saw that they were keg-bodied and menacing, but not in uniform. She couldn't believe such huge men had been able to keep themselves hidden.

Ara let go of Teth and took Ironbranch in both hands, readying herself for a confrontation.

Only defense. Only defense.

Teth bent his head close to her ear. "You won't need the stick."

"It is not a stick," Ara snapped. She didn't move an inch.

"Tinno. Wulg." Teth greeted each of them, then splayed his hands to show he had no weapons. "I thought I smelled you."

Ara took a step back. *Teth knows these men?*

They didn't make an appealing pair. Tinno moved stiffly, like he was built of bricks. His shirt was mottled with stains, and he wore a leather cap with ear flaps that was much too small for his square head. An iron-headed mallet was in his right hand. Wulg was tall and shaggy as a bear. Ara could just make out beady eyes and a nose within the thick hair sprouting from every other part of his head and face. She didn't see a weapon, but she guessed Wulg could simply give a person a squeeze and break all their bones.

They both reeked of ale. At least that would make it easier to knock them off-balance. Ara just had to be sure she kept out of Wulg's reach.

"Lucket told us to keep an eye out for you," Tinno said to Teth. "We're supposed to bring you in."

He smacked the head of his mallet against his left palm. He tried to do it a second time, but missed his hand and staggered sidewise.

Ara started to think Teth was right about not needing her stave. *Stick, my foot!*

"Let me see if I can explain this," Teth said in a pleasant voice. "I'm here."

He lifted the key. "I was about to open the door."

Tinno frowned, his bleary eyes fixed on the key as if he was transfixed by its shininess. "We're supposed to bring you to Lucket."

"Yes, but that's no longer necessary," Teth replied. "I'm going to see him. Look, I even brought a friend."

He patted Ara's shoulder.

Ara didn't know if she was meant to smile, but she wasn't about to. Teth might be flippant with these two, but she wouldn't take any chances.

Tinno's face screwed up in confusion when Teth pointed out Ara. "Who's this?"

"Someone Lucket wants to meet."

Tinno had given up making threatening motions with his mallet, but he appeared to be at an impasse regarding what to do with them.

"Would it make you happy if you unlocked the door and we followed you through it?" Teth suggested.

Tinno thought about it. "Okay. Wulg, you block the door after they're through so they can't run."

Nava's mercy, Ara thought.

Teth sighed.

It took a while for Tinno to find his key; in fact it took until he remembered that Wulg had the keys. Wulg had not remembered that either.

Ara had concluded they were not a threat and returned Ironbranch to its harness.

Tinno opened the door, swaying on his feet as he did so. Teth and Ara followed him. Wulg kept watch outside, which *was* quite intimidating. He was bigger than the doorframe.

They were only a few feet inside when Tinno turned and waited.

"We're not going to run, Tinno," said Teth.

Tinno looked disappointed. "Tell Lucket we found you."

"You have my word."

That made Tinno squint at Teth as though it was some kind of trick. "I'll tell him."

"Hmpf." Tinno hiccupped and went back outside.

The warehouse smelled of sweet grains and spices, sacks of which were piled from floor to ceiling. They were joined by barrels, casks, crates, and boxes. Rows and rows of goods waiting to be shipped wherever the empire ordered. Teth led Ara through the maze of stacks and shelves until they reached a stone staircase descending to a cellar, which Ara thought strange. A cellar in a warehouse struck her as superfluous.

At the bottom of the steps, Teth brought out another key. They came into a room that held a few rolled-up rugs, but was mostly empty. Another door waited across the room, this one featuring a large brass knocker.

When Teth knocked, a thin strip of wood slid back and a pair of bright blue eyes stared at them from the other side of the door.

"It's me, Bib," said Teth.

"You have to say the password," Bib whispered. He looked at Ara, eyes narrowing as if she were guilty of something by just standing there.

She smiled at him, and he scowled.

"Ugh." Teth passed a hand over his eyes. "What is today? Thursday? Salmon."

The wood slid back into place, and a moment later the door swung inward.

A slender man with wispy gray hair and a lightly lined face waited on the other side.

"Welcome back, Teth."

"Thanks, Bib." Teth's smile at the man was genuine.

"He know you're coming?" Bib asked.

"More or less."

Bib chuckled as he closed the door and returned to his post.

Doors, stairs, thugs, passwords. A thief's world, Ara thought. She'd wanted to know more about Teth. He'd granted her wish.

Teth and Ara walked through arched corridors that frequently branched off into dim passageways. It was a place one could too easily get lost in. Faint voices came in ghostly waves from time to time. Ara caught sight of a person here or there, but no one stopped to greet or even look at them. Ahead, Ara could see a gentle light growing brighter as they walked.

She discovered the source of that light when the corridor ahead opened up into a massive chamber. Hundreds of candles gleamed throughout the room, though the most eye-catching feature was a massive iron chandelier that dangled above the center of the room. A hodgepodge of furniture inhabited the chamber. In one corner plush couches and velvet love seats were drowning in silk pillows. In another corner a great hearth was home to a blazing fire. The group of people huddled in front of it was throwing dice. A long wooden table, holding inkwells and scrolls, and flanked by straight-backed chairs, occupied another corner. The walls beside the table were covered with maps and printed notices.

The last corner differed from the others. A brief set of steps led to a half-circle landing from which rose another short set of steps, where an ornate piece of furniture sat that was not quite a throne, but more than a chair. Upon its velvet cushions lounged a man with neatly shaped silver hair, a likewise finely trimmed beard, and sharp features. He was sumptuously dressed in a dark velvet coat over a tailored shirt and black suede breeches. His long body draped over the massive seat. While his position appeared casual to the point of negligence, he had eagle eyes upon the old woman beseeching him.

"It is the third time in six months." The woman's voice was ragged. "It cannot be borne. This last was Foli's child, her first, and she's aggrieved to the point of wishing herself dead. She's threatened to stop eating, and I fear she will make good on those words."

The woman dabbed her cheeks with a handkerchief.

The third what? Ara thought, taking in the woman's stricken face.

"It shan't be borne," said the man, flexing his long fingers until his knuckles cracked. "I promise you we will uncover the source of this plague. Pertha will see you home and will also visit the grieving mother to be sure she has all she needs."

A woman in a dark gray dress materialized from the shadows and nodded to the older woman.

Dipping into several curtsies, the woman babbled her thanks. "Your majesty's kindness will save us. Gods bless you. Such a great man."

Pertha led the sniffling woman from the room.

Your majesty? Ara peered at the man. She knew of no king other than

Dentroth, who'd been executed by the Vokkans soon after his capture.

Could it be a jest? A nickname of sorts? Only the woman had spoken in a respectful, almost reverent tone. Something else was afoot in this place. Ara's curiosity harassed her like an itch that was out of reach.

Teth and Ara took the woman's place on the landing.

The silver-haired man's gaze touched Ara briefly before he turned his full attention on Teth.

"Tinno and Wulg tracked you down then?" The man's tone was neutral, his expression blank.

"In a way," Teth replied, his face also unreadable. "They were waiting by the warehouse side door."

The man put his face in his hands, making a sound of disgust. When he looked up his mouth twitched with annoyance.

"They were meant to go find you."

Teth smiled slightly. "You weren't specific enough, Lucket."

This is Lucket, thought Ara, *and Teth didn't call him "your majesty." Maybe a nickname after all, but that doesn't explain how obsequious that townswoman was.*

With a sigh of resignation, Lucket said, "I need to stop trying to make them do more than intimidate people. It never works out. I'd let them go, but they are peerless when it comes to a shakedown. All they have to do is stand there, and my debtors fall all over themselves to make amends. Only a fool tries to fight them, and one dead fool always means a sharp drop in late payments."

"True," said Teth. "They are very good at that."

Lucket shifted in his chair, leaning forward to let his elbows rest on his knees. "Much afoot in Silverstag of late. Rebels at the Antler and Tusk, much too eager about their rendezvous with royalty. The children . . ."

Lucket's eyes had gone distant, but he suddenly straightened, holding Teth in a fixed gaze.

"I've been waiting for *those two* to show up. But it was a surprise to see you riding in with them."

This man knows about the twins. He's been expecting *them.* Her skin prickled. Perhaps Teth had lured her here to set a trap for the twins where she would be the bait. Ara wondered if she could have Ironbranch in hand before Teth had a dagger at her throat. Unlikely.

"You shouldn't have sent those stump heads after me," Teth complained.

"You didn't come in as quickly as usual," Lucket told him with a shrug. "Passed a whole day without so much as a note. Gives a man reasons to worry."

"It was insulting," Teth complained. "If I don't come in right away I have *my own* reasons."

Lucket gave him a long look, then shifted his gaze to Ara.

Sizing her up, he gave a dismissive "Hmpf."

To Teth he said, "She's no one. Why is she here?"

Ara's insides seized up. She'd never thought of herself as particularly worthy of notice, but she'd never been called "no one" before. It stung more viciously than she would have imagined. And it festered when Teth didn't have an immediate reply.

Lucket paused, assessing Ara again. "Not particularly pretty, but not unpleasant to look at. Quite short, isn't she? I suppose I could turn her out."

"Senn's teeth, no," Teth replied with a nervous glance at Ara.

"Turn me out—" Ara began, then comprehension jolted through her. "How dare you!" She glared at Lucket. "I didn't come here to be insulted."

"Insulted?" Lucket became livid. "I offered you a job! If you knew anything about anything you'd know working for me means any person who raises a hand to you will lose that hand. I'd suggest you talk to my employees to hear the truth of it. But now I'm of a mind that I don't want a girl of such poor manners ruining my good name."

"I don't want your job," Ara snapped.

"Easy now," Teth said quickly. "That was Lucket's idea of being friendly. It takes getting used to."

"You don't say," Ara muttered.

"Why are you bringing me a troublesome shrew, boy?" Lucket stabbed a finger a Teth. "Is this your idea of a joke?"

Brow furrowing, Lucket eyed Ara once more. He began to chuckle. "Oh, I see. You walking out with her? No surprise there; you like your girls plucky."

Ara's cheeks flared with heat. "I am not *his girl*."

"Of course you aren't." Lucket chuckled.

"She's not," Teth said, tugging at his collar in discomfort.

"I am no one's *girl*." Ara took a step toward Lucket, eyes defiant and chin lifted. When Teth tried to pull her back, she shook him off.

Lucket raised an eyebrow, but his gaze became admiring. "I can see that now."

Ara rolled her shoulders back, feeling much better.

Teth had been watching Ara with disbelief. He coughed nervously.

"Lucket, I need to you stop talking and start listening."

"Well, then tell me what I need to know." Lucket stretched, then slouched, hanging one arm over the back of his chair.

"This is Ara of Rill's Pass," said Teth. "She's a friend."

"Rill's Pass, eh?" Lucket threw Ara a brief smile. "Dying village at the edge of the world. Pretty place. Obscenely cold."

"You've been to Rill's Pass?" Ara asked, startled.

"I'm from everywhere and I've been everywhere, my dear." One side of Lucket's mouth twitched up. "Though I only visited Rill's Pass once. Never could get comfortable in the mountains. It's a place apart from society up there. And I deal in society." He frowned briefly. "I didn't think any children of the mountain villages avoided the Embrace. How did you manage that?"

"I can become invisible," Ara replied matter-of-factly. She was tired of being the mouse to Lucket's cat.

He stared at her, and color leached from Teth's cheeks.

Lucket slowly leaned forward. His lips parted, and a roar of laughter burst from his chest.

"Senn's teeth," Teth swore. He jabbed a finger at Ara. "Don't do that to me."

Ara smiled, rather pleased to know Teth had been so worried for her.

"I might like her," Lucket said to Teth.

Jumping on her advantage, Ara asked, "Why would you call Rill's Pass a dying village? People still live there."

Lucket replied, "All the villages are dying, little one. Haven't you been paying attention?"

Ara bit her lip, wanting to object to his calling her "little one," but also smarting from the answer to his question. She'd been hidden away. Old Imgar and Elke had kept her safe while the rest of the world fell apart.

I have to make that worth something. Ara closed her hands, making them tight fists. *All that pain. All that loss. I'm the one who can put Nimhea on the River Throne so Saetlund can live again.*

Ara swore to herself, in that moment, to give all of her being to prove her worth to the gods.

Lucket noticed; curiosity sharpened his gaze, but he said nothing. He abandoned his chair and came down the stairs. When he crossed the room to a table bearing wine and plates of fruit, Teth and Ara followed.

"I brought Ara here make introductions," Teth told him. "Because I believe we have mutual interests."

"Eh?" Lucket poured himself a glass of wine from an ornate gold pitcher. "Can I offer you refreshment while we talk?"

Ara and Teth both declined.

"Just remember I'm not a poor host," Lucket said. "Go on."

"Ara is escorting the pair of visitors you're interested in," Teth said as they walked with Lucket to a cluster of chairs.

"I know." Lucket sank onto an overstuffed divan and looked at Ara.

Ara looked at him sharply, realizing that he'd known all along. All that prodding when she first appeared had only been a way for Lucket to get the measure of her.

A growl of frustration rumbled from Teth's throat. "You. Knew."

"I always know," Lucket quipped. "If I didn't, someone else would take my throne. I'm a little hurt that you thought you'd brought me a surprise."

While Teth stewed, Lucket returned his attention to Ara.

"Back to our royal friends then. Tell me how you came into such a position; you're too small for muscle."

Ara's mind flooded with questions for Lucket, the most pressing being how he knew about Nimhea and Eamon. But Lucket had made a mistake; he knew she'd arrived with the twins, but Ara believed that was the extent of his information. His little show had been about some personal contest between him and Teth. For the moment Ara decided to keep it that way. Rather than say anything, Ara sat tight-lipped with her hands folded in her lap.

Lucket waited, then shrugged. His attention turned to Teth. But Teth shook his head.

"Truly?" Lucket frowned, but quickly recovered his smile. "A mystery, then. Fortunate for you, Ara of Rill's Pass, that I'm very fond of mysteries. You'll have time before I lose my patience."

Ara noted that he didn't indicate how much time.

"Are you losing your edge, Teth?" Lucket swirled his wine in his glass.

Teth laughed nervously. "I hope not."

He glanced at Ara, and she knew his mind was tracking backward to the night she'd discovered his hiding place. She also knew he didn't want Lucket to know about that. She gave Teth a quick nod that she hoped was reassuring.

"Perhaps as you get to know your *friend* better," Lucket snickered, "this clouded mirror will clear."

The look Teth gave Lucket had a warning in it, but Lucket smiled serenely. Neither of them spoke, and Lucket eased back upon the divan, savoring his wine. At the break in conversation, Ara let her eyes wander around the room. It was much brighter and more pleasant than she'd expect a buried room to be. There was constant movement from light to shadow to light going on around them. Men and women passed through and by the room often, and she hadn't seen the same person twice. There were more people here than she'd seen in all of Silverstag.

"You're not familiar with the Below." Lucket caught Ara with his steady gaze.

She shook her head.

Smiling, Lucket swept his arm, indicating the expanse of the room and beyond. "The Below is the place where things happen that need to happen, but are often best unseen."

"Like thievery?" Ara said archly. She didn't look at Teth, but she could feel his eyes on her.

With a low chuckle, Lucket nodded. "Thievery is only one branch of the many trades that compose the Below. We're the watchers of society."

"You mean spying," said Ara.

"If you prefer," Lucket said. "As well as smuggling, forgery, extortion, blackmail, slander, and, of course, assassination. I could give further examples, but you appear to understand."

Ara hadn't expected the last and was chilled by Lucket's casual admission. More unsettling was how obviously Lucket felt no worry about Ara's knowing about his criminal pursuits. She began to see that Lucket had wide-reaching power.

"In many ways the Below is a province unto itself, an underground river that flows through each of the provinces and shapes them in myriad unseen ways," Lucket continued. "Our operations affect everything that occurs above ground, but rarely are the good people of Saetlund aware of all that we do."

A man emerged from one of the adjoining corridors and came swiftly to Lucket, leaning down to whisper something in Lucket's ear.

Lucket gave a brief nod, and the man disappeared back into the corridor. After finishing his glass of wine, Lucket rose.

"That will be all for now," Lucket said.

"Before you go." Teth stood up. "I took care of Braegan."

"And that's a mystery solved." Lucket smiled at Teth. "It explains the arrows, but not the hacked limbs."

Scratching his beard, Lucket fixed a challenging gaze upon Ara. "Courtesy of you?"

When Ara didn't respond, he looked pointedly at Ironbranch. "That's a big stick you have, but I don't see a blade."

"It is not a stick!"

"Our princess is blooded, then." Lucket laughed softly. "I'll take that as a good sign."

Lucket turned to leave, but Teth said, "One more thing: two soldiers took liberties with Helti tonight. Their names are Malvo and Tretter."

"They will be seen to." Lucket gave a curt nod.

Teth added, "And I have a bonus coming for finding the twins."

Not bothering to turn around, Lucket said, "You'll get it."

Without another word, he walked away.

That's it? Ara had been shown a single page of a book and now she wanted to know the full story and why Teth had wanted to offer her that glimpse.

Teth obviously thought the meeting was important, but Lucket hadn't offered them aid or information. She knew more about Saetlund's seedier side, but she didn't see how that mattered. Maybe Teth had been trying to impress her . . . That was flattering and annoying.

Ara was frustrated that Teth would take her on a pointless side trip when she could be using the time to prepare for the next stage of her journey.

But what kind of help can he offer when he doesn't know who I am? The thought chastened her. *He has no idea what the stakes of our quest are. I only told him that I was guiding Nimhea and Eamon to Silverstag. What if he thinks I'm returning to Rill's Pass in the morning?*

Ara smiled at the notion of Teth wanting to recruit her for his line of work, but holding back the truth from him began to bother her. Keeping her secret had been a safeguard, but now it felt like a hindrance.

"We should go," Teth said.

He surprised Ara by taking her hand. His fingers wrapped around hers, firm and reassuring, but when he led her toward a different corridor from the one by which they'd entered Lucket's receiving room, she hesitated.

Turning to look at her, Teth said, "You never leave the Below the same way you came in."

He let go of her hand and waited for her to fall in beside him. As they walked into the unfamiliar, yet identical, arched passageway, Ara knew Teth had released her because he didn't want to pull her somewhere she didn't want to go. And that it was kind.

Her hand still felt empty.

9

he corridor led to a trapdoor. It opened into a bedroom of a house that appeared to be occupied only by furniture. They left by the front door of the house, returning to Silverstag's dark and quiet streets.

Teth set a much slower pace than when they'd left the inn. Ara sorted through the questions this strange meeting provoked, trying to decide what would be best to ask first. But Teth began offering his own questions before she had the chance.

"Why are you traveling with those two?" Teth kept his voice low, and he didn't look at Ara when he posed the question. "You're putting yourself at risk, and you don't seem well suited to their company."

"Preordained obligation," Ara said, with a twinge of regret. He'd earned her trust, and she still hadn't given him the truth. "A bit like yours when guiding us."

"That's the worst kind," Teth grunted, but a smile had sneaked onto one corner of his mouth, like he was laughing at himself. Or both of them.

"I suppose it is," Ara said with a sigh.

Not wanting to be too hard on Nimhea and Eamon, she added, "It's not so bad. They've learned a lot about being on the road in a short time."

"Your first night must have been a disaster." He risked a breath of laughter.

Ara swallowed her own laugh, but she couldn't stop a broad smile.

"It really was."

"So—" Teth began.

Ara cut him off, not only wanting to question him, but sensing that Teth's inquiries were less about curiosity and more like a hunt for answers. Albeit, a polite one.

"Why did that woman call Lucket 'your majesty'?"

"He's the Low King of Fjeri," Teth answered simply, as if that was explanation enough.

Irritated by his unhelpful reply, Ara snapped, "Tell me what a Low King is."

Teth shot her a sidelong glance, taken aback by her short temper. "The Low Kings rule the Below. Remember how Lucket called the Below 'a province unto itself'?"

Ara nodded.

"It's more like the Below constitutes the shadow side of each province," Teth told her. "Just as the provinces of Saetlund have chancellors, there are five Low Kings that rule the Below. The Low Kings negotiate trade routes, percentages, regulations and limitations affecting their operatives, and issues of discipline and punishment. You witnessed the last in Braegan."

"The way Braegan died was horrible," said Ara, flinching at the memory.

"Braegan was a horrible person," Teth said in a cold voice. "He killed innocents without restraint or regret. Killing isn't often part of my job, but when it needs doing I don't wring my hands over it."

Quiet followed, then Teth asked, "Do you think I should?"

"Wring your hands?" Ara considered that. "If it has to be done, then no . . . but I hope it isn't an easy thing for you to do."

She held her breath, worried she'd gone too far, but needing to hear his answer.

His voice was very soft. "Killing is never easy."

They were walking even more slowly and closer to each other. Occasionally, Teth's arm would brush Ara's and give her a start that she never grew accustomed to.

Unable to bear the silence, Ara asked, "Why does it matter that Lucket knows about me?"

"I wanted you to know that you have friends," he said.

With a nervous laugh, Ara said, "The Low King of Fjeri is my friend."

"If he wasn't," Teth told her, "you would never have walked out of there."

She knew he wasn't jesting.

His voice lowered. "The Below may have things to offer you that the Resistance can't."

"Of course you know," Ara murmured, more to herself than to him. He thought she'd come to Silverstag to join the rebels. In a way, she had.

"I know more than most," Teth replied. "The most important commodity in the Below is information."

He's trying to recruit me.

Ara smiled slightly. *My grandmother outdid herself, keeping such a secret from the Low Kings.*

Teth hesitated, then said, "I have something to confess. I also brought you to Lucket because I hoped he might know who you are. I still haven't figured it out."

"You know who I am," Ara answered reflexively.

"Where you're from is a sliver of who you are," Teth countered.

They continued to stroll along, but the air between them had tightened.

"My second name is Silverthread," she offered.

"Your mother was a weaver." His tone was thoughtful. "I'm glad to know your second name, but it still reveals little about who you are."

As he'd been talking, Ara's heart had climbed into her throat. *I told Lucket where I'm from.*

Lucket knew about the Resistance, and now the rebels knew about her Loresmith heritage. He'd find out soon enough that the twins had gone out of their way to find Ara in Rill's Pass. It was only a matter of time—days if she was lucky, hours more likely—before Lucket tugged on those threads to unravel her past. He'd discover who she was. She didn't know if Teth had access to all the information acquired through the Low Kings' espionage or if weighty secrets were kept from him. Given his apparent comfort trading barbs with Lucket, Ara suspected that Teth was privy to more intelligence than other employees of the Below.

Testing this notion, Ara said, "You don't call Lucket 'your majesty.'"

"I'm sorry?" Teth was spun by the abrupt shift in topic.

"Lucket," Ara continued. "He's a Low King, but you don't talk to him as if he's royalty."

"Lucket and I have an unusual relationship," he explained in a wry tone.

That was enough to convince Ara that if Lucket knew she was the Loresmith then Teth would know soon after. As much as she'd tried to keep the purpose of her journey a secret, she didn't want Teth to hear it from someone else. The thought of Teth discovering the truth through his ties to the Below made her stomach wobble.

Ara searched the street and buildings they passed. When she saw what she wanted, she grabbed Teth's arm and dragged him into a narrow gap between two buildings. The space had only been created for drainage, and the tight quarters left them standing less than a foot apart.

"What's wrong?" Teth asked, peering at the vacated street. "What did you see?"

"Nothing," Ara replied. "I need . . ."

The words stuck in her throat. What if this was the worst possible decision she could make?

He brought me to his hidden world. He wants me to be part of it. He honors Eni.

A new, more practical idea sprang into her mind.

Maybe the Below can help us, if not in the way Teth intended.

Teth rested his hand lightly on her shoulder. "What is it?"

Genuine concern infused his voice, and the vise around Ara's chest loosened.

"I need to tell you who I am."

She felt him tense, and he drew his hand away, but stayed quiet.

Little light could reach between the buildings, and despite their closeness Ara could barely make out Teth's face.

"Nimhea and Eamon came to Rill's Pass to find me. Eamon believes that I'm the only way to win a war against the empire."

The shadows made it easier to confess.

She stopped to take a breath. Teth remained quiet and still.

"My father was the last Loresmith," she said. Speaking those words, she felt like a stone thrown into the center of a pond with ripples of power emanating from her bones. Admitting to Teth who she was felt like embracing both her past and her future. "His name was Yos Steelring, and he served King Dentroth. He died in the conquest, but made sure I'd been sent away before the Vokkans reached Five Rivers."

Teth had yet to speak, and though Ara paused, he offered neither comment nor question.

"I travel with Nimhea and Eamon because I become the next Loresmith only when I prove to the gods I'm worthy. It's only been a handful of days since all of this began, and all I know is that our next step is to go to Daefrit . . . to find Ofrit."

That was the worst of it, the line that Teth would either cross to believe her or stay behind to dismiss her wild tale.

"Ara . . ."

He didn't say anything more, but his fingers curled around hers. Just as quickly they dropped away.

"Do the rebels know?" His voice was taut.

Relief spilled through Ara.

He believes me. He believes.

That moment of respite was immediately replaced by the desperate need to interpret every nuance of his tone and inflection in his words.

"Eamon told them," she answered.

She heard him exhale sharply, but he failed to explain what that sound meant.

A new question bloomed in Ara. "You didn't suspect, did you?"

A broad swath of possibilities rested between Teth's superstitions about the gods and believing that lore could be true.

"I knew you must be . . ." Teth shook his head. "No. Not this. I would never have guessed this."

"But you accept it," Ara said tentatively.

"I don't have a good reason not to," Teth told her. "There were signs, but even if I'd been paying close attention I still wouldn't have come up with what you just told me."

"What signs?" Ara had gathered signs of her own: flying through the woods after Fox, Teth's belief in Eni's curse, her dreams. None of these could have figured into the minds of her companions. She quickly reviewed their journey to Silverstag, but came up with nothing else that hinted of the gods.

Teth leaned in to the wall at his back; a little tension bled out of his limbs.

"Fox leading you to my hideout," Teth said. "The ruin shaking. And then that woman showed up at our camp."

"What does the old woman have to do with signs?"

A self-mocking laugh drifted in the space between them. "Oh, it was more than a sign."

"I don't understand." Ara frowned.

"Nava's mercy save me." Teth sucked in a deep breath. "I don't think that was an old woman . . . I think it was Eni."

His voice was nervous, even vulnerable.

Ara was distracted by the fact that her heart had skipped several beats. "Eni . . . you mean . . . you think a god visited our camp."

"Yes." He spoke stiffly, as if not wanting to acknowledge his own suspicions. "I've heard tales."

"But you saw her," Ara protested. She knew the old stories about Eni following, or even joining travelers, but Teth spoke as though he'd heard *recent* stories. "The old woman. She ate with us. She made us tea."

"She said she was on her way home and got lost," Teth replied. "I know those woods as well as anyone, and I've never come across an isolated cottage, home to an elderly couple. There never was a cottage. The old woman was a disguise."

Ara didn't say, *But they're only stories*, only because she stopped the words from slipping out. She was in Silverstag because stories were not just stories any longer. And if she was to become the Loresmith she had to accept that lore and myth were now her life. That meant the gods would be in her life, too. Ara had been growing accustomed to that idea, to fantastical things like her dream about Wuldr hunting with Senn. But a dream was altogether different from a deity being physically present at one's supper.

"Eni can appear however Eni wants to." Teth presumed she didn't follow his last comment. "The form of the visitor is always different."

Ara's eyes had adjusted to the dim light; she could make out Teth's face now, and the familiarity of its curves and angles reassured her. He believed her. She didn't want shadows to hide them from each other. This honesty, this pouring out of secrets, soothed her spirit. She'd held her truths so close that her soul ached from the effort. But she didn't have to struggle any more. Ara had a new ally and a friend she could trust.

"Why?" Ara asked, awed and troubled by the possibility she'd been in the company of a god and had no clue.

With a sidelong glance, Teth said, "I have a couple of suspicions about that. One: you've been awfully fond of invoking Eni's oath the past several days."

"You think I drew Eni to our camp."

"You could have." Teth shrugged. "Eni is known to be curious. With you speaking Eni's name over and over, Eni might have wanted to see what that was all about."

Ara tried to get comfortable with that idea. She couldn't.

"If you didn't like that," Teth said, "you definitely won't like the second reason Eni might have come."

"Tell me." Ara sighed.

"It might have been a test." His cloak rustled against the wall when he shifted his weight. "You say you have to prove your worth to the gods?"

"Yes." Thinking about it made her weary.

Teth made a soft noise indicating he was lost in his own thoughts.

Ara reached Teth's conclusion before he did. "Ironbranch. The test was Ironbranch."

"What's an Ironbranch?" A few moments later he asked, "There's something special about your staff, isn't there? I've seen Eni's sign, but it's more than that."

"It is." The question surprised Ara. "I can show you."

To free her stave from its harness, Ara had to step forward, putting her so close to Teth she had to tilt her chin up to look at him. Any breath or small movement meant a rustle at the friction of their cloaks tangling or the slight touch of his arm against hers. Her skin grew warm, despite the cold night, and she was glad Teth couldn't see her face.

When the stave was untethered, Ara stepped back. "Hold out your hands."

Ara carefully laid the stave upon Teth's palms. When he closed fingers around it, Ara felt a strange pang of loss or envy.

"What do you notice about it?" she asked him.

Teth turned the stave in his hands and ran his fingers along the grain of the wood. He even lifted the stave to his face and sniffed it, something Ara would never have thought to do.

"It isn't like any wood I've ever encountered," he admitted. "And while its scent is very pleasant, I can't seem to place it. Or even compare it to another fragrance."

Ara nodded, then moved closer. Her fingers were shaking slightly when she covered his hand with her own. Gently guiding his touch, she moved their hands to one end of the stave so he could find the carved mark.

"Eni's sign." There was a hoarseness to Teth's voice, and he cleared his throat.

Removing her hand, Ara said, "Find the sign at the opposite end."

She watched his fingers move and could almost feel the shape of the sign beneath her fingertips as Teth traced it.

"Ofrit."

He offered the stave and Ara took it, relieved to have it back in her hands.

"This is the Loresmith's stave, Ironbranch," Ara said softly. "It was crafted by Ofrit and Eni for the first Loresmith, and it has passed to each new generation." Her throat tightened. "My father left it for me."

"You offered the Loresmith's stave to an old woman in need," Teth whispered. "Something priceless given out of compassion. An act both selfless and reckless."

Wincing, Ara said, "I didn't mean to be reckless. It happened so quickly."

"It was meant to," Teth told her. "The test wasn't about the power of the stave, but the measure of your character. Eni looked into your soul, and you passed."

You must prove yourself worthy to the gods. Ara shivered.

She brushed up against Teth a second time when she returned the stave to its harness. Before she could return to her place against the opposite wall, Teth's hands encircled her upper arms. He held her lightly, his grip tentative.

"I can't imagine—" His already tense voice choked off.

Ara wanted to lean in to him, to hear what he would say next. She listened to his breath, worried when it became jagged. Then, to her shock, she realized he was laughing. When he began to laugh aloud, Teth let go of her arms. And she moved away from him, irked that her struggle had become his entertainment.

"You've got me, Ara," Teth said between laughs. "I've never come across a situation where I don't know how to maneuver. With you, I have no idea."

"You don't have to maneuver around me." Ara's reply tasted bitter. *He makes me sound like a job, or worse, a trap.*

Teth stopped laughing. "Don't be angry. I mean that as a compliment."

"It's a strange compliment," Ara said tartly. She wasn't ready to forgive him, but a nudge in her mind hinted that her irritation had nothing to do with what he'd just said.

"Do not be angry, sacred Loresmith." Teth laced his fingers together, pleading and prayerful.

He looked so foolish Ara couldn't help but laugh. "You're forgiven."

"Thank Nava." He beamed at her.

"You said that I have friends in the Below." His antics may have been ridiculous, but his words sparked an idea. "Does the Loresmith?"

"I'm not sure I follow," Teth said cautiously.

"Nimhea, Eamon, and I have a long journey ahead," Ara told him. "I suspect we'll have more than bandits to contend with. Do the Low Kings have an interest in our survival? If so, what can they do to increase the odds of our success?"

Teth gave a low whistle. "You only learned of the Below tonight and you're already trying to leverage it. I think that's impressive . . . or else you're mad."

"So what are you going to do?" she asked drily.

"I'm going to think about what you've said. Probably talk to Lucket." Teth gestured to the street. "After you're back at the inn."

"Go talk to Lucket," Ara told him. "I can make it back to the inn on my own."

"I know you can," Teth said softly. He offered his hand.

Ara hadn't known her heart could tremble.

Though it took another quarter hour to reach the inn, no conversation passed between them. Ara's entire body seemed to exist only in her fingers that were twined with Teth's. He stopped in the shadow of the building across the street from the Antler and Tusk and released her hand.

"Try to get at least a few hours' sleep." His voice was matter-of-fact, even a bit brusque. "Tomorrow will be an interesting day."

Ara stared at the inn, her insides quivering with a question she was afraid to ask, but had to.

"Is this goodbye?" Her chest was burning, like she'd eaten too many smoldering plum cakes.

After a long pause, Teth said, "I hope not."

Instead of leaving, Teth stood quietly, watching her with eyes that seemed puzzled, intrigued, and slightly unnerved. The moment stretched on, and Ara became tense in a way that made her fingers tremble . . . but was inexplicably pleasant.

Then he simply nodded at her, and with silent steps he faded into the night.

Despite Teth's urging, Ara returned to her bedroll certain she was too full of unformed questions and fledgling notions to sleep soundly. The last she remembered, her mind had been tumbling with distractions, but she'd somehow fallen asleep. Low voices speaking unintelligible words reached her ears as she woke, along with a scent that made her mouth water.

Sitting up, Ara rubbed the drowsiness from her eyes. Her nose led the search for breakfast. It was waiting for her on a tray: cooked eggs, bacon, buttered toast, and fresh berries.

"Oh good, you're up," Eamon said cheerily. "I didn't want to wake you, but I was afraid your food would get cold."

Ara was too ravenous to reply. She flashed a smile at Eamon then cut into her eggs, feeling blissful as she dunked a corner of toast into golden yoke.

"I think this is the first time we've been awake before you," Eamon added.

He and Nimhea were sitting on the floor beside their beds with empty trays that matched Ara's next to them.

Ara nodded and continued to eat. The bacon was perfectly crisped, and the berries burst with sweetness.

"Have you seen any of our friends this morning?" Ara asked before picking up another piece of bacon.

Nimhea shook her head. "The innkeeper brought our meal. I expect the others will come for us shortly."

"Then I'd better hurry." Ara happily returned her full attention to breakfast.

She was chewing on the last bit of toast when the wall panel slid open and Xeris stepped into the room.

"If you'll join us downstairs."

They returned to the same storeroom. The table was gone and chairs had been brought; they formed a ring and everyone had a place to sit.

Before Ara could pick a seat, Nimhea whispered quickly, "I want you and Eamon to sit on either side of me."

Ara waited while Nimhea chose her place. Eamon sat to his sister's right, so Ara took the chair on the left.

As the others found their seats, Ara tried to read the room. Edram smiled slightly when Ara caught his eyes. Xeris wore a neutral expression.

When Ara looked at Ioth, he arched a brow at her, likely wondering what she'd gotten up to the night before. He'd still been on watch when Ara had returned to the back door of the inn, but he hadn't said a word. Now she cursed the blush creeping onto her cheeks. Quickly looking away from Ioth, Ara's gaze settled on Suli, who had taken the chair opposite Nimhea. Suli's face was serene, but her eyes hard. Ara sneaked a worried glance at Nimhea only to discover the princess returned Suli's gaze with a look of steel. Ara braced herself for what was to come.

It began with pleasantries.

"Did you pass the night well?" Suli asked.

"Very well, thank you," Nimhea answered.

With a bland smile Suli began, "About this journey to Daefrit . . ."

The morning devolved rapidly from that point on. After a repetition of the previous day's arguments, Suli and Nimhea's rancor toward each other escalated as each dug in to defend her decision. Suli remained firm, insisting that Nimhea remain in the care of the rebellion and that should the princess fail to do so she put the fate of Saetlund at risk.

Enflamed by Suli's suggestion that her choice was selfish, Nimhea drew upon the legends of Saetlund and the powers of its gods. Given that Eamon was the fount of knowledge when it came to the kingdom's lore, Ara was deeply impressed by Nimhea's ability to cite story after story of the Loreknights and their pivotal place in protecting Saetlund from its enemies.

Anticipating this conflict, Ara had expected that she and Eamon would flank Nimhea, offering her support and their own arguments. Nimhea had another strategy in mind. It soon became clear that this would be a duel. Either Nimhea or Suli would conquer the day. The rest of them were spectators.

Ara at times turned her attention from the combatants to the other rebels. Watching their reactions offered insights into the mood of their group. Ara noted with interest that when Nimhea spoke, Edram leaned forward, his eyes alight with interest. Ioth couldn't stop fidgeting and looked like he'd rather be anywhere than in this room, while Xeris watched with a cool detachment. To Ara's surprise, none of the rebels' expressions reflected a burning allegiance to their leader. While Edram, Ioth, and Xeris were deferring to Suli's authority, beneath the surface the rebels did not present a united front. Ara tucked that observation away, knowing it could work in their favor.

What began as a skirmish became a siege. Suli was the wall at which Nimhea hurled boulders tirelessly. Ara's early impression of Nimhea was her penchant for petulance, borne out of always getting what she wanted. In this venue, however, the princess revealed a talent for persuasion. She argued with the agility of an acrobat, and her voice rose and fell as she wielded words as weapons. Nimhea achieved such octaves at the peaks of their parley that Ara thought the princess might be an exceptional singer.

Despite Nimhea's efforts, Suli blocked every argument. Both women were standing now, and choreographed gesticulations accompanied their words.

"I hate arguments first thing in the morning." A new voice cut through the room, shocking Nimhea and Suli into silence. "That makes me delighted to break this one up."

Edram, Ioth, and Xeris were instantly on their feet, weapons drawn.

The silhouette in the doorway stepped into the light.

"Teth." A little flutter of joy moved through Ara at his appearance.

Teth caught sight of her and one corner of his mouth twitched into a smile.

She could offer only a bemused smile in return. Ara was happy to see him, but he'd put himself in mortal peril by entering the room.

To that point Xeris had slid out of the ring and was slowly making her way toward Teth. She moved like water, lithe and silent.

Teth glanced at the Vijeri warrior, but had no apparent reaction to being stalked. Ara watched him and grew more confused. Teth was no fool, but coming here unannounced was terribly reckless. She looked to Nimhea and Eamon for help, but the twins had been similarly stunned by his arrival.

Showing no fear, Teth strolled up to the ring of chairs.

"How did you get in here?" Suli demanded. She shot a hard, questioning look at Ioth.

Ioth shrugged his shoulders. "There are guards."

"There still are," Teth supplied cheerily, as if he were being incredibly helpful.

Ara found herself admiring and cursing his gall.

"It's not their fault," Teth continued drolly. "I'm very good at getting into places I want to be. And if I can avoid a fight, I will."

He turned suddenly and pointed his finger at Xeris, who was closing on him. "I'm not here to fight."

Xeris froze and looked at Suli. Suli motioned for Xeris to stand down. Xeris stepped back, but kept a calculating gaze on Teth.

Sword in hand, Edram moved to stand beside Suli. Quietly, Ioth took up a position on Suli's other side. Both warriors kept defensive stances, but the taut mood of the room had eased slightly.

"Who are you?" Suli asked Teth.

"He's a friend," Ara said firmly. She wanted the weapons put away.

"It's true," Eamon added. "He guided us through the forest to Silverstag."

Nimhea nodded when Suli looked at her for confirmation.

"My name is Teth," said Teth. "I'm here today as an emissary, seeking an audience with the rarely seen rebellion Command."

Suli frowned. "You have us at a disadvantage. Few know who we are."

"I only know who you are because of who I represent," Teth told her. "I bring a message from Lucket, Low King of Fjeri."

Talk to Lucket.

Ara sucked in a quick breath, suddenly wondering if she was responsible for Teth's surprise visit.

Edram lowered his sword. "What business does a Low King have with us?"

"Quite a lot of business." Teth smiled at him. "If you prove amenable."

Nimhea looked from Edram to Teth. "What in Nava's Ire is a Low King?" Clearly unsteady after being abruptly pulled out of her fight with Suli, Nimhea tried to reorient herself.

"A leader of Saetlund's underworld," Edram replied. "Thieves, charlatans, smugglers, assassins—the dregs of society."

He turned his eyes on Teth, waiting for an objection.

"It's accurate," Teth said simply.

"There's a Low King in every province," Ara told Nimhea. "From what I've learned, they seem to be quite powerful."

Nimhea's eyes narrowed. "You *knew* about this?"

Biting her lip, Ara silently cursed her misstep. She needed to hold her tongue. Who knew what Nimhea would do if she figured out Ara had put this idea into Teth's mind. Fortunately Suli drew Nimhea's attention again.

"Your friend is right," Suli said. "The Low Kings are very powerful."

Teth cleared his throat. "And they would like to use that power in service to the rebellion."

He is here because of me. Ara was pleased that Teth had taken her seriously, but he'd grabbed the horses and was running away with the carriage.

With a rough laugh, Ioth returned his sickle to his belt. "I find that hard to believe."

"If I were you, I'd feel the same," Teth replied.

Suli tilted her head, regarding Teth with more curiosity than suspicion. "You have my attention. Why don't we be civil and sit."

With the addition of Teth they were one chair short, but Xeris insisted she preferred to stand. Ara watched her, worried Xeris would be too eager to pounce on Teth if this meeting went awry.

Nimhea tried, but failed, to hide her alarm at the sudden change. "Pardon me, Suli. Teth was a fine guide, but what could we possibly want from an . . . organization of lowlifes and murderers?"

Teth scoffed at her. "The Below doesn't harbor murderers."

"Edram said assassins," Nimhea told him pointedly.

"Assassins aren't murderers," Teth replied. "They're professional killers."

"That's hardly a difference." Nimhea folded her arms across her chest, glaring at him.

Teth smiled blandly. "It is to the assassins."

Ara covered her mouth to stifle a giggle.

"Technicalities aside"—Suli broke into their spat, speaking to Nimhea—"the Low Kings have the best intelligence network in Saetlund, far better than any government could claim. More importantly, they've proven impervious to all Vokkan attempts to root them out."

"How good can they be?" Nimhea sniffed.

Teth winked at her, then said to Suli, "We know about your inside man."

Suli stiffened and Xeris gasped, unable to hide the horror on her face. Unconsciously, Ioth's hand had gone to the hilt of his sickle.

"That's impressive." Edram remained the picture of calm.

Nimhea was looking at the rebels in alarm. "What's wrong? Who is this inside man?"

"We told you about our commander." Suli recovered her composure. "That his identity is secret—"

Teth leaned toward Nimhea and whispered loudly, "We know that, too."

Suli's flat stare showed she was not entertained.

With a polite cough, Teth said, "Please go on."

"The Hawk's identity will remain secret until we're ready to attack," Suli said. "The same goes for his counterpart. Someone high in the ranks of the Vokkan Empire. He's referred to as the Dove."

"There's a traitor in the empire?" Nimhea's eyes widened. "Someone with power? That's wonderful."

Suli gave Nimhea a direct look. "It's wonderful only so long as our asset's identity remains protected."

"The Hawk and the Dove," Ara murmured to herself. Names that sounded like legends. Maybe someday they would be.

"Only we four have had knowledge of the Dove." Edram cast a calculating glance at Teth. "Or so we thought. We never speak of the Dove outside of this group."

He looked at each of them in turn. "It needs to stay that way."

"We understand," Nimhea answered, while Ara and Eamon nodded.

"The Low Kings are exceptional at keeping secrets," Teth said with a flourish.

Suli's jaw had a grim set. "Give us a moment."

The four leaders withdrew to a corner of the room. Nimhea let out a huff, displeased at being left out of this discussion and being shown, yet again, that though her title was respected, she was not in charge.

Eamon sidled up to Teth with a sidelong glance full of bewilderment. Teth chuckled.

"You don't have be nervous, Eamon," he said. "I'm still the same person."

With a blush, Eamon replied, "This Below. Is it like a guild?"

"Much more complex than a guild," Teth told him, scratching his neck absentmindedly. "But its members do swear fealty. Breaking that oath means exile, or more likely death."

"Doesn't it scare you at all?" Eamon asked. "To always be surrounded by . . . those kind of people?"

"It's all I've ever known," Teth replied. "And 'those kind of people' are just people who for one reason or another couldn't find a place in your world but did find a home in the Below."

Chastened, Eamon cast his eyes to the ground, but the crease between his eyebrows spoke of his unease about Teth's revelation.

Still quietly seething, Nimhea found a target in Teth. "This proposal of yours is ludicrous."

"It's really not," Teth countered.

"The rebellion needs warriors," Nimhea snapped. "Honorable women and men. No upright ruler would ever consort with cutthroats."

"Do you think any real war has been won without assistance from the Low Kings?" Teth asked with a quiet laugh. "If nothing else, they'll be paid to stay neutral, which, as it happens, was exactly what the Vokkans did."

"Treason!" Nimhea gasped. "They should be hanged. All of them."

With a chuckle, Teth said, "While I can appreciate your fervor, princess, what the Low Kings did was survive. Saetlund would have lost a war to a force half—no, an eighth—the size of Fauld's invading army. Dentroth's army was nothing more than an ornament. When the Vokkans arrived Saetlund wasn't conquered, it collapsed under the weight of its own helplessness. Without the aid of the Low Kings, Saetlund's economy would have been ruined. They may have turned their back on the king, but they saved the people."

"Ridiculous." Nimhea shook her head. "Commerce and trade should have been ruined; the empire would have reaped no rewards from the conquest."

"The people would starve," Teth shot back. "Is that the kind of ruler you plan to be?"

Nimhea balked; a crease matching her brother's formed between her eyebrows. The frustration on her face showed how desperate she was to form a suitable response, but couldn't.

The rebels broke from their small conference and returned to the ring of chairs. Edram, Xeris, and Ioth sat, but Suli did not.

"I expected the Low Kings would stay neutral when the war comes," said Suli. "It's their safest course, and they've dismissed all attempts we've made to treat with them."

Nimhea sucked in a sharp breath, incredulous. "You've *already* tried to form this alliance?"

Suli and Teth ignored her.

"We've been keeping tabs on the growth of unrest toward the empire," Teth told Suli. "A rebellion may no longer be a doomed enterprise."

"How kind of you to say," Ioth muttered.

Teth doffed an imaginary hat at him, then continued. "But it's the return of the princess that truly changes things."

He leaned against a barrel and examined his fingernails. "That's why I've come bearing a proposal from Lucket today, made on behalf of the five Low Kings."

Suli's eyebrows lifted. "Why would the Below turn its back on the empire so early? History tells us they'd prefer to wait until the odds of a conflict become clear."

"Despite promises to the contrary, the Vokkans haven't turned a blind eye to the activities of the Below." Teth pushed away from the barrel. "In addition to their stranglehold on commerce and closure of too many trade routes, they've made thievery a hanging offense. Now they're insisting on placing an administrative agent in each major outpost."

Edram chuckled. "Imperial oversight of the Below? That's novel."

"I'm sure you can imagine how popular the idea is among the Low Kings." Teth smiled at him.

Suli threaded her fingers at her back and began to pace slowly. "Very well. What are Lucket's terms?"

"The Below will provide what intelligence we have on the Vokkans, regarding their knowledge of your rebellion and their readiness for war," Teth said. "We'll also inform you immediately if we learn there are moles among your ranks."

"Moles?" Eamon asked.

Ioth answered from where he sat. "Spies for the empire, planted within the rebellion. It's a reality no one likes to think about, but that we must inevitably prepare for."

"And in return?" Suli stopped pacing.

Teth drew himself up, meeting Suli's piercing gaze. "You'll release the Loresmith to pursue her quest, and you'll allow the princess and her brother to accompany Ara on the journey."

Ara started at his words. That the Low Kings had an interest in her future both pleased and unnerved her. Was Teth the driving force behind this proposal, or did Lucket actually believe in the Loresmith?

Suli stared at Teth, mulling over the request.

Xeris, who'd been sitting crosslegged in her chair, frowned at Teth. "I didn't take the Low Kings to be religious. What do they want with the Loresmith?"

"I can't answer that," Teth confessed. "All I can convey is that they are deeply curious about Ara's pursuit of her bloodright."

How many strings are attached to this deal? If the Low Kings thought the Loresmith could be compelled to serve them, they were going to be very disappointed.

Edram and Xeris exchanged glances of dissatisfaction at Teth's answer, but offered no further objection.

Suli shook her head slowly. "We can't knowingly risk the princess."

"From what I've gathered," Teth said carefully, "the only way you'll keep the princess in your company is to drag her from this establishment in chains."

Suli's jaw tightened, but she did not deign to ask how Teth had come by such information.

Teth took her silence as an opportunity to make his case.

"If you ally with the Low Kings you'll have access to supply caches and safehouses, and we'll take care of provisions. Not only will you preserve resources, but you'll also save yourselves the risk of resupplying the travelers. The empire is trying to find *you*. They won't be looking at us."

"She needs protection," Ioth interjected. "Warriors to accompany her."

"She needs anonymity," Teth replied. "If you surround her with bodyguards the empire will be on to you in a matter of hours."

When Ioth scowled, Teth added, "You should also consider that unlike you, I've seen Nimhea fight. Any skirmish we might encounter won't pose a problem for her."

"We?" Suli arched an eyebrow at him.

"Oh." Teth smiled winsomely. "Did I forget that one of Lucket's terms is that someone from the Below accompany our three adventurers?"

Edram looked more closely at Teth, assessing him. "And you are the person for this job?"

"I'm not too shabby in a fight." Teth cracked his knuckles. "That aside, I'm still the one you want for this job. Lucket trusts me more than anyone else."

"Why would the Low King of Fjeri have so much faith you?" Edram asked pointedly.

Teth paused for a moment, and then said: "Because he's my father."

Gasps and startled exclamation buzzed through the room. Only Ara didn't react, because she didn't dare.

It was a lie. Teth was lying. The first time she'd met him, he'd told her he'd been orphaned. Or maybe he was lying then and telling the truth now. She didn't know if one was better than the other.

She had the merest thought that she should immediately call Teth out, but in truth she'd come to trust him more than anyone else in the room. So she kept quiet and tried to make her expression neutral.

As if he knew Ara was thinking about him, Teth slid a glance over to Ara. And smiled.

Ara drew a short, sharp breath, wanting to rebuke, yet marveling at his audacity.

Producing a scroll, Teth handed it to Suli. "The truth of it is in there, along with the terms set down by the Low Kings."

Suli examined the image stamped in black wax on the scroll, then said to her cohort, "This *is* Lucket's seal."

"You'll find one more issue addressed in Lucket's proposal." Teth's expression hardened. "More than imperial slights pushed the Low Kings to action. Something strange has been happening, and we're beginning to suspect it's been happening much longer and is more wide-ranging than we'd like to think. The Low Kings hope you'll collaborate with them to investigate the matter."

Mail rustling as she crossed her arms, Suli nodded for him to continue.

Teth took a moment to meet the eyes of each of the rebellion's emissaries. "Have you heard talk of missing children?"

He waited through a nervous shuffling of feet and several darting glances.

"Our commander," Suli finally said. "The one we call the Hawk. His grandniece and grandnephew, infant twins, were taken from their crib three years ago."

Ioth regarded Teth for a moment. "In Kelden there have been rumors of missing children, but they remain simply that—rumors."

"Traders from Vijeri have brought news of disappearing children." Edram rested his elbows on his knees and steepled his fingers. "But this affliction—if it is real—has yet to reach Daefrit."

Xeris, whose eyes were on Edram, nodded and said, "I've heard tales. Not enough to arouse suspicion, but the whispers are real."

To Ara the question was jarring, though she could not draw from personal experience. She was barely three years old when soldiers armed with swords and the emperor's decree rode into Rill's Pass.

"They promised an Embrace would never be issued again," Ara murmured to herself.

She'd been speaking softly and was surprised when Teth replied, "I wouldn't count on imperial promises if I were you."

Speaking to the group, he said, "I'll be plain with you. The Below has no information other than that children have gone missing, and it seems to be happening in every province of Saetlund. What the Low Kings request of you is to share any accounts, rumors, suggestions regarding the disappearance of children or any talk of another Embrace. With any luck our combined efforts will help us to discover the truth of it more quickly."

Suli nodded. "Of course we will assist in this matter. Saetlund still grieves those lost in the Embrace. We cannot allow such a horror to befall the kingdom again."

"We're agreed then." Teth offered his hand. "On all terms."

"Isn't anyone going to ask what I think?" Nimhea demanded. Her cheeks bore a touch of red, signaling her awareness that she sounded sullen. Nevertheless, she let the question stand without apology.

Suli addressed the princess wearily. "You're getting what you want. Unless you want to object and accompany us to a secure location."

Nimhea's lips formed a thin line. She shook her head.

Clasping Teth's hand, Suli said, "The terms are struck."

At those words, a familiar sound filled Ara's ears, the ring of a hammer on steel. She felt the vibrations of its strength in her limbs. She glanced around the room, waiting for the others to react to the sound.

But no one did.

10

 flurry of activity, but little discussion, followed Teth and Suli's handshake. Nimhea fell into a half-sullen, half-bewildered silence. Eamon was likewise quiet, but his muteness seemed to come from a place of wonder. Ara had yet to speak because the person she most wanted a word with was still deep in conversation with the rebels.

When Teth at last broke away from the four warriors, Ara quickly pulled him aside.

"What happens now?" she asked.

"We leave as soon as possible," he answered. She thought he looked a little too pleased with himself. "There are arrangements to be made, of course—that horse of yours for example—"

Ara lowered her voice to a harsh whisper. "Why did you lie?"

"I didn't."

His flippant reply made her seethe. "You did. Either to me or to them. You told me you're an orphan, and you just told them Lucket is your father."

"Ahhhhh." Teth's expression filled with mischief. "I see the problem now. Neither what I told you nor what I told the rebels was a lie."

"But—" Ara began.

"What I actually said to you about my provenance was that I'm an orphan who was taken in by someone powerful," Teth said. "That powerful someone is Lucket. While I admit we aren't an ideal portrait of a father and son relationship, we still regard each other on those terms . . . for the most part."

Grinding her teeth, Ara snapped, "You could have mentioned that when I met Lucket."

"I thought it would be obvious." Teth grinned at her. "Now about your horse . . ."

What remained of the day was overtaken by the necessity and tedium of preparing for a lengthy journey. Traveling from Rill's Pass to Silverstag entailed a handful of days on the road. The trip to Daefrit would consume the better part of two weeks. They could take the main road, and shorten the length of their journey, but that meant following the eastward track. The larger cities to the east had become the seats of the Vokkan conquerors and needed to be given a wide berth; thus, their path would take them south, again on hunters' tracks until they reached Midford—the halfway point between Silverstag and the border steppes.

Ara's thoughts often drifted to all that had come together in a matter of days. Eamon and Nimhea had found Ara in Rill's Pass. The heirs of the River Throne and the Loresmith were together. Ara caught a thief. That thief had connections to an underworld with a long reach and deep pockets. An underworld that now said it wanted to help her and aid the Resistance.

It was so much Ara would have thought she'd be frightened. But she wasn't. If anything she felt more sure of her choices than ever. Like Wuldr's appearance in her dream and Eni's presence in the ruins, Ara believed, this unlikely tangle of alliances was another sign that this was her fate.

With the alliance struck, Lucket would supply what they needed for the onward journey, which made Teth responsible for arranging said supplies. It was in this role that he'd presented Ara with a reasonable argument that Tekki had no business in the desert. Ara was quick to agree. The bulky, hairy-as-a-bear draft horse belonged on a northern farm. Teth's first impulse was to sell the gelding, but Ara insisted that Tekki and the packhorse who'd come from Rill's Pass be returned to their home. After a few minutes of grumbling, Teth assented to her request. He spoke to Eamon and Nimhea in turn, then left them with instructions to gather their things and directions to a safe house where they were to meet him.

The rebels requested that Nimhea speak with them in private, so Eamon and Ara returned to their room and began packing. Eamon snatched his belongings in a frenzy, as if he couldn't get them into his pack fast enough. His eyes were bright, almost fevered.

"It's happening," Eamon breathed. "It's truly happening."

Ara didn't know if Eamon expected a response, but she was worried he might begin to hyperventilate. "Yes, it's good news. Are you all right?"

She'd had similar thrilling moments when becoming the Loresmith seemed truly within her grasp. Eamon's excitement, however, had a flavor of madness.

His answering laugh didn't ease her fears. She heard no joy in the high-pitched cackle.

Eamon glanced at her and abruptly sat on the bed. "I must seem mad to you. I don't know how to describe what I'm feeling."

"You can try," Ara urged. Maybe if he talked about it, he could calm down.

"Your kindness honors me." Now Eamon looked like he could weep. She would have asked if he'd eaten anything that morning, but she'd seen his finished breakfast plate.

To her relief, he did not cry, but smiled at her. "I'm sorry to be in such a state, but this . . . it's as if all I've dreamed of is about to come true."

Ara didn't grasp what he meant, but Eamon continued to explain.

"All of my life, it's been Nimhea: her future, her prowess, her commanding presence. And she deserves all that. I love who my sister is. But the people who raised us adored Nimhea and had no time for me. If not for Nimhea's insistence, I think they would have ignored me completely."

"That's horrible," Ara murmured. She heard the deep well of lonelinesss behind his words.

"I didn't care about them," Eamon said dismissively, but Ara knew that he had. "All I wanted was to help my sister fulfill her destiny. For the longest time, I couldn't find any way to do that. I was a poor swordsman, bowman, spearman. I can keep my seat on a horse, but I'd be no boon to a cavalry unit. Where Nimhea was strong and graceful, I was weak and awkward. I had a mind that wouldn't stop churning, and I didn't know what to do with it. And then I began to read."

Ara watched as he began to drift into his past, eyes dreamy.

"Mind you, I was taught how to read at a very young age," Eamon continued. "But what they gave me were letters, pronouncements, speeches—all types of administrative literature, as if they expected me to become Nimhea's personal secretary."

When Ara gave a dry laugh, Eamon smiled at her.

Then consternation briefly clouded his face. "I don't understand why no one thought to give me a book."

Ara nodded. There was no excuse for the way Eamon had been neglected. He'd been a child needing guidance and affection.

Eamon's attention returned to the present, and he said to Ara, "I found the library myself, you know. No one showed me."

"How odd," said Ara, though she meant it more as a means to keep him talking than a genuine observation. Her thoughts kept returning to a little boy wandering through endless halls, waiting for someone to notice him.

"The irony is our caretakers were thrilled once I was ensconced among all those books," Eamon laughed bitterly. "It kept me out of the way, and they could focus on Nimhea."

He leaned toward Ara, his tone becoming conspiratorial. "But the library is where I found it. The answer I'd been looking for: a way to assure Nimhea's return to the throne. Magics that have been lost for centuries. If I could restore that power on behalf of my sister, I wouldn't be useless anymore."

"I'm certain Nimhea never thought you were useless," Ara said softly.

"I know that." Eamon smiled at Ara. "She's a good sister. All the more reason I want to do all I can for her."

"Of course," Ara agreed. She felt a twinge in her chest at Eamon's raw vulnerability. He was so open. So earnest. The kind of person too many would try to take advantage of.

"I was afraid for so long," Eamon confessed. "Even after I'd convinced Nimhea that the tales of Saetlund's gods weren't stories for children, they were history. I believed, but I couldn't be sure I was right . . . until we found you. Now I know we cannot fail."

Ara felt a hard stone in her throat.

"But Eamon." She didn't want to say it—she could taste her own fear—but she had to. "I could fail."

He took her hands. "You won't."

Eamon's expression was so earnest, so innocent, that Ara couldn't help but smile back. While she'd become fond of the young prince, she'd assumed they had little in common. She saw now that they shared a struggle with purpose. Eamon having always lived in the shadow of his sister's purpose; Ara with a destiny she'd lost hope for.

Clasping Eamon's fingers, Ara said, "If you help me, I won't."

An hour passed before Nimhea joined them. She was uncharacteristically quiet as she began to pack. Itching to know what transpired between the princess and the rebels, Ara expected the three of them to immediately fall into conversation. Instead, Eamon held his tongue, not even greeting his sister. Impatient as she was to know Nimhea's mind, Ara followed his cue and kept her questions to herself.

The princess still hadn't spoken—apart from terse one-word answers to practical questions about the imminent journey—when the time came for them to leave the inn. Ioth met them at the back door, and Ara was surprised that he was alone. In Rill's Pass goodbyes took forever, at least a quarter of an hour, even if you'd be gone only a single night. She assumed that Suli, Xeris, and Edram had taken proper leave of Nimhea when their meeting ended. But did they hold Eamon and Ara in such low regard that they wouldn't deign to give them a few parting words?

"It's not an affront," Ioth said, reading Ara's expression. "We always stagger our departures. I'm the last to go."

"Oh." Ara cast her gaze down, humbled by having assumed the worst about the rebels.

"Don't fret," Ioth told her. "We're all still getting to know one another."

Ioth escorted them to the appointed safe house. Ara wondered if they'd return to the house she'd been in with Teth the previous day, but his directions took them to another part of Silverstag entirely.

"I leave you here," said Ioth. "Know that the hopes of the rebellion go with you."

"You have our thanks," Nimhea replied.

When Ioth was gone, Eamon stepped up to the door and gave it several sharp raps just as Ara said, "Wait!"

Eamon looked at her quizzically, but Ara felt quite sure that one didn't knock at a safe house; she was baffled when a plump middle-aged woman in a frilly bonnet and apron decorated with blue ribbon opened the door.

"Welcome!" she exclaimed. "Come in, come in."

The cherry-cheeked woman ushered them through the door and into a room where chairs had been arranged near a cheery hearth fire.

"I have tea and spice cakes for you." She motioned for them to sit. "Make yourselves at home."

She scurried from the room, and the sound of clinking dishes soon reached them.

"Who was that?" Eamon asked.

"I have no idea," Nimhea replied. "Did she even tell us her name?"

"I don't think so," said Ara.

The stairs separating the hearth room from the kitchen creaked under the weight of footsteps, and a second woman joined them near the fire.

"We do love having guests," the woman said, not bothering to introduce herself. She looked to be of similar age to the first woman and had the same soft, rounded shape and warm bearing. She likewise wore a frilly bonnet and apron, this time decorated with a red ribbon.

Nimhea stood. "We thank you for your hospitality, Goodwoman . . ."

"No names, no names," the woman said with a tinkling laugh. "A good bit of advice, dear: do not use names unless you absolutely must."

"Of course," Nimhea answered uncertainly, slowly sinking back into her chair.

The woman smiled kindly. "You won't be accustomed to it, but it is the best way. We've been at this for years."

Blue Ribbon returned to the room bearing a tray laden with small cakes, three teacups, and a teapot. Red Ribbon clapped delightedly and hurried to place a low table in front of their guests.

"You're in for a treat," said Red Ribbon. "Her spice cakes are scrumptious."

"Not as delicious as your apple tarts," replied Blue Ribbon.

"Pishposh." Red Ribbon waved a dismissive hand.

The door to the cupboard beneath the staircase swung open, and Teth stepped into the room.

"Good evening." Teth smiled broadly at the Ribbons.

The Ribbons dipped into curtsies. "Good evening, sir."

"Sir?" Nimhea offered Teth a mocking smile.

"Only on certain occasions," Teth remarked.

"The tubs have been prepared," said Red Ribbon. "They're in the guest quarters."

"Thank you." Teth eased into a chair and stretched his legs out. His gaze fell on the tray.

"Are these your spice cakes?" he asked Blue Ribbon hopefully.

When she nodded, he scooped up three. "Marvelous."

With another curtsy, the Ribbons retired to the kitchen.

"Try the cake," Teth told them between bites. "It's amazing."

Eamon politely took a cake to nibble on, but Nimhea was taking in their surroundings.

"Why are we here?" She gave Teth a pointed look.

Ara couldn't blame her for the question. The house didn't seem a likely starting point for a covert journey. Unlike the skeletal house Ara had visited the night before, this place was a home. Floor scrubbed, wood polished, tables and shelves decorated with cozy knickknacks and lace doilies.

"Witness the first benefit of aligning yourself with the Low Kings," Teth replied. "If you'd eat some cake you'd understand how fine a benefit."

When Nimhea answered with a frosty stare, Teth chortled. "I'll answer your question, but only after you've eaten a cake."

"They really are quite good," said Eamon as he reached for his second cake.

Grudgingly Nimhea picked up a cake and took a bite. Her eyes widened, and she looked at the cake in surprise.

"I told you." Teth was on his fourth cake.

Ara wasn't inclined to eat; anticipating the journey had set her stomach to fluttering. Curiosity overpowered her nerves, and she selected her own cake. Her teeth sank into the soft crumbs that immediately melted on her tongue. Not overly sweet, the cake was an explosion of flavors. Cinnamon, cardamom, a hint of almond. With the flavors came an overwhelming sense of well-being, like hot drinking chocolate after a romp in snow drifts.

"These are magic," Ara murmured, savoring another bite.

"Not literally." Teth was watching her with a smile that made the room feel much warmer. "But that's a good description."

Nimhea cleared her throat. "We all love the cakes. Now answer my question."

Ara felt a twinge of disappointment when he looked away.

"Our path out of Silverstag begins here," Teth told Nimhea. "But there's a matter to take care of first."

He brought out a glass bottle filled with an inky liquid.

"What's this?" Nimhea asked.

"Dye," Teth answered. "For your hair."

Nimhea stared at him, unblinking, and Ara felt the air go out of the room. She was certain Nimhea was about to scream or faint. Ara expected a scream, as Nimhea likely didn't believe in fainting.

The princess must have been holding her breath because instead she exhaled explosively. "Why?"

"You already know," Teth told her. "Your hair is a signpost. Only the Dentroth bloodline produces *that* combination of red hues. If it's noticed too many times, people who've always believed you died in the conquest will start believing you're alive. A time will come when we want that to happen, but not before the Resistance can build a real army. Too soon and the Vokkans will flush every last rebel out and put your head on a pike."

Nimhea's eyes bulged. Clearly the image of her head on a pike didn't sit well.

"And that's why we must dye your hair," Teth reasserted.

"I keep it covered," Nimhea protested, her hand moving protectively toward her hair.

Teth sighed and shook his head. "Not well enough. I've spotted it numerous times when you've tried to tuck it away."

Ara had noticed Nimhea's hair too. It liked to catch the light and flash like rubies.

"You'll need to make a change as well," Teth said to Eamon. "Your hair isn't a problem, but we should try to make you look older. Can you grow a beard?"

Cringing, Eamon replied, "Yes . . ."

"But?" Teth lifted his eyebrows.

"They're so itchy!" Eamon scratched his jaw at the thought and scowled.

Ara's brow furrowed as she tried to imagine Eamon with a beard. He had such a young face. She didn't think any beard he could grow would seem natural.

"Discomfort can't conquer necessity," Teth said. "Sorry, my friend. Stop shaving."

Eamon slumped in his chair and grumbled for a moment. Then he took another cake.

Teth turned back to Nimhea. "Stop that. You look like you're in mourning. It's not permanent."

Nimhea was indeed wearing a rather pitiful expression of despair.

Ara was tempted to make light of the situation and say, "It's just hair." But in Nimhea's case it really wasn't.

"You're sure it's not permanent?" Nimhea asked, eyeing him warily.

"Yep," he answered.

A little too quickly, Ara thought.

Teth poured himself a cup of tea. "You'll find the tubs and water you need upstairs. We have time to spare because we won't leave for another couple of hours, but I'd get started now if I were you. It's important to make sure the dye will take."

It took Ara a moment to realize Teth was speaking to her. "*I'm* dyeing Nimhea's hair?"

She suddenly couldn't remember why she'd thought anything nice about Teth.

"You come from a line of weavers," Teth replied. "Surely you know about dyes."

"I'm a smith," Ara countered, trying to maneuver a way out of this. "Not a weaver."

"But you do know about dyes," Teth pushed.

She didn't appreciate his presumption, and considered lying, but she nodded. She'd spent enough time helping her grandmother card, spin, and dye wool to grasp the basics.

Teth gave Nimhea a reassuring smile. "I'm certain Ara will do an excellent job."

"Fine." Nimhea stood. "Let's get this over with."

As the princess walked to the staircase, Ara leaned over to Teth.

"Why am *I* doing this?" Ara hissed at him.

Teth whispered back, "If I ruin her hair, she'll kill me. I don't think she'll kill you."

"You don't think." She held him with a flat stare.

"I can't be sure."

Ara decided she should start a list of things she didn't like about Teth. This would go at the top of the list.

"Ugh." Ara picked up the bottle of dye and went after Nimhea.

"Try not to make it streaky," Teth called to Ara as she began to climb the stairs.

Ara pivoted to face him and hissed, "Stop making it worse."

"You're very good at speaking through clenched teeth," he replied.

Nimhea was halfway up and spun around. "Streaky?!"

Teth winked at her, and she stomped her foot but didn't say anything.

When Ara had first met the princess, she would have dismissed Nimhea's reaction as vain or ridiculous. Having spent more than a week in Nimhea's company, Ara better understood that despite the eye-catching beauty of the princess's red hair, its attractiveness wasn't her primary concern. Nimhea's distinct hair was a symbol, proof that she was the embodiment of the flaming crown that marked the Dentroth dynasty. To mask that symbol would be akin to losing her identity.

"It won't be permanent," Ara said firmly to Nimhea. "And you know why it needs doing." At Teth she growled, "Stop baiting her."

"Who, me?" Teth feigned wide-eyed innocence. "It's the door on the right, by the way."

All in all Ara thought she'd done a fine job with Nimhea's hair. She could say with confidence that Nimhea absolutely did not look terrible. There were no streaks.

Was the new shade of her hair becoming? Not quite, but Ara worked hard to convince herself, and Nimhea, that the color only seemed dull in contrast to the exceptional liveliness of Nimhea's natural hue.

Ara couldn't say what color the dye was meant to be, but on Nimhea's hair it came out as a sullen brown. Not a hint of red or gold came through, making the disguise ideal. Unfortunately, it no longer brought out the warmth of her deep bronze skin.

Nimhea had taken the whole process stoically, only speaking with Ara once as they waited for the dye to set.

"How much do you trust this alliance with the Low Kings?" Nimhea had asked.

"Just enough to take a chance on it," Ara answered. "*Everything* before us is unknown." She paused before saying, "But I've come to trust Teth. And this alliance with the Low Kings offers the best means to continue our journey, amply supplied, without drawing attention to our little party."

"I go where my brother goes," Nimhea said with a long sigh. It wasn't clear if she was speaking to Ara or herself.

That was the end of their conversation.

At the moment, it was too dark to discern the color of anyone's hair. The only light came from Teth's lantern as he led them along the tunnel they'd accessed through the basement of the safe house.

Unlike the stone corridors leading to Lucket's offices, this tunnel had been roughly dug from the earth. Roots poked through the dirt on all sides, revealing the secret lives of trees, and only the regular support beams reminded Ara that the pathway had been created by humans and not some enormous mole. The dank, rich scent of living soil drenched the air.

They walked in a little cluster to stay close to Teth's light, but Eamon and Nimhea were slightly behind and had fallen into their own quiet conversation.

"Do you know their names?" Ara asked. She'd been wondering about the two homemakers in Silverstag since they departed.

Teth glanced over his shoulder to look at her. "Whose names?"

"Red Ribbon and Blue Ribbon."

"Clever." Teth chuckled and turned back to the total darkness ahead. "I know a few of their names."

"'A few of their names.'" Ara pushed string-like roots away from her face. "What does that even mean?"

"In our line of work," Teth said, "it's best that you keep your real name to yourself."

"Isn't Teth your real name?" She kept her gaze on the bobbing lantern. "Plenty of people in Silverstag seemed to know it."

"In Silverstag, having my name well known is an asset." Teth ducked to avoid knocking his head on a support beam. "It's the name Lucket gave me, and my connection to Lucket opens a lot of doors, literally and figuratively, in his territory."

Ara frowned. "Does that mean you have other names?"

"Many other names," Teth responded. "To be used as best fits each circumstance. I'm sure you'll learn some of them over the course of our journey."

While Ara chewed on that answer, another question formed. She felt a bit uneasy asking it, and lowered her voice.

"Do you remember a name before Teth?"

"I don't know if I had a name," Teth said. "My earliest memory is a market filled with giants. The sun was too bright. I was thirsty and hungry. There was a cart full of apples. Green apples. So many apples it seemed like a few were about to spill onto the ground. I took one of those precarious apples, and the sun disappeared, blotted out by one of the giants' shadows. The giant squatted beside me so he wasn't so giant. He pointed to the apple in my hand and said, 'That's not how it's done.'"

"That was Lucket," said Ara.

He nodded.

"Does Lucket have any ideas about where you're from?" Ara asked. "Who your parents might be?"

"His only guess is that one of my parents was from Vijeri and the other from Daefrit," Teth told her. "Because I have features from both."

"Do you think you'll try to find them someday?" Paying too much attention to the conversation and not enough to the ground, Ara's foot hooked on a knot of roots.

She lost her balance and would have fallen, but Teth caught her arm, steadying her.

They kept walking and she waited for him to answer her question, but he didn't.

Ara tried again. "Do you—"

"No." He cut her off rather sharply. "I have no memories before that market and Lucket. As far as I'm concerned there is nothing else to remember."

His tone was that of a stranger, and the lantern light that reached his face revealed a tightly drawn mouth and tense jaw.

"Are you all right?" Ara asked.

"Sorry." Teth stopped, and when he looked at her he was smiling. "I think my elbow is about to permanently lock into an angle. Would you mind leading for a while?"

He handed her the lantern. "This is the only path, so just keep on as we have been."

Baffled, Ara began walking.

"How much farther?" she heard Eamon ask Teth.

"Not much," Teth answered.

"Thank you for that ever so specific, completely unambiguous answer," Nimhea grumbled.

Teth laughed. "I aim to please."

With her companions chittering at her back, Ara moved on, lantern aloft, and waited for something other than darkness to greet her.

11

hen Ara came to the end of the tunnel, shafts of daylight speared the shadows, revealing a ladder that climbed the wall of a ruined well. The top of the well was a jumble of cut stones blanketed with dark moss.

Teth signaled that they should wait near the edge of the well and keep quiet. He slunk into the brush. A moment later, Ara heard two short fluttering whistles, and a moment after that an answering whistle.

"You can come out," Teth called to them.

Making their way through the dense brush, Ara, Nimhea, and Eamon joined Teth in a small clearing a short distance from the well. Another man was untying the ropes linking four saddled horses and two packhorses. Ara recognized the twins' mounts, but the other horses were unfamiliar. When the horses were free, the man mounted his horse, nodded briefly at Teth, and rode away.

"You two." Teth pointed at the twins. "Get your horses ready. Eamon, take one of the packhorses' leads: I'll have the other."

While Nimhea and Eamon saw to their mounts, Teth gathered the reins of the new horses and brought them over to Ara.

"Daefritian steeds for our use," Teth told her. "Courtesy of Lucket's stables."

To Ara these horses were beautiful, but strange. If the horses of

Rill's Past were best described as hardy, the ones Teth brought forward should be called flashy. Their glossy coats caught the morning sunlight, flaring it back at the world. They were roughly the same size as Eamon and Nimhea's mounts, but the twins' horses were built of straight lines. Curves seemed to define these new animals; bowed necks draped by silky manes, and tails that arched up before flowing out like a pennant behind their long, tapering legs. Their small, well-shaped heads were crowned by ears that curved into points.

Pretty as the new horses were, Ara eyed their slim legs with suspicion. Tekki's legs were sturdy as tree trunks, while this pair appeared to balance on twigs that could snap at any moment.

"Do you have a preference?" asked Teth. "They're both geldings—though not as sensible as the geldings you're probably used to. Daefritian horses can be a bit flighty. They excite easily."

"I believe that," said Ara as she looked into the horses' eyes, finding an intense eagerness and daring that was more than a little unsettling.

She looked at Teth critically. "If they're not sensible, why are we riding them?"

The horses snorted and stamped their feet as if insulted.

"Because they're fast," Teth answered. "And they'll bear the heat. Plus, they're especially fun to ride . . . once you've adjusted."

Pointing at Eamon and Nimhea, who were already mounted, Ara complained, "Why don't they have new horses?"

"Their horses are Keldenese," Teth explained. "Keldenese horses are both strong and agile; that's why they're the most common cavalry mounts. Since Nimhea and Eamon are already accustomed to their mounts I didn't see a point in changing. Time to pick. We need to get going."

Ara shot him a skeptical glance, then compared the two horses.

One had a deep gray coat dappled with white, like snowflakes against a storm front. The second had a coat like ochre contrasted with ebony mane and tail. Both were stunning, but the first horse, despite being from the desert, made her think of home. That horse also looked a smidge shorter, and Ara thought it wise to be closer to the ground.

When she gestured to the gray, Teth handed her the reins. "He's called Cloud."

Ara stepped up to Cloud and cupped her hand beneath his nose. Cloud's breath blew warm on her palm as the horse took in her scent. When he began to lip at her fingers, she laughed and stroked his cheek, then his long, arched neck. Ara had enjoyed petting Tekki because it reminded her of comforting thick fur rugs. Cloud's coat was like velvet.

"That means it's you and me again, friend," Teth said to the other horse.

Looking at him sharply, Ara said. "You know that horse?"

Teth nodded. "He's my favorite of all the horses in Lucket's stables. His name is Dust."

"If he's your favorite, why did you let me choose?" Ara frowned at Teth.

Rubbing the back of his neck, Teth looked away. "Well, I didn't want to deny you the chance to ride him if you wanted to."

A little smile crept onto Ara's lips as she adjusted her stirrups.

Cloud was pawing at the ground with impatience as Ara began to mount. She didn't have her right leg over the saddle when Cloud bounded forward, leaving Ara on her butt in the dirt.

"Easily excited," Teth called from his seat atop Dust.

As Ara swiped debris from her breeches, Cloud walked back to his would-be rider. He had the courtesy to look embarrassed.

Taking the reins in a firm hand, Ara said to the horse, "I would like us to be friends, but if you insist on acting silly, things will not go well between us. Do you understand?"

Cloud snorted, and Ara decided that was good enough. Her second attempt to climb into the saddle was much more successful. When Ara was seated, Cloud turned his head and neck to make sure she was there before he took a single step.

Despite the choice to avoid the main roads, their route south consisted of pleasant tracks that were much wider, with more even ground than the hunting paths north of Silverstag. They rode through soft spring drizzle at times, but no downpours or thunderstorms intruded, and they made good progress. They passed the time with light conversation, and Ara began to feel strange about how normal the journey seemed to be. Amid the tense meetings and negotiations in Silverstag, their trip to Daefrit had sounded momentous, but as a regular pattern of travel each day and camping at night established itself the thrill of embarking on an adventure waned. It all suddenly seemed unremarkable. At times it was even boring.

To take her mind off the monotony, Ara spent most of her time adjusting to her new horse. It wasn't that she disliked Cloud. He was intelligent and eager to please, but he required a much more active type of riding than Tekki, who'd happily plodded along in whatever direction he was pointed and frequently paused to snatch whatever green leaf or clump of grass he could get his teeth on. In stark contrast to Tekki, Cloud had a mad enthusiasm for speed. He was frustrated by the slow pace demanded by the meandering forest trails they were facing. In the horse's opinion, faster was always better. Ara quickly learned that giving him anything other than the gentlest cue would cause him to leap into a full gallop. Fortunately, Cloud also had an instant response to being reined in, so they never got too far ahead of the others. The first time she stopped him, Ara nearly went over his head, but after that she knew how to keep her seat.

Despite his sometimes frustrating tendencies, Cloud's gait was a dream; it was like riding the current of a swift, smooth river. Ara had never imagined one could trot without the constant jolting. After a few days' riding, she wondered just how fast Cloud could run and looked forward to reaching the open grasslands of northern Daefrit, where she'd be able to find out.

On the day they reached Alderspring, which marked the border between Fjeri's highlands and lowlands, Teth took the packhorses into the town for resupply, while the rest of them waited at the edge of town. Standing in her stirrups, Ara craned her neck in the hopes of getting a better look at Alderspring. Though it was hard to tell from a distance, Alderspring seemed to have less of the chill and caution that characterized Silverstag. Alderspring was smaller and unconnected to the main trading routes of the province. Ara supposed that meant it might garner less attention from the empire and could afford an ease that Silverstag could not.

Teth returned an hour later, the horses bearing packs laden with fresh goods.

"We can join the southern route to Midford here," he told them. "Only local merchants use that road. The empire gave up patrolling it years ago when the Low Kings offered to maintain it."

The road bore only slight differences from the hunting tracks they'd been following. A bit wider, enough to accommodate a wagon, and straighter, the road was grass-covered and absent the trampled quality of major thoroughfares.

As they rode on Ara noticed Teth glancing frequently at either side of the road as well as behind him.

"Are you looking for something?" She pulled in her horse beside his.

"Fox," Teth admitted, looking rather embarrassed. "Honestly, I hoped my little friend wouldn't follow us. Fox belongs in the north, but I thought it might try to tag along anyway. It couldn't have followed us through the tunnel, but Fox knows the scent of Nimhea and Eamon's horses, and could have used that as a guide."

He gazed into the thick forest and gave a wistful sigh. "Now that I'm sure the little beast isn't coming with us, I'm a bit sad. Fox is an excellent co-conspirator."

"I'll miss Fox, too." Something about the creature's odd behavior and comic antics perfectly matched the strange quality of Ara's life at the moment. "I'm sure it will be waiting for you when you return home."

"And when will that be?" Teth said quietly, and Ara held her tongue. It was a question neither of them could answer.

Despite Teth's assurance that he could make peace with Fox's absence, Ara thought he seemed oddly restless when they set up camp for the night. At dinner, Teth put a question to the group.

"I'm accustomed to traveling alone," he told them. "And I usually design a journey to my personal liking. But in our case, I think certain decisions are best made as a group."

"What are we deciding?" asked Eamon, cutting himself another slice of ham.

"When we reach Oakvale, we have two options." Teth picked up a stick and poked at the fire. Sparks jumped into the night air. "We can continue on our own or join a trade caravan."

Nimhea's brow furrowed. "Why would we join a caravan?"

"It would be a good cover." Teth continued to pester the campfire. "Oakvale is the junction of western, northern, and southern trade routes. It will be brimming with caravans. I should be able to find one tied to the Low Kings that would guarantee us safe passage."

"Would you stop that?" Ara said when the stacked pieces of wood collapsed due to Teth's poking. "Leave it be."

"It's fine," Teth muttered.

"No. It's going to burn out faster now." Ara tried to grab the stick, but Teth snatched it back, holding it protectively.

"Poking fires with sticks is a time-honored practice," Teth said. "You can't take my joy away."

Ara scoffed. "Your *joy*?"

Nimhea rolled her eyes at them. "What's our other option?"

Teth made a face at Ara, then answered, "To continue as we have been: staying off the road, avoiding encounters."

"And you don't think we should do that . . ." Nimhea waited for an explanation.

"It would be faster," Teth admitted. "But to reach Daefrit we have to pass through the Midland Steppes. That's rough terrain, and there are few ways through. The steppes are full of tight corners and dead ends—perfect for ambushes."

"Bandits?" Eamon asked, eyes wide with memories of their last run-in.

Teth stared at the fire, which was starting to die down. "Lots of bandits."

With a last longing look at the campfire, he shot a resentful glance at Ara and went to fetch more firewood.

"We can handle bandits," Nimhea told Teth as he restacked pieces of wood.

"We can," Teth answered. "That doesn't mean we should."

He looked critically at his construction, then at Ara. "Anything to say?"

She put on a mask of feigned innocence. "What could I have to say?"

"I don't like bandits," Eamon offered, and Ara guessed that would be the closest he got to casting a vote in this decision.

He scratched at the thin, spiky scruff on his jaw. Eamon's beard *was* coming in, but in a rather haphazard way. He looked miserable.

"If we strike out on our own, we won't just have one run-in with bandits." Teth returned to his place beside the fire. "We'll have several. That means we'll be leaving bodies or witnesses behind. Neither would be good for us."

"Won't bandits strike the caravan as well?" Ara asked. Her eyes narrowed as she noticed Teth's fingers twitch toward the poking stick.

"Possibly," Teth replied. "But they prefer attacking small groups. Large caravans always have hired guards. Unless the bandits know a caravan is transporting something so valuable it's worth risking their lives for, or if they're absolutely desperate, they don't harass merchant convoys. There's also the risk of running into imperial patrols on the trade route. They keep an irregular schedule, which makes it impossible to know when they'll be where."

"But those patrols will be a problem for us," Eamon said. He was fidgety that evening, casting frequent glances at the woods around them.

"That's where your alliance with Lucket will prove its worth," Teth replied.

"How much slower will it be?" Nimhea asked.

"Three, maybe four days longer," Teth answered. "But that's assuming we wouldn't run into trouble traveling on our own."

"The caravan sounds like the better choice to me," Ara said.

She watched with disbelief as Eamon picked up Teth's stick and tentatively poked the fire. Feeling her gaze, Eamon looked up.

"Sorry," he said, though he kept poking the fire as if he couldn't help himself. "It really is fun."

"I told you," Teth quipped.

"You're a bad influence," Ara grumbled.

Teth smiled sweetly. "Isn't it great?"

"I agree with Ara." Nimhea's voice was tinged with disappointment, which Ara thought odd.

A sudden spray of sparks rose from the fire, which had just collapsed again.

"Oops," said Eamon.

He met Ara's baleful eyes. "I'll fix it."

"You do that." Teth stood up. "Ara and I have another matter to discuss."

"What matter?" Nimhea placed her sword in her lap and drew a whetstone from her pack.

Ara wanted to know the same thing.

"It doesn't concern you," Teth told Nimhea.

Nimhea didn't object, but as she looked from Teth to Ara a sly smile played on her lips. "Very well."

Ara could suddenly feel her pulse in her throat.

Teth, however, was completely unruffled. "Let's go, Ara."

As she followed Teth away from the campsite, Ara heard a yelp. Then Nimhea was shouting.

"What are you doing? Don't pick up the pieces that are on fire with your bare hands!"

"Amateur," Teth said with a chuckle.

"Where are we going?" Ara asked.

"Not far."

Ara groaned inwardly at his characteristic vagueness, but her body was trembling with anticipation. The tender quaking of her limbs made her feel silly. She wished she could stop it, but didn't know how. She looked at Teth, who was only slightly ahead of her. If she reached out, she could take his hand. She wondered what would happen if she did.

"Here we are," Teth announced, snapping Ara out of her musing.

He'd led her to a small clearing in the wood. The sky was cloudless, and a bright moon shone on the space, making it surprisingly easy to see.

Teth was looking at her. The sight of his face bathed in moonlight made her want to rest her fingertips on his cheek. She tried to lift her hand, but her body was frozen in place. Time had stopped. The moment stretched forever. The moment when Ara thought Teth was about to kiss her.

"I have a proposal for you," Teth said.

Ara choked on her next breath. After she was done coughing, she said, "I'm sorry?"

"I noticed something about you," he told her. His hands were behind his back, and she realized he was keeping some object out of sight.

Ara didn't answer. She was making sure she still knew how to breathe properly.

Teth brough his hands forward. He was holding Ironbranch. Her stomach clenched; she hadn't even seen him pick it up at their camp.

He noticed her incredulous expression and added, "Never forget I'm the best at what I do. You might lose something important."

His tone was teasing, but Ara fumed and grabbed the stave. "Not funny."

She didn't understand why he would have taken Ironbranch. Maybe Teth considered pranks romantic. She wouldn't put it past him.

"It's a little funny," Teth said, looking a bit injured.

She ignored him.

"After the fight with Braegan," Teth continued, "you weren't afraid or in shock. You were frustrated."

Still irked, Ara wondered why was he talking about Braegan.

Ara had been anticipating a kiss. Her *first* kiss.

"I think I know why." Teth was still talking. "You've a curious mind and impressive determination."

I guarantee you have no idea why I didn't attack.

Ara stared at him; the fizzing excitement in her veins drained away. Whatever Teth intended in bringing her here, it was not for a kiss. In that moment, she despised him.

"But it was absolutely the right thing to do," he went on. "Throwing yourself into a fight without any experience is a good way to get killed."

"I have experience," Ara said flatly. For some reason she wanted nothing more than to slap that pretty, moon-blushed cheek of his and walk away.

Teth gave her a puzzled look. "I didn't mean to offend you."

Exasperated, Ara let out a huff. "My grandmother taught me to use my stave. I know how to defend myself."

"I saw that when you were fighting Braegan," Teth replied. "But you can do more."

"Like what?" Ara didn't want to be curious, but she was. A little.

"You don't have to be tall, or built like a warrior, like Nimhea, to fight well," Teth told her. "Being small has its advantages. It means you can be quicker and more agile than your opponent. You might even have skills already that you don't realize would be useful in a fight."

Ara's irritation couldn't stand up to the strange turns of this conversation. She felt silly for ever thinking Teth would want to kiss her.

It's so unfair I can't even kick him in the shin.

"What skills?" she asked impatiently.

Teth looked rather relieved at her change in mood.

"Are you good at climbing trees?" he asked.

"Why?" Ara frowned at him.

"Children don't climb trees in Rill's Pass?" Teth said, tapping his chin. "I suppose it's too cold. Icebergs, then."

"Very funny," Ara said sourly, but she smiled. "Come to think of it"—she considered his question—"I did climb trees when I was younger. Before I could apprentice at the smithy I would sometimes go with Old Imgar to harvest wood. I climbed while he chopped."

"Were you any good?" Teth asked.

"Hard to say," Ara replied. "I didn't fall."

"You're either very good or you didn't climb enough," Teth remarked. "Even the best climbers have usually fallen and broken something in their early years. The scars on your arms are the mirror of every blacksmith's arms. Have you broken bones? Had accidents?"

Ara briefly wondered why her answer would matter, but her mind fixated on the fact that Teth had been looking at her, noticing details about her. A warm shiver crept from her toes all the way to her cheeks and took away any lingering stings from the absent kiss.

Maybe he doesn't deserve a kick in the shins after all.

"Ara?" Teth looked at her quizzically.

"Accidents, of course; I grew up in a smithy," she said quickly. "There are a few other scars—"

Teth raised an eyebrow, and Ara cursed the sudden, blooming heat in her face.

"And I broke fingers and toes," she continued, looking away from him. "Once I was certain I'd broken my foot, but it was only very, very badly bruised. Imgar had to fashion crutches for me. It made for a very disappointing summer."

"What happened?" Teth's lips parted in a half grin. "Drop a hammer?"

"It didn't even happen in the smithy," Ara replied, laughing ruefully at the memory. "I was helping one of our neighbors prepare to plow the fields, and when I wasn't paying attention one of the draft horses stepped on my foot."

Teth didn't even try not to laugh. He laughed until the stars heard his glee.

"It's not that funny," Ara muttered. "I thought you were going to teach me how to use this." She pointed Ironbranch at him.

When he saw the stave leveled at his chest, Teth forced his grin away. "I'm not going to teach you how to use a stave. I'm going to show you new ways to use your body with the stave."

He walked a few steps away then turned so he stood facing her. He laced his hands behind his back. "Attack me."

Not this again.

Ara returned to standing on two feet. She took Ironbranch with both hands.

"I can't."

"Don't worry," Teth assured her. "You won't hurt me."

"I know," Ara said, frustrated. "Because I *can't* attack you."

Teth frowned at her. "I'm missing something, aren't I?"

With a sigh, Ara held the staff horizontally and gazed at it. "The Loresmith stave can only be wielded in defense. If I attack, I forfeit the gods' gift."

"Can you attack with other weapons?" Teth asked.

Ara shook her head.

Teth laughed drily. "Who made that rule?"

"The gods," Ara replied.

"Right." Teth smirked. "Not about to argue with them. Though if I were you, I'd lodge a complaint. Considering how likely you are to be attacked, limiting the ways you can fight seems unfair."

"I think it's so the Loresmith won't be corrupted." Ara wanted to explain. "Otherwise I could make weapons and armor for myself and become invincible."

"Kill whoever you want, take whatever you want," Teth mused. "Tempting for some, I'm sure. You're not that type, though, unless you've been keeping your cards very, very close."

Ara smiled at him. "I'm not that type. But I'm pretty sure the rule isn't on a case-by-case basis."

"May I see that?" Teth reached for Ironbranch. Ara handed it to him.

Teth turned the stave over in his hands, held it close to his face to examine the wood grain. He began to toss it lightly from one hand to the other.

"Its lightness belies its strength," Teth observed. He stabbed one end of the stave into the earth, then leaned his full weight into it. "It's not too stiff either."

He gave Ara a puzzled look. "This was a gift from Eni and Ofrit to the first Loresmith."

Ara nodded.

"But not for fighting . . ." Teth stepped back to assess the stave again.

"For defense." Ara needed Teth to understand that she wasn't making excuses or afraid to fight. "When the gods came to Saetlund they taught the peoples here to strive for peace and shun violence. The Loreknights were created to repel invasions, but never did they seek to conquer other lands."

Teth paused, scratching absentmindedly behind his ear, while he thought. "That sounds vaguely familiar. Like a bedtime story."

"Mmm-hmm." It was a wry sound. Ara knew the feeling of bedtime stories coming to life too well.

"As far as defense goes . . ." Teth took Ironbranch in both hands and began to weave its ends through the air. "You couldn't pick a better weapon than a stave."

Ironbranch whirled faster and faster, until its original shape had vanished and Ara could only see a wheel spinning in the air. "It's quick."

The spinning stopped, and Teth began to move. With light steps he glided across the clearing, ducking, twisting, jumping. All the while Ironbranch moved with him, an extension of his limbs: swift jabs, long thrusts, sweeping strokes. Then he sprinted to the center of the clearing, stabbed the stave to the earth, and catapulted himself into the air. The stave went with him, drawn close to his body. He flipped three times then landed perfectly.

Teth walked back to Ara and said with an absolutely straight face, "See? It's very useful."

Ara grimaced. "You were showing off."

"True." He broke into a grin. "But don't you want to be able to do all that?"

Ara saw the dare in his eyes and knew she was going to take it.

❈ ELSEWHERE: THE MESSENGER ❈

he men in the room had blood on their hands and were not happy. The blood didn't trouble them—it had completed its task perfectly—but the news was not good. There had been a surprise within the message. The wizards were not fond of surprises. They were even less fond of informing the head of their order of a divergence in the plan. The ArchWizard would not be pleased. Soon after he learned what had happened, he would have blood on his hands, too. But that blood would come from someone among them.

At least the elders could protect themselves by forcing the novices to draw straws. The poor lad who won the short straw gave an audible moan of despair. His peers all stepped away from him, as if he carried the plague. The chosen man didn't plead or protest. After his initial outburst he'd fallen silent and left the room without a word. When he'd gone the other novices huddled close together, whispering reassurances to one another that each of them was destined to be spared.

Alone now, the messenger began the long climb from the Chamber to the ArchWizard's study. He barely heard the cries of the prisoners when he passed the dungeons. He didn't notice the brightness of daylight as he exited the bowels of Vokk's temple. Nor did he see the bright blooms and bubbling fountains as he crossed the courtyard. The guards he walked past didn't greet him. They recognized the face of a condemned man.

Standing before the ebony doors of the study, the messenger's legs began to tremble. A sickly sweet taste filled his mouth. Here was his last chance to turn away. To run.

But he would not run. If he ran it would be worse. He had seen what happened to people who ran.

Two sound knocks on the door and the ArchWizard's voice called, "Enter."

The messenger pulled the thick door open and stepped into the study. The ArchWizard had his back to the room. He gazed upon the courtyard gardens, where two children were chasing a butterfly.

"Yes?"

"I bring news of the travelers," the messenger said. He was surprised he could hear his own voice so clearly over the swarm of flies in his mind.

"Tell me."

"A fourth has joined their company." The bad news. Even worse, "We don't know who he is."

The ArchWizard's shoulders rose and fell with a sigh. "What a shame."

He began to turn.

The messenger closed his eyes.

12

In the days that passed as they rode toward Oakvale, the conifer-dominated forests of the north gave way to trees with broad trunks and long, twisting branches dressed in broad green leaves. The sun rose earlier and set later. The lingering chill that had accompanied their nights ebbed away.

While their journey progressed Teth picked Eamon's brain about the precise location in Daefrit they hoped to reach. Ara didn't catch much of their conversation, but when she did it was because Teth had raised his voice in objection, peppering the air with creative, but startlingly impolite, language.

In the evenings, Ara's training sessions with Teth continued. After his showy demonstration of the skills she would master, his teaching technique was something of a disappointment. Teth insisted that Ara first master balance before moving on to anything else. She spent most of her time during a lesson standing, crouching, jumping on one foot, all without even having the stave in her hands. While she hopped on one foot with her other leg stretched in front of her, it was too tempting to suspect Teth's methods were less about Ara's progress and more about making fun of her.

An hour or so after sunset on the eve they would arrive at Oakvale, strange noises began to wind their way through the forest. Nimhea, at the lead of their group, slowed her horse from a canter to a walk. She lifted her hand, signaling caution. As they followed the road, the sounds grew louder and took the shape of music. Fiddle and fife accompanied by racing drumbeats. Between the trees Ara could see flames jumping from a massive fire. As they drew closer, the scent of roasting meat made her mouth water.

"Imperial Players!" Ara exclaimed with glee. Her initial delight was quelled by worry. "We should find another way."

"No, we shouldn't—and the empire gave them that name. Don't use it," Teth said sharply. "They call themselves Eni's Children."

His rebuke stung. Ara had a vague notion that the Imperial Players were sometimes called Eni's Children, but that fact hadn't been emphasized in lessons with her grandmother or Imgar's tales. Nor did she remember the musicians and dancers who'd come to Rill's Pass being called anything but Imperial Players by the other villagers.

Teth rubbed his hands together in anticipation.

"That's good luck, coming across their camp. We'll feast tonight."

Nimhea reined her horse in. "You want to stop? I thought the point was to avoid people until we found a trade caravan."

"I would *never* avoid a camp of Eni's Children," Teth replied. "And you don't have to worry about them blabbering to anyone else about us. As followers of Eni they take the hospitality of the campfire very seriously. Not only do they happily invite strangers to share their meals, but they never pass on information about other travelers they encounter. We'll be safe there."

"How can that be true?" Ara objected, still stubborn. "They're the *Imperial* Players."

Teth shushed her. "I already told you: do not use that name when we're with them. That's what the Vokkans forced Eni's Children to call themselves after the emperor outlawed all worship but that of Vokk."

Chastened, Ara held her tongue and regretted having called Eni's Children by a false, unwanted name.

"Since you're practically drooling, I suspect your stomach is speaking instead of your brain," Nimhea said, still skeptical of Teth's enthusiasm.

"They're making a collaborative effort," Teth admitted, patting his belly.

When Nimhea leveled a cool gaze at him, Teth continued, "We'll have dinner, enjoy some music, and then make our own camp in the woods so we won't be just off the road like Eni's Children are."

"A fresh roast would be nice." Eamon cast a hopeful glance at his sister.

"Very well." Nimhea clucked her tongue and her horse walked on.

The music emanating from the camp could be described as nothing less than ecstatic. Driven by frenzied beats and sustained by soaring melodies, the song made Ara's toes drum in her boots. Cloud's ears flicked back and forth, and he began to prance, likewise compelled by the lively tune. Teth brought Dusk alongside Cloud, and both geldings tossed their heads in time with the music.

"Do you think if I dropped the reins, he'd spin around in circles?" Ara asked Teth, laughing.

"I'd wager he would."

Cloud lifted his head and gave a high, piercing whinny. Dusk kicked up his back hooves.

"They agree with you," said Ara.

When the riders rounded a bend in the road, the music became an accompaniment to a riotous scene. Five wagons formed a semicircle in a broad swath of grass to one side of the road. Two of the wagons had been opened, side doors swinging outward and platforms erected before them creating a stage. One of the stages was occupied by musicians. The other stood empty.

The roaring bonfire was one of the largest Ara had ever seen, its flames spiking to the heights of nearby trees. Men, women, and children danced around the fire, laughing and shouting. All were dressed in vibrant colors. Long coats that flared out, light layered skirts that floated as they spun. The camp was like a gathering of Saetlund's people writ small. Ara saw faces that were ice pale, deep olive, sun-touched gold; in shades of the earth ranging from sienna to ebon, proving that those who heard Eni's call hailed from every province in the kingdom.

Teth swung down from Dusk. "Wait here. I'll make our presence known. It's best to have an official invitation before we settle in."

"I thought they loved visitors," Nimhea muttered.

The trio watched Teth approach a group near a smaller fire over which a roasting goat turned on a spit. The conversation was short, and Teth walked back with a bit of jaunt in his step.

"We'll tether the horses near their wagon horses," Teth said. "They're delighted to have dinner guests."

"Wonderful!" Eamon had been soaking in the music and mood of the camp. He was obviously ecstatic about spending the evening with Eni's Children.

As they tethered their horses, Nimhea took Ara aside.

"Have you encountered Eni's Children before?" she asked in a low voice.

"A caravan came to Rill's Pass once," Ara told her. "But it was years ago. I begged my grandmother to let me watch them. I had to hide under blankets in a wagon so I wouldn't be seen. What I remember most is how much I loved their music and dances."

Nimhea's lips pressed into a thin line. "I trust Teth, but I can't help feeling that stopping here is unwise. Can we really believe none of them have become loyal to the Vokkans? It's been fifteen years. The past fades. Loyalties shift."

"I understand your concern," Ara said. "But Teth has traveled more than any of us. He knows what he's doing."

Nimhea made an ambiguous sound and looked away.

Ara made another effort. "Eamon seems happy to be here."

"*Shockingly*, he's read about Eni's Children," Nimhea said with a little laugh. "I'm sure he can't wait to see how the real thing compares to his studies."

Ara laughed, too. "He is predictable that way."

"Is is true that all Eni's Children do is travel?" Nimhea hung her bridle on a low branch.

When Ara nodded, Nimhea shook her head.

"Don't they want a real home?" Nimhea asked.

"What I've been told is that the road is their true home," Ara replied. "That's what makes them Eni's people. Eni is the god of travelers and journeys."

"It's so strange." Nimhea fell in step with Ara as they made their way to the camp. "My whole life I've longed to live in my real home. I've been imagining the palace in Five Rivers for as long as I remember."

Ara glanced at the princess and saw that worry had left Nimhea's face and she now wore a thoughtful expression.

"That makes sense," Ara said to her. "More than anything else you were told how important your legacy is, and returning to Saetlund is at the heart of that legacy."

Teth and Eamon, the most eager of their foursome, had already found seats beside the smaller fire and were being handed plates heaped with food.

"It does smell scrumptious," Nimhea admitted.

Ara grabbed Nimhea's hand. "I'm starving!"

They ran to join the boys.

"Ara, Mea!" Teth set his plate aside and stood up. "Let me introduce you to our hosts."

"Mea?" Nimhea asked, all the while keeping a wide smile on her face.

"Just go with it," Teth murmured.

Teth brought them to an older woman and man who were savoring the roast and lounging on cushions.

"Hewa and Banir are the elders of this caravan," Teth explained.

Hewa was brown and wrinkled as a walnut. Her hair was a crown of silver braids. Banir's hair was dark, his skin olive, and likewise bore the lines of ages. They both had laughing eyes.

Ara knelt beside them and took Hewa's extended hand. "We're grateful for your hospitality."

"To share our bounty with guests is to honor Eni, who protects and blesses us," Hewa replied. Her voice had a warm, rich timbre that filled Ara with ease.

Banir smiled broadly. "Enjoy our food, our music, our fire. As long as you are here our home is your home."

Nimhea's voice was tremulous when she softly said, "That's very kind, sir."

Banir's laugh was a roar. "I'm no sir, young lady. Just an old man who's had a fine life."

"Thank you, Banir," said Nimhea with a bashful smile.

Ara managed to keep her mouth closed; otherwise she'd have been gaping at Nimhea. She'd never seen such demure behavior from the princess.

After their greetings were exchanged, Ara and Nimhea found seats of folded blankets near Teth and Eamon. No sooner had they reclined than their hosts appeared out of nowhere with plates overburdened by food. Ara's stomach had been complaining for the last hour, and she tore into the food like a ravenous wolf. The roast goat was succulent; the pickled vegetables served alongside the meat were blooms of flavor and spice. Ara couldn't remember a better meal.

Having eaten beyond her fill, Ara snuggled into the piled blankets to savor memories of the exquisite flavors and digest.

Teth had other ideas.

"Time to show me how much you've learned about balance," he announced, taking her hands and hauling her to her feet.

Ara laughed as he pulled her along until she realized he was towing her toward the ring of dancers surrounding the enormous fire.

"Oh no," Ara said. "I'll be sick. My belly is full to bursting."

"No excuses," Teth countered. "You haven't danced until you've danced with Eni's Children."

"I have danced with Eni's Children," Ara mused, though that dancing had only been in her imagination. As a little girl she'd been buried under blankets, peeking through the gaps in the wagon planks to watch the players, but her feet had ached to patter to the rhythms and her hands begged to clap along.

She'd been speaking to herself, not Teth, but he laughed.

"You haven't danced with me," he whispered hoarsely, suddenly pulling her close.

Ara's breath fled when her body pressed into Teth's. His eyes held hers and she desperately wished she could pull thoughts from his mind. Was his heart also racing? Was his blood as hot as the towering flames beside them, the way hers was?

"Are you ready?" Teth asked.

"For what?" Ara replied, her question honest.

Teth, whose expression had been full of mirth and mischief, hesitated. His hand came up, palm fitting to her jawline. His thumb followed the outline of her lips. Ara didn't know how she was still standing. Her bones had all melted.

They stayed like that for what was probably seconds, but felt like an eternity.

Then they were moving. Ara didn't know how their dance began, but her feet were flying. Her body twisted and spun as Teth guided her through the steps of an unfamiliar dance. She didn't stumble. She didn't balk. The drumbeats drove her on, teaching her the dance as she moved.

And Teth's hands were always there. Supporting her. Encouraging her. Never forcing. Never insisting. He let her unfold into the rhythm on her own.

It was glorious.

Ara had never felt so alive. As she danced, she was aware of everything around her. The heat of the fire. The rise of the flames. The laughter and shouts of the other dancers. The stars glimmering high above.

Without warning the music stopped. Ara and Teth stood like statues, ossified in the middle of their steps. Eni's Children began to clap, whooping and shouting their approval to the heavens.

Breathless, Ara asked. "What happens now?"

Teth held her against him, "What do you want to happen?"

Ara didn't know the answer, or rather, she did, but it wasn't possible. She wanted that moment to last forever. The warmth of Teth's body against hers. The way his hand curled around hers. The way he looked at her.

"I—" Ara somehow found her voice.

Suddenly silence fell all around them. The lingering energy of the drums stilled. The laughter of the other dancers vanished. A new feeling spilled over the camp. Anticipation. Even the massive bonfire seemed to quiet.

Teth let Ara go as they both turned to watch.

The stage the musicians vacated now held a lone woman. She wore a long-sleeved dress that wrapped around her torso and tied at the waist. The skirt of the dress flared out. In the firelight the Ara couldn't make out the color of the fabric, only that it was dark, as was the woman's hair.

All eyes were on her. Eni's Children held a collective breath, waiting.

The woman began to sing.

Her voice rose in a pure, lyric soprano that poured into the night. The ballad she sang was slow, mournful, and unlike any song Ara knew.

The fading time
When the moon goes dark
They fly away
As the moon goes dark
How long? How long? How far away?
Till the moonlight comes again.

Each note sank into Ara's bones. Though the words were unfamiliar, they made her throat close and her eyes prick, like she'd been touched with a sadness that was eternal.

She stole a glance at Teth to gauge his response. It was clear he'd been likewise captured by the song, but the tiniest pinching at the corners of his eyes told Ara he was also puzzled.

The musicians reappeared, forming a half ring around the singer.

They took up their instruments, offering harmonies when she began to sing again. This time she was not alone in her song. All Eni's Children sang with her.

"This would be a good time to make our exit," Teth whispered.

They found Nimhea and Eamon savoring a dessert of fresh berries. They were alone; the whole of Eni's Children were gathered around the stage lifting their voices with that of the woman.

"Is it time to go?" Nimhea asked.

"That's the idea," Teth replied.

"But this is so wonderful," Eamon protested. "I want to hear more of their songs."

"Another time," Teth said rather brusquely. "We should go."

Nimhea frowned at him. "Is something wrong?"

"It's probably nothing," Teth told her. "But let's get the horses."

Teth led them a few miles away from where Eni's Children camped. When they reached a crest of a hill, Ara could see lights in the towers of Oakvale's wall. To Ara, the city appeared enormous. A sprawling bulwark that stood between the forest of the Fjeri lowlands and the Midland steppes.

They set up camp in a glen another mile off the road. Ringed by oaks, it was an appealing place to pass the night. The stoic, watchful trees gave Ara an odd sense of security.

It was late, and having already eaten, the travelers needed no fire of their own.

Before they bid one another good night, Nimhea called the small group together.

"I want to know what troubled you at the camp," Nimhea said to Teth.

"As I said before, it was probably nothing," Teth replied. "But it was the song."

"What about the song?" Nimhea's forehead wrinkled

"They're ill advised to sing it," he told her. "That's a very old song, and it's forbidden."

"But that's why I was so excited to hear it," Eamon piped up. "I know the story behind the song. The fading of the gods. Why is it forbidden?"

"No song is officially forbidden," Teth said. "But all Eni's Children know that their verses about the gods can bring the wrath of the empire. Right after the conquest, when the Vokkan army was making its way through the provinces to subdue any lingering resistance, they encountered Eni's Children. Some of Fauld's wizards seized on the idea that Eni's Children could not be trusted because unlike the rest of Saetlund, they still clung to the ways and worship of the gods."

"What did they do?" asked Ara.

"Rumors began to circulate among the soldiers that Eni's Children were sorcerers and assassins," said Teth. "That their travel allowed them to evade any accusations of nefarious deeds. Caravans were seized. People imprisoned or killed. It's said that Zenar the Exalted, who's both the ArchWizard and Fauld's younger son, was about to decree the existence of Eni's Children illegal and disband all remaining groups. Individuals would have been forced to move to cities or villages or face execution."

"Someone stopped it," Nimhea suggested. "They must have. Who had the authority to overrule the ArchWizard of Vokk?"

"His brother," Teth replied. "Commander Liran, the elder of Fauld's sons. There are several versions of how it happened. The most oft-told and dramatic, which hints that it might lack accuracy, is that Liran was present when some caravans were being rounded up and escorted to Five Rivers. During their breaks on the road, Eni's Children would play and sing. According to the story, Liran was so moved by their music that he altered the decree. Eni's Children would be able to continue their itinerant lifestyle so long as they no longer sang or told stories related to the former gods of Saetlund and if they stopped at major cities to offer performances of songs praising the exploits of the Vokkan Empire, its history, its heroes, and most of all, Emperor Fauld."

"Wait," said Ara. "They're forced to perform?"

"Even the clothing and drapings on their wagons and stages aren't their own," Teth answered with a shake of his head. "The colors, the styles—all were designed to give Eni's Children a new identity as Imperial Players. Their origins were meant to fade with time, leaving only a traveling group of people who entertained the public and reminded the empire's citizens of the great legacy they were a part of."

He looked back wistfully in the direction of the camp. "What we witnessed tonight is rare. The music, the dancing, it was all for their own enjoyment. It was a glimpse of who they really are. They're likely on their way to Oakvale, where they'll hold performances for a week before moving on. Were you to watch one you'd see how different it is."

What had been blurry but happy memories of the Imperial Players' stop in Rill's Pass were soured.

"The decree was over a decade ago," Teth continued. "But the Below's intelligence makes it clear that Eni's Children continue to be a contentious subject between the imperial brothers. Eni's Children are known to be especially cautious of the plays they perform and the songs they sing because the ArchWizard still presents a threat."

"Then why?" Eamon asked, bewildered. "Why would they be singing that song?"

Teth shook his head. "I have no idea. But I didn't think it wise for us to linger."

"Agreed." Nimhea offered a tight but encouraging smile. "We should seek our beds. Tomorrow we hunt a caravan."

"That's a fine way to put it," Teth said with a light laugh. "Good night then."

Eamon and Nimhea offered their good nights. When they were tucked into their tents, Ara's heart beat faster. The thrill of her dance with Teth simmered at the edges of her mind, but what she'd learned about Eni's Children troubled her deeply. She didn't know if it was right to stay with Teth, hoping for what started with the dance to continue.

"Ara," Teth said softly.

She heard her name on his lips and sent a silent wish to the stars that Teth would convince her not to sleep just yet.

Ara could barely see his face in the darkness.

"Sleep well."

Disappointment was a fist in her stomach, but she said, "You too."

❈ ELSEWHERE: The Sending ❈

he initiates were nervous. They stank of fear, and the elders wanted to spit on them for their cowardice. At the behest of their emperor, the wizards had newly invited a handful of young men and a few women into their ranks. The elders resented the command, each loath to dilute their individual power. Fauld the Ever-Living, who had the greatest magic of all, would never share his gift. That made his wizards all the more infuriated that the emperor demand they give away theirs.

There were some sly smiles among them, despite their sour mood. The ritual to be performed was taxing, demanding a union of will, spirit, and malice. Should an initiate falter amid the work, there would be consequences. If the right sequence of events fell into place, it could prove delightful.

Elder Byrtid stood on a dais with four of her peers flanking her, two on each side. The ten initiates stood in a semicircle facing the elders. The novices and elders not participating in the ritual kept watch from alcoves and balconies that looked down on the chamber.

Byrtid took a ceramic vessel in her hands, and the chamber fell silent. She began to chant. The initiates echoed her words. One by one she tossed the elements demanded by the ritual to the center of the semicircle. First, the pelt. Then, the bones. The teeth. Finally, the earth.

The chamber shook, and the iron chandelier hanging above the initiates began to sway. From the corners of their eyes, they glimpsed shadows. Shadows that chased one another around the room. With the shadows came snarls. The hot breath of unknown creatures touched their ankles and elbows. Snapping teeth closed just shy of their calves.

A few of the initiates began to glance around, still chanting, but trying to follow the shadows that never took full form. Beads of sweat formed upon their brows. One of their number began to trip over the strange words of the chant.

The watchers leaned forward.

The initiate whose chant fell out of rhythm with the others now felt the brush of wiry hair against his shins. He'd been told time and time again not to move after a ritual had begun, but he swore a muzzle had pressed against his low back. When a rough, wet tongue tasted his palm, he shrieked, abandoning the chant altogether.

The chamber floor rumbled with the power of the spell. The frightened initiate stumbled and fell into the center of the room atop the earth, the teeth, the bones, the pelt.

Snarls filled the chamber. Claws rasped against the stone floor. The fallen man began to scream. He reached toward his peers, first begging for help, then mercy.

The remaining initiates kept their eyes on Elder Byrtid, who was shouting now. Their chorus swelled until they could no longer hear the man's screams. Byrtid raised the vessel over her head then threw it to the center of the circle, where it shattered.

The chanting stopped and was replaced by howls that rose until the initiates thought their ears would bleed. Then silence.

Elder Byrtid bowed her head and led the other elders from the chamber. The initiates filed out after them. The last to leave were the watchers, who permitted themselves to gaze a bit longer on what was left of the forsaken initiate. Pieces of flesh, gobs of gore, splashes of blood. They had witnessed his body ripped apart by beasts none of them could see, called forth from a place of which none of them dared speak.

13

he first howl startled Ara out of her blankets. When it was followed by a second baleful cry, her surprise and confusion became something visceral. Fear with spikes. The others had woken at the sounds and scrambled from their tents, Teth bearing a hooded lantern.

"Wolves?" Nimhea asked.

Teth had his head cocked, listening. A third howl came.

"That doesn't sound like any wolf howl I've heard," Teth told her. "And we're too far south for the forest and mountain packs, but too far north for the desert packs."

"If not wolves then what?" Eamon's eyes were wide.

With a frustrated grunt, Teth said, "I don't know."

A fourth howl sounded, long and hollow. It hung in the night sky, making the hair on Ara's arms stand up.

Teth slung his quiver over his shoulder and picked up his bow. "But we need to leave the camp now. Leave everything but your weapons."

Hearing the admonition, Eamon half turned his body toward his pack, filled with books and scrolls. "But—"

"No." Teth's face hardened. Within those carved lines, Ara saw something else flickering that she recognized as fear—an emotion she'd never witnessed in Teth. Her belly filled with stones.

The moment they were all ready, Teth said, "This way."

Running at a steady, straining pace, they followed Teth out of the glen.

"What about the horses?" Ara asked. The thought of leaving Cloud and Dust to face wolves on their own made her ill.

"We're leaving for the sake of the horses." Teth shot her a knowing glance. "If we draw the wolves away from camp, we can fight them off on the road. If the horses are in the mix, there's too much chance one of our mounts will be injured."

"So that's why you're leading us toward the howls," Nimhea said drily.

Teth offered the princess a grim smile.

"Oh dear," said Eamon. He carried a short-sword that Ara doubted he knew how to use effectively. "Oh dear, oh dear."

When they reached the road Teth opened the lantern's hood, bathing their group in light.

The howls sounded more frequently and were much closer. Teth had been right. These weren't wolf howls. When Ara heard the calls of mountain wolves, they would sometimes make her shiver, but it was in wonder. The calls pressing on them now didn't have the songlike character of wolves. These howls had a rough but shrieking quality that made Ara's insides curdle. She gripped her stave, wishing she were farther along in her lessons.

Grating, piercing, the beasts' cries seemed to be all around them, but wherever Ara looked she found no sign of the animals.

All at once there was silence more terrible than the howls.

"Form a circle," Nimhea ordered. "Face out, shoulder to shoulder."

Ara stood between Nimhea and Teth, Eamon at her back.

"Where are they?" Eamon's voice trembled. "Why did they stop?"

Within the trees, Ara noticed lights flickering. Coming closer. Moving in pairs. Burning like hot coals, one set of lights stopped moving at the tree line opposite Ara.

"Nava's mercy," Ara breathed.

Eyes. The burning lights were eyes, and they were staring at her.

"I see them," Teth murmured.

What stepped out of the forest into the lantern light did not belong in Saetlund or in the natural world. An awful amalgam of dog and wild boar, the creatures were the size of wolfhounds. They had long legs and stout bodies. Tufted ears crowned their blockish heads, and what resembled both a muzzle and a snout sprouted from the center of their faces. Tusks jutted from their mandibles.

Despite such terrible features, the most alarming thing about the beasts was the absence of flesh. Their bodies undulated and flickered, dark and ethereal. Smoke swirled around their legs, rose from their backs and their burning eyes.

"No," Teth uttered, his whisper petrified.

"What are they?" Ara's voice cracked.

Eamon's answer was remarkably calm, his tone almost curious. "Shadow hounds."

More of the beasts stalked out of the woods. A dozen. They began to circle their prey.

"What do we do?" Nimhea hissed.

"There's nothing we can do." Teth swore under his breath. "If the stories are true."

"I don't understand." Ara felt the tension in his upper arm pressing against her shoulder.

Eamon's whisper came in answer. "In accounts of the shadow hounds, the beasts are truly made of shadows. They can't attack us or bite us, but if they pass through us the wizards receive a vision of exactly who and where we are. They can then use that vision to continue to track us. It's a linking spell cast using the hounds as proxy. Vokk's wizards can deploy it from great distances."

"Did it say anything in your books about how to fight them?" Nimhea snapped.

"Yes."

Hope flared in Ara's chest.

"But nothing we have at hand will work," Eamon finished. With a sigh, he added, "At least they won't hurt us."

"Giving the wizards a window into our every move hurts us," Teth snarled.

"I know, but—"

Eamon was cut off by a series of yips and a keening cry. A small creature dashed out of the woods, between the pacing shadow hounds, and began racing in circles around their tightly clustered group.

"Fox?" Teth gasped.

Fox continued to run in circles but turned its face to gekker stuttering screeches at the shadow hounds. Fox's screeches made the hounds snarl and bark, but they moved no closer.

"What is it doing?" Nimhea asked.

"I have no idea," Teth replied.

Fox stopped in front of Teth to crouch down, its tail brushing Teth's feet. The circle of hounds broke as all of the beasts bore down on Fox. Fox bared its teeth and held its ground.

As Fox screamed its displeasure at the hounds, another startling light caught Ara's eye. A person silhouetted by a swirling, golden nimbus was coming down the road. The stranger approached from the direction opposite the snarling, slavering hounds.

"State your purpose!" Nimhea commanded.

The heavily cloaked stranger stopped just beyond the reach of Nimhea's sword. They didn't reply, but spread their arms wide and turned their palms up. The nimbus that surrounded the stranger brightened and grew. The light spread forward. Nimhea gasped as it flowed over her. When the shimmering gold touched Ara, it tickled, and she had the ridiculous impulse to laugh and smile.

"What's happening?" Teth jumped as the nimbus engulfed him.

The golden, glimmering light spread outward and upward until it formed a dome around them. Ara gazed in wonder at the swirling barrier, and her eyes widened.

"Fireflies," Ara whispered. "It's fireflies."

"How is that possible?" Nimhea murmured.

Fox turned away from the hounds and jumped up to put its front paws on Teth's legs. Fox pressed its nose briefly against Teth's hand then raced out of the dome and into the woods, disappearing as suddenly as it had arrived.

"Fox!" Teth called.

The shadow hounds didn't give chase when Fox fled. They lifted their muzzles and bayed at the sky, triumphant. Moving as one, they charged at Teth. He loosed an arrow that passed right through its mark. With a sigh of resignation, Teth lowered his bow.

The hounds leapt, mouths gaping, and though Ara knew they wouldn't physically touch her, she couldn't fight the instinct to shut her eyes and brace herself.

A flood of sharp crackling and pained yelps snapped her eyes wide. She glimpsed a shadow hound midleap hitting the dome of light and sizzling into a cloud of steam. All the other hounds were gone.

The dome began to lift. Swirling fireflies rose into the sky, higher and higher, as if they planned to join the stars. Only the lantern light remained.

Nimhea's sword arm was shaking, but she demanded of the stranger, "What was that?"

"Help," the stranger answered. "One should always help one's companions if able."

When the stranger pushed back their hood, Ara drew a sharp breath. Standing before them was the singer from the camp.

"I am Lahvja," she said. "And the time has come for me to join your quest."

The four travelers were so dumbfounded that when Lahvja ordered them back to their camp and to the beds to sleep, they obeyed mutely. To Ara, the entire episode felt like a dream. She went to sleep believing it probably was.

But when she stepped out of her tent the next morning, Lahvja puttered around a campfire preparing a breakfast of stewed fruits and hearty baked rolls. In the sunlight Ara could see that Lahvja was young, no more than a handful of years older than Ara. Ornate silver combs kept her wealth of lustrous black hair from her face, its length falling in waves down her back. She had deep olive skin and a softly curving body. Her dress was pale blue and the same wrapped style as she'd been wearing the night before.

"Good morning, Ara," Lahvja said.

"You know my name." Ara took the bowl of fruit and warm roll Lahvja offered.

Smiling, Lahvja answered, "You seek your legacy, the gift of the Loresmith. A long journey lies ahead."

"It's already been long," said Ara. The day she'd left Rill's Pass felt like a lifetime ago. "How do you know who I am?"

"I am a servant of the gods," Lahvja replied. "I do as they bid, and they bid me join you."

Teth staggered out of his tent, indulging in a long yawn and languid stretch. When he noticed Lahvja at the campfire, he immediately tensed.

"Good morning, Prince of Thieves." Lahvja spooned fruit into another bowl. "Break your fast with us."

Warily Teth accepted the bowl and bread before sitting beside Ara.

"No one has ever called me that," Teth said a bit tartly. "Who are you?"

"You're the son of a king," Lahvja quipped. "That makes you a prince."

Teth frowned. "I still need an answer."

Lahvja looked directly at Teth. Her eyes were lavender gray and piercing.

"It's best if we wait for the twins," she told him. "They'll be here soon enough."

No sooner had the words passed her lips than a bleary-eyed Eamon came out of his tent, blinking at the light. Nimhea emerged a moment later, her usual composed self. Both of them startled when they saw Lahvja.

Eamon bumbled over, looking confused but curious. Nimhea approached cautiously.

"Scholar." Lahvja smiled warmly at Eamon. Then she curtsied gracefully. "Princess."

Nimhea glanced at Ara with alarm.

"You seem to know all of us," Ara said to Lahvja. To be polite Ara put a spoonful of stewed fruit in her mouth and almost swooned at the velvet texture and spices that wrapped around her tongue. "This is absolutely delicious."

"Thank you, Ara." Lahvja offered breakfast to Eamon and Nimhea. "As for knowing you, I was told you were coming."

Nimhea accepted the bowl of fruit and warm bread, but Eamon declined.

"Am I the only one who went to bed thinking all of last night was a dream?" Teth asked, though he tore of a chunk of the roll Lahvja had given him and chewed it contentedly. His brows rose slightly, and he shook the roll at Lahvja. "Very good!"

Her answering smile was serene. "Thank you."

"I thought it was a dream, too," Ara answered Teth.

Nimhea continued to stand, while Eamon sat at Ara's other side.

"I was inclined to believe it a dream, as well," Nimhea said. She eyed Teth critically. "You seem awfully calm after finding out last night was real."

"I trust her for the moment." Teth shrugged. "She saved us, after all . . . Plus, breakfast."

Eamon was shaking his head. He looked at Lahvja with narrowed eyes. "Except for how they were driven away. Are you some kind of sorceress?"

"There are too many words that try to name people with gifts like mine," said Lahvja. "But you may think of me as a Summoner."

"Ugh." Teth put his roll aside. "You bring back the dead."

"That's a necromancer," Eamon said in a short voice. "Summoners commune with spirits of all kinds."

Lahvja nodded. "I can speak with the dead, though I'm rarely called upon to do so. Calm your stomach, Teth, I do not trade in bodies."

"Well, that's something of a relief." Teth picked up his roll again and dunked it in the stewed fruit.

"How do we know you're a friend?" Eamon demanded. His arms were tight across his chest.

"Perhaps it will reassure you to know a trusted friend brought me to your aid last night," Lahvja replied, delight dancing in her eyes.

With a yip, Fox ran into their camp, paused to stick its nose into Teth's unguarded bowl, then continued to run until it stopped in front of Lahvja. She held out her arms and Fox leapt into them. Lahvja sat down and Fox snuggled into her lap while licking fruit juice from its muzzle.

"So that's how it is, eh?" Teth said to Fox. "You steal from me and I don't even get a proper hello."

Fox left Lahvja's lap, trotted over to Teth, and gave a loud, screechy bark in the thief's face.

"I guess that's what I asked for," Teth muttered, but smiled when Fox crawled into his lap. He also pretended not to notice when Fox continued to drink fruit juice from his breakfast bowl.

"How did you know Fox was our friend?" Ara asked.

"As I said, I don't often commune with the dead," Lahvja answered. "But I frequently commune with nature. Fox told me you were in danger."

"Where have you been all this time?" Teth scratched behind Fox's ears.

"Fox has been keeping an eye on you," Lahvja told him. "Albeit from a distance."

Ara looked at Lahvja in amazement. "You summoned the fireflies that protected us."

"They weren't precisely fireflies," Lahvja replied with a kind smile. "You're right in that I summoned spirits of nature to drive the hounds away." Her face clouded. "Awful things, those shadow hounds. They belong to another realm, and their presence causes a great dissonance with nature. It can be used against them."

"We appreciate your coming to the rescue," said Teth. "And if Fox wants you here, I have no objections. Anyone else?"

"All that's happened speaks to the necessity of your presence," Nimhea said. "I welcome you."

"So do I." Ara thought Lahvja's words, bearing, and actions demonstrated that the Summoner was wise and powerful, but also kind.

"Eamon?" Teth looked over to where Eamon sat, wearing a sulky expression.

Eamon made a grunting noise more ambivalent than affirmative. His behavior was so out of character, Ara wondered what had come over him.

"It's settled then," Teth announced. "Huzzah to our new companion!"

With a huff, Eamon got up and trudged back to his tent.

Nimhea frowned and said to Lahvja, "I apologize for my brother. This is so unlike him. I'm sure he's simply unsettled after last night."

"I'm sure," Lahvja murmured in reply, but her eyes were on Eamon's tent, and Ara could have sworn what she saw in that gaze was regret.

❊ ELSEWHERE: MEDDLING GODS ❊

lder Tich stepped aside to give the guards room enough to drag the body from the Exalted's study. The bearers of bad news never knew that an elder always followed close behind. It was usually Tich. He'd developed a reputation for his deft handling of the prince's moods. While not entirely without fear, Tich entered the study confidently. Once the initial outburst had passed, the danger of an attack was significantly lessened. Zenar could be temperamental, and didn't bother to learn any of the novices' names, but he valued those among his wizards who advanced to Elder status. The prince wasn't reckless with his most powerful adherents' lives.

"I thought the point of observation was to stave off pitfalls like this," Prince Zenar said as Tich approached.

Zenar the Exalted had straw-blond hair that fell to his shoulders. His decision to wear it severely pulled back at the nape of his neck made him look far older than his thirty years. With the exception of ceremonies, Zenar forsook the dark robes of Vokk's wizards for a wardrobe befitting his royal station. He'd chosen an ivory linen shirt and black suede trousers, over which he donned a sleeveless coat of emerald green silk embroidered with silver thread. None of the Vokkan royalty wore crowns, but Zenar favored a silver talisman in the shape of a dagger with a hooked blade that rested above his heart. Elder Tich knew the talisman to be wrapped with enchantments, but he could only guess what spells hung from the prince's neck.

Zenar gestured to a high-backed chair opposite his broad desk of the same polished ebony as the doors. Tich sat, and Zenar proceeded to fill a crystal goblet with water. The prince opened a tall cabinet behind the desk and selected a small glass vial containing a viscous blue substance. Measuring two careful drops, Zenar swirled the liquid in the goblet until it was the color of a summer sky.

The prince arched one eyebrow at Tich. "Care to join me?"

"Another time," Tich answered with a placid smile.

With a knowing laugh, Zenar tipped his head back and drained the goblet in a single gulp. On one occasion alone Tich had taken one of Zenar's concoctions. Whatever had been in that glass chased his mind to places he had never imagined and never wanted to visit again.

The elder wizard knew that his demurring from these libations signaled a kind of weakness to the prince, but Tich preferred his sanity to petty impressions. He'd known wizards who valued the latter. Some of them still shrieked and gibbered in the cells beneath the temple.

Zenar's eyes were closed. He had settled into the seat at his desk. His arms were outstretched. He flexed and unflexed his fingers like talons. After a long, blissful sigh, he looked at Tich.

"I feel much better."

Tich inclined his head. "I'm pleased to hear that, your highness."

"This newcomer." Zenar drummed his fingers on the polished wood. "How much of a threat does she represent?"

"Hard to say," Tich admitted. "Her ability to deflect our hounds shows power, but if that is the extent of her abilities she is but a flea."

Leaning back in his seat, Zenar observed, "She's another youth. The third who somehow escaped the Embrace to now join our travelers."

"I noticed that as well, your highness." Tich spoke carefully. The prince was leading him along a dangerous path. "It is possible . . ." The elder shifted in his chair. "That there has been meddling we did not foresee."

"Meddling by whom?" The question sounded innocent, but Tich knew better.

"Your highness will not like my suggestion." Hedging was a risk, but seemed safer than assertions.

"Pah!" Zenar wiped his mouth with his hand, as if he'd tasted something foul. "You believe *their* gods have arranged it to be so?"

Tich raised his palms in supplication. "Mere speculation, Exalted."

Zenar nodded, but his face was troubled. "I wonder . . ." The prince's expression cleared abruptly. "I must give your idea further consideration. For now, continue your observations and reports."

"As you command." Tich hid his relief. For a moment he had been certain he'd gone too far.

He quickly bowed and went to the door as swiftly as he could without the appearance of fleeing.

"One more thing, Elder."

Tich's hand was on the door pull. Without letting it go, he looked back at the prince. Zenar carried a covered basket to a gray velvet couch near the study's fireplace. Tich could hear dry susurrations coming from within the basket.

"Send me one of the novices." Zenar placed the basket on the couch, and the rustling sounds became more frequent. "I'll need assistance working through my thoughts."

14

he wagons creaked in the ruts of the southern road. On either side of the road an endless sea of grass undulated. The sky above was likewise endless. An expanse of blue that curved to each corner of the earth, revealing the rounded shape of the world. When Ara first set eyes on the Daefritian plains the landscape made her dizzy. No trees or mountains disturbed the horizon. What little variation appeared came in the form of small herds of cattle or horses who only sometimes looked up when the line of wagons passed.

Ara did not enjoy travel by caravan. The wagons moved at a tediously slow pace. Even when crossing difficult terrain, Ara and her friends had managed a swifter speed. Now the ground was flat, the road straight, and yet the caravan could only trudge along. Ara had taken to grinding her teeth too often, and her jaw ached.

Their winding journey through the Midland steppes had been uneventful. Passing most of their days in the two private wagons Teth had rented, Ara had at first enjoyed gazing up at the bands of color that wrapped around the steep hills. Once they reached the grasslands, however, it took only a matter of hours for the scenery to become rather bland.

Teth had hired the wagons to give them shelter each night while saving them from setting up camp. Ara wished he hadn't. Setting up camp would at least give her something to do. Fox apparently shared Ara's opinion of caravans and had made itself scarce from the moment they joined the wagons. The rest of her companions adjusted to caravan life in their own ways. Eamon was happy enough to spend day and night in the wagon with his books. Nimhea split her time between keeping her brother company and stretching her limbs by walking alongside the caravan. Lahvja disappeared for large portions of the day, devoting her energies to walking up and down the length of this snake made of carts and wagons. She returned each night for dinner, and with each evening conversation, Lahvja ingratiated herself with their small company.

It helped that Eamon's inexplicable anger toward Lahvja had vanished. He'd done the same thing before. It was a strength of Eamon's, Ara thought, that he could shrug off whatever had troubled him in a particular moment and become his affable self once more. He engaged the Summoner as often as anyone else, and he raised questions about her mysterious art that Ara would never have thought to ask.

"Have you always had your powers?" Eamon swiped his sleeve over his chin.

That evening Lahvja had prepared two chickens, which she'd purchased from another trader in the caravan. She'd cooked the chicken with aromatic herbs by burying a small clay oven in burning coals. It was so good, no one spoke until all of it had been devoured.

Lahvja smiled as she poured cups of ginger and blackberry tea. "I was aware at a very young age that I could see and hear things others couldn't. The elders of my caravan learned of it when I was ten, and I was sent to another caravan to apprentice with a master Summoner. For five years I steeped myself in the natural world, learning to commune with spirits and wild creatures. When I turned fifteen my teacher declared me a true Summoner in my own right. I traveled for another year, seeking a new home, until I joined the caravan you met outside Oakvale."

"I've long been curious about the art of summoning," Eamon told her when she handed him a cup of tea. "But there are surprisingly few texts on that branch of magic, and none of them are instructional."

"With good reason," Lahvja replied as Ara accepted a cup from her. "Summoning cannot be learned from books; it comes from within. It is a spark that lives in a person's spirit. With the right teacher, that spark will become a blazing fire."

"Like your rabbit stew," Teth quipped, taking a sip of his tea.

They all laughed, and Lahvja grinned. Her cuisine could be wickedly spicy. Fortunately her teas cooled the tongue and settled the stomach.

Eamon made a frustrated sound. "But you must be able to read instructions somewhere."

"Even if there was a scroll or book with descriptions of the practice, it would do no good." Lahvja settled beside the fire and poured her own cup of tea. "Summoning is manifesting one's own spirit and loosing it into the world. Without guidance a novice could easily turn oneself into a wild creature or become lost in the spirit world."

Nimhea, who was sharpening her sword, asked, "Will you always be able to protect us from the wizards' magic?"

"I wish it were otherwise, but no," Lahvja replied. Her eyes grew troubled. "They've gathered so many forms of magic through their conquests that I cannot hope to counter all of their spells."

"What do you mean 'through their conquests'?" Ara asked.

Teth followed with, "And how come they have many forms of magic and you only have one? That hardly seems fair."

The grim cast of Lahvja's face gave way to laughter. "The answer to your questions is the same. The Wizards of Vokk take their magic. They pore over tomes and scrolls, searching for sources of power, and when found they will wring magic from that source until they've drunk every drop it had to give. When they encounter a people that have magic, but no books, they draw the magic directly from those with power. I have no idea how they're able to do so. As the Vokkan Empire consumed the world, the wizards devoured its magics. Fauld's wizards are mirrors of their god's greed."

"What terrible power they have," Eamon murmured.

"Their crimes do not end there, for their greed is a jealous greed," said Lahvja, wrapping her cloak more tightly around her body. "Once the wizards have taken all they can of a culture's magic, they go on to destroy all evidence and knowledge of those mysteries. They demolished Saetlund's shrines quickly, because it was easy to do. The libraries at Zyre and Isar, however, have survived because it will take Vokk's wizards decades to consume the vast knowledge in those archives."

"That's why the wizards destroyed Saetlund's shrines," Ara said softly to herself, remembering the ruin that was Teth's hideout. "To prevent anyone in the future from seeking knowledge of the gods."

"You believe that?" Eamon asked Lahvja in a sickened voice. "That they'll raze the library?"

"More likely both universities," Lahvja answered, steel in her eyes. "They've already reassigned scholars of the arcane and esoteric to positions within the Temple of Vokk. Those who've refused have been publicly executed, or they simply disappeared."

Eamon shrank back against the stump, curling into himself; even the imagined loss of centuries of scholarship devastated him.

Lahvja kept her eyes on him; her face was calm, but her gaze verged on interrogative—yet she stayed silent.

"Do they hoard all of this magic because they never had magic of their own?" Ara asked.

"No," said Lahvja. "Their own magic is their most closely guarded secret. No one has discovered its origins or what type of power it is."

"They use stolen magics and hide their own." Nimhea held up her blade to judge its sharpness. "That's quite churlish of them."

Teth snickered. "The Wizards of Vokk aren't known for their gallantry."

"The hounds that hunted you were not Vokkan magic," Lahvja told them, ignoring their banter. "They were stolen from the Bridden people, who created the shadows hounds to seek any who were lost."

After a long sigh, Lahvja said, "Not only do the wizards steal magic, they twist and mangle it to serve their own purpose."

"How is that possible?" Eamon leaned in, rapt with interest.

"Magic is simply power." Lahvja gestured to Nimhea. "Like your sister's sword arm. Power itself is neutral, but it can be used for good or evil. Nimhea has chosen to strike with her sword in the service of redemption and justice. She could have also raised her weapon in tyranny. A choice lies in each use of power; in such choices we sculpt our fates."

Teth snorted with incredulity. "I thought the whole point of fate was its finality. To resist one's fate is always futile, and such and such. I find the idea rather tiring."

"Fate isn't static," Lahvja answered in a solemn voice. "Fate is fluid. Its shape changes with every decision a person makes. At every crossroads infinite fates exist. People claim fate cannot be altered because it spares them responsibility for the choices they make. But they are lying to themselves. The map of one's fate isn't drawn until that person returns to our Mother."

"How are mothers involved?" Teth guffawed. "You lost me."

With chiming laughter, Lahvja said, "Not mothers. The first Mother: the universe. Mother of all life, even the gods. The universe is the source of all mysteries. I could not be a Summoner without calling upon the wisdom of the Mother."

The rest of them stared at her, stunned by this revelation.

Teth rubbed his eyes. "That's a bit too philosophical for my taste. But I have a different question for you."

"Please," said Lahvja.

"So the hounds were stolen magic that the Vokkans used to hunt us." Teth rested his forearms on his knees. "But how did they find us?"

"That's what the hounds were for," Nimhea answered.

"Yes," Teth replied. "But how did they know where to look?"

Ara and Nimhea exchanged a troubled glance.

"The only way I can think is that the wizards loosed hundreds of those things all across Saetlund and hoped to get lucky," said Teth. He looked at Lahvja. "Is that what they did?"

"No," she answered. "Bringing forth shadow hounds is a compli- cated ritual, and the hounds themselves aren't easy for the wizards to control. They don't like serving the Vokkans."

Teth grumbled and threw a rock into the fire. "Then I don't under- stand how they knew where to look."

"Do you know?" Nimhea asked Lahvja.

"I can give you no answer," Lahvja said in a sad voice.

Eamon, who'd been silent for some time, spoke up. "Do you think only the wicked seek knowledge from books and scrolls?" He didn't look at Lahvja after asking the question.

Ara gazed at him with curiosity, surprised by the abrupt shift in subject.

"Like power, knowledge itself is neither good nor evil, but can be used for either," Lahvja, who didn't seem surprised at all, told him. "As I said, a person's choices chart the course of their fate."

Sliding her sword into its scabbard, Nimhea said, "I'm quite fond of that idea."

Lahvja smiled at her. "That doesn't surprise me."

"I'm very tired." Eamon used the wagon to pull himself to his feet. "I think I'll go to bed now."

"I'm right behind," said Teth. "I just hope I don't dream about those hounds. I've been doing my best to not remember what they looked like."

When the boys were gone, Lahvja turned to Nimhea.

"This journey has brought great strain upon your brother."

"He doesn't have a strong constitution to begin with." Nimhea pursed her lips. "I worry about him."

Lahvja placed her hand atop Nimhea's. "The bond between you is very powerful."

"I've never thought of it in those terms." Nimhea gave Lahvja a quizzical look. "Sometimes I wish he'd stayed in the Ethrian Isles, where he'd be safe instead of having to endure this journey. But I also know I couldn't see this through without him by my side."

"You're capable of more than you imagine," Lahvja murmured.

Ara noticed that Nimhea had turned her palm over so she could hold Lahvja's hand. She also noticed the way Lahvja's gaze lingered on Nimhea's face.

"I'll say good night then." Ara got to her feet.

The princess and the Summoner wished Ara sound sleep. She hurried to the wagon in which she slept, climbed into her bunk, and buried her face in blankets, overcome by a fit of childish giggles. When she got hold of herself, Ara stared at the ceiling and couldn't stop smiling. It might have been nothing, or it might have been something. Either way Ara took comfort in knowing she wasn't the only one tangled up in unexpected attraction.

The next morning Teth waylaid Ara before breakfast.

"Good morning." He sat in the back opening of the wagon, swinging his legs.

Ara had been musing over what she'd seen at the campfire and feeling embarrassed that she'd made too much of a small thing. Or she was projecting her own confused emotions on her companions.

When Teth called to her, in the middle of these thoughts, a fiery blush rushed onto her cheeks.

"Yes?" Ara considered freeing her hair from its usual tie in the hope of hiding her face.

"The horses are restless." Teth hopped down from the back of the wagon. "Let's go for a ride."

If he'd noticed her flaming cheeks, he didn't mention it, and Ara was happy to turn her attention to something else.

"Let's."

It was obvious that Cloud and Dust detested the plodding pace of the caravan. When they spotted Ara and Teth carrying saddles, the horses began to snort and prance.

"I'll hold the horses while you saddle them." Teth untied the horses from the wagon. Cloud reared immediately. Dust kicked out his back legs and gave a reprimanding whinny.

"Yes, yes," Teth said. "Your complaint is noted."

Saddling frisky, impatient horses was no easy feat.

"If you don't keep still we're not going anywhere," Ara said through gritted teeth as Cloud pranced away from his saddle for the third time.

When both horses were finally saddled and bridled, they were quivering with excitement.

"Be careful when you mount and hang on," Teth warned. "They're both going to want to take off."

"I already noticed that," said Ara.

Teth swung up onto Dust's back. *"Whoa!"* Dust charged forward, throwing clods of dirt into the air.

Ara watched as he galloped away with Teth only halfway in the saddle.

She sighed as she watched Cloud's envious gaze follow horse and unfortunate rider.

"Cloud." Ara took a firm grip on the bridle and pointed at Dust. "If that happens to me I will be very, very cross. I promise that you can run, but please wait until I'm properly in my saddle. I'll let you run as fast as you want if you'll stay still for me."

Cloud blew warm breath onto her shoulder and whickered.

"I hope that means yes."

Holding her breath, Ara grabbed a fistful of Cloud's mane and climbed into the saddle. She tensed up, waiting for Cloud to explode beneath her. But the gelding stood in place, muscles trembling. Ara let her breath ease out as her feet found the stirrups.

"Thank you." She patted Cloud's neck. "I'm almost ready."

Ara made sure she was balanced in the saddle. "Let's go."

Her heels had barely touched Cloud's sides when he shuddered and then barreled forward.

It was lucky that Ara hadn't let go of Cloud's mane, else she would have been on the ground with a very sore behind. Clinging to mane with one hand and reins with the other, Ara gripped Cloud's body with her thighs and tried to adjust to this shock of speed. Cloud streaked through the tall grass, and wind pulled tears from Ara's eyes. She decided she had the most control if she leaned forward with her torso parallel to Cloud's outstretched neck. Ara bit her lip and released Cloud's mane. She gasped with relief when her body remained steady in the saddle.

Taking the reins on both hands, Ara shifted her focus from staying on the horse to actually riding the horse. She'd intentionally given Cloud free rein, but now she put gentle tension in the reins, pulling them back ever so slightly with the hope that Cloud remembered she was still there.

Cloud snorted but shifted from a flat run to a swift gallop, allowing Ara to sit up a bit. Cloud's attention to her cue boosted Ara's confidence, and the speed became exhilarating. They flew across the plain, racing the wind. Ara laughed then gave a joyful shout.

She saw Teth and Dust a short distance away and turned Cloud toward them. Cloud lifted his head and gave a long, piercing whinny. The wind carried Dust's answering call.

Teth and Dust and galloped to meet them. Ara slowed Cloud to a trot, and Dust matched Cloud's jogging steps.

"How is it?" he asked.

Ara grinned at him. "Once I knew how to stay on it was amazing."

"You got in the saddle more successfully than I did." Teth laughed.

"Thanks for noticing." Ara patted Cloud's bowed neck.

"Let's walk for a bit." Teth reined Dust in.

Having burned off their pent-up energy, the horses were content enough to walk. It didn't hurt that they could snatch mouthfuls of fresh green grass as they pleased.

"How are you?" Teth asked.

"Well enough," Ara replied. "A little bored."

"Caravan life isn't for you?" Teth smiled wryly.

"Definitely not." Ara looked toward the caravan. Cloud had covered an impressive distance. From Ara's vantage point, she could see the full length of wagons slowly rolling along the road.

Teth cleared his throat. "I've been wondering—"

Ara tensed, her mind returning to the moment beside the bonfire. *What do you want to happen?*

"What do you make of Lahvja?" Teth finished.

"Oh." Ara tried to cover her suprise. "I don't know what I make of her because so much about her is mysterious. But I like her." She thought about Lahvja for another moment. "My gut tells me she belongs with us."

"Mine too." Teth swatted a fly away. "And it's very strange. I can't remember ever feeling that way."

"You mean you didn't feel like a part of our group from our first meeting?" Ara teased.

Laughing, Teth replied, "I'm sorry, of course! The moment Nimhea drew her sword I thought, 'There's no other place for me.'"

Ara laughed with him, then asked, "So what do *you* make of Lahvja?"

"I like her, too," said Teth. "But I'm not used to someone knowing who I am when I have no idea who they are. I can't say I like that."

"Now you understand how the rest of the world feels about you," Ara teased.

Teth smiled slyly. "I didn't know who you were."

"And you couldn't bear it!" Ara replied. "Proving my point."

"I don't like surprises," Teth admitted. "Since I met you I've been bombarded with them. Are you trying to make me paranoid?"

"Wouldn't you like to know," she said.

Teth looked at her curiously. "When I asked about Lahvja you seemed surprised. Was there something else you thought I was going to ask?"

"No," Ara said too quickly, heat rising in her cheeks.

"Hmmm." Teth's face filled with mischief. "What if I try to guess?"

Ara decided that wasn't a good idea. "Let's run some more!" She put her heels to Cloud, and the gelding charged forward.

She heard Teth shout, "Hey!"

They rode for the bulk of the morning, only turning back to the caravan when their stomachs grumbled, wanting lunch. Dust and Cloud were drenched in sweat, but seemed blissfully content after their run. Ara wiped sweat from her forehead. Spring in the grasslands felt like summer in Rill's Pass, and the sun burned high and bright above.

When they were within a quarter mile of the lurching wagons, one of the caravan guards rode out to meet them.

Reining his horse in, the guard asked sternly, "What are you doing out here?"

"Just exercising our horses," Teth answered, patting Dust's shoulder.

With a look of disapproval, the guard said, "Word must not have reached your wagons."

"We are toward the far end of the line," Teth replied. "What word?"

"There's concern a pack of wild dogs might be trailing the caravan," the guard told them.

"Wild dogs?" Ara went cold with the thought that shadow hounds might be close. "Someone has seen them?"

The guard shook his head. "None have been spotted, but we've been finding carcasses not far from the caravan."

"What kind of carcasses?" Teth's brow knit.

"Small creatures," the guard replied. "Rabbits, quail. Wild dogs are no threat to our oxen or horses, but it's unusual for them to range so close to the road. Their packs are few, and they normally avoid contact with humans. We don't believe they'll attack a grown person, but if they're bold they might snatch a goat or chicken, even a small child."

Ara squirmed in her saddle at the suggestion. The idea of anything hunting children repulsed her.

"We've asked that everyone stay close to their wagons," the guard continued. "You'll have to forgo your morning rides until we're past Aerindross." The guard's eyes narrowed. "And Lucket said we're to keep you out of harm's way. I'm not going to lose my hide because you're bored."

"Noted," Teth replied.

With a brief nod, the guard wheeled his horse around and rode back to the caravan.

Pulling her fingers through Cloud's mane, Ara sighed. "Here I thought I'd been freed from all the monotony."

She looked at Teth, expecting a snappy remark. But Teth was lost in thought, his face captured by a troubled expression.

"What's wrong?" Ara asked.

Teth passed a hand over his eyes. "Nothing. It's just . . . wild dogs."

His gaze turned skyward, searching.

"There." He pointed to a ring of carrion birds circling near the end of the wagon train.

They rode at a moderate pace until they spotted a cluster of ravens squabbling with one another. So many birds had gathered that it was impossible to see what they were fighting over.

Teth moved Dust forward at a walk, stopping a few feet away from the squawking mass. He slid out of his saddle and handed Dust's reins to Ara.

"Stay here."

Waving his arms and shouting, Teth rushed at the birds. Startled, they rose into the air, a noisy cloud of beaks and feathers. Teth crouched to examine what was on the ground.

Ara stood in her stirrups, straining to see what Teth was looking at. All she could make out was a swath of red against the yellow grass. Teth stood up and stared at the ground for another minute. Some of the braver birds had landed along the edges of the red stain, taking wary hops toward Teth.

When he returned to Ara and the horses, she couldn't read his expression. She gave him Dust's reins and looked back to the place he'd just left. It had only taken moments for the ravens to return. Their glossy black bodies completely hid the reddened grass.

"What was it?" Ara asked.

"Animal remains," Teth replied, clucking at Dust, who began to walk. "Like the guard said."

Ara moved Cloud to ride alongside him. "Why did you want to see them?"

Teth was quiet for a moment, then he said, "I needed to see if they were the same as something I've seen before."

"Were they?" Ara asked.

"Yes."

"What does that mean?" she pressed, frustrated by his reticence.

Teth rolled his shoulders back. "Maybe nothing."

She waited for him to say something more, but Teth passed the remainder of their ride in silence.

Teth remained distant that evening, barely touching his food at dinner. He excused himself early and left the campfire seeming troubled. The animal remains had touched on something that worried him, Ara thought. She wished he would share what it was so she could help solve whatever problem he'd run into.

He's used to working alone, Ara reminded herself.

It was hard to know where the line was between being helpful and interfering.

When the rest of them had finished eating, Eamon announced he was going for a walk.

"I'll go with you," Nimhea said, standing up.

Eamon frowned at her. "I don't need a chaperone."

"I didn't mean it that way," Nimhea told him. "I'd like to stretch my legs."

"I'd prefer to be alone." Eamon looked at the ground.

Nimhea shrugged. "If that's what you want."

He lifted his head, encouraged that she wasn't irked by his seeking solitude. "It is."

She pointed to the front of the caravan line. "I'm walking this way. You go wherever you want."

Eamon mumbled something and went off in the opposite direction.

As he walked away, Nimhea shook her head. "I never know what he wants. Sometimes he needs to talk and talk until I can't take any more strange facts or outlandish tales. But then he's like this, bristly and aloof."

Ara had noticed that about Eamon as well. She thought the swings in his mood had become more frequent since Lahvja joined the group.

Is he jealous of the fast friendship between Nimhea and Lahvja? For most of their lives the twins only had each other. It must take an adjustment to be in close company with new friends.

"That can be the way of scholars." Lahvja gathered the dinner dishes. "Their scrolls and tomes are jealous masters, demanding sole focus. But they're still human and need companions. It's a difficult balance."

"I suppose." Nimhea sighed. "I really do need to stretch my legs. I'll be back soon."

Ara and Lahvja had nearly finished washing dishes when the shouting began. At first the two girls exchanged puzzled glances, not recognizing the sounds muffled by distance. As the cries grew sharper, becoming clear they were human voices, Ara realized they weren't louder—they were closer.

A rumbling sound like far-off thunder accompanied the shouts, but the night sky wasn't hidden by clouds. Ara let her dishes clatter to the ground and ran to the side of the wagon.

"Look!"

Lahvja joined her and gazed in the direction Ara pointed. At the front of caravan, flames danced in the air, offering glimpses of figures moving swiftly alongside the column of carts and wagons. Men on horseback waving torches.

At the sudden battering of hooves rushing up behind them, Ara pulled Ironbranch from its harness. Drawing on the techniques Teth had drilled into her, Ara planted the stave then kicked her legs up and to her left. Her feet hit the side of the wagon, and she launched herself into the air, taking Ironbranch with her. She landed a few feet behind Lahvja, facing the opposite direction, and braced herself as horse and rider bore down on them.

The rider gave a cry of surprise and hauled back on the reins so hard his mount reared and stabbed its hooves at the sky. Ara heard Lahvja gasp.

When the horse came down, Ara recognized the guard who'd warned Teth about wild dogs.

"Stop!" He struggled to settle his horse. "I'm not one of them."

"Not one of who?" Ara let her grip on Ironbranch loosen.

The guard waved toward the ruckus at the front of the caravan. "The soldiers! You need to get in the wagon now!"

Instead of going for the wagon, Ara turned around in a circle, hoping to see Nimhea, Eamon, and Teth reappear.

"Get in the wagon!" the guard screamed at them. "That's a conscription column."

Lahvja dragged Ara toward the wagon.

"The others—" Ara objected.

"Will be here," Lahvja replied as she opened the back door and scrambled inside. "We must stay hidden while we wait for them."

Ara climbed into the wagon.

"Shutter all the windows. I'll lock the side doors," Lahvja ordered.

They closed up the wagon until the only light was from the dwindling cooking flames that reached through the open back door. A shadow blocked the light, and Nimhea joined them in the dark space.

"I don't know where Eamon is," Nimhea whispered. Her voice was on the verge of breaking.

The shouting of soldiers had been joined by shrieks of fear.

"We have to stay calm," Lahvja said softly. "Did you see Teth at all?"

"No." Nimhea started to move. "I have to go find them."

Lahvja's voice was like iron. "No."

"Eamon can't defend himself," Nimhea pleaded. "He needs me."

The light disappeared again. "They're almost here." It was the caravan guard. "Don't make a sound."

"What about the others?" Horror crowded Ara's chest.

"There's nothing I can do for them," the guard said. "Lock this door."

He slammed the back door shut, and darkness covered them. Ara crawled to the door and felt for the bolt that would lock the door. She slid the bolt home, feeling a dreadful finality as she did so.

In the dark the sounds from outside were worse. The screams louder, the wailing more piercing. Heavy hoofbeats made it sound like an army surrounded the caravan. Ara could understand the shouting soldiers.

"Volunteers! Volunteers for the imperial army!"

The three girls huddled closer together. Ara could tell they were each trying to keep their breath quiet.

"Your emperor requires your service! The uprising in Penra must be quelled!"

"Volunteers!"

There were loud hoofbeats, then a horse snorting on the other side of the wagon wall. "You!"

"Your servant, sir," replied the caravan guard.

"Open this wagon," the soldier commanded. "We have orders to identify all able-bodied men and women in this caravan."

"There is nothing of use to you in this wagon," the guard said.

Along with the shouting all around them, Ara heard splintering wood and the squealing of frightened horses.

"Did I ask you a question?" the soldier bellowed. "No! Open this wagon or I'll have you chained with the rest of the conscription line."

There was a long pause.

"The sun sets here." It was the guard's voice.

"What?" The soldier was growing angry. "Are you some kind of idiot?"

Another round of hoofbeats rushed up to the wagon.

"Is there a problem?" A new voice, smooth and more assured than that of the first soldier.

"I commanded this guard to open the wagon, Sergeant," the blustery soldier replied. "He refuses. I was about to arrest him."

The caravan guard said again, "The sun sets here."

"I think he may be wrong in the head, sir," the first soldier complained.

"I'll deal with this, private," the sergeant told him. "Move down the line."

"Yes, sir."

There was another pause as the private rode away. The din of soldiers' voice, trampling horse hooves, breaking wagons, and terrified conscripts' cries continued to fill the air.

"Do you have payment?" the sergeant asked.

Ara could barely recognize the tinkling of coins.

"The empire thanks you." The sergeant's warm voice sounded obscene amid the chorus of fear.

The caravan guard replied, "At your service, sir."

No one troubled their wagon again, but the shouts and chaos continued for hours. Through it all they had neither sign nor word of Eamon or Teth. Every sinew in Ara's body ached from being clenched with fear, and her mind swam with terrible visions.

At last came sharp raps on the wagon door. "It's safe now. You can come out."

It was Teth's voice.

Ara unbolted the door. Squinting against the early morning light, she tumbled out of the wagon and into him. Without a thought, Ara threw her arms around Teth and buried her face against his neck.

"It's good to see you, too," said Teth. "But you might want to keep your distance."

That was when Ara noticed that Teth's neck, in fact all of Teth, was very wet and a little slimy. She stepped back and saw that he was covered from boots to the tips of his hair in gray mud.

"What happened?" Ara wiped mud from her cheek. Her nose wrinkled at the odor of rotting eggs. "Senn's teeth! What is that smell?"

"It's us." Eamon stood behind Teth, a sheepish expression on his face. If anything, he was filthier than Teth. And Teth was incredibly filthy.

"Eamon!" Nimhea was climbing from the wagon when she heard her brother's voice. She started toward him, but stopped when she saw the state of things.

"We hid in a mud hole," Eamon answered before Nimhea could ask.

"Not just any mud hole," Teth piped up. "A sulfuric mud hole."

Nimhea shot an accusing glare at Teth. "Why did you put my brother in a mud hole?"

"It's not Teth's fault, Nimhea." Eamon stepped between Teth and Nimhea's dagger eyes. "If he hadn't found me the soldiers would have."

Lahvja had emerged from the wagon, and she put a hand on Nimhea's shoulder.

"Tell us what happened, Teth," Lahvja said quietly.

"I was doing what I do." Teth picked at mud that had dried on his arms. "By which I mean snooping. When I heard the conscription column approaching, I came here to check on the situation and saw that the three of you"—he gestured to Lahvja, Nimhea, and Ara—"would be hidden in the wagon. I waited for Eamon to show, but it became clear he wouldn't get to the wagon before the column did. So I went looking for him."

"Why didn't you tell us what you were doing?" Ara resented having been wrung out with fear while Teth had known the three of them were safe.

He offered an apologetic nod. "Things were moving too quickly. Once I realized Eamon was at risk, I had to go after him."

"And where were you?" Nimhea's hands were on her hips. Her eyes blazed with fury as she fixed them on her brother. Eamon quailed, but Ara could see the depth of fear disguised by Nimhea's anger.

Eamon looked away, unable to suffer his sister's rage. "The lights from the wagons hide the stars. The grassland skies have more stars than I ever imagined I would see. I wanted to get away from the light."

"You. Went. Looking. For. Stars." Nimhea's eyes bulged.

"I know . . ." Eamon hung his head.

Ara couldn't blame Nimhea for being angry. Eamon's dreaminess was often endearing, but he clearly didn't understand how much danger he could put himself in.

"How did you know where to find Eamon?" Lahvja asked. "He could have gone anywhere."

Teth glanced at Eamon. "Don't take offense to this, friend."

"Not likely to," Eamon mumbled. His downcast eyes suggested regret, but he was kicking the ground with the toe of his boot as if in resentment, too.

Lahvja watched Eamon's behavior with a deepening frown.

"I'm an observer of people," Teth went on. "What I've come to expect from Eamon is, well, let's call it an earnestness of purpose."

Eamon grunted. "You can say *naive*."

"That honestly wouldn't be my word of choice," Teth replied. "What I mean is that Eamon will do things that aren't very sensible, but he is sensible about the way he does them."

Nimhea rolled her eyes. "That's ridiculous."

"Not really," Teth countered. "Eamon wanted to see the stars, so he went away from the caravan. However, he wouldn't want to get lost, so he would walk in a straight line directly away from our wagon so he could take the same path back."

Ara considered that, then asked, "How did you know what side of the wagon he would walk away from?"

"I didn't," Teth admitted. "That was a lucky guess."

Eamon's head snapped up at Teth's words. He looked queasy as he comprehended what might have been.

"We were also lucky he chose the side that took him close to the mud holes," Teth added. "The smell alone kept any ranging soldiers away. Speaking of which, I'm going to find a barrel of water to dunk myself in. Eamon, I think you'd better join me until your sister is less likely to boil over."

Teth took a moment to look up and down the caravan line. "We need to leave as soon as possible. Pack up quickly and quietly."

Ara had been so focused on Teth and Eamon that she hadn't given attention to the aftermath of the soldiers' visit. Up and down the length of the caravan, smoke rose, here in wisps, there in pillars. She spotted the carcasses of goats and cattle. The sound of weeping was soft, but clear.

"It shouldn't have happened," Teth said. "Low King trade caravans aren't supposed to be harassed. Lucket will be furious when he hears about this."

Wrapping her arms around herself, a shield against the devastation she'd witnessed, Ara said, "But we were protected. When the guard gave one of the soldiers a pass phrase, the soldier took a payment and we were spared."

"I know." Teth frowned. "If anything, that's more troubling. The mixed message. The empire might be bungling its business affairs, or something more insidious is at work. I don't like either option."

15

he Zeverin Gorge was an angry scar running south of Aerindross until it disappeared into the Ghost Cliffs. They'd left the broken caravan line and taken a south-easterly route. Their destination: the great maw that cut the southern plains in two.

It took all day to reach the gorge. The setting sun painted exquisite colors along the rock walls on its opposite wall. They made their camp a good distance from its edge. When Nimhea started to walk toward the gorge, Teth called her back and asked everyone to gather at the half-built campfire.

"If you must look over the ledge, do it crawling on your belly," Teth warned them. "Wind shears come out of nowhere all along the gorge. If you're standing they'll sweep you right over the edge."

After that no one seemed very interested in investigating the gorge.

For the next several days, they followed the gorge's path south, though always riding a good distance from its edge. The landscape around them gradually shifted. The grass became shorter, until it disappeared altogether. Beneath Cloud's hooves the earth was parched and cracked, and the wind lifted red dust that collected in the folds of Ara's clothes. Stunted shrubs dotted the ground, and unfamiliar varieties of lizards and rodents scurried in and out of their cover. The high desert made their destination more real. The Ghost Cliffs. The Scourge. Places of legend. Places of death.

Ara didn't want to run or turn from her path, but dry winds whispered to her of danger, and she had to harden herself against the fear trying to scratch its way inside her.

The farther south they traveled the more bizarre the wildlife became. Another signal that as they closed in on the Ghost Cliffs, they'd entered another world.

They passed a group of long-necked, broad-bodied creatures with spotted coats that Ara thought looked a cross between an elk and a cow. On closer inspection she saw they were covered not with fur, but feathers.

Watching the strange beasts, Eamon sighed happily. "They say that of all the lands, Daefrit is home to the most wondrous creatures because Ofrit loves puzzles. He fit the oddest pieces together to form all manner of things strange and beautiful."

"And frightening," Teth added. "I'd be very happy to go the rest of my life without seeing a butcher crow. There's a reason everyone travels to Isar and Zyre by sea. Most who go into the desert never come out."

"Butcher crows aren't real," Nimhea scoffed.

Ara looked at Nimhea, surprised that after all they'd seen the princess remained a skeptic.

"I'm sorry," Teth replied. He appeared to be of the same mind as Ara. "I thought we were on a quest to find a god who will tell us where Ara's magic hammer is. Or better yet, he'll just give Ara the magic hammer and we'll be all set."

"What are you blathering on about?" groaned Nimhea.

"I'm just saying we're now operating in a world with gods and magic hammers," Teth shot back. "In that world I'm pretty sure butcher crows are real."

"There is no magic hammer," Ara snapped at Teth, but for a moment she worried and glanced at Eamon for affirmation.

"No hammer," said Eamon with a smile. "At least not in what I've read. And I've read a lot."

Lahvja was laughing softly.

"Doubtless there are fearsome beasts in the Scourge," Nimhea said to Teth. "But they will be no more than desert lions and venomous lizards."

"Unlikely," Ara murmured, but Nimhea didn't hear her.

Teth gave the princess a long look. "I hope you're right." He noticed Lahvja's shaking shoulders.

"Care to weigh in?"

Lahvja shook her head and smiled. "I hate to ruin a surprise."

A flurry of fluff burst from the shrubs as Fox flushed out a burrow of rabbits with miniature rams' horns curled next to their long ears.

"That was a cute surprise." Teth pointed at the fleeing ram-rabbits. "For the record, cute surprises are fine."

No bridges spanned the Zeverin Gorge. The chasm separating its walls was over two miles wide. Its depth had yet to be discovered as no one had successfully scaled its walls. The gorge stretched to the edge of south central Daefrit where it formed the Marik Delta and emptied into the Southern Sea. It was commonly held that there was no central passage between northern and southern Daefrit given that the Ghost Cliffs dropped directly into the Zeverin Gorge, and the cliffs themselves had long been declared impassable. Some referred to the northern edge of the Ghost Cliffs as Ofrit's Wall.

Despite all of this, they rode directly toward the western edge of the cliffs. All of Saetlund claimed there was no way through, but according to Teth there was. Every day the Ghost Cliffs loomed larger, and from Ara's perspective one of the sandstone towers blocked the way forward.

As their journey progressed Eamon had become increasingly agitated. He fell into a pattern of pestering Teth about setting up camp earlier and earlier each day. His initial excitement about Daefrit's odd beasts faded away and he rode quietly, but constantly fidgeting in his saddle. Eamon's inability to remain still compelled his horse to frequently turn its head and watch him with one eye, as if waiting for its rider to jump out of the saddle and scurry away.

He broke his silence only to ask: "How soon till we camp?"

When they did camp that night, Eamon scarfed down his dinner and then disappeared into his tent, begging forgiveness for the demands of his studies. Hours later, when Ara sought her bed, she saw lantern light still winked behind the flaps of Eamon's tent.

I hope he doesn't fall off his horse when we ride tomorrow. Ara thought before she ducked into her tent.

Ara's bladder woke her just before sunrise, begging for relief. She left her tent and was met by traces of gray light that saved her from stumbling in the dark. The dry soil discouraged trees and Ara had to go further from camp than she liked to find a shrub that afforded some privacy. It was likely no one else was awake to see her, but she preferred not to take that chance.

A few moments later as Ara tugged up her trousers she noticed a dark shape in the distance. A shape that was coming toward her. She hurried to the opposite side of the shrub and dropped into a crouch. As the shadowy form drew near Ara could make out the shape of a human silhouette.

Someone had been following them.

Ara cursed under her breath. She'd thought this would be a quick trip outside and hadn't brought Ironbranch with her. Without its protection, she had hope whoever it was would pass by without seeing her. The soft light that had guided her to the shrub now seemed treacherous.

The stranger was running. As they drew closer, Ara could hear huffing breath as if they were strained by the exertion. When they were only ten feet from Ara's hiding place, the tired runner tripped over a stone and went sprawling. The hood of their cloak flew back.

Ara jumped to her feet. "Eamon!"

Eamon gave a little yelp as Ara hurried to him.

"Are you hurt?"

"What are you doing out here?" Eamon asked in a trembling voice.

Gods, I must have frightened him.

"I had to pee." She helped him up.

Other than a few scrapes on his palms, he appeared unhurt.

"Why are you out here?" Ara asked.

He answered quickly. "The same reason."

Of course that was it, Ara thought. But she didn't know why Eamon had gone so far from the camp.

It would be in keeping with Eamon's character, Ara reminded herself. *That he'd tend toward extreme modesty.*

She frowned at him.

All the same, Eamon shouldn't be risking himself like that. Especially after what happened at the caravan.

"Don't go so far next time," Ara chided gently. "We can't be sure what's out there."

"Of course." Eamon bobbed his head in apology. "I wasn't thinking."

She took his arm. "Come on. We can probably nab another hour's sleep before breakfast."

As they rode, Ara found her eyes often wandering to Eamon. Deep shadows haunted his eyes, and Ara wondered if he was sleeping at all. He didn't look well. Despite the bright sun, his bronze skin had taken on a grayish cast.

Maybe Lahvja should look at him. This hasn't been an easy journey. Perhaps he's taken ill.

By the afternoon they'd drawn close enough to the cliffs to ride in their shadows. Teth brought the group to a halt. A few hours of daylight remained, and the stop came as a surprise.

"We should camp here tonight and cross over tomorrow," Teth told them.

Eamon was already out of his saddle. "Wonderful!"

"Could we reach the passage yet today?" Nimhea asked Teth.

"We could," Teth answered hesitantly. "But it's better if we cross in the morning, when there's better light."

A prickling suspicion rose on the back of Ara's neck. *He's hiding something.*

"Do you want to tell me why?" Nimhea pressed.

"Not really."

Shaking her head in exasperation, Nimhea went to unburden the packhorse.

Ara didn't like it either. Teth was in the habit of keeping things to himself, but they all relied upon one another now. She would have to help him break that habit.

When they settled around the campfire for dinner, Teth looked at Eamon.

"Don't run off until we're done talking."

"But—"

Teth shook his head. "It's important, and we'll need you."

Eamon looked very unhappy but didn't argue further.

After Lahvja handed out dark bread, cheese, and sliced ham—an unfortunate result of having left the caravan was that Lahvja no longer had fresh goods to cook with—Teth cleared his throat.

"Before we cross into the Scourge tomorrow I want to discuss the potential obstacles we'll face," he said. "We need to be as prepared as we can."

The rest of them shifted on their seats of blanket and boulder with uneasy anticipation.

Teth's face was grim. "I have no idea what's in there. But between what I know from the Below and all the books Eamon's read we can at least get a sense of the possibilities. Eamon?"

"Yes, I can help with that," Eamon replied, but not cheerfully.

"Once we cross the passage we'll step right into the Scourge." Teth tore his bread into pieces but didn't put any in his mouth. "Here's what we have to watch for: predators that are exceptional hunters—cliff panthers leave their dens to stalk at night, and butcher crows swoop down from the sky without warning. Another threat comes from smaller creatures with deadly venom. Sand spiders. Swarming scorpions. Dune vipers."

Ara's skin crawled. The spiders and scorpions frightened her more than big cats and crows.

"What a lovely place it must be," Nimhea muttered.

"I know remedies for a variety of venoms." Lahvja appeared to be the only one actually eating her food. "I'll prepare them before I sleep."

Ara suddenly wanted to hug Lahvja.

"Thank you." Teth brightened. "That's very helpful. I have two vials of antivenom in my pack, but if things go badly we might need more."

He popped two pieces of bread in his mouth.

"Is there any way to avoid these crawling things?" Ara asked.

"We're going to try," Teth answered. "Scorpions and spiders live in dens they build in rock clusters, so we'll give those a wide berth. Dune vipers live, well, in dunes. Most of the dunes are on the southwestern side of the Scourge. With luck we can ride around, rather than over, any dunes we run in to."

He took several swallows from his waterskin. "As far as the large predators go, we should be able to reach the Bone Forest before sunset, eliminating the panthers as a threat. Unfortunately, there isn't anything we can do to hide from butcher crows."

"I'm still wagering they're not real," said Nimhea. She'd assembled a sandwich of bread, cheese, and ham. It looked appealing, so Ara did the same.

"I hope you win that wager." Teth dug an apple out of his pack. "Eamon, if you have anything to add, please do. Also I have nothing to offer about the Bone Forest, so I'll hand that to you."

Eamon had been turning a chunk of bread over in his hands as though if he stared at it long enough it would turn into a book. "I can confirm what you've said about the Scourge. The butcher crows do hunt there, but they've only been known to kill humans inside the Bone Forest. In the Scourge they're looking for food."

"And you're sure we're not food?" Teth's eyebrows went up.

"We shouldn't be." Eamon shrugged. "And we should be given safe passage through the Bone Forest."

He frowned suddenly, and his fingers began to twitch. "That's all I have to say."

"Don't you want to tell us why we'll be safe in the forest?" Teth asked. "Because I'd like to know."

Eamon was already on his feet. "Tomorrow."

He dashed to his tent before anyone could object.

Ara didn't understand Eamon's sudden departure, but she did appreciate someone keeping a secret from Teth for once.

Teth threw the core of his apple into the fire. "Is it just me or has he been acting very strangely the past few days?"

Ara stood up. "I'll go talk to him."

"Would you rather I did?" Nimhea asked.

"I'm the reason we're here," Ara replied. "Maybe he'll be willing to share more with the Loresmith."

Nimhea offered a grateful smile.

Ara walked to Eamon's tent. "Eamon?"

"I meant it when I said I don't know anything else," he grumbled from inside.

Taking his reply as her cue to enter, Ara ducked under the tent flap. He didn't look up.

Eamon sat surrounded by books and scrolls. As far as Ara could tell, he hadn't bothered to unpack his bedroll. His eyes bored into the scroll in his hands, and his face was screwed up with concentration. With a groan, he suddenly put the scroll aside and pinched the bridge of his nose with his fingertips.

"Are you all right?" asked Ara.

He looked at Ara, squinting as though he didn't recognize her.

"You seem unwell," she said quickly. "I've been worried about you."

"I'm fine, Ara." He moved his fingers to rub his temples. "I wander away from the rest of the world when I'm reading."

Ara sat beside him. "Do you have a headache? I know how to make a tea that eases them. Lahvja could probably make something even better."

"That's kind of you," Eamon replied. "But does it also make you sleepy? Many remedies seem to."

"Yes," she admitted. "It's meant to help you sleep as well. But what's wrong with that? You need to rest."

Shaking his head, Eamon picked up the scroll. "I can't afford to sleep."

He rolled up the scroll, trading it for a book.

"Haven't you read all these a hundred times or more?" Ara flicked the cover of the book.

"Or more." Eamon's laugh was shaky. "But it doesn't matter. I need to be sure I haven't missed anything."

"I'm sure you haven't," Ara replied a bit flippantly.

He turned on her with angry eyes. "Don't you understand? The Bone Forest could kill us. I think I know a way through, but if I'm wrong we all die. I have to be sure I didn't miss anything. That I didn't misinterpret—"

Wincing, he pinched the bridge of his nose again.

"You have a headache?"

It was Ara's turn to jump. Nimhea's head poked through the tent flaps.

"It's not bad." Eamon dropped his hand from his face like he'd touched a hot stove. The book slipped out of his other hand.

Nimhea leaned down and picked it up.

"Give it back." His voice was almost a growl.

Unflinching, Nimhea said, "You know the healers said to stop when you feel the headache coming on. We've talked about this."

"I know," Eamon complained, some of the harshness leaving his tone. "But tonight I have to make an exception."

He looked to Ara for support.

Ara put her palms up, signaling neutrality. "I don't know anything about these headaches."

"There are no exceptions," Nimhea said with finality.

Muttering under his breath, Eamon pushed past Nimhea and stormed off. She watched him leave and sighed.

"I've never seen him like that," said Ara. "He seems so afraid."

"He's not afraid," Nimhea replied, picking up books. "At least not in the way you're thinking. Help me put these away. I'll keep them in my tent tonight."

Ara helped Nimhea gather up the mess of writings. If Eamon had put them in some kind of order, Ara couldn't see it.

"Eamon and I have this fight over and over," Nimhea said.

Ara slid scrolls into one pack and books into another as she listened.

"His headaches aren't simply headaches," Nimhea continued. "They consume his whole body, causing him so much pain. I stay with him if he lets me. I don't want him to suffer alone, but seeing what he goes through takes its toll. It's like watching him be tortured."

"What causes it?" Ara asked.

"No healer has been able to explain it," Nimhea said. "I didn't realize how bad his condition was because he tries to hide it. It wasn't until I came upon him trembling and so dizzy he couldn't walk that I understood how serious it was."

"How long has he been sick?" Ara glanced down at the title of the book she held, *The Occult in Saetlund's History.*

She frowned, wondering how different a scholar's interpretation would be from the stories passed down to her from Old Imgar and her grandmother. Might the erudite minds of the universities at Zyre and Isar have something to more to offer than the old tales?

Nimhea shook her head and gave a frustrated sigh. "He's never had a strong constitution, but the headaches and weakness began in the last year. Eamon claims he has no idea what brought it on."

"That's . . . very unusual." Ara didn't know how to describe Eamon's behavior and accompanying illness. She'd never heard of anything like it.

"Ever since we arrived in Saetlund I've been consumed by my place here, the rebellion, all this." She ran her fingers over the scroll then shook her head. "He's my brother. I should have been paying attention."

"But he's been fine," Ara said, putting her hand on Nimhea's shoulder.

"No, he hasn't," Nimhea countered. "I could tell how much pain he was in tonight. That takes time to build up."

They'd cleared the floor of Eamon's tent. Each hefting a pack, Ara and Nimhea moved Eamon's collection to Nimhea's tent.

"Is there anything else I can do?" Ara asked.

Nimhea shook her head. "If I think of anything, I'll ask."

Ara left the tent and returned to the campfire, where Teth and Lahvja were visiting. As soon as Ara sat down, Lahvja excused herself and went straight to Nimhea's tent.

"Hmmm." Ara retrieved her unfinished sandwich.

"Hmmm, what?" Teth moved around the fire to sit beside her.

It was hard to swallow the chunk of sandwich she'd just chewed. "Nothing."

Teth looked her in the eyes, then laughed. "If you say so."

Ignoring him, Ara continued to eat. It didn't help that her stomach had decided to do flips. She stared at the fire, willing her nerves to settle.

"I need you to promise me something." Teth leaned close to her.

Ara wished she wasn't eating a sandwich. She was quite sure she had crumbs on her lips.

"Promise what?" She hoped she was wrong about the crumbs.

"When you see the path tomorrow," Teth whispered into her ear, "don't hate me."

"How could the path make me hate you?" Forgetting about the potential crumbs, she turned to look at him.

Teth's face was mere inches from hers.

"You'll know." He brushed his lips across her forehead, then hopped up and walked to his tent.

The strip of ground that connected the grasslands and the Scourge was narrow. One side of the trail dropped off into the darkness of the gorge. The other pressed back against a towering cliff face. At the end of the crossing was a small gap beyond which another cliff rose. There was only room enough for one person or horse to cross at a time. It was true that there was no central passage to southern Daefrit. This wasn't a path; it was a nightmare.

"We'll lead the horses," Teth said, dismounting. "Leave the pack-horses tied to their guide horse; it'll keep them calmer."

Ara stared at the crossing and understood why Teth had kept the path to himself. They would have spent all night demanding that he find a *different* path.

"This can't be the way."

"Believe me, I wish it wasn't," Teth replied.

She hated him a little.

Nimhea slid off her horse, leading it closer to the gap. "But you've crossed it before."

With a self-mocking laugh, Teth said, "No. But I know people who have. Or people who claimed they have."

Claimed they have? Eni save us.

"What about the wind shears?" Eamon frowned at the path.

"There won't be wind shears," Teth said unconvincingly.

"You're certain this is the only crossing." Lahvja had dismounted. Her face was ashen, and her hands shook even while she clung to her horse's reins.

"It's the only approach from the eastern side of the Ghost Cliffs." Teth gave her a worried look. "If we'd gone west we would have passed through Dothring, which has an imperial checkpoint. We also would have been forced to cross a much wider swath of the Scourge."

Lahvja pressed her hand to her stomach. "I did not anticipate this test."

"It's not a test," Teth said. "It's just a terrible path that's our only option."

"It is a test for me," said Lahvja, shaking her head. "I do not fear the things others dread. But the very sight of this place rips away any courage I possess."

Ara began to fear for Lahvja. A crossing like this one had to be taken on with courage. With the belief that one *would* make it to the other side. Doubts could be deadly.

Nimhea came to Lahvja. "You have trouble with heights?"

"Not only the height," Lahvja answered. "But being trapped between death and a wall of stone."

Teth eyed Lahvja nervously. "Maybe try not to think of it in those terms."

Nimhea took Lahvja's hand. "You'll be fine."

Lahvja smiled at her weakly.

Twins be with her, Ara prayed. She'd grown up in the shadow of the Ice Mountains, where the Twins dwelled. The Ghost Cliffs were not cold and icy, but the ferocious winds reminded her of squalls coming down the mountains. If any gods should walk with Lahvja it should be Ayre and Syre, keepers of the mysteries.

Perhaps by some magic they can float her to the other side. Ara laughed nervously under her breath. Even if the Twins answered her, Ara suspected that wasn't how it worked.

"Ara," Teth asked. "Since Lahvja is nervous about the crossing, would you please tie her horse to yours and lead them across?"

"Of course," Ara replied. "Don't be afraid, Lahvja. The gods are with us."

Lahvja was holding on to Nimhea like a sailor clinging to floating pieces of a shipwreck, but she smiled at Ara. "They are."

The question of who would cross first was answered by Fox, who bounded along the cliff, yipped with delight, and bounded back to them.

"Fox puts us to shame," Lahvja murmured. She closed her eyes, but her lips moved soundlessly.

Teth crouched down to scratch Fox's chin. "It's hard for us. We're bigger."

Fox barked at him.

"I'll go." Ara walked to the edge of the crossing, Cloud's lead rope in her hands and Lahvja's horse tied behind.

"Are you sure?" Teth was at her side.

"I want to get it over with," she said.

Teth put his hand on her shoulder. "Keep your eyes ahead. One step at a time. Remember to breathe. Do not look down."

The giant lump in Ara's throat kept her from answering.

He lowered his voice and squeezed her shoulder. "If either horse starts to fall, let go of the rope."

Ara had to close her eyes for a moment, waiting for her breath to slow. She nodded.

"See you on the other side," said Teth.

It wasn't very far. Three hundred feet at most.

Ara made sure the right side of her body was always brushing against the cliff wall. Not looking down was so hard, it was almost painful. She tried to distract herself by looking at the features of the wall. That didn't help because the wall had no features. It was perfectly smooth. No crevices to use as handholds. No jutting bits to grab if one slipped. Blood roared in her ears as they strained for the sound of crumbling rock or falling scree.

She kept moving. *The others must think me such a coward. I've been out here for so long.*

Ara controlled each breath. Deep slow inhale, easy exhale. She knew the horses would sense every emotion she felt. If she flinched or panicked, so would they. And then it would be over for all of them.

And then she stepped onto the other side of the cliff.

The gap widened a few feet beyond the crossing, opening into a trail that wound westward between the cliffs.

Shouts and cheers bounced off the cliff walls.

Ara turned and waved to her friends. She still felt shaky.

How long was I out there?

"Huzzah for the Loresmith!" called Teth, making her laugh.

Leading the horses a safe distance along the trail, Ara left them there and returned to the end of the crossing.

Eamon had started across with his horse. His face was frozen in an expression both determined and terrified. Barely a minute passed, and he was at Ara's side.

She gaped at him in disbelief. *Had it taken so little time to cross?* Ara felt like she'd spent an hour on that ledge.

Nimhea followed her, leading her mount and a packhorse. Her face wasn't a mask of terror, but had the same fierce cast as when she went to battle.

As soon as she was across, Nimhea handed her reins to Eamon and went back to the edge.

Lahvja stood at the other end of the ledge. She pressed one hand against the wall and began to cross. Ara could see that Lahvja's entire body shook with each step. Step by step Lahvja willed herself forward. Passing the midway point, Lahvja began to walk faster, her confidence growing.

A blast of wind rose from the gorge and whipped across the cliff toward the gap. The swirling air grabbed Lahvja's skirt, dragging her forward. She screamed. Pushing herself against the sandstone wall, Lahvja curled in on herself and covered her head with her arms.

As suddenly as it appeared the wind died. Lahvja didn't move.

"Lahvja!" Teth called. "You're almost across."

Lahvja didn't move.

"I'm going out to her," Nimhea said grimly.

Ara's heart jumped into her throat.

"Nimhea!" Teth shouted when the princess stepped onto the ledge. "What are you doing?"

"Shut up, Teth!"

Nimhea crept along the wall until she reached Lahvja. The princess gently took hold of Lahvja's wrists and drew her arms away from her head. Lahvja slowly lifted her face. Nimhea stayed on the ledge, crouched beside Lahvja for several minutes. They were speaking, but Ara could hear nothing they said.

Helping Lahvja to her feet, Nimhea clasped her forearms as Lahvja clasped Nimhea's. Lahvja's eyes locked on Nimhea's face, and they began to move. Lahvja continued forward along the ledge while Nimhea walked backward.

Ara couldn't breathe. She grabbed Eamon's hand. Eamon watched his sister's every step back, terrified. An eternity passed as they waited for Lahvja and Nimhea to finish the crossing.

Nimhea stepped into the gap and Eamon darted forward, grabbing his sister around the waist to drag both women away from the gorge. Lahvja collapsed, and both Eamon and Nimhea caught her and helped her to sit.

When Ara went back to the crossing, Teth had already reached the midpoint with Dust and the second packhorse behind him. Fox trotted a short distance ahead, as if leading a parade. Teth's lips were moving as he talked to Fox, the horses, or himself. She knew whatever conversation he was having served to keep him calm. Ara wished it could do the same for her.

Eni protect him. Please keep him safe. Ara envisioned the pendant Teth wore. She focused her thoughts on Eni's symbol. *Protect your thief.*

Teth reached the gap without a misstep. The horses were as calm as if they'd been led through a pasture.

Fox immediately ran over to Lahvja and snuggled into her arms.

Teth stopped in front of Ara. She rested her fingers against his pendant. In contrast to the rising heat of the day, it was cool, soothing.

Thank you.

"Nava's mercy," he whispered, covering her hand with his. "Tell me I will never, ever have to do that again."

Having had time to recover, Ara smiled impishly at him. "I'm not the one who decides such things."

"Cruel woman," Teth said, but he grinned at her.

16

he trail cut between massive, curving cliff walls that pressed close, letting little sunlight in. To Teth's delight, it was a short passage, and within half an hour they stood at the edge of a new world.

Stretching before them was a desert landscape marked by golden sands. The air shimmered with heat, and wind picked up the sand, spinning it into miniature tornadoes that danced erratically along the ground. Southward, in the distance, Ara could make out a line of tall dunes that marked the border of the Punishing Desert. Directly ahead the terrain was relatively flat. No shrubs eked out their existence on this side of the Ghost Cliffs, nor any other plant life Ara could see. Clusters of white boulders were the only distinct features in the landscape. Despite its fearsome reputation, the Scourge presented itself as a quiet, empty place.

What a deceptive mask it wears.

Lahvja had called the gorge her test. Ara's limbs were taut. She had no doubt the Scourge would have its own tests.

Teth was standing in his stirrups, gazing into the distance. He gave a low whistle.

"I think I can just make out the edge of the Bone Forest," he said. "It's closer than I dared to hope."

Ara peered at the horizon. She could see a band of bright white in the distance, but no distinctive details.

Our goal. Ara's pulse quickened. *The place that holds secrets I must know.*

The Scourge, whatever its horrors, wouldn't keep her away.

Nimhea, who'd been riding at the back of the group with Lahvja, pushed her mount forward. She also stood in her stirrups, shading her eyes with her hand.

"I can see it, too," she said. "I'd say half a day's ride at most."

"Good." Teth relaxed into his saddle. The strain etching his face eased slightly. "When we reach the Bone Forest, we'll need to make some more decisions about how to progress. The sooner we get there, the better."

He jumped down from Dust's back. Walking a short distance forward, out of the cliffs' shade and into the bright sunlight, Teth soon began to nod.

After leading Dust back to the group, Teth said, "There's a faint trail. It's not much, but I think we'd be wise to follow it."

"Lead the way," Nimhea replied.

"We should ride in single file to reduce the chance of stirring up something nasty from beneath the surface." Teth swung into Dust's saddle.

Teth took the lead with Dust and the first packhorse. Eamon followed, then Ara and Lahvja. Lahvja seemed to have fully recovered from her panic on the ledge. It probably didn't hurt that Fox had insisted on riding in her lap. Lahvja's horse tolerated the beast, but craned its neck frequently to eye Fox with suspicion. Nimhea rode at the rear with the second packhorse tied to her mount. They started out at a cautious pace, an easy walk.

The moment she passed the line from shade to sunlight Ara gasped as a blistering wave of heat slammed into her. This heat was unlike any warmth Ara knew; the closest comparison she could muster was how bread must feel inside her grandmother's oven. Sunbeams hit her skin, pulsing on its surface—a strange and disturbing sensation.

"Ara, you should cover yourself," Lahvja called to her. "Especially your arms and face. Your skin won't tolerate this intensity and will soon burn."

Windburn Ara was familiar with, but the wool she'd wrap herself in for protection would smother her in this burning place. She needed to find something else to do the job, and soon, considering that the skin on Ara's forearms was already tightening against the heat.

"Lahvja!" Ara called. "Do you have any spare silks?"

"Hold a moment!" Lahvja reined in her horse, dismounted, and rummaged inside one of her packs. She withdrew something rolled and pale blue.

Fox sat contentedly in the saddle by himself. Lahvja's horse looked at Fox and gave a snort of distrust.

At the front of the line, Teth turned in his saddle, watching with curiosity.

Leading her horse close behind Cloud, Lahvja said, "Climb down."

Ara dismounted and Lahvja came over, unwinding the blue roll. It was lustrous silk four feet in length and two feet wide.

Smiling, Lahvja said, "I should have thought of this myself. Your pale skin will scorch here."

"We shield ourselves from cold at home." Ara took the silk from Lahvja's hands. It was like cool water running over her fingers. "This should be perfect."

"Would you like to use the wrap you're familiar with?" asked

Lahvja. "Or would you like to try the style worn in the sweating jungles of Vijeri? I'll don my own after I've finished here."

"I'd like to learn that style." Ara paid attention while Lahvja talked her through the steps of the southern wrap.

"There." Lahvja stepped back to check Ara's work. "You learn quickly. How does it feel?"

Falling loosely over her arms and shoulders, the wrapped silk shawl afforded plenty of movement. The more closely wrapped fabric that hooded her face offered shade, but didn't impede her vision.

"It's lovely," Ara said. "Thank you."

"You did me a favor. I shouldn't be riding exposed either," Lahvja told her. "I would never have forgiven myself if we were sunsick for the next two days."

"What's sunsick?" asked Ara. She wondered if it was similar to snow blindness.

"I'll tell you another time," Lahvja replied with a laugh. "And I hope it's something you never have to experience."

After Lahvja had donned her own wrap they returned to their horses, and Teth started Dust along the trail once more.

When the first hour passed without incident, Teth pushed Dust into a jogging trot. Wilting in her saddle even with the protection of Lahvja's shawl, Ara was grateful for the faster pace and the light wind it created. She took small sips from her waterskin, knowing water was precious and must be preserved.

Ara could make out the silhouettes of the Bone Forest now. From a distance the trunks looked like wrists and the spread of branches like fingers clawing at the sky. The sight of it made her shiver in the heat.

⟨━━⟩

Another hour passed, and they stopped to water the horses. Dust and Cloud were thirsty and sweaty, but not troubled by the heat. Eamon and Nimhea's Keldenese mounts, as well as the packhorses, had begun to droop.

Despite her regular sips of water, Ara's mouth had become parched and her throat dry.

Teth walked to the middle of the line to check on her.

"I don't think the desert likes me," Ara told him with a weak smile.

"It hasn't gotten the chance to know you yet." Teth returned her smile, but his eyes were worried. "How are you holding up?"

"Tolerably," Ara answered. "Though I might be a dried, wrinkled apple by the end of the day."

"We should reach the Bone Forest in another couple of hours." Teth sounded apologetic. "I would have liked us to ride at night, when it's cooler, but I didn't want to risk any run-ins with cliff panthers."

Ara shook her head. "You made the right decision. I'll be fine."

"Take another waterskin off one of the packhorses," Teth told her. "If you get sunsick we'll have to rest in the Bone Forest for at least a day."

"Lahvja mentioned sunsickness, too." Ara frowned at him. "Is it really so bad?"

"Yes."

The sky was cloudless, but a massive shadow blotted out the sun momentarily.

"Senn's teeth!" Teth stared up in dread.

Eamon gasped, and Nimhea gave a startled shout. Lahvja remained silent but lifted her face to the sky.

Ara watched the shadow slide along the ground beside them and wheel around in a long, slow circle. Then she too looked skyward.

High above them, the massive bird floated on air currents. Black as pitch, the bird shared the features of a crow but was the size of a wolf-hound. On the ground it would be as large as their horses.

"A butcher crow!" Eamon marveled at the creature. Fascinated rather than afraid, Eamon grinned at the sight of this mythic bird come to life. He smirked at Nimhea. "I told you they were real!"

It wasn't clear if Nimhea heard him. She stared at the crow with wide eyes. Her hand was on her sword hilt. Shocked or not, Nimhea was ever the warrior.

Ara looked at Teth and saw his face was ashen.

"Should we run?" Teth asked. The tilt of his face made it seem like he was asking the sky.

"No," Ara answered. "We stay still until it passes. Think like a hunter. You know what to do if you meet a bear in the forest. Right now it's simply curious about us. If we run we look like prey."

"You're right." Teth let loose a tangle of curses. "I really wanted butcher crows not to be real."

Lahvja said gently, "They have a place in this world. Do not judge them too harshly."

"My judgment rests solely on whether or not they eat us," Teth said with a strained laugh.

"I think that's fair," Ara agreed.

"I'll tell Nimhea what we're doing," Lahvja said, and walked to the back of the line.

Nimhea hadn't mounted, but her sword was drawn and her gaze was trained on the circling bird. Drawing Nimhea's attention, Lahvja spoke with the princess, after which Nimhea eased off her defensive stance, but her sword stayed out of its scabbard.

The butcher crow circled above them for a quarter of an hour before it lost interest and flew away.

Eamon let out a dreamy sigh. "Wasn't it beautiful?"

"I think it's better if I don't answer that." Teth returned to the front of the line.

Teth varied their speed between a swift walk and moderate trot. He glanced up at the sky frequently. The desert sun was unrelenting. Ara finished her waterskin and started on a second, but there would never be enough water to slake her thirst in this place.

They stopped twice more to water the horses. On the second, and hopefully last, stop of the day, Teth visited Ara again.

"Are you dizzy at all?" he asked her. "Nauseated?"

Ara shook her head. "Is it as close as it looks?"

"I have a feeling the trees in the Bone Forest are of a different size from normal trees," Teth said. "And it's farther away than our eyes want to perceive. But we should reach it by midday or a little after." Laughing quietly to himself, Teth said, "I'd be tempted to make a run for it, but the horses are too wearied for sprinting."

"And the butcher crows supposedly live in the Bone Forest," Ara reminded him. "Running toward it is probably a bad idea."

"Good point."

They'd barely continued on the trail when Fox's piercing bark made Ara turn in her saddle. Fox leapt out of Lahvja's lap and hit the ground running. Still barking, Fox wove between the horses' legs, snapping its jaws as if trying to harass them into a gallop.

Whinnying and prancing with irritation and nerves, the horses tugged at the reins and champed at their bits.

"Fox!" Teth shouted the beast. "Boredom is not an excuse for frightening the horses! Stop that now!"

Fox ignored him, running and jumping at the horses' flanks.

"What's gotten into Fox?" Ara asked Lahvja.

Lahvja's mouth was set in a thin line. She didn't answer.

The horses snorted and tossed their manes, jostling up against one another in agitation. An earsplitting squeal of fright sounded at the back of the line. The last packhorse struggled to move forward as the sand beneath its back legs had dropped away. The lead rope of that packhorse was tied to Nimhea's mount. As the panicked horse scrambled to regain its footing, Nimhea's horse became frightened by the desperate whinnies at its back. It reared up, striking at the sky with its hooves. Nimhea grabbed her horse's mane and threw her weight forward, trying to bring the horse down.

"Come on," Teth called to the others as he jumped out of his saddle. "We have to get the packhorse away from that sinkhole."

Eamon and Ara slid off their horses.

"I'll make sure the other horses don't bolt," Lahvja called to Teth before she rode to the front of the line.

Teth, Eamon, and Ara reached Nimhea and the packhorse only to see more sand collapse beneath it. The packhorse fell to its knees, blowing and snorting with fear. Nimhea's mount was dragged backward. Nimhea cried out in alarm, clinging to her horse's neck.

"Try to stay on," Teth shouted at Nimhea. "We need your horse to keep moving forward!"

Nimhea nodded, driving her heels into her mount's sides. The horse lunged forward.

"Grab the rope," ordered Teth.

Ara and Eamon took hold of the length of rope that linked the packhorse to Nimhea's mount. Teth grasped the terrified horse's halter, hauling the beast to its feet. The horse struggled forward a few feet.

A few more feet. It was free of the sinkhole. Teth pulled it farther up the trail.

With another squeal, the packhorse's back legs went out from under it again. Ara stared in shock at the horse, then at the sinkhole as she realized it was moving, following the packhorse. Had it been stationary, they should have been out of danger. It was as though the sinkhole had chased after the horse.

"Teth!" Ara shouted. "The sinkhole! Look at it!"

Teth's focus had been fully on the packhorse. Now he shifted his gaze to the crater of sand and swore when he saw what Ara had seen. At the lowest point in the depression, something was moving. A dark mass churned below.

"Borer ants!" Eamon called. "This is how they hunt!"

What they had thought was a sinkhole was instead a funnel. A whirlpool of sand spinning faster and faster, dragging down anything that slipped over its edge.

The packhorse let out a desperate whinny and fell to one side.

Teth yelled as he lost his grip on its halter and slid into the swirling sand.

On instinct Ara let go of the rope and threw herself forward to catch Teth's forearms, dragging him out of harm's way. When she had him out of the funnel, they crawled back to Eamon. Ara and Teth grabbed the the rope and hauled on it, but the packhorse could hardly move its legs. It wheezed and shuddered, overwhelmed by exhaustion. Its eyes rolled back with fright.

"We have to save it!" Ara shouted at Eamon.

Eamon nodded, but his expression was one of helpless horror.

Ants began to spill out of dark hole at the bottom of the funnel. They were the size of cats. The ants skittered in circles, running with the whirlpool's current and using its speed to hurl themselves up the funnel toward the horse.

Freeing Ironbranch from its harness, Ara took a fistful of the packhorse's mane. When any ant jumped from the spinning funnel, Ironbranch was there to meet it before it could land.

Ant carapaces thudded against Ironbranch, and the stunned ants fell back into the hole. The ants kept coming no matter how many Ara knocked back. Recognizing that it was Ara who kept them from their meal, the ants began to hurl themselves at her rather than the horse.

An ant landed on her forearm. She swept the ant away, but the feeling of its weight, its scrabbling toward her shoulder, haunted her. More and more ants spilled out of the hole, throwing themselves at Ara and the horse. Too many for her to keep back.

"Nimhea!" Ara shouted. "We can't stay here!"

At Ara's cry, Nimhea began to scream at her mount, commanding it to press forward, but her horse's hooves were losing purchase on the ground. It had begun to slide inexorably backward.

Eamon yelped and dashed away, leaving Teth to hold the rope on his own.

The solid sand beneath Ara slipped away. She screamed as she fell, no longer pulling on the horse's mane, but hanging from it. She wrapped her legs around the horse to keep from falling any farther.

No! No! No! Her added weight made any rally from the packhorse unlikely.

"Ara!" Teth shouted curses at the futile efforts he made to drag Ara and the horse up the funnel.

One of the ants reached the packhorse's tail. With a new surface to grip, the ant scurried up the tail and onto the horse's flank. With a strangled cry, Ara lifted the ant with one end of Ironbranch and shook it loose. The ant dropped to the bottom of the whirlpool, where it was swallowed up by the churning darkness.

"Ara!" Teth wrapped his arm around the taut rope and reached out with his other hand. "You have to climb out of there! Swing Ironbranch up and I'll catch it."

Ara clenched her teeth. If she did what Teth wanted, it would leave the horse defenseless. She felt the creature's fear, and its desperate need to live, as if it were her own.

She continued to sweep the ants away.

They dropped farther into the whirlpool of sand, and Ara heard screams from above.

Nimhea is almost at the edge.

An ant clamped down on her boot. Ara shook her foot until the boot slipped off and the ant fell.

I have to save Nimhea. The Resistance needs her.

"Use Ironbranch to reach me," Teth called. "I'll cut the rope. If the borer ants are feeding they'll stop."

His words made her stomach curdle. *I'd be sending the horse to an unimaginable death.*

"I can pull you up with Ironbranch." Sweat poured down Teth's brow. "But you have to let go of the horse."

The packhorse squealed as an ant bit into its flank. Ara swept it away.

She gazed into the horse's liquid brown eye, and time seemed to stop.

I have a choice. I can save myself by sacrificing this animal. But what gives me the right to judge my life worth more than its life? How would I feel if it were Cloud or Dust instead of a packhorse? What would I do if it was Eamon or Teth?

I'm not leaving you. Ara pressed her cheek against the horse's neck. *Fellow traveler.*

Ironbranch tingled in her grip. When she looked down at the stave, it was glowing.

The Loresmith stave has hidden powers.

"Teth!" Ara swung Ironbranch up, and Teth caught the far end of the stave.

He drew a dagger from his belt.

"Put that away!" Ara shouted. "Let go of the rope and pull us!"

"I can't—" Teth began.

"Just do it!"

His face twisted with anguish, but he gripped Ironbranch with both hands and began to pull.

The packhorse began to move, taking Ara with it.

Teth's eyes went wide with disbelief, but he kept pulling back.

The horse squealed again as ants landed on its legs. They skittered toward Ara. She kicked them away with her booted foot. The horse's head rose above the edge of the funnel.

Then its shoulders were out of the trap, and Ara flung herself forward, rolling away from the devouring sand and freeing the packhorse of her weight.

Ara ran to help Teth drag the horse up and a few feet away from the borer ants. The packhorse lay on its side, drenched in sweat and wheezing. Ara crouched beside the beast, holding Ironbranch close.

"We have to try to get that horse up." Teth drew his dagger and severed the rope tied to Nimhea's horse. "Get out of here!" Teth shouted at the twins.

Nimhea and Eamon spurred their horses into a gallop.

Ara took the halter of the fallen packhorse with one hand and called to Teth. "Help me!"

Ara pulled the packhorse toward her while Teth wedged his arms beneath the beast's right shoulder. With a weak whicker, the horse rolled onto its stomach.

"That's it, friend," Ara murmured to the horse. "Just a little more now."

Bringing a waterskin to the horse's mouth, Ara waited for it to drink. Then she stroked the horse's neck, making soothing noises, as she tugged on its halter. The horse put its front hooves on the ground. Shaking, it struggled to lift its chest and stomach, giving its back legs space to find solid ground.

The horse rose on trembling limbs. Lathered and still breathing hard, the packhorse stood up. Its eyes were wild with fear. It could only take slow, unsteady steps forward.

Glancing behind her, saw the sand funnel moving toward them.

"It's coming for us."

"I know," Teth said. He laid his arm across the horse's back and pressed his body against the horse, trying to support it. "Come on. You have the strength for this."

The horse pushed itself along the trail, walking faster.

"That's it!" Teth patted its neck. "See your friends ahead? You'll be with them in no time."

Snorting, the horse reached a pace where Ara and Teth had to jog alongside it. Ara looked back. The borer ants were no longer gaining on them.

The packhorse gave a horrid, shrieking cry and collapsed to its knees.

"No!" Ara knelt beside the horse. "Please get up. Please."

Face full of despair, Teth began to untie packs from the horse. "It can't go any farther. Its heart is ready to give out."

He gestured to the packs. "Take as much as you can carry, but still run. Water takes priority. We'll die without it."

Ara found the pack filled with waterskins and draped it over her shoulder. She looked back and saw the sand funnel bearing down on them.

She her hand on the horse's neck. "I'm sorry. I'm so sorry." Her voice cracked as tears spilled down her cheeks.

Watching her, Teth continued, "I'll cut its throat before we leave. It won't suffer."

The borer ants were only a few yards away.

"You should go," Teth told her. "I'm right behind you."

"I will not leave without you," Ara said through gritted teeth.

Teth knew better than to argue.

Suddenly, Fox was there. After yipping at Teth and Ara, Fox bent its muzzle and sniffed the exhausted packhorse. Fox gave a small sad cry. The horse answered with a strained whinny.

The little beast trotted around Ara and gazed upon the approaching whirlpool of sand. Fox snarled and gave a vicious bark, then ran directly at the sand trap.

"Fox!" Teth jumped to his feet.

Reaching the edge of the swirling sand, Fox began to race around its perimeter. Faster and faster, Fox sped along the circle, eyes darting at its center.

Ara cried out as Fox leapt into funnel. A moment later Fox was running around the edge once more.

"What the—" Teth stared in astonishment.

Fox jumped into the whirlpool again, dashing along the inside of the traps, then using the trap's speed to fling itself back to solid ground. Repeating this pattern, Fox appeared to be bouncing in and out of the funnel. The whirlpool spun faster and faster, reflecting the borer ants' frustration with their erratic prey. Ants spilled out of the sinkhole, desperate to catch Fox, but none succeeded.

The packhorse blew hard into the sand, startling Ara and Teth, and sending a spray of dust in the air. Collecting its legs beneath it, the horse staggered up. Giving a hard, mane-to-tail shake of its body, the packhorse started forward. Its breathing had steadied, and its muscles no longer shook with exhaustion.

"That's unexpected." Teth gave the animal a hard look.

The packhorse set out at a swift walk, looking back once to see if Ara and Teth followed.

Incredulous, Teth shook his head then turned back toward Fox.

"That's enough, Fox!" Teth shouted. "Time to go!"

Fox leapt out of the whirlpool and ran a few feet up the trail. Locking eyes with Teth, Fox gave several sharp, playful barks. Then Fox wheeled around and raced back to the swirling sand trap. Fox sprang high into the air . . . and dove directly into the funnel's churning black center.

The world around them went silent. The whirlpool stopped spinning, and the wind began to fill the gaping hole with sand.

Moments later it was all gone. The whirlpool. The borer ants.

And Fox.

17

 eth's cry of anguish was almost inhuman. The sound clawed at Ara's heart. He dropped to his knees.

"Why?" he shouted at the desert. "Why did you do that?"

Grabbing fistfuls of sand, Teth hurled them toward the spot where the whirlpool had been.

"You didn't have to do it!" Teth yelled. "We were safe."

His voice broke, and he buried his face in his hands.

Ara was about to go to him when Lahvja's voice pierced the iar.

"You were not safe."

Lahvja sat astride her horse. Dust and Cloud stood a short distance behind, watching the Summoner with curious eyes. Oddly, no lead ropes tied them to Lahvja's mount.

"How—" Ara began to ask.

"You," Teth was on his feet. His word a snarl.

"We must not linger here," Lahvja told them. "Our companions await us in the Bone Forest."

"Why weren't you here?" Teth stalked toward her. "You could have stopped it!"

Ara thought the accusation unfair. Teth didn't know the extent or bounds of Lahvja's magic.

"No," Lahvja replied calmly. "My power exists in harmony with nature. To command a predator to quit its prey violates natural laws."

"Senn devour your natural laws!" Teth shouted. "Fox was our friend. You said Fox was *your* friend."

"Fox is my friend," replied Lahvja quietly.

Teth glared at her. He stumbled toward Dust and climbed into the saddle.

"There is something wicked in you," Teth said with bared teeth. "Stay away from me."

"Teth . . ." Ara knew his anger was driven by grief, but Lahvja hadn't earned such harsh words.

Lahvja remained still. Sadness touched her eyes as she watched him.

Wheeling Dust around, Teth urged his horse into a gallop. He didn't look back.

Numbly, Ara took the waterskin pack to Cloud and tied it behind her saddle.

This could have been a moment of triumph. Ironbranch brought about the impossible.

But the miracle was marred by death.

She returned to do the same with the packs Teth had removed.

"Place those upon the mare's back," Lahvja said. "She is fully restored."

Ara hesitated, staring at the packs in confusion, but ultimately was too bewildered to do anything but comply.

"Should I water her?" Ara asked Lahvja, petting the packhorse's soft nose. The horse pushed its head against Ara's shoulder and whickered.

"It's not necessary," Lahvja replied. "We should be on our way."

Climbing onto Cloud's back with her booted foot in the stirrup and her bare foot dangling, Ara let Lahvja set their pace as they continued on the trail. The horses moved at a swift walk; ahead, the Bone Forest grew larger and larger. Though the sun still blazed overhead, Ara ignored the pressing heat. And tried to understand Fox's choice. The little beast had intentionally given itself to the borer ants. An action that spared Teth, Ara, and the packhorse. What could compel an animal to sacrifice itself? Ara couldn't make any sense of it.

Gazing at Lahvja, Ara asked, "What just happened?"

"What had to." Lahvja didn't look at her.

"Could you have stopped it?" Ara could still see Fox floating above the swirling funnel, then plunging into its depths.

After taking a long breath, Lahvja answered, "Not without attacking that which I'm sworn to protect."

"Couldn't you have made an exception?" Fox was an extraordinary creature. Surely it deserved to be saved.

"Exceptions are like cracks in a dam," Lahvja said quietly. "A few may seem harmless, but eventually the river will burst through."

Ara fell into silence, grieving, confused. She'd saved the packhorse only to lose Fox. It didn't seem fair. And worse, Ara knew that whatever sadness she felt, it was nothing compared to Teth's loss.

The border between the Scourge and the Bone Forest was so stark and confounding, Ara knew it couldn't be natural. Approximately ten yards before the treeline, the sand simply stopped, giving way to grayish, chalky earth. The strength and direction of the wind had no bearing on the movement of the sand. Not a single grain blew into the Bone Forest.

The second uncanny change upon leaving the Scourge was an inexplicable drop in temperature. The midafternoon sun was high and bright, but the near the Bone Forest was comfortable, neither hot nor chilling.

Observing Ara's reactions, Lahvja smiled and said, "The places of the gods have their own rules."

Nimhea and Eamon had set up what they could of camp without the supplies borne by the second packhorse. They greeted Ara and Lahvja soberly. Nimhea came to them with sympathy in her eyes, but Eamon watched Lahvja with a guarded expression that verged on hostile. Fortunately, Ara's spare shoes hadn't been lost in the fray.

"Where is Teth?" Ara asked, remembering her lone boot and putting on leather shoes.

Eamon pointed to the edge of the trees, a small space apart from the camp. Teth sat with his back to them. Dust was beside him, snuffling at Teth's shoulder every so often.

Ara started toward him, but Eamon caught her arm.

"He told us he wants to be alone."

Eamon's warning stung. Ara wanted to believe that Teth's *alone* didn't include her, but out of respect she had to assume it did. Eamon threw a disparaging glance at Lahvja. He clearly had taken Teth's view of Fox's death. Nimhea, on the other hand, stood close to Lahvja. The two women smiled as they talked to each other. Ara was caught between them. The loss of Fox was a spear in her heart, but she could understand Lahvja's position.

"They can finish making camp," Eamon said with a dismissive air. "Let me show you the forest."

"I thought we weren't going in yet," Ara replied.

"We're not," Eamon said, pulling her along. "But we can stand on the edge and look inside."

Ara walked beside Eamon toward the Bone Forest. They stopped a foot from the closest trees. Caught up in the distress of fleeing the borer ants and Fox's death, Ara hadn't turned her attention to the features of this strange place. Even now that she did, her mind struggled to interpret its otherworldly character.

The only trees of the Bone Forest were like bleached white skeletons left unburied in the desert. Every tree gave its neighbor a wide berth, creating broad, open spaces on the forest floor. No ferns or brush grew beneath the trees.

The trees' immense trunks ranged from huge to enormous, with some too large for five people to form a ring around. The trees stretched toward the sky at heights of one hundred to three hundred feet. No leaves decorated their branches, which grew out and up in twisting but symmetrical shapes. Each branch ended in a thornlike tip, most of which were as long as javelins.

Intermittent gashes marred the white trunks, from which thick red sap oozed.

"The sap is what gives butcher crows their size." Eamon's voice was a reverent whisper. "It also bestows them with the knowledge to judge seekers of Ofrit as worthy or unworthy."

Ara glanced at him. "That's what the lore says?"

"Yes," Eamon said. "I can tell you the story if you'd like."

"Please." Ara sat cross-legged on the ground. "I want to understand what we're getting into." In truth, Ara wanted a distraction from the horror of the borer ants and the pain of losing Fox.

With a wan smile, Eamon replied, "I hope you don't regret asking. The tale goes like this . . ."

After the gods had sworn fealty to one another and settled
with their peoples in Saetlund, four of them questioned the wisdom
of including the fifth, Ofrit, in their company. For Ofrit was ill-
tempered and reclusive. The other gods worried he would soon

neglect his people or refuse to take counsel with his peers. But they were grieved to lose him, for there was no wiser god than Ofrit. His mind was labyrinthine, his imagination boundless. Doubtless Ofrit would bring wonders to his people . . . if only he kept an interest in them. The Sower, the Hunter, the Twins, and Eni took counsel with one another to decide if they should plead with their brother or intervene directly with his people, the Daefritians.

The words of Eni at last swayed the other gods in Ofrit's favor, for all the gods loved Eni.

"I am the Traveler," said Eni. "My realm is that of the courier, the messenger, the page. I will carry our thoughts to Ofrit and remind him of his responsibilities to his people and the world, should he join with us."

The other gods assented, for where Ofrit might have been affronted by a demand made by any other among them, they were certain he would heed the words of Eni.

Eni sought out Ofrit in his apothecary, where the Alchemist would easily lose himself in research for eons. Eni knew it was imperative to win Ofrit's interest in and commitment to his people before that could happen.

"My brother," Eni entreated. "You have retreated from the world and into this place for many months. Your people struggle without your presence and blessings."

"I gave them language," Ofrit replied sourly.

"Yes," Eni agreed. "As we all did."

"Isn't that enough?" Ofrit said. "I chose the people of this province because they had cunning, curious minds. With language they can speak and read and write. They can work the rest out for themselves. Knowledge isn't a gift; it's earned."

"Then let them earn an audience with you," urged Eni. "Your people will lose their way without your blessings. Do you want them to suffer?"

"Don't be ridiculous," Ofrit told his sibling. "I would not have chosen them if I wished them ill."

"There must be those worthy of you, whom you should teach," argued Eni. "They can return to their people as leaders, holy men and women, who will take what they have learned and shape their society according to your wisdom."

Ofrit stroked his beard. "I admit, I like the sound of that. A society devoted to learning. That would be a marvel to see."

"It would indeed," said Eni.

"But I can't have every puffed-up fool who thinks they're worthy showing up to petition me," Ofrit snapped. "I have important work to do here."

"Of course," Eni replied, then mused, "Perhaps there should be a test. A way to sort the unworthy from those truly devoted to you."

Ofrit regarded his sibling with suspicion. "What kind of test?"

"A puzzle to be solved," Eni suggested. "Or hardships to overcome."

"Both!" Ofrit exclaimed with delight. "A puzzle to test their cleverness, but also treacherous ground barring the way so that they must prove their dedication."

"An excellent solution, my brother." Eni smiled.

"What an enjoyable task this will be." Ofrit moved to his drafting table. "I shall begin immediately."

Eni returned to the other gods to celebrate Ofrit's new scheme. Eni had invited Ofrit to join them, but Ofrit was already consumed by the work that lay ahead.

First, Ofrit created a pathway from Daefrit to his apothecary, which exists out of time, but the god in his cleverness fashioned a bridge linking the human world to this extraordinary place. Ofrit placed this pathway in the Ghost Hills, a place steeped in frightening lore, with origins that stretched back to a time before the gods. Thus, he ensured only those whose minds could overcome their primal fears would seek him.

Next, the god devised a puzzle, the only way to reach his Bridge Between Worlds. This puzzle he made in the form of a great labyrinth. Its solution could be discovered by only the most cunning of seekers.

Finally, Ofrit brought forth from the desert landscape a forest of trees unlike any other. Bleached and leafless, this strange wood became known as the Bone Forest. Ofrit filled the Bone Forest with strange, deadly creatures who could see into the heart of any person. These forest guardians kept all, save those with pure intentions, from reaching the labyrinth.

When word reached the people of Daefrit that their god had opened a path for them to reach him, many made the pilgrimage to the Bone Forest. A good portion lost their lives long before the forest was in sight. Many succumbed to the hardships of the Punishing Desert. Others fell to the nightmarish beasts that populate the Scourge. Of those who did reach the Bone Forest, not many were judged worthy of Ofrit's blessings; thus, their corpses decorated the white tree branches. Those remaining that found Ofrit's path and the entrance to the labyrinth labored at this puzzle. Most perished in the process.

The few who passed all of Ofrit's Trials and crossed the interdimensional bridge found themselves in the god's apothecary

*and were welcomed by Ofrit himself. Having completed their
pilgrimage, these select women and men became Ofrit's disciples.
They spent years in the company of their god. Their families and
friends presumed them lost to the perils of the journey.*

*When Ofrit deemed it the right time, his disciples returned
to their homes, bearing Ofrit's sign on their palms. Known as the
Scribes of Ofrit, these wise men and women shared Ofrit's wisdom
with all who came to them. Their immense knowledge inspired
a new wave of pilgrims to make the trek to the Bone Forest.
With each attempt, news returned to the cities of Daefrit of the
trials' difficulty. Soon only the most dedicated embarked on the
pilgrimage. As the years passed, new Scribes returned from Ofrit's
Apothecary, taking their place as Daefrit's great teachers. Every so
often a boastful warrior or glory-seeker would face the trials. None
survived.*

*The repuation of Ofrit's Scribes drew sojourners from every
part of Saetlund, and their fame grew. The teachings of holy men
and women, and the actions of those who sought to emulate them,
were the catalysts for the establishment of Daefrit's renowned
centers of scholarship: the Great Libary of Talia, the universities of
Isar and Zyre, and the Halls of Contemplation. Thusly did Daefrit
become widely proclaimed as the most learned of the provinces.*

"Do you regret asking?" Eamon gazed at Ara with earnest eyes.

Of all the gods, Ofrit was the one Ara knew the least about. The god
of Daefrit was reclusive. Like Ayre and Syre, Ofrit didn't appear in many
of Imgar's tales. They were the gods who lived apart from the world:
Ofrit in his apothecary and the Twins at the Wells. Gods of the mysteries
Ayre and Syre held the secrets of magic; while Ofrit dealt in the hidden

powers of plants, earth, and minerals. His knowledge could offer life, but always walked close beside death.

Having spent so much time laughing at Eni's tricks and imagining hunts with Wuldr, Ara was intimidated by Ofrit's solitary nature. He forced those who sought him to prove themselves through life-threatening trials and asked them to take on reclusive lives dedicated to study. Ara thought Ofrit a harsh god and feared he would reject her for judging him so.

Ara drew a long breath and answered Eamon honestly. "I haven't decided yet."

When Eamon and Ara returned to camp, Lahvja was waiting by the fire. She gestured for them to sit beside Nimhea. Ara cast her gaze toward the place Teth still sat and Dust continued his watch. She wanted to go to him. To listen to him and take on the burden of his sorrow.

With a sigh, Ara sat down. No matter what she felt, her focus had to be Ofrit's Trials.

"We must talk of your journey on the morrow," Lahvja said. "The strain of this day weighs heavily on you, and I would advise you to sleep as the sun does."

Ara was still reeling from Eamon's tale. She looked at the sky. The sun was sinking toward the horizon. "I doubt I'll be able to sleep that early." Her mind was a knot of nerves.

"I've prepared a tonic that will give you long, restorative sleep," Lahvja told her. "You'll need to call upon the sum of your wits and be sustained by the fullness of your fortitude to find Ofrit."

Eamon barely concealed his scowl. "And I supposed you'll also tell us what we must do to complete our quest."

"No," Lahvja replied solemnly. "That is not my task; it is yours."

"Oh." Eamon blinked at her, then ducked his head, chagrined.

"The depth of your learning is the map that will guide you," Lahvja told him.

That brought a little smile to Eamon's face.

Nimhea turned to her brother. "You know the way?"

"Yes." Eamon nodded quickly.

"Do you know how long it will take?" Ara asked. They'd had to estimate how much water and food they would need for their time in the Bone Forest. If the trials weren't a matter of hours but of days, they wouldn't have enough.

"No," Eamon admitted. "The directions I've gathered aren't literal. They don't speak of distances, but signs."

"Wait." Ara held up her hand. "We should get Teth before we talk further. He'll want to know these things."

"Teth should be left alone," Lahvja said in a firm voice. "It's what he desires."

"But—" Ara looked at Lahvja, confused and somewhat put off by Lahvja's presumption that she knew what he wanted more than Ara.

"He will not enter the Bone Forest," Lahvja said, cutting her off. "Neither will I."

Shaking her head, Ara argued, "We shouldn't break up the group. It's too dangerous."

"There would be greater danger should Teth and I join you." Lahvja took Ara's hands in hers and gave them a reassuring squeeze.

Releasing Ara's hands, Lahvja took a moment to look at each of them in turn.

"The Queen," Lahvja murmured, meeting Nimhea's gaze.

"The Scholar." Lahvja nodded to Eamon.

When she turned to Ara, Lahvja's gray eyes were full of mystery. "The Loresmith."

The Summoner fell silent, letting these titles rest upon them like mantles.

Ara didn't like leaving Teth and Lahvja at the camp, but at least she wouldn't be alone.

"Where are you getting this information?" Eamon's expression kept switching from amazement to suspicion. "It's not in any of the scholarship."

"It wouldn't be," Lahvja replied. "I share with you what is whispered to me from the air and the earth."

Eamon frowned. It wasn't the explanation he'd hoped for.

"This piece of the journey is for you three and no others." Lahvja spoke with finality. Then a smile twitched onto her lips. "Besides. Someone has to watch over the horses."

The morning sky was red as the sap that seeped from the trees. Ara dressed in her usual suede breeches under a long, sleeveless tunic, belted at the waist. The Loresmith stave hung from its harness across her back. She carried a small satchel in which she'd placed the blue silk scarf and a long-sleeved tunic.

Upon waking, Ara had briefly wondered if the occasion of meeting a god warranted more formal dress. She quickly dismissed that notion. No fine clothes were at her disposal, and if the gods were to judge her it should be as herself. No costumes or trappings. Simply Ara Silverthread: daughter of the last Loresmith.

Though dawn had barely spread across the Scourge, Eamon and Nimhea were already breaking their fast.

Ara's first glance went to the place Teth had spent the previous day. He was gone, and Dust was picketed with the other horses. Ara hoped he was asleep in his tent and that rest would provide him some relief.

She joined Nimhea and Eamon at the fire. "Did you sleep?"

The twins nodded.

"I never sleep soundly," said Eamon. "Lahvja's tonic brought me rest more pleasant than . . . well, than anything besides the night that old woman in the forest made us tea."

Nimhea smiled at the memory. "I slept and did not stir till dawn."

Ara looked at the crumbs on their plates. "You've already finished."

"We'll wait for you," Eamon said quickly.

"No." Ara picked up the roll that had been set aside for her. "I'll eat this as we go. I can't bear waiting here any longer."

In truth her stomach was twisted so tightly, Ara didn't know if she'd be able to eat at all.

"Thank Nava." Nimhea stood up and adjusted her sword belt.

Surprisingly Eamon wasn't overburdened by a pack full of books. He had only a small bag slung over his shoulder.

"Lahvja packed food for us," Eamon told Ara when he saw her gaze fall on the bag. "Since we don't know how long this journey will take."

Ara nodded. "Let's go then."

The three of them walked to the edge of the trees. They gazed up at the tall, thornlike branches and watched red sap seep onto pale trunks. Though Ara knew it was not, the Bone Forest looked endless. A place where one would inevitably become lost, or be lost forever.

Ara steeled herself and stepped between the tall trees and into the forest. Instantly something had changed. Wheeling around, Ara looked for Eamon and Nimhea, fearing they might be gone. But the twins were only a few steps behind her. Beyond them, Ara could make out the camp, but it was blurred like she was looking up at it from beneath rippling water.

"There's a barrier between us and the camp," she murmured. She could see its translucence stretching from the ground to the sky.

Nimhea turned around and retraced her steps till she stood close to the undulating surface. "We walked through it easily enough, so it can't be meant to protect the forest."

She lifted her hand.

"I wouldn't touch it!" Eamon called to his sister.

Looking over her shoulder, Nimhea asked, "Why not?"

"Because I don't know what will happen if you do," he told her. "I don't think it would kill you, but it might hurt you. No reason to risk it."

Nimhea let her hand fall to her side and came to back to join Eamon and Ara.

"Did you know about this?" Ara demanded of Eamon.

"No," he said earnestly. "But I'm not surprised by it. Only those seeking Ofrit enter the Bone Forest. I think once you cross over, you've committed to being judged."

Nimhea's eyes narrowed. "You're saying we can't leave."

"I'm saying there is only one way we can leave," Eamon replied. "By passing Ofrit's Trials."

There's no going back. Ara was grateful for the familiar weight of Ironbranch against her back.

"All right then." Nimhea scanned the forest that lay ahead. "Which way do we go?"

Eamon smiled brightly. "It doesn't matter."

"How can it not matter?" Ara asked, though as she surveyed the area around them it all looked the same.

"We have to keep walking," Eamon told them. "Farther into the forest. That's where we'll be judged. We can't find Ofrit's Path unless we're judged. If we are the path will find us."

Nimhea walked ahead. "I choose this way."

Laughing, Eamon followed, and Ara ran a few steps to catch up.

How many others have walked to their judgment?

"I'm not fond of all this ambiguous mysticism," Nimhea grumbled. "I'd much prefer a straightforward sword fight."

Ara smiled at her. "That does sound less complicated."

The three of them walked, and walked, and walked some more. Nothing around them changed. Each of the trees had a unique size and shape, but the ground remained bare. No other distinctive features appeared in the forest. Though they should have been making progress toward somewhere, Ara had the uncanny feeling that time wasn't passing. Whenever she looked up to gauge the height of the sun, it wasn't there. The sky was there. Blue, cloudless. But the sun was nowhere to be found. Nor could she estimate the hour by the weariness of her body. The satchel slung over her shoulder didn't grow heavier as she walked, nor did her stave become a tiresome burden. Her legs seemed not to tire.

CAW!

Ara, Nimhea, and Eamon froze.

The sound was clearly a crow's call, but along with it came a visceral sensation like the vibrations of a giant bell that had been rung.

The call had reverberated in the branches of the trees around them. Out of habit Ara looked for scattering songbirds and startled rabbits, but only their trio stirred in the forest.

Slowly, Ara looked up. A butcher crow perched on a branch ten feet above her head—a branch Ara could have sworn was empty a moment ago. The massive bird tilted its head, peering at her. *CAW!*

Ara could feel the force of its cry in her bones.

Nimhea's sword hissed out of its scabbard, and Ara freed her stave from its harness.

"Keep walking," Eamon murmured. "It's begun."

Ara wondered what form the judgment would come in, how she would know it had happened. Would it confront her or pass through her like a ghost? If the gods found her wanting would there be any warning or would the crows deliver the message with their beaks and claws?

Eamon began walking at a stately pace, as if leading a holy procession. Ara and Nimhea followed slightly behind, holding their weapons defensively while they kept wary eyes on the surrounding forest.

A loud fluttering of wings came from Ara's right.

CAW! CAW!

Two more butcher crows had landed in nearby trees. With dark, piercing eyes they gazed upon the trio below.

More birds landed. Some remained in the highest branches, drinking the red sap of the trees. Others were bold enough to dive low, perching where their taloned feet could easily grab Nimhea's shoulder or Ara's head.

As the butcher crows gathered in the trees, something else in the forest had changed. Objects dangled from the thornlike tips of the branches. At first they were too far away for Ara to discern what they were.

Nimhea gasped. She stopped and stared at something hanging from a low branch.

Ara followed Nimhea's gaze.

"Eni protect us," Ara murmured.

Impaled on sharp tip of the branch was the carcass of what Ara suspected was a cliff panther. Chunks of the big cat's flesh had been torn away, but enough remained to make it clear what was being devoured.

"That's where their name comes from."

Eamon's voice made Ara jump.

"They hang their prey in the trees," Eamon continued. "Saving it."

"Ara—" Nimhea's voice was rough. Her gaze locked on the trees ahead, where more carcasses hung.

A wave of nausea crashed through Ara's stomach.

"We must continue," Eamon whispered.

Nimhea looked to Ara, who clenched her teeth and nodded.

More and more crows filled the trees, but their piercing cries had stopped. For Ara, the silence was worse; it amplified the only other sound, that of branches weighted by bodies, creaking though there was no wind.

The bone-white trees that had been eerie were now ghastly. Ara tried not to look closely at the bodies. Panthers, giant toads, lizards, and oversized insects in varying states of decay hung all around them. Dry bones fallen from on high now littered the once-empty forest floor.

Her foot caught on something and she stumbled.

Nimhea took hold of Ara's upper arm, steadying her. "Are you all right?"

Ara nodded, then looked down to see what had tripped her. It was a desiccated arm. A human arm. Shreds of fabric still clung to the leathery flesh.

Choking on a cry of horror, Ara faltered. Nimhea had to hold her steady.

When Eamon came back to see what was the matter, he looked at the arm and said, "Oh."

"Is that all you have to say?" Nimhea snapped at him.

Ara couldn't speak; nor could she stop her eyes from climbing the trees. Scattered among the carcasses were human bodies. Unlike the animals, the human dead were mostly intact. Thorns pierced their sternums, keeping the bodies upright, but the normal process of decay hadn't transformed them into skeletons. Hair sprouted from their scalps, and husk-like, wrinked skin clung to their bones. Most wore tattered clothing that hung loose upon their shrunken forms.

"The unworthy," murmured Eamon. "This is their fate."

Nimhea glared at the hanging bodies. "What kind of god does this?"

"Ofrit must be cruel," Ara said.

"What kind of hubris must a person possess to believe they can cheat a god?" came Eamon's retort. "The lore is filled with warnings. Only those who ignore them die here."

"You think they deserved this?" Nimhea stared at her brother in disbelief.

"It's not about what they deserved," Eamon replied. "This is what they chose when they came to this holy place under false pretense."

Ara was taken aback by Eamon's absolute lack of sympathy for the dead in the trees and the way his eyes flared with indignation. The adventurers and fortune-hunters who came here might not be worthy of Ofrit's blessing, but she was still horrified that they had met such an end. Such a cruel punishment for what might have been simple foolhardiness and not some insidious aim. The expression on Nimhea's face told Ara the princess was in agreement. Only Eamon could gaze at the hanging corpses with eyes cold and unflinching.

A mind of a scholar might demand that, Ara thought. *A dispassionate gaze that could analyze evidence objectively.*

But she wondered how a person could look at the world with such eyes and still remain human.

"I don't want to linger here." Ara turned away from the twins and continued walking but at a swifter pace. She kept her eyes ahead, ignoring the horrors in her peripheral vision as best she could.

All at once the butcher crows burst into a cacophony of cries.

CAW! CAW! CAW!

The calls layered upon one another, a never-ending echo. The noise shook the ground and rattled the trees. Ara planted Ironbranch in the ground and braced herself. The sounds hit her like physical blows. She heard the flapping of wings and was soon buffeted by fierce winds from every direction.

Ara closed her eyes, but lifted her face and stood tall.

CAW! CAW! CAW!

The sound stopped. The winds died.

Ara slowly opened her eyes. Nimhea and Eamon were crouched together beneath a tree.

They were still in the Bone Forest, but the butcher crows and bodies were gone. The white trees stood empty and austere.

Nimhea and Eamon helped each other up. Eamon's face suddenly filled with triumph.

"Look!" He pointed at Ara's feet.

Instead of gray earth, she now stood upon granite blocks that were set in an alternating pattern of dark and light stone.

"Ofrit's Path." Eamon's voice trembled with exhilaration. "We've been chosen."

18

 hosen.

When little Ara had dreamed of becoming the Loresmith she hadn't imagined that fulfilling one's destiny required being chosen more than once. That it wouldn't be enough to be her father's daughter.

Looking at Ofrit's Path, Ara felt a thrill but also a trickle of cold dread. This wasn't the last trial. She would have to be chosen again. And again. Ara pushed the burden of that thought aside and started walking.

The path led out of the Bone Forest, bringing Ara, Nimhea, and Eamon to a courtyard in the shape of a half circle. The dark and light stones of the path covered the ground to become the courtyard floor. A curving wall of red sandstone marked the dimensions of the space. Rising twenty feet high, the wall was at its widest where it met the Bone Forest—fifty feet from one side to the other. Towers of stone loomed behind the wall, leading Ara to believe Ofrit's Path had returned them to the Ghost Cliffs.

The labyrinth must be hidden within the cliffs. Or beneath them.

The wall opposite the Bone Forest held two massive doors. One of blood-red cherry, the other darkest ebony, both ornately carved. Set into the sandstone, the doors were framed on three sides by an alternating pattern of dark and light sandstone blocks identical to that of the courtyard floor.

"You should investigate," Nimhea told Ara and Eamon. "I don't like having this forest at our back. I'm going to keep an eye on it for a bit."

Ara gazed at the doors in wonder. "Do you know what this is?"

"Both doors give entry to the labyrinth," Eamon said as he crossed. "But only one leads to Ofrit's Apothecary; the other offers eternity within the maze."

With a tight laugh, Ara said, "Tell me you know what door to choose."

When he didn't answer, Ara looked at him with disbelief that quickly became fear.

"You don't know?" Her voice jumped an octave.

The depth of your learning is the map that will guide you. That was what Lahvja had said to Eamon. *Where does that leave us when his knowledge proves too shallow?*

Nimhea shared Ara's alarm. She abandoned her watch of the forest and came to face Eamon.

"Surely you know something," Nimhea pressed her brother. "An account of someone who's been through the labyrinth."

Eamon stared past his sister to the immense doors, his face drawn. "There is no such account."

"There must be." Nimhea gestured to the satchel Eamon carried.

"No one has returned from the labyrinth." Eamon adjusted the bag's strap on his shoulder, uncomfortable with this sudden scrutiny.

"What about the Scribes?" Ara asked desperately. "Don't they have access to Ofrit's Apothecary?"

Eamon nodded. "The Scribes share Ofrit's wisdom, but never his secrets. They're Ofrit's followers. They wouldn't reveal the solution to his puzzles. That would be heresy."

"Ugh." Nimhea threw up her hands.

"It's okay." Ara didn't want an argument. "Eamon, you must have some idea about what I'm supposed to do."

Her anger flared. She'd proven herself in the forest only to run into a wall. Literally.

It was Eamon's good fortune that he answered. "I have a couple."

"What are they?" Nimhea asked.

"There's a phrase that's repeated in all stories about the labyrinth," Eamon said. "'All who seek Ofrit must follow his path; only the wise will find him.'"

Ara's heart gave an unpleasant thud. "That's not very helpful. The path could be on the other side of either door."

"I agree," Eamon replied. "But I think we might be able to find the answer on the doors."

"How would we find an answer *on* the doors?" Nimhea asked.

Excitement crept into Eamon's voice. "Within the carvings. Since there is nothing in the literature to help us, there must be something about the doors themselves that can help you choose. A riddle. Images that relate to Ofrit."

"It's a place to start," said Ara. "Nimhea, I think you should stand guard while Eamon and I try to interpret the carvings on the doors. I don't know if anything keeps cliff panthers away from here. Or if Ofrit has any other surprises lying in wait."

Nimhea nodded and began a patrol around the courtyard.

As Ara and Eamon drew closer, the etched pattern of dark and light sandstone appeared to stretch out toward them. A trick of the eye had made the pattern appear flush with the wall from a distance, when in fact the dark and light stones composed decorative dividers, separating the two doors. The contrasting blocks climbed at a forty-five-degree angle, with the first waist-high block set a few feet away from the wall and the last block matching the height of the wall.

"Clever," Eamon said admiringly.

Ara made an ambivalent sound, too wary to be appreciative of design.

"I'll take the ebony door," Eamon told Ara. "You have a look at the red door. Keep in mind, this is a puzzle any worthy petitioner should be able to solve. It's not specific to the Loresmith."

The door built from the wood of a cherry tree was divided into four panels. The carvings within each panel were intricate and beautiful, so detailed they almost leapt off the wood.

The first panel was filled with the image of a tree, more specifically a tree from the Bone Forest. Ara had been running her fingers over the grooves in the wood and suddenly snatched them back, suspicious that the door was not cherry, but carved from the innards of a Bone Forest tree. The red hue of the wood matched that of the sap that leaked from those trees.

With a shiver, Ara moved on to the next panel. It depicted the interior of the Bone Forest, replete with bodies hanging from the branches. Ara's stomach turned, and she quickly looked at the third panel. A butcher crow was its occupant, wings spread wide. Ara was grateful it wasn't eating anything.

The fourth panel was a precise replica of the courtyard they had just entered.

Drawing no conclusions from her inspection, Ara went to see what Eamon had found. They almost walked into each other as they came around the dividing wall, as Eamon had been on his way to find Ara.

She described the four panels of the red door to Eamon.

"Interesting." He scratched his beard absentmindedly.

"What was on your door?" Ara asked.

"The five signs of the gods," Eamon replied.

Ara waited for him to illuminate her on the significance of either door's carvings, but he was quiet.

"Do you have any ideas about what door we should take?" she pressed.

Eamon frowned at her. "Unfortunately, I could make a case for either."

Ara's shoulders sagged. She'd been thinking the same thing.

Senn's teeth, I'm a blacksmith, not a puzzle master. She would have preferred a test of how quickly she could unshod and reshod a horse.

"Let's talk with Nimhea," Eamon suggested. "Maybe the three of us can work it out together."

Nimhea was confident the red door would open to safe passage through the labyrinth. Eamon, however, had been leaning toward the ebony door and its signs of the gods. Ara had no opinion whatsoever. Both doors depicted things of equal significance.

"But it makes sense," Nimhea argued. "Those are the trials we just completed. Behind that door is the reward for being deemed worthy."

"That's a fair point," Eamon replied. "But it's redundant. That part of Ofrit's Trials is over. What we seek is the blessing of the gods. The way forward, the future, lies behind the black door."

Nimhea shook her head. "We seek Ofrit's blessing. One god. These are Ofrit's Trials. We had to find Ofrit's Path. I don't think the other gods are involved."

"The Loresmith must be judged worthy by all the gods," Eamon countered. "The signs carved into the ebony door could be in reference to that."

"Could be." Nimhea squared her shoulders. "What happens if we open the wrong door?"

"Nothing good."

As they continued to argue, Ara wandered back toward the doors, intending to examine them both. Her eyes followed the pattern on the floor of the courtyard. She frowned, noticing something for the first time. At the point where the floor met the first block of the dividing wall, the pattern continued up the wall without interruption. On first glance, Ara had perceived the pattern on the walls as complementary to that of the courtyard. In truth, its distinctive feature was its continuity. Ara moved to the other two decorative walls and found they likewise continued the pattern from the floor stones, yet that pattern did not appear anywhere on the doors.

"All who seek Ofrit must follow his path . . ."

"Eamon!" Ara shouted.

The twins' voices had been growing louder, but their argument broke off when Ara called out.

"What is it?" Eamon asked, hurrying to her side.

"'All who seek Ofrit must follow his path,'" Ara said. "That's the only direction you've found in your research."

Eamon nodded.

"Nothing mentioned about doors," Ara continued. "Not anywhere."

"No," Eamon said hesitantly. "But that doesn't mean—"

"I have an idea." Ara turned away from him and walked up to the first block of the center wall. Her gaze followed the angle of its climb, then looked at the proportions of the blocks.

They could be stairs. Very, very tall, narrow stairs. But climbable.

Stepping onto the first block, Ara began to scale the wall. She climbed with her hands and feet, keeping her center of gravity low so she wouldn't lose her balance.

"Ara!" Nimhea called to her. "What are you doing?"

Ara didn't answer. She could only concentrate on the climb, as she was quite high up now.

Don't look down. Don't look down.

It wouldn't be the instant death like if she fell from the gorge, but Ara was quite certain she would still break in several places.

She made it to the top of the wall, her heart slamming against her ribs. Her knees and shins were on the top step of the wall, but her palms rested on the same stones that decorated the courtyard floor. Directly ahead, Ofrit's Path stretched toward the cliffs.

Ara shouted to the twins as her blood sang in triumph. "I solved the riddle!"

19

nother door. This time set into a cliff face.

At least there's only one.

The door was plain, though made from the red wood Ara had found on one of the other doors. It had a simple brass handle.

When Ara grabbed the handle, Eamon cried, "Wait!"

"What?" Ara looked at him.

"You can't just open the door," he told her.

"Why not?" Ara was happy to find something straightforward in the midst of Ofrit's Trials.

Eamon cast about for an answer. "It's too simple."

Ara laughed. "I'm not going to complain."

If she'd had an ominous feeling or heard something behind the door, Ara would have been cautious. But she sensed that this door was just a door.

Ara turned the handle, and Eamon cringed as though he expected something to explode from within. The door swung inward.

No surprises yet.

"What's inside?" Nimhea asked.

Ara took a few steps forward, moving out of the sunlight so her eyes could adjust. Ofrit's Path continued then dropped off into a stone staircase. Walking to the edge of the steps, Ara peered down. The tight spiral of steps prevented her from seeing where they led, but she was encouraged by torches blazing in iron scones on the stair walls.

We won't be stumbling in the dark. That's something.

Ara went back outside. "The path ends at a staircase."

"I guess we're going underground," Nimhea said. "How difficult will the climb down be?"

"I don't know how long it will be," Ara told her. "But it's lit by torches. We won't be risking a fall with every step."

Nimhea nodded. "That's something."

Ara smiled.

She led the twins into the short corridor. Before they began their descent Eamon went back and closed the door.

Ara lifted her eyebrows at him.

"It seemed like the polite thing to do," Eamon explained.

Her eyes were still adjusting to the drastic shift in light, but Ara suspected he was blushing.

The stones coiled tightly around a central pillar, forcing them to proceed single file. Nimhea volunteered to lead the way, and Ara agreed it was best to have the princess's sword at the front.

Torches continued to appear at regular intervals as they descended. Nothing about the stairs changed. Turn. Turn. Turn. Down. Down. Down.

Ara lost all sense of how long they'd been descending. The constant repetition verged on maddening; it made her feel like she was fruitlessly turning in a circle. Going nowhere.

She was grinding her teeth and fighting dizziness when the air began to change. The courtyard and the path had been dry like the desert. The air here had a distinct dampness and carried the scent of caves. The familiar odor lightened Ara's mood.

The staircase ended abruptly, spitting them out in front of a broad sandstone wall with a single opening. The wall spread in both directions as far as Ara could see.

Nimhea pointed up. "Look at that."

Hanging above the wall was a bank of shimmering silver cloud that bathed the wall in something akin to moonlight. Ripples of brighter light occasionally raced through the cloud, but it was otherwise motionless.

"Ofrit's Labyrinth," Eamon murmured in an awed voice.

Nimhea made a sound of disgust. "I haven't seen a labyrinth since I played in the estate gardens where we grew up. It's awfully fanciful."

Eamon threw her a reproachful look.

She spread her hands helplessly. "That's how I feel about labyrinths."

Ara had not played in any labyrinths as a child. She'd read about them in books, but they'd never featured in her imagination. Like Nimhea, Ara considered labyrinths a type of entertainment for people who didn't have anything better to do.

Ara gazed at the wall. *It's a maze. How hard can it be to get through a maze?*

"Do you know anything more about the maze than the doors?" Ara asked.

It was obvious Eamon felt slighted, and Ara wished she'd chosen her words more carefully.

"The lore speaks of Ofrit's Labyrinth as a physical structure," Eamon told her. "But most scholars concluded that it was probably metaphorical." He gestured to the wall. "Clearly they were wrong."

Eamon hurried on, determined to prove he was of more use than those scholars. "The only consistent evidence about the labyrinth is that it always changes."

"Changes how?" Ara envisioned walls moving while they were inside the maze. Doors appearing, then disappearing.

What a nightmare.

"The solution to the maze is personal for each petitioner," Eamon replied. "Unlike the Bone Forest and Ofrit's Path, the labyrinth re-creates itself. Any person who makes it this far will encounter a different maze from their predecessor. Anyone who comes after will yet again find a new labyrinth."

He adjusted the strap of his satchel, wincing at an ache in his shoulder.

"This is your quest, Ara," Eamon said. "The puzzle of the labyrinth will be for you."

Ara nodded grimly, feeling the burden of her role. *It falls to me.*

Despite the weight of responsibility, she was resolute in purpose. She wasn't fearless, but she felt balanced in a way that was almost serene. Calmed by the truth that this was exactly where she needed to be.

"Let's go," Ara said. She entered the labyrinth with the twins a few steps behind.

The silvery light from the cloud was enough to see clearly. The opening in the wall stretched into a long, straight corridor. The walls on either side of them were unmarked. There was no ceiling above their heads, only the strange cloud.

The labyrinth was eerily quiet, making their regular footfalls sound like stomping. The corridor didn't exactly end, but they reached a point where three choices were presented. Each opening was framed by the same sandstone of the walls, but the frames were marked.

To their left, Eni's symbol had been etched into the stone. The opening to their right bore the mark of the Twins. Straight ahead, Wuldr's mark framed their path.

"Three of the gods." Ara traced the shape of Eni's symbol on the left opening.

This puzzle is for me. One of these gods is the answer to a question in my life.

Eamon coughed politely. "I'd like to offer advice, but only you will understand the puzzle."

"If you'd like to talk through it," Nimhea said gamely, "I'm happy to listen."

Ara appreciated her offer. Talking about her ideas with the twins would help her keep her thoughts in order.

"Eni seems like the most obvious choice," Ara said. "The god of travelers would move with us between provinces. This quest has been a journey more than anything."

Eamon tugged at his downy beard. "I agree."

"What about the other two?" Nimhea asked. "Is there any way they could be right?"

Ara pressed her lips together. "They could. Wuldr is the god of Fjeri, and I grew up on the pilgrim's path to the Twins' Well."

Nimhea folded her arms over her chest. "You and Eamon are right. Eni is the best choice. The others haven't had anything to do with our journey."

"It's settled then." Ara took Ironbranch in her right hand and stepped through the frame bearing Eni's mark.

Nothing happened as she continued forward. Somewhere close by, Ara heard a metallic click followed by the whirring of a wheel. Ara launched herself back, tumbling toward the opening. Nimhea and Eamon grabbed her and pulled her out as flames spouted from hidden openings in the walls where Ara had just been standing.

Thank the gods Teth has been teaching me.

The spears of flame continued to roar as Ara got to her feet.

"Not Eni," she said, and dusted off her clothes.

I can't let myself be shaken. There is no going back.

"Second choice?" Nimhea asked nervously.

"Wuldr. The god of my homeland." Ara couldn't waste time mulling over the choice. This was only the first juncture in the labyrinth. She had no idea how many more they would encounter. She'd dreamed of Wuldr in the forest. That was enough.

Ara started toward Wuldr's opening, but Eamon jumped in front of her.

"Let me go."

"But it has to be me." Ara tried to move around him, but he blocked her.

"I don't think it does," Eamon said. "The gods know we're together. The puzzle is for you, but there will always only be one correct door. It doesn't matter who goes through first."

Ara let out an exasperated breath. "Why should you go instead of me?"

"You could be hurt or worse," Eamon answered. "It doesn't make sense to risk you when we don't have to."

"Risk me?" Ara wanted to shake him for this ridiculous show of gallantry. "This is my quest. I'm meant to take risks."

"You are," Eamon blurted. "You will. But hear me out. To take Saetlund back you and Nimhea have to survive. The Loresmith and the Queen."

"Lahvja didn't say anything about sacrificing the Scholar," Ara shot back.

"And hopefully you won't," Eamon replied, his eyes pleading. "But better me than you or my sister."

Nimhea had been listening to the exchange in silence, but her face was a thundercloud. "Don't you dare, Eamon. I won't allow this."

"I'm sorry," Eamon said.

Before either Nimhea or Ara could react, Eamon rushed through Wuldr's frame.

"No!" Nimhea shouted, but Eamon was already well into the space beyond the opening.

He stopped, panting. A few seconds passed.

"I think—"

A groan filled the air, like the bellow of a giant.

"Eamon, get out of there!" Ara ran to the opening. She had one foot through the door when the ground heaved, throwing her back.

Eamon fell to the floor.

"Nava's mercy," Nimhea gasped. "The cloud."

The silver cloud hanging over the labyrinth began to descend, but only above the space Eamon had entered. It was changing, transforming from mist into a solid mass that resembled steel. In another few seconds Eamon would be crushed.

"Crawl to me!" Ara put one foot in through the frame again. The ground surged, but she was ready for it and braced herself to stay on her feet. She took Ironbranch in both hands, holding it vertically, and watched the ceiling rush down.

Eamon had lifted his head when Ara called to him, but he hadn't moved toward her.

He's stunned from the fall.

"Nimhea!" Ara caught her arm. "Something's not right. You have to bring him out."

Nimhea glanced up at the mass of metal then took in the way Ara had positioned her stave.

"Will it hold?" Nimhea asked.

"We're about to find out."

Nimhea ran through the doorway. Immediately the ground rumbled and shook, but the princess kept her footing. She reached Eamon at the moment the descending steel hit Ironbranch.

The shock of the impact surged through Ara. She gripped her stave tighter. The ceiling screeched.

Nimhea had Eamon on his feet. She guided him back to the opening. As soon as they were through, Ara called upon a strength she didn't know she had. Willing Ironbranch to come free, she jerked the stave with all her might. Ironbranch sprang loose and Ara fell back.

The ceiling slammed down with a noise that shook the walls.

The three of them sat there, breathing hard, while dust settled around them.

"Are you hurt?" Nimhea asked Eamon.

"No," Eamon replied, touching his chest. "When I fell, the wind was knocked out of me."

Ara stood up and went to Wuldr's frame. Where the opening had been was now solid metal.

"I chose poorly."

It was hard to muster the confidence she'd had when they first entered the maze.

"No worse than either of us would have," Nimhea said. She helped Eamon to his feet.

Eamon smiled gingerly at Ara. "At least the only option left is the right one."

"Are you sure I'm not already disqualified?" Ara asked. "I picked the wrong way twice."

"If you're clever enough to keep breathing, you get to keep going." Eamon patted her on the shoulder.

"But try to pick better," Nimhea added, and walked past Ara toward the frame decorated with the Twins' marks.

As Eamon promised, there were no consequences for walking through the Twins' doorway. They moved through another corridor with plain stone walls. They turned once. Then again.

"Here it is," Nimhea said, stopping.

It was identical to the last juncture. Three frames. Three choices.

"Is it the same gods?" Ara asked.

Eamon shook his head. "The left side is Ofrit."

"But Wuldr is the middle option again," Nimhea corrected.

Ara went to the right-side opening. "Nava."

"Did we learn anything from the first time?" Nimhea asked. She was trying to sound friendly, but Ara heard the sharpness buried in the question.

Ara pressed her lips together. Something about what Eamon said bothered her.

If I'm clever enough.

Those words nagged her, like they should mean something.

Taking Ara's silence as fear, Eamon piped up. "All we can do is pick one and see what happens."

"I had so much fun with that last time," Nimhea muttered. She glanced at Eamon with an irked expression.

Ara didn't doubt Nimhea was angry, but when the princess looked at her brother, Ara saw how frightened Nimhea was. That Eamon could have been lost had shaken Nimhea to the core.

Ofrit. Wuldr. Nava.

This was Ofrit's Labyrinth, so he could be the right choice. Ara still considered Wuldr the god she knew best—at least before calling up Eni so many times during their travels. Nava didn't seem right. Ara's grandmother had taught her to give thanks to Nava at each planting and each harvest. But Ara didn't have a personal connection to the goddess.

"Wuldr," Ara said.

"You can take more time," Nimhea suggested. "Don't rush yourself."

"I'm not," Ara replied.

She didn't give Nimhea a chance to reply. She strode through the opening with Wuldr's marks and waited. This time she'd relied on her instincts. The answer that came from her gut.

There were no sounds. The walls didn't move. The ceiling didn't drop.

Nimhea and Eamon peered at her through the frame.

"It's right," Ara said with relief. "Wuldr is the right choice."

"Then we keep going." Eamon stepped through Wuldr's frame.

Nimhea nodded, following her brother. "We keep going."

Ara should have been happy, but she wasn't. As they walked down another corridor, she contended with her troubled thoughts. Her instincts had served her at the last juncture, but Ara knew that instincts didn't solve puzzles. She'd made the right choice, but not using the right method. Each choice had a meaning, and she hadn't figured out what that meaning was.

The Twins. Wuldr.

First. Second.

Ayre and Syre's Well was physically closest to Rill's Pass. Then Wuldr's Tree. Nava's Bounty was closer than Ofrit's Cavern. But where would Eni fit in? Eni didn't have a sacred site. Roads and camps were Eni's holy places.

Physical distance also seemed too banal for a riddle of the gods.

The meaning. What's the deeper meaning?

They reached the next juncture.

"Nava. Ofrit. Eni," Eamon announced. "That's too bad."

Ara looked at him. "What?"

"Wuldr's marks appeared in the center opening twice," Eamon said. "I thought that maybe the markings that stayed in the same location might be the right choice."

He frowned at the openings. "But none of these matches a previous location."

"Ara?" Nimhea leaned against a wall.

Ara rubbed her temples. "I don't know. Ofrit or Eni, I think. I don't know any special way Nava fits into my life."

"Between Ofrit and Eni." Eamon looked at the opening in the center and on the right.

Even if Ara thought her instincts were reliable, she had no gut feeling this time.

If I'm clever enough.

She didn't feel very clever.

Ofrit. Eni. Ofrit. Eni.

Clever.

Clever Ofrit.

Ara felt a wave of giddiness that made her want to giggle.

Gods. I'm so exhausted I can't think straight.

Ofrit. Eni.

Clever Ofrit. Cunning Eni.

Ara's head snapped up.

"What's wrong?" Nimhea pushed off the wall, watching Ara with concern.

Ara raised her hand, asking for silence. She'd caught a glimpse of something, and she couldn't let it get away.

Clever Ofrit. Cunning Eni. Where have I heard that?

Ara drew a sharp breath. "I think we've been coming at this wrong."

"Wrong how?" Eamon asked.

"When you said the labyrinth would be personal, I focused on me," Ara said. "My life. My past."

"But that makes sense," Nimhea said, frowning.

"It does," Ara agreed. "But what if the puzzle isn't for Ara the person, but Ara the Loresmith?"

Nimhea paced back and forth. "How is that different?"

"I've been looking for connections to myself," Ara told her. "But I think I should be looking for connections to the Loresmith."

Eamon was nodding, but he stayed quiet.

"Eamon, when you said if I was clever enough to keep breathing, I'd get to keep going, I couldn't let go of that phrase." Ara was speaking quickly now. "If I'm clever enough."

Eamon's brow furrowed as he listened.

"We're in Ofrit's maze," Ara continued. "The god known for his cleverness."

Comprehension dawned on Eamon's face. "The cleverness of Ofrit."

"Yes!" Ara clapped her hands. Eamon was beaming.

"What is going on?" Nimhea demanded.

"Sorry. Sorry." Eamon took Nimhea's hands. "It's in the story of the Loresmith. A list of the gods' traits a Loresmith must embody."

"The wisdom of the Twins!" Ara shouted.

Eamon laughed. "The steadfastness of Wuldr."

Ara spun in a little circle. "The cleverness of Ofrit!"

"The cleverness of Ofrit!" Eamon echoed.

"The Twins. Wuldr." Nimhea ticked off the gods' names. "The first two paths. You think this list means Ofrit is the next choice?"

"It's the order of the traits." Ara grinned at Nimhea.

"What comes after Ofrit?" Nimhea asked.

"The generosity of Nava," Ara answered.

"And Eni's own curiosity and cunning," Eamon finished, and then bowed.

Nimhea thought it over. "If Ofrit is correct, then only Nava and Eni will be left."

"This the solution, Nimhea." Ara had never felt so alive. "I'm sure of it."

Ara gave Eamon a hug then walked through the opening framed by Ofrit's marks.

Nothing. She'd done it!

"Come on!" Ara waved at the twins.

By the time they were through the doorway, Ara was running for the next juncture.

20

ra's confidence was rewarded. They passed under Nava's marks then Eni's and came out of the labyrinth unscathed. They were all laughing as they jostled each other through the exit.

"Congratulations." Nimhea clapped Ara on the back. "Let's not do that again."

Ara laughed and rested her hands on her thighs. They'd been running since the third juncture, and she needed to catch her breath.

"Of all the wonders of Ayre and Syre." Eamon was gazing at what lay ahead.

Ara straightened to find out what had so impressed him.

On the other side of the labyrinth was an enormous cavern. The light from the silver cloud reached only its edge, and even that seemed to be slipping away.

Ara turned back. What she saw made her pulse jump.

"The light in the cloud is going out."

Nimhea spun around, confirming what Ara said.

"Do we have any light?"

They looked at each other.

"Well, that wasn't very clever of us," Eamon said with an uneasy laugh.

Ara pivoted back toward the cavern, searching for any sign of light ahead. Any landmarks.

Then, as if a giant candle had been snuffed out, they were plunged into darkness.

"Eamon, take my hand," Ara ordered. "You too, Nimhea. I don't want us to lose one another in the dark."

When their hands were joined, Nimhea asked, "How long do we stay like this?"

"We don't," Ara said, keeping her voice calm. "We keep walking."

"Where?" Nimhea jerked Ara's hand. Ara didn't think it was on purpose. "We can't see anything."

"Ahead." Ara took a step forward, tugging on the twins' hands. "Away from the labyrinth. We passed that trial. The only way is forward."

The twins were moving with Ara, but reluctantly.

"Eamon?" Nimhea said.

"The labyrinth is the last trial," Eamon answered.

"We go forward," Ara said firmly.

Their voices sounded louder in the dark.

It was black as pitch all around them. Ara forced herself to keep moving, but at more of a shuffle than a walk. She willed something to appear. Anything.

A note sounded in the dark. High and resonant, it had the qualities of both a bell and a flute.

"What was that?" Nimhea whispered.

A second note followed the first, lower but in the same tone. It hung in the air with the original sound.

The third note was very low, almost rumbling.

Three tones echoed through the cavern, bringing new light with them. Three crystal spheres floated in the air just ahead of Ara. Tiny points of light at their center expanded until they illuminated the cavern like miniature moons.

Beyond the glowing spheres was a simple stone bridge; at the end of the bridge was a door.

"Ofrit's Apothecary is through that door." Eamon gasped. "That's the Bridge Between Worlds."

The bridge spanned a narrow chasm that separated one side of the cavern from the other. A subtle gleam emanated from deep within the chasm as if a river of light flowed far below.

They reached the bridge, and Ara trembled with each step. A god awaited them.

Ara let go of her companions' hands.

Unlike the ornate doors of the courtyard, the door on the other side of the bridge was unassuming. Ara grasped its iron handle and pulled it open. Nimhea and Eamon followed close behind, watching Ara for cues to guide their steps.

The room on the other side of the door was small and very cluttered. One wall of the room was stacked floor to ceiling with books. Another with shelves holding glass, copper, and silver containers in all shapes and sizes. The third wall brimmed with sealed jars of unidentifiable substances.

In the center of the room was a long, tall workbench covered in scrolls and a single stool. Sitting on the stool was Ofrit.

He had a cloud of snowy white hair and a very long beard. His dark skin was deeply wrinkled.

"It's been a long while since anyone has attempted my trials." Ofrit had a thin, gravelly voice. He was bent over the workbench, writing, and didn't look at them. "Much less overcome them."

Setting his quill aside, Ofrit lifted his gaze. He had a pinched face and knife-sharp eyes that glittered like stars. They widened when he saw Ara, Nimhea, and Eamon standing before him.

"Three of you at once!" Ofrit exclaimed. "That doesn't seem likely. *All* of you want to be Scribes?"

The god leaned across the table and peered at them over his long, pointed nose. "No, no. This isn't right."

Suspicious and sullen, Ofrit pointed at Eamon. "You might belong here."

He then wagged the same finger at Ara and Nimhea. "But these two? A warrior and a . . . whatever you are . . . you have no business with me."

Eamon's face made plain his conflicting emotions. He was deeply pleased by Ofrit's assessment of himself, while perplexed by the god's dismissal of his friends.

"No business here?" Nimhea was having none of it. "Do you know who we are?"

"Should I care?" Ofrit snapped at her. To Eamon, he said, "If you want to be my Scribe your first task it to get these pests out of my apothecary."

"Pests?" Nimhea's voice climbed toward a dangerous octave.

Ara did not care for being called a pest, but she was much more concerned that Nimhea had forgotten she was speaking to a god.

There came a sudden noise and a flurry of movement from a dark corner of the room. A small shape darted from the shadows and leapt onto the workbench, knocking several scrolls to the floor. The invader began to scold Ofrit with sharp barks.

"Fox!" Ara gaped at the furry beast.

"Stop!" Ofrit shook his finger at Fox. "Stop that right now! You know I hate it when you show up as one of your irritating little beasts."

Fox gekkered at Ofrit then jumped off the table, but didn't land on the floor. Where Fox should have landed stood a tall figure wrapped in cloaks that swirled despite there being no wind. A broad-brimmed hat cast a shadow over the figure's face, but a pair of eyes that gleamed like Fox's gazed upon Ofrit's three visitors.

Ara stared back at those eyes. "Eni."

Eni bowed with flourish. "An honor to meet you, Ara Silverthread. Though we have met many times before."

"You were Fox?" Eamon gaped at the tall figure. "Fox was a god? I mean, you?"

"You know well enough, Prince Eamon." Eni laughed. "I travel in many, many forms."

Eamon blushed, looking at the ground. "Of course I know that. But . . . *you* traveled with *us*."

He lifted his eyes to gaze at Eni in wonder. Then he quickly looked away again. His face clouded over with something that looked like fear.

Eni turned to Nimhea. "Saetlund has not been what you expected, princess."

"It has not . . . ummm . . ." Nimhea struggled to find the appropriate form of address.

"Eni or Traveler are the only names I need," Eni told her. "All I want to ask is if you are disappointed by the tasks that have been laid before you."

"No," Nimhea said reflexively, then she frowned. Her lips pursed, and slowly a smile crept onto her face as if she understood something that had eluded her. "No, Eni, I am not."

Eni nodded.

"What is the meaning of this? My apothecary is much too crowded. I cannot have it!" Ofrit slammed his fist down on the table. "You know these people, sibling? Is this your doing?"

Turning to Ofrit, Eni said gently, "The appointed time has arrived, dear brother. The Queen seeks her throne. The Scholar guides her steps. And the heir to the Loresmith seeks to prove her worth."

Ofrit gazed at Eni in amazement. "Is it time already?" Turning from Eni, Ofrit squinted at Ara. "So you're the one."

Ofrit abandoned his stool and came close to Ara. He was very thin and very tall. He leaned down to peer into her face. This close, the god's wrinkles were canyons. His eyes pools of oblivion. His messy shock of snow-white hair and beard crackled with energy that made Ara's skin prickle. Little hairs stood up on her arms and at the nape of her neck, as if a thunderstorm was closing in.

Ofrit took Ara's chin in his hand, and she felt as though she were no longer standing on solid ground. The apothecary was gone. Nimhea and Eamon were gone. She was floating. Caught in a bubble with only the blackness of eternity and flickering of stars around her. She could no longer see Ofrit, but had the sense of being watched. And she saw herself, a tiny point in a web of the universe that stretched in every direction to infinity. She was so small against that vastness. And yet, in her smallness, she glowed. A beacon. A sign.

The apothecary came rushing back, and Ara keeled over. The room bobbed and swayed as she hit the ground. On her hands and knees, she gasped and coughed.

Eni was at her side. "Here, water."

Ara took the cup Eni offered, though it was several more moments of coughing and gulping air before she could take a sip.

When she'd gotten some water down, Eamon came to help her up. She was grateful to find the ground beneath her feet stable.

"Hrmphf!" Ofrit scowled at her. "I suppose you'll be wanting an apology now. I forget how delicate you little creatures can be."

He turned back to his workbench with a dismissive wave of his hand.

If Ofrit had spoken such to Ara when she first encountered the god, she would have quaked with fear. But in her brief glimpse of herself—whether through the god's eyes or the gaze of the universe itself—she had been changed.

"I need no apology." Ara spoke with quiet strength. "I have sought this place, faced your trials. Now I ask you to set me on my path."

The words came easily, but Ara knew they only came partly from her. The voice that spoke was that of the Loresmith. Of all Loresmiths.

The god straightened and turned back. A slow smile pulled the wrinkles around his mouth tight.

"She has teeth," Ofrit said. "That shows promise."

"I agree," Eni murmured.

"Do you acknowledge me?" Ara asked, not knowing where the question came from, but also innately understanding its importance.

She was filled with hope, surrounded by the support of all who'd come before her. They lifted her up now. Claimed her as one of their own.

Ofrit continued to smile. "Suppose that I do? After all, you carry my staff. Such a thing has a strong sense of itself and takes care not to fall into the wrong hands."

"The Loresmith stave belongs in my hands," Ara answered. The chorus of Loresmiths made her voice resonant, musical. "My cause is just. I seek the path of restoration."

"Indeed." Ofrit wrapped the length of his beard around his neck and shoulders, like a stole. "It truly is time then. I have been out of the world much longer than I believed."

The god sighed, gathering scrolls into his arms. "I could ponder my absence many more years and be content. What say you to that?"

"Saetlund has fallen," Ara told him. A deep sorrow took hold of her. The grief of so many generations. "Vokk continues to devour the land."

"All true," Ofrit replied. "But what does that matter to me? One who has been abandoned by Saetlund's peoples."

Here, Ara faltered. The steady supply of responses that welled from within her suddenly dried up. The Loresmiths of the past offered no answers.

I am the Loresmith. Ofrit has acknowledged as much. Isn't it the god's turn to tell me what to do?

While Ara frowned, searching for something to say, Nimhea stepped forward.

"The people have failed you," the princess said to Ofrit. "They are lost without your wisdom and guidance. We ask for mercy, that champions might once more prove to you that we are worthy. That Saetlund must be saved."

Ofrit listened to Nimhea but didn't respond. The god's gaze shifted to Eamon.

"By will, word, and sword," Eamon said. "We walk the path of restoration. We lay down our lives should they be demanded. To this task alone, we dedicate ourselves."

Eamon fell silent, but his eyes were wide. Ara knew that he and Nimhea had spoken words heretofore unknown to them; she heard the echoes of other voices speak with them. Other Scholars. Other Queens.

Ofrit was still for several moments, then began to nod. "Very good. I like to get that archaic nonsense out of the way. Now we can get down to practical matters. Eni?"

"To fulfill your quest, you must overcome the darkness that drove the gods from Saetlund," Eni told them.

"The Vokkans will be defeated," Nimhea said proudly.

"That is another task to be completed in time," Eni replied. "But the darkness of which I speak is that which dwells in the gods themselves. Each of us has a weakness, that when indulged, can overwhelm our strengths and consume us. In our sorrow we allowed this to happen, and it severed the bond between gods and Saetlund's people."

Ara's brow furrowed. "I don't understand."

"You do not need to, for the moment," Ofrit told her. "There are hidden places in Saetlund. Places where our faults have been allowed to fester."

Ofrit leaned so close his nose almost touched Eamon's face. "Use these as you decide best."

He placed two scrolls in Eamon's hands. Eamon drew the scrolls to his chest protectively. His expression became drawn.

"Seek out these places, Loresmith," Eni said to Ara. "Unravel the mysteries in the dark. That is your task."

Though puzzled by Eni's cryptic words, Ara looked at the god hopefully. "I am the Loresmith now. How will I bring the Loreknights back to Saetlund? Where will I forge their weapons?"

"You will find the forge when the first Loreknight has been chosen," said Ofrit.

And when will that be? Ara wanted to ask, but she felt like a child begging for sweets. If these were the answers Ofrit offered, she would take them. For now.

Observing her frustrated expression, Ofrit said, "You have what you need to *begin* your quest. And that is enough."

Ara felt like she knew little more than she had before the trials. She knew the scrolls Ofrit had given Eamon would have answers. She wished she could hold them and instantly know every word.

"Stay strong in spirit," Eni added. "And you will prevail."

Ofrit snorted. "Eni is optimistic about your chances. I'm quite certain you'll fail."

"Ignore him," Eni said. "He's always been cantankerous."

"Why are you still here?" Ofrit stomped back to his stool. "I have work to do."

Eni beckoned Ara, Nimhea, and Eamon to stand apart while Ofrit grumbled over his scrolls.

"As the Traveler I would be pleased to assist you back to your friends," Eni told them. "Though sour in disposition, my brother speaks true. Your task here is finished and you must go."

"Eni." Ara spoke hesitantly. "Teth will be overjoyed that Fox didn't die, but he'll also be very confused by your role in this."

Eni sighed. "I am sorry for the Thief's pain at what he perceived was the death of his dear friend."

"You let them think you'd died?" Ofrit snarked from his workbench. "And they call me the mad one."

Ignoring him, Eni said to Ara, "Tell the Thief he need not grieve. I took the form of Fox when you left northern Fjeri that I might travel with you without causing suspicion or alarm. The creature that has long been his companion remains in the Highland forests, awaiting his return."

"Knowing that will be a great relief to him," Ara replied.

Regarding her, Eni added, "Tell him this as well: you must hasten your lessons with the Loresmith stave. He teaches too slowly."

"I will tell him." Ara laughed, but Eni's words reminded her of another question. "If I may, Teth has been trying very hard to figure out what the Loresmith stave is made of. Will you tell me?"

"He won't understand," Ofrit barked from his perch. Unable to resist inserting his opinions, the god left the workbench to properly join the conversation.

"In my years of wandering with our peoples," Eni said to their brother, "I've found it can be useful to tell them things they don't understand. Think of it as a puzzle they might never solve."

Ofrit's expression brightened. "Ah, puzzles. I do like puzzles."

"I know." Eni smiled gently.

"Very well." Ofrit turned to Ara. "Young Loresmith, you may tell the Thief that our stave is made of the heartbeat of the earth, the memory of a tree, and the laughter of a star."

21

ni's offer to assist Ara, Nimhea, and Eamon in their journey back to camp was not what Ara expected.

Gazing up at his three friends, Teth blinked several times then rubbed his eyes.

"Senn's teeth," he sighed, scowling. "I'm really losing my edge. How'd you sneak up like that?"

Ara stared at him, then glanced at Eamon and Nimhea to either side of her. The twins appeared as befuddled as she was.

They were standing over Teth. The horses were tethered a short distance away.

Trying to orient herself, for the last thing she remembered was Ofrit revealing the strange composition of the Loresmith stave, Ara turned to look at the landscape. It took a moment for her to accept that she didn't recognize anything. There was no Bone Forest. No Scourge. All around them were low dunes spiked with salt grass. Somewhere nearby Ara heard waves crashing onto a shoreline.

"Where are we?" Nimhea had taken notice of their strange surroundings as well.

Teth stood up. "What kind of question is that . . . ohhhhhh."

He looked at the three of them accusingly. "Care to explain this?"

"Eni helped us travel," Eamon told Teth.

Their encounter with Eni and Ofrit had taken a toll on Eamon. His shoulders sagged, and his skin had an ill cast. He held Ofrit's scrolls to his chest like they were the only thing that kept his heart beating.

"Apparently for Eni that meant sending us to a surprise location," Nimhea added. "I don't know why that would be considered helpful."

Teth stared at the twins, brow furrowed. "Eni? Weren't you trying to find Ofrit?"

"Teth!" Ara's confusion had faded, and all that transpired in Ofrit's Apothecary flared to life in her mind. "Fox isn't dead!"

After flinching at Fox's name, Teth frowned. "What did you say?"

In her excitement, Ara had to work to keep the words from tumbling out. "Fox was Eni. Not your Fox, but the Fox who was with us after Silverstag. Your Fox is still in the Highlands. Alive, safe."

"Are you sure?" Teth gazed at her in astonishment.

Ara nodded. Her eyes were burning with tears, but not from sharing this news with Teth. Everything that had befallen them on the journey to Ofrit's Apothecary surged within her, battering her heart.

Seeing the emotion break on her face, Teth gathered Ara into his arms. He didn't speak, but held her tightly.

Teth. She reveled in the warmth of his skin, its scent of pine and riverstones.

"My friends!" Lahvja stood a short distance away, atop the crest of a dune. "Come see!"

The dune didn't have much height, but it still offered a much better view of their surroundings. Turquoise waters rushed onto a pristine beach not half a mile away. Following the coastline, Ara spotted a city in the distance and a harbor filled with ships.

"Marik." Teth laughed and shook his head. "I'll have to thank Eni the next time we meet. It should have taken us a week to reach this port."

Nimhea looked at him in amazement. "You planned for us to come here?"

"I hoped to," Teth told her. "If we survived our second crossing of the Scourge."

He laughed again, deep belly laughs. Soon they were all laughing. Doubled over. Falling into the sand. Laughing and crying.

Amid her own laughter, Ara found two truths. *This is joy. This is happiness.*

Only Eamon kept himself apart. He quietly turned away and went back to camp.

Does the Scholar ever celebrate? Does he ever rest?

Ara knew if she followed Eamon she'd find him poring over the scrolls he'd received. His focus was incredible, but Ara hated that Eamon was so willing to make himself suffer.

The longer we're together, the more we can help him. We'll be the strength he needs.

Teth helped Lahvja to her feet.

"I'm sorry for the way I treated you. It wasn't fair."

Lahvja offered him an understanding smile. "You were in pain."

"Still . . ." Teth paused, considering Lahvja's expression. "You knew, didn't you? You knew Fox was Eni."

"I wanted to ease your grief," Lahvja said quietly. "But it is not my place to reveal the secrets of the gods."

"I wouldn't spill a god's secrets either." Teth chuckled.

Turning to all of them, he grinned broadly. "Who else wants to get a closer look at that beach?"

They raced down the dune, shrieking with delight. Teth stripped his shirt off, then hopped on the sand as he took one boot off then the other. Ara sat down and tugged her shoes from her feet. The sand was warm and velvety between her toes. She freed her hair from its braids then pushed herself up and ran into the sea.

Teth dove into the small waves while Nimhea and Lahvja splashed each other and danced like water sprites. Ara waded into the water until it reached her chest. She let herself fall back, completely submerging. She rose up again, savoring the sensation of the water sliding through her hair and down her neck, easing all the tension harbored there.

Teth emerged from the waves a few feet away from her. He shook water from his hair, spraying sparkling droplets around his head like a halo. Ara watched rivulets run down the planes of his back and etch out the taut muscles of his abdomen.

The water was cool, but heat began to build beneath Ara's skin. A low, curling, sinuous heat. Ara quickly turned away and sank into the water again. These new sensations were so strong, so insistent, she felt overwhelmed. The water felt safe. It could quench any fires that tried to run wild.

Ara looked for Nimhea and Lahvja, but they had disappeared. That meant Teth and Ara were alone with the sea. She shivered, but not from cold.

"Ara." His voice was so near she knew he was just behind her. When she turned, he'd be close enough to touch.

Ara breath quickened. Something was about to happen. Something she wanted, but didn't know how to prepare for.

She rose from the water and slowly turned to face him.

When her eyes took Teth in, Ara knew his beauty in that moment would be forever etched upon her memory. His amber eyes rivaled the colors of the sunset. His sandalwood-toned skin gleamed in the sunlight. Everything about him was perfect. The cut of his jaw. His full lips. The slope of his shoulders. The sleekness of his torso.

Ara wanted to touch him, but at the same time she was afraid. To put her hands on him here, now was something different than the casual affection they shared as friends. She lifted her hand and reached for him. Her fingers trembled.

Teth caught her hand in his and lifted it to his lips. He kissed each of her fingertips. Each gentle touch of his mouth sent a shock of exquisite sensations all the way to her toes. He held her eyes in his sunset gaze.

When he let go of her hand, Ara took a step forward. She placed her palms against his chest. She could feel his heartbeat, fast, like hers, beneath her fingers. She slid hands up to his shoulders, around his neck.

Teth bent his head to lean his forehead against hers. He spoke in a rough, low voice.

"I've never wanted anyone—" His words broke off, as if whatever he was about to say was too great a confession.

His hands were on the small of her back, pressing her closer.

"Kiss me," Ara murmured. "Please kiss me."

Teth's lips brushed across hers gently, like a question. Ara parted her lips in answer. She wanted to taste him. He kissed her again, lingering this time. Ara tightened her arms around his neck. She was melting. She would melt into the sea.

His kisses moved to her cheek. Her jaw. Her throat.

"Ara." She heard her name on his lips and knew he was melting with her.

A fit of coughing came from the beach. Startled, Teth and Ara broke apart.

Nimhea carried on with her pretend coughing a bit longer, then feigned surprise to see them.

"Oh! Hey, you two," she called. "I don't mean to interrupt, but time for dinner."

When Nimhea tromped back up the dune, Teth and Ara looked at each other. They started to smile. Then they started to laugh. They fell into each other, a tangle of limbs and laughter.

Ara and Teth returned to camp hand in hand. Nimhea grinned at them like a cat in cream. Ara couldn't stop herself from blushing.

Lahvja had turned up a bed of clams on the shore. They now simmered with herbs over the campfire. In all their nights on the road, Ara had never felt so at ease. There was nothing looming, nothing to keep her on edge. This peace wouldn't last long. She wasn't going to pretend that it would. Soon Eamon would share with them the secrets contained in Ofrit's scrolls, and their next task would begin. But that was for tomorrow.

Eamon had been absent from the beach, but he joined the group for dinner. Ara studied his face, looking for signs of improvement or deterioration.

Moving to sit beside him, Ara asked, "How are you feeling, Eamon?"

"I'm fine," said Eamon with an unconvincing laugh and a wan smile. "Just very tired."

"We've been through so much." Ara hoped she sounded sympathetic and not condescending. "It's exhausting. It's overwhelming. I think it's important to step away from all of it. Even for a short time."

Eamon cast a sidelong glance at her. "How can we do that?"

"Only in little ways," Ara admitted. "But it helps. For example, I've decided tonight I will not think about fate, or being the Loresmith, or where we'll go next. I will be grateful that we fulfilled our first task, that my friends are well and safe . . . and that we don't have to cross the Scourge a second time."

That drew a genuine laugh from Eamon.

"You should try it," Ara urged.

He gave her a quizzical look.

"For example, the scrolls Ofrit gave you . . ."

Eamon's expression grew wary. "What about them?"

"Have you looked at them yet?" she asked.

"Only the first." Eamon let out a long sigh. "I know where you . . . we . . . need to go next. It's in Vijeri; a place known as the Tangle—"

He was about to continue, but Ara interrupted.

"I don't want to think about what's next. Not now. Not when we've just accomplished so much. We need to savor this moment." Ara took his hand and squeezed it. "Don't read anything more. Don't think. Not tonight. Enjoy being with your friends. The world can crash down on us tomorrow."

Eamon looked at his hand in hers. "Tomorrow."

Ara smiled at him. "Is that a promise?"

Handing an empty bowl to her, Eamon said, "If you get me some clams."

Eamon stayed true to his word. After they'd eaten, he lingered at the campfire, volunteering to recount his journey with Nimhea and Ara through Ofrit's Trials. The story Eamon told was much better than what Ara remembered living through. There was a narrow escape from butcher crows, a battle with the undead unworthy, and at one point Ara dangled from a cliff while Nimhea grasped her with one arm and fought off a giant lizard with the other.

Ofrit was even crankier than he'd been in real life. Eni kept changing forms through the entire episode in the apothecary. Ara's favorite moment was when Eni changed into a duck and laid an egg on Ofrit's head.

A few times Nimhea tried to interrupt with a correction, but Ara jabbed her with an elbow. Eamon's retelling of their adventure was priceless.

By the time Eamon brought his epic performance to a close, they were all wheezing with laughter.

"You, my friend," said Teth, "have the gift of the bard."

With a self-deprecating chuckle, Eamon said, "Not even close. I belong in a library where everything happens in whispers, instead of shouting like a fool in the wild."

"Teth speaks the truth," Lahvja countered. "Among Eni's Children you would be treasured. Few people can make stories come to life."

"You're kind," Eamon said softly. "But I'll take my bow. Sleep beckons."

Eamon went to his tent, and Ara was pleased when lantern light didn't glow from within.

Much later, when all the others had gone to bed, Ara and Teth remained by the fire. Sometimes they spoke, but mostly they sat quietly. That night Ara craved nothing more than Teth's presence. The assurance that he was near. She snuggled under his arm and rested her head on his chest.

"I just remembered something about Eni," Teth said, troubled.

"What is it?" Ara asked.

"Eni licked my nose."

"Who?"

"Fox," Teth said. "But it was Eni Fox, not Fox Fox. That means a god licked my nose."

Ara sat up to look at him seriously. "Yes. I suppose it does."

"I really don't know how to feel about that."

"Wait till you hear what the Loresmith stave is made of." Ara broke into a grin.

"Spare me for tonight." Teth shifted close to her, folding her back into his arms.

Basking in warmth and hope, Ara felt at peace. She watched flames dance in the campfire until her eyelids became too heavy to keep open.

Ara didn't know what had woken her. Now that she was awake, she realized she also didn't know how she'd gotten into her tent and her bed. She was still fully dressed.

A high, keening sound came from outside. It was an awful sound.

Ara left her tent. The sun told her it was midmorning. The late night had encouraged an overlong sleep. She looked around, trying to find the source of the sound. The camp looked much as it had the previous day. Walking the perimeter of the camp, Ara noticed the sound grew louder as she approached Nimhea's tent. Alarmed, Ara ran to the tent and drew the flap back.

"Nimhea?"

A piercing wail rose from Nimhea, who was curled into a ball in one corner of her tent. Ara crawled to her side.

"Nimhea." Ara gently touched the weeping girl's shoulder. "What's wrong? Did something happen?"

Nimhea shuddered and let out a sound that was both a sob and a scream. The raw agony of it made Ara's limbs crackle with fear.

"Nimhea, please." Ara tried again to draw the princess out of her pain. "Tell me what's wrong. Let me help you."

It was as though Ara wasn't there. All Nimhea knew was her sorrow.

Ara crawled out of the tent, intending to go to Lahvja for help. But Lahvja was already there, standing a few feet away as if she'd been waiting.

"Something is wrong with Nimhea," Ara told her. "She wouldn't speak to me. I don't know if she's injured or ill."

"She isn't either," Lahvja said. Her face was calm, but her gaze was melancholy. She drew a folded piece of paper from the pocket of her skirt and held it out to Ara.

Ara stared at the paper for several breaths before she took it. The sight of it filled her with an irrational dread.

Lahvja remained silent as Ara unfolded the page.

It was a brief, scribbled note.

> *Nimhea,*
>
> *I have to go to them. It's the only way.*
> *I know you'll never be able to forgive me,*
> *but everything I've done was for you.*
>
> *Eamon*

"What does this mean?" Ara demanded of Lahvja.

"It means the Scholar is gone," Lahvja replied. "He has gone to his masters."

"What masters?" Ara's heart was pounding.

Lahvja looked past Ara to Nimhea's tent. "Get Teth. I'll meet you at the firepit."

Teth was coming out of his tent, stretching his arms. His slow smile made her heartbeat skip, but when he reached for Ara, she shook her head.

If only we could go back. Ara's emotions became ragged when she thought of the joy of the previous night and the devastation brought by the morning.

"What is that sound?" Teth asked, frowning.

"It's Nimhea," Ara told him. She gathered in her feelings, holding them tightly. She couldn't break down.

All the drowsiness vanished from his face. He started toward Nimhea's tent.

"What happened?"

Ara grabbed Teth's hand, stopping him. "Eamon's gone."

"What?"

"Lahvja wants us at the campfire." Ara pulled him along as she walked.

"Ara, none of this is making any kind of sense."

"I know."

They stood beside the cold, gray ashes in the firepit, waiting for Lahvja.

The sun was warm upon the sand, but Ara felt a creeping cold and emptiness all around her.

"Read this." Ara gave Teth the letter.

Teth read the short script. Read it again. "Am I meant to understand this?" he asked. "Because I don't."

She looked at him sadly. "I don't either."

Lahvja arrived at the firepit still wearing a mask of melancholy.

"Would you like breakfast?" she asked them.

"I would like you to explain this." Ara took the letter from Teth.

Lahvja sank to the ground. "I can't stand any longer. Will you please sit?"

Ara and Teth sat opposite Lahvja.

"Nimhea is sleeping now," Lahvja told them. "She'll sleep for a long time. She needs to. When she has rested, we can discuss what to do. For now, I can share with you what I know. I'm sorry to say it's very little and may bring you more confusion than answers."

Teth frowned at her. "Where has Eamon gone?"

Looking away, Lahvja laid her fingertips at the base of her throat. "To the Temple of Vokk."

No answer could have shocked Ara more. "That's impossible. They'll kill him."

"They won't," said Lahvja. "He is their servant."

Teth shook his head. "I don't believe it."

"It's true." Lahvja met his angry gaze with an unyielding one. "As much as I wish it weren't."

"How can you be sure?" Ara asked. A sick feeling joined her sadness.

"It's no coincidence that the wizards' hounds happened upon your camp," she said. "Or that a conscription squad raided the caravan. Your movements have been tracked."

Teth's face was stricken. "The entrails near the caravan. I knew I recognized the way they'd been arranged. That was Eamon?"

"Blood magic is favored by Vokk's wizards," Lahvja said with regret.

The vise gripping Ara's heart tightened and her revulsion grew. "No."

"The wizards' magic leaves a shadow upon anyone who uses it," Lahvja told her. "I saw that shadow clinging to Eamon the first time I met him."

Teth swore and clenched his jaw.

Ara's disbelief was plain on her face. "Why didn't you say anything?"

"I understand your anger," Lahvja said sadly. "But I am beholden to laws beyond this plane. I answer to gods and spirits. I was forbidden from interfering with Eamon's choice."

Lahjva had already proven she was unshakable when it came to matters of the divine. Pushing her for further explanations would be fruitless.

Furious but resigned, Ara asked, "Did you know he would leave?"

Lahvja suprised Ara by shaking her head. "I knew it was a possibility. But several choices lay before Eamon. I did not know what path he would take."

Ara and Teth fell silent, absorbing the magnitude of what had befallen them.

Ara's mind went to Eamon's habit of disappearing at odd hours and the animal carcasses. Teth's description of the entrails.

Blood magic is favored by Vokk's wizards.

Ara's stomach wrenched and she almost gagged. What had Eamon been doing all this time?

"All hope for Eamon is not lost," Lahvja said quietly, observing the disgust in Ara's expression. "His was an act of desperation, not evil."

Teth asked, "How do you know that?"

"The letter," Ara answered. Those few words on the page revealed a broken soul.

But why did Eamon do any of this? What did he hope to gain?

"He left one of Ofrit's scrolls behind," Lahvja said. "Eamon left that scroll, and he chose to leave now. Before he knew too much. He's placed us in much less danger than he could have."

"If he left one scroll, it's because he read it," Teth scoffed. "Haven't you noticed he reads multiple books each day?"

"I have," Lahvja answered. "But he could have taken both scrolls to Vokk's wizards. Instead, he left one with us."

Teth gave a dry chuckle. When he spoke there was a terrible weariness in his voice. "So where you're going with this is: Eamon betrayed us horribly, but he could have betrayed us *more* horribly."

Lahvja shrugged. "It's something to consider."

Teth seemed ready to snap at her, but he held his tongue.

Looking at them both, Lahvja said, "I need time to read Ofrit's scroll. But we should plan to leave in two days."

"We leave now," Teth told her. "You can read the scroll in one of Marik's safehouses. We'll need to gather new provisions there anyway."

"Very well." Lahvja nodded then returned to the tent where Nimhea slept.

22

hen Lahvja was gone, Ara and Teth sat in a silence that was a mockery of the joyful quiet they'd shared the night before.

"This can't be real," Teth murmured. He drew his knees to his chest and put his head in his hands.

Ara's mind turned to Eamon. Trying to understand how and why he had become entangled with the Wizards of Vokk. The pain of Eamon's betrayal was like a twisting knife in her belly. But in her suffering she was not alone. She had Teth, Nimhea, and Lahvja. This was a pain they shared.

Eamon had exiled himself from them. He was alone. Ara knew that in some way, his suffering might be greater than theirs.

She read the letter again, then folded it. Nimhea's name stared back at her. Ara followed Eamon's looping script with her gaze. She paused to look at the discolored places, the streaks and smudged ink. Evidence of Eamon's grief when he'd put his sister's name to the page. His tears.

The fire danced behind the paper, blurred and unfocused. It drew Ara's gaze. Grief from Eamon's betrayal wanted to anchor her in despair, but her mind struggled to grasp threads of hope that they might still prevail in their quest. She took some comfort from the flames. Fires never failed to remind her of the forge. Of home.

She stared into the flames, letting memories of Imgar's smithy seep through her troubled thoughts. Ara closed her eyes when she began to hear the strike of hammer on iron and the hiss of steam. She drew scents of smoke and leather in with her breath, easing the strain from her neck and shoulders.

Regretfully, Ara opened her eyes. She blinked. She blinked again.

The fire was gone. As was the beach. And Teth.

Ara got to her feet and slowly looked around. Eamon's note was still in her hand, and she tucked it into her pocket.

The space she found herself in was a peculiar blend of nature and artifice. It appeared to be a cave with rough stone walls studded with quartz crystals. The roof over her head was a perfect dome divided by curving stone ribs into five sections. At the apex of the dome was a source of light Ara couldn't identify, but it made the crystals flash their varied hues throughout the room.

Another test?

She stood at the top of a short flight of stone steps that ended at a stone bridge. Ara crossed the bridge to reach a broad, round platform with a smooth stone floor. Opposite the bridge was a forge in which fire burned brightly. She could hear it calling to her.

As Ara approached the forge, the energy of its heat reverberated through her skin. Along with the forge were an anvil and worktables. Ara found her own tools laid out on one of the tables, as well as her apron. She ran her fingers over each tool and felt each one welcome her to this place.

"Have I found it?" she whispered.

The Loresmith Forge.

"I've been waiting for you to ask, dear."

Ara whirled around. At the center of the platform stood the old woman from the forest.

"Eni?"

The woman toddled forward, beaming at Ara. "It's so nice to see you again. Are you hungry? I can bring cakes."

"No, thank you," Ara replied, wondering what could be more bizarre than talking about cake with a god. "Why are you like that?"

"Like what?" Eni asked, smoothing her apron.

"Like the woman from the forest," Ara answered.

"Don't tell me you don't like her." Eni sounded disappointed. "I thought you two got on very well."

"We did," Ara said, flustered at the thought she'd insulted the god. "I do like her . . . but why her?"

A chair appeared and the old woman sat. She laced her fingers and rested her hands in her lap.

"Fox can't speak," Eni said. "At least not in a way you understand. And most people find my natural form . . . intimidating. It tends to distract people from what's important."

Ara nodded, remembering the sight of Eni's swirling cloaks and gleaming eyes.

"I'm very pleased to see you again," Ara told the old woman.

"Thank you." Eni was now stirring a cup of tea. "Would you like some?"

"No, thank you," Ara said again. "Are you going to tell me if I've found what I've been seeking?"

The old woman sipped tea; the spoon she had been stirring with had vanished. "I think you should guess."

Ara bit her tongue. Eni wanted her to guess? It sounded ridiculous, but that didn't seem like something she should tell Eni.

"I enjoy a good guessing game." The old woman smiled at Ara. "Take a good look around, then tell me where you think you are."

Ara returned the smile weakly. "I can do that."

"Of course you can," Eni encouraged.

Walking to the edge of the platform, Ara looked down. She immediately jumped back, her heart in her throat, trying to process what she'd seen. She could swear it had been stars. Her pulse had gone wild.

Ara lowered to her hands and knees and forced herself to crawl back to the edge.

"Caution is always advisable," Eni called.

Though her body screamed against it, Ara peered over the edge. She had seen stars. Millions of them twinkling against an inky expanse. She couldn't see where they began or ended. Nor could she see what, if anything, supported the platform. She became very dizzy and pushed herself away from the edge.

Lying on her side, Ara pressed her cheek against the cool floor and waited for her sense of up and down to return to normal. Her head felt like a spinning top. When the dizziness passed, Ara pushed herself up with care. She stood very slowly, making certain she was steady on her feet.

"Any guesses yet?" The old woman was now in a rocking chair, knitting a wool blanket. It stretched away from her and spilled over the side of the platform.

Ara shook her head. She made her way back to the forge and leaned against the anvil. Looking up, Ara examined the ceiling more closely. She hadn't noticed before that each of the five sections of the dome bore a sign of the gods. Eni—the Traveler, Ofrit—the Alchemist, Wuldr—the Hunter, Nava—the Sower, the Twins—Keepers of the Mysteries. All deities accounted for.

A ceiling above and stars below.

A forge. An anvil. Everything Ara needed to smith. But nothing else.

"It is the Loresmith Forge," Ara said.

Of all the wonders in the old tales, the Loresmith Forge had been the only one that Old Imgar and Ara's grandmother had admitted skepticism about. It appeared only a few times in the stories and never with any detail. No Loresmith had described it, nor left any clues as to its location. Imgar had gone so far as to tell Ara it was a metaphor.

"The Loresmith Forge represents a forge within you," he'd said. *"It is the manifestation of your skill and power."*

"He wasn't wrong."

Ara jumped.

Eni had appeared beside her, still bearing dimpled, rosy cheeks.

"You know what I was thinking." Ara stared at the old woman.

Her nose scrunched up, like she smelled something unpleasant. "I try not to do it. And when I do, I usually don't admit it. But in this case, that crotchety old man deserves credit. He was closer to understanding the Loresmith Forge than most ever do."

Ara gazed around the cavernous space. "I'm inside myself."

"In a way," Eni replied. "Only the Loresmith can travel to this place, and it is the power within you that brings you here. The Loresmith Forge doesn't exist on the temporal plane."

"I don't know what that is." Ara frowned.

The old woman was now wearing eyeglasses, and she pushed them up the bridge of her nose. "It's the world you live in. This is somewhere else."

Ara began to feel dizzy again.

Eni clucked her tongue. "None of that. Save the pondering of your existence for later. You have work to do. The first Loreknight has been chosen—by me, I'm pleased to say—and you need to forge their weapon."

Ara's eyes widened as she took in Eni's words.

Who? Who has been chosen?

"I'll leave you to your task." The old woman patted Ara's cheek. "Don't hesitate to call for me should you need anything."

Then Eni was gone.

Ara sat in a chair that had appeared close to the forge.

A Loreknight has been chosen.

Ara wrestled with the statement. *Who could it be?*

It would make the most sense for the person to be among Ara's companions. Nimhea was the obvious choice. Unless the task in Ofrit's scrolls was to find the Loreknight and give them the weapon.

She put her fingers to her temple and leaned forward, hoping to clear her addled mind. Instead, a noise caught her attention. The sound of paper crinkling in her pocket.

Drawing Eamon's note from her pocket, she read the letter again. Looked at Nimhea's name again, the streaks and stains around it. How difficult it must have been to write her name, knowing the message within would break her heart. No matter what Eamon had done, Ara had seen time and again how deeply he loved his sister. She knew that hadn't changed.

And he had wept for her.

A traitor's tears. Five of them.

Could she?

Ara touched one of the smudges. A tear rolled onto her finger, quivering and perfect. Raising the tip of her finger, Ara watched the tear slide into her palm, not become a streak of liquid, but keep its shape. Ara touched the next smudge, and another tear freed itself from the paper. She drew out the next tear and the next until she had five glistening tears in her palm.

She gazed at them in wonder.

This is the craft of the Loresmith. A forging of metal and spirit, material and memory.

The chorus of Loresmiths whispered secrets to her.

With a sweep of her arm, Ara threw the tears at the ceiling. They hung in the air, lining up with the five sections of the ceiling. She watched as the gods' symbols burned within each tear, and Ara knew what they would be.

The tears floated back into her palm. When she came to the worktable, a satin-lined box appeared. Ara placed each tear in the box and closed the lid. She would return to them later.

Ara donned her apron and moved to the forge. She was unsurprised to find two stacks of ingots waiting for her. One stack Ara identified as iron. She picked up an ingot from the second stack. It was the same material from which Ironbranch had been forged. Ara returned the ingot to its place at the top of the stack.

Gathering the iron ingots required, Ara set about creating the molds she would need.

The work wasn't any less grueling or sweaty than when Ara had labored at Imgar's forge. She wasn't aware of time passing, but when she grew hungry, food would appear on one of the tables. When she tired, a feather mattress with pillows and blankets was waiting for her. She worked and ate. Worked and rested. She was utterly consumed by the task at hand.

When the molds were finished Ara melted down the unusual ingots. She poured the molten liquid into the first set of molds and one very large mold. While they cooled, Ara retrieved the box of tears. One by one she placed a tear in a long-handled iron bowl and set the bowl inside the forge. One by one she withdrew the fired tears and poured each into its unique mold.

She slept.

By the time Ara woke, the pieces had cooled.

She finished the bow first. Though crafted of the same substance as Ironbranch, the bow had a springiness and life that was altogether different from the qualities of her stave.

Ara set the bow aside. She began to assemble the arrows. Five shafts. Five tips.

The shafts shone silver-gray like the bow. The tips had a dazzling brightness. Their teardrop shape ended in a point that drew blood at the slightest touch. They were clear as diamonds save for the symbol stamped into their surface. Five arrows. One for each of the gods. Eni, Ofrit, Wuldr, Nava, and the twin gods who are one, Ayre and Syre.

When Ara fitted the last tip to the last shaft, a very slender quiver appeared on the worktable. She slid the arrows home, though they were without fletching. The task of fletching fell to the archer. Fletching was too personal a craft to be undertaken by anyone else.

Ara set the quiver beside the bow and stepped back to admire them. They were the most beautiful things Ara had created at a forge. But her heart was troubled. There was no doubting whom this weapon was intended for.

Then Ara knew Eni was standing beside her.

"Why him?" she asked.

"Who else did you think I would choose?" the god replied.

"Are you sure?" She felt guilty for asking the question and cast a sidelong glance at the god.

Eni's lips curved with mischief. "You doubt him?"

"No," Ara replied without hesitation.

"Not all knights require shining armor." Eni looked pleased. "Particularly Loreknights."

In a formal tone, Ara said to Eni, "I present to you this weapon I have forged, Tears of the Traitor."

"I bless this weapon you have forged," Eni replied in the same formal speech.

The old woman clapped her hands. "Very good. Now that that's taken care of, do you have any questions before you go back?"

"Does it have a name?" Ara asked. "What Ironbranch is made of, what I forged the bow and shafts from?"

"It's called godswood," Eni told her. "But that's for you alone to know, as is this place. Guard it in your heart."

Ara nodded. "I will."

"You'll find your way out through there." The old woman pointed to the bridge and the stairs. At the top of the stairs a door appeared. It reminded Ara of Ofrit's Bridge Between Worlds.

Eni said, "That's not a coincidence."

"You read my mind again," Ara chided.

"I apologize." Eni sounded sincere. "Would you like to take a pie with you?"

The cheerful old woman offered Ara the steaming pastry. It smelled like apples, and Ara's mouth watered.

Regretfully, she declined. "It would probably raise questions."

"I suppose you're right," Eni agreed, and was gone.

Ara removed her leather apron and reorganized her tools. She picked up the bow and quiver of arrows. When she crossed the bridge and climbed the steps, Ara readied herself for what would happen when she returned to the world. With her companions' help, she would find the next task the gods asked of her. She would not let Nimhea despair. Ara understood the meaning of Eamon's tears, and clung to the belief that there was still hope for him.

She would tell Teth that he'd been chosen by the gods. He could become the first Loreknight in the battle to restore Saetlund. He would bear a weapon that had no rival. A gift from the gods.

Her grandmother's voice came to her. *Gifts from the gods are complicated.*

Ara saw that the gods offered not only a gift, but a burden.

A just, honorable burden. But a burden still.

Teth had a choice, just as Ara had a choice.

She didn't know what choice he would make.

Ara opened the door and walked between worlds.

❖ EPILOGUE ❖

The Dove

---

iran, fiftieth of his name, the Dark Star, Commander of Imperial Armies, Beloved Elder Son (this generation) of Fauld the Ever-Living, was making his weekly inspection of the Imperial Stables in Five Rivers. The stables had become something of a refuge for Liran, ever harassed by administrators who believed he could be bribed to curry his father's favor on their behalf. Despite Liran's consistent record of having never accepted a bribe, the vultures wouldn't stop circling.

Liran had discovered, however, that such men seemed to share a universal dislike of animals. Thus, whenever the Commander made his inspections of the stables he was guaranteed a bit of peace. Unfortunately, the handful of hours—the stables were large, and Liran made sure his inspections were thorough—he could spare that week for the cavalry had come to an end.

His final stop of the day was a brief appointment with the stables' master farrier.

"Here's my tally and notes." The farrier handed Commander Liran a small satchel.

"Your account will be credited promptly," Liran told the man.

The farrier bent his head. "Many thanks."

His inspection completed, Liran rode back to the palace. He

returned to his rooms, locking the door behind him. He passed through the receiving room and unlocked the door to his personal study. Once in the study, he locked its door again.

Opening the satchel, Liran pulled out the farrier's papers and put them on his desk. He returned his attention to the satchel, reaching inside and rolling back its false bottom. He took the envelope from its hiding place and set the satchel aside. Liran sank into his chair, taking a moment, as he always did, to gaze at the image drawn in ink on the face of the envelope.

A dove.

ACKNOWLEDGMENTS

All books come to life thanks to an enormous effort by an exceptionally talented group of people. This book in particular exists thanks to the patience and dedication of extraordinary individuals to whom I can never offer enough thanks. Penguin Young Readers Group has been my publishing home for a decade, and I am ever grateful for their support of my work. Thanks to Felicity Vallence and Tessa Meischeid for spreading the word and getting *Forged* into the wild. Philomel is my writing family, and I want to especially thank Ken Wright, Cheryl Eissing, and Kelsey Murphy for helping bring this novel into the world. My editor Jill Santopolo continually amazes me with her insights and helps me keep faith with her encouragement. My agent Charlie Olsen knows how to pick up the pieces when I fall apart and is my knight champion. I've benefited from the presence of incredible writer friends who have made me laugh and offered priceless advice, particularly Jessica Spotswood, Beth Revis, Marie Lu, Carrie Ryan, Gwenda Bond, Jessica Brody, Jessica Khoury, Jenn Johansson, Morgan Matson, Suzanne Young, Elizabeth Eulberg, Stephanie Perkins, David Levithan, and the attendees of SPATL 2019. My family continues to be my greatest source of inspiration, and are ever-failing cheerleaders without whom I would be lost. The past several years have been a difficult journey, but also filled with the brightest light in the form of my husband, Eric, who brings joy to my heart with its every beat.